in the flesh

PORTIA DA COSTA

in the flesh

HQN™

Recycling programs
for this product may
not exist in your area.

ISBN-13: 978-0-373-77716-7

IN THE FLESH

Copyright © 2012 by Portia Da Costa

This edition published by arrangement with Harlequin Books S.A.

For questions and comments about the quality of this book
please contact us at Customer_eCare@Harlequin.ca.

® and TM are trademarks of the publisher. Trademarks indicated with
® are registered in the United States Patent and Trademark Office, the
Canadian Trade Marks Office and in other countries.

www.Harlequin.com

Printed in U.S.A.

To my dear friend and critique partner Saskia Walker,
who's cheered me on throughout
the writing of this story and many others.

CHAPTER ONE

Eyes of the Devil
London, 1890

"WHO IS THAT MAN over there?" demanded Charlie. "See the one I mean? The tall impertinent-looking fellow by the ballroom door, talking to Sir Horace Rumbelow."

Beatrice Weatherly suppressed a sigh. Her brother could be a bit of a bear sometimes when he drank too fast, and the champagne was disappearing down his throat tonight at an alarming rate.

"I asked you to wear a more conservative dress. Something dark and modest, maybe one of your mourning gowns," Charlie went on. "But of course you wouldn't, and now look what's happened. I swear that if he doesn't stop ogling you this very minute, I'll go across there and box his ears for him!"

I'd like to see you try, brother dear. He looks as if he could swat you like a gadfly with just one hand.

"Please, ignore him, Charlie. He isn't bothering me in the slightest, so I don't see why he should bother you." Keeping her face carefully averted, Beatrice sipped her own champagne. She was determined to make every glass last as long as she could tonight. Just look what had happened the last time she'd drunk fizz.

But, truth be told, her bold scrutinizer across the reception room *did* bother her and it wasn't an urge to box his ears she felt. No, it was something far more alarming. Her heart pounded and her entire body felt deliciously restive every time she caught his hot gaze on her. Something that seemed to happen every few moments or so because try as she might, she couldn't help looking back at him. And *he* hadn't taken his eyes off her since they'd entered the room.

Of course, when she and Charlie had been announced, it seemed as though almost *everybody* had swiveled around to stare at them. *Oh look,* she imagined them all saying, *There she is, Beatrice Weatherly, the Siren of South Mulberry Street, the shameless hussy who posed naked for those scandalous cabinet cards.* Men who probably owned copies of said cards had eyed her with salacious interest when their wives weren't looking. The women had frowned and pursed their lips as if worried that their men would be so overcome with lust that they'd flock around the indecent Siren, unable to help themselves. Even the discreet servants circulating with their trays had seemed to study her covertly.

Now, though, the first reaction was over and the hubbub of gossip had returned to its normal clatter. Some wives had won the battle for propriety and a few groups had self-consciously cut her and Charlie, but most of the other guests seemed far more free and easy.

I suppose a fast set like this is more forgiving of transgression, sexual or otherwise, and scandals are two a' penny, something new every day, she thought.

But the tall man with dark eyes and blond hair continued to stare.

The temptation to glance around at him again was a physical force. It bore down on Beatrice's chest, making her breathless, and it seemed to be affecting other parts of her anatomy, too. It was as if she'd suddenly appeared in Lady Southern's salon dressed exactly as she'd been in one of her ex-sweetheart Eustace's racy photographs.

That was, in nothing but her birthday suit.

Trying to appear not to be moving, she inched her head around, then blushed crimson when he nodded his head in acknowledgement.

Hateful man! I've had enough of this!

Beatrice glared back at him, adding a curt nod of her own for courtesy's sake. He looked vaguely familiar to her somehow, as if she'd seen his image recently, too. An artist's impression in some periodical or other, although obviously not a nude study. Her face and chest turned rosy pink at the thought of that, too. Especially as the elegant cut of his suit couldn't entirely mask the rangy power of his body, making the job of her imagination dangerously easy.

Her oppressor gave her a smile. A dazzling, daring smile, so much more arresting than a mortal man's should be. A smile that had her gulping her champagne as if it were lemonade, regardless of her resolve to be cautious.

His lips were sultry. In a clean-shaven face that was neither young nor older, but somehow strangely both, they were strong and firmly outlined, hinting at voracious appetites never denied. Beatrice imagined him savoring rich food and fine wine, but always in moderation, appreciating every pleasure without going to excess. Lips like that would kiss a woman just as hungrily and with equal calculation. Lips like that would kiss a woman until she gasped.

Lips like that would kiss a woman into doing anything.

Across the room, it was impossible to see the color of the man's eyes, but they were dark, dark as night, glittering with mystery and menace, his stare unwavering.

Almost suffocated, Beatrice had to look away, barely

able to breathe. Had Polly laced her too tight? Much
as she disliked corsets, hers hadn't seemed excessively
oppressive tonight, not until she'd arrived here and set
eyes on *him*. Now she wanted to rip open her bodice and
wrench the entire miserable thing asunder, laces and all.

Taking small breaths so she didn't appear to be panting over the strange, aggravating man, she turned smartly
toward Charlie and found him frowning at an alternative
source of vexation.

Their recently acquired friends, Monsieur and Madame
Chamfleur, were talking and laughing with a small but
rather animated group, a few feet away. Watching them
discreetly, Beatrice envied the way Monsieur Chamfleur
kissed his wife's gloved hand with a decidedly French
flair. It spoke of other kisses she'd imagined the two of
them sharing, especially if the hot looks they kept ex-
changing were anything to go by.

"My God, those two are a rum couple, aren't they?"
Charlie swigged down his champagne and took another
glass from a passing waiter. "When you first introduced
them, I thought them to be persons of quality, but there's
something decidedly fishy about the way they look at each
other. Don't you think so?"

Sometimes Beatrice wanted to give her brother a good
shaking. She loved him dearly, because he was a sweet
man in his own way and she knew he loved her, but he
could act like a towering hypocrite at times. "Well, I think
they're charming, and the way they exhibit fondness for
each other is most refreshing. If more couples were as
tender in their affections toward each other the world
would be a far happier place."

Charlie clucked in irritation, the expression far too
stuffy for his twenty-five years. "I think the less you
talk loudly about 'exhibiting' and 'affections,' the better.

We're trying to retrieve your reputation here, sister dearest, not damage it further."

"Don't be such a stick-in-the-mud, Charlie!" Nerves atwitter, Beatrice tossed back the rest of her champagne and took another glass, too. Better that, to take the edge off her apprehension, than be drawn into a public argument with her sibling. "We both know I'm completely beyond retrieval or redemption in most people's eyes, so we'll just have to make the best of it somehow." She narrowed her eyes at him, keeping her voice low. "I think the sooner you relinquish thoughts of me making a good marriage to mend our fortunes the better. Maybe you should think about getting a job? I'll work, too. I'm a quick learner and there are plenty of things I could do."

Her brother looked as if he were about to explode. "No sister of mine is going to *work!* I'm a gentleman, for heaven's sake!"

"Goodness, don't take on so, brother dear. I was only thinking of learning how to operate a typewriting machine and enrolling at an agency. Anyone would think I'd just offered to walk the streets of Whitechapel at a shilling a tumble."

Charlie opened his mouth, no doubt to reprimand her again, but no words came out. He stared over her shoulder, frowning furiously, and as she watched him, a silvery shiver descended the length of Beatrice's spine. She hadn't a doubt in the world who she'd find when she finally turned around, but like Charlie, she was frozen too.

Don't be afraid, Bea. He's just a man. Just a man...

"Such a modest sum?" A husky, measured voice rumbled with humor. "If it were me, I'd pay upward of a hundred guineas for such a splendid opportunity."

"I beg your pardon, sir!" Pink in the face, Charles

started to bluster, then shut his mouth again, as if turned to stone by the Medusa's frightful gaze.

Slowly, as if in a strange, floating dream, Beatrice turned on her toes. Her chin came up, almost as if *she* were preparing to box some ears, just as Charlie had threatened to, but inside she was quivering to her core.

It was him, of course. The blond man of the dark, intimidating eyes and smooth, hard jaw. The man who'd stared at her so insolently. In an elegant flowing gesture, he bowed low, and it was only when he took her small gloved hand in his larger one that she realized she'd automatically held it out to him.

She could feel his mouth through the satin. The touch of it, the heat of it, burning like a flame. And at the same time she felt it elsewhere too, the sensation so vivid that she almost imagined she was back in the dreamy, drifting stupor Eustace had inflicted upon her when he'd sweet-talked her into letting him take those accursed photographs. A liberated state where she could do anything, feel anything, enjoy anything.

Between her legs, her sex fluttered as if her new admirer stroked it.

"I'm Edmund Ellsworth Ritchie, Miss Weatherly." He straightened up and stared her directly in the eye, his gaze unwavering.

It's like drowning. Drowning but wanting *to drown...*

Beatrice couldn't look away, couldn't be modest the way she knew she should be. His eyes were darkest blue, almost black. The color of India ink, fathomless and gleaming. "I won't say that I hoped to meet you here tonight," he continued, "because I *knew* I would. You were invited especially so I could meet you."

It was Beatrice's turn to be lost for words. She had

them, plenty of them, but what was happening to her body shocked her into silence.

"I say—" Charlie tried to rally, then he too shut up when Edmund Ellsworth Ritchie quelled him with a look almost as disturbing as the hot one he'd given Beatrice.

"Weatherly, I wonder if you'd allow me a moment of privacy with your sister, if I may?" It sounded courteous enough, but it was delivered like a velvet slap in the face, and before Charlie could answer, the ruthless barbarian had Beatrice by the elbow and was steering her away toward a concealed corner between a pair of potted palms.

I should shake him off. I should walk away. I should ask for a carriage to be called and leave this place immediately.

The danger was so acute she almost did it. But she couldn't. Deep in her body, some demon imp of sweet licentiousness was capering, roused to madness by the delicate touch of Ritchie's hand on her gloved elbow.

She knew him by reputation. Edmund Ellsworth Ritchie was a famous figure, who featured often in publications such as *Town Talk* and the scurrilous but fascinating *Marriott's Monde,* as well as the society pages of other more distinguished papers. He was a man of enormous wealth, an entrepreneur, owner of properties and businesses and the most notorious reputation with the ladies. He was always described as squiring some famous beauty or other, and the less salubrious periodicals, the sort Beatrice's maid Polly favored, hinted heavily at a string of affairs.

Yet because he's got money, he gets away with it all. He's done far worse than me, but society adores him.

Now away from the throng, she expected Ritchie to launch into a flirtatious conversation in keeping with his notoriety, but he said nothing, not a word, and just stared at her. Beatrice realized she was still clutching her champagne glass, and wished it full again, not for the alcohol, but just for something to do with her nervous hands. As if he'd heard her, Ritchie plucked crystal vessel out of her fingers and set it on a shelf beside them.

High-handed beast!

"Kindly explain yourself, Mr. Ritchie." Beatrice schooled her voice to project the same kind of unruffled authority the man in front of her exuded. It was a tall order, but she managed it after a fashion. At least she didn't squeak like an outraged mouse. "What exactly did you mean? That you *arranged* for our invitation here. What do you want from us, sir, that you would do such a thing?"

Ritchie laughed, a low, thrilling chuckle that seemed to roll across her exposed skin and her covered parts, too. If it wouldn't have caused even more public awkwardness, Beatrice would have slapped him then and there she felt so angry.

But was it just anger? She felt confused. All awhirl. Astonished by the way her body was reacting and betraying her. There was heat in her face and her décolletage, every hidden delicate portion of her anatomy tingled, and her breasts ached in the confines of her gown and its underpinnings. Yet at the same time, the sensations were undeniably pleasant. More than pleasant. In her drawers, her sex felt agitated and hot…as if, oh goodness, it were in need of *touching?*

"I don't particularly want anything from your brother, Miss Weatherly. I only want you." Ritchie paused, and his long, elegant, tapered fingertips rested against the lapel of his perfectly cut tailcoat. Watching him like an adder hypnotized by a mongoose, Beatrice jumped when, with a swift, almost showmanlike panache, he flung open his coat to reveal the inner pocket in its dark satin lining, and the gilded edge of what looked like a cabinet card.

Oh no! So that's *why he wanted to meet me. He's seen the accursed things rather than just heard about them.*

"I wanted to see if the real woman lives up to the promise of this image." His jacket still open, he ran a forefinger over the card's sliver of gold edging, slowly and lasciviously. "To see if you really are a siren." Appalled by the implications of what lay against him, Beatrice experienced a delicious but alarming ripple in the pit of her belly.

I've gone quite mad. I only met the man a few moments ago and he's turned me into a bedlamite!

"A gentleman wouldn't bring such an item to a social gathering." She gave him a hard stare, even though every single bit of her felt as if it was melting like a meringue before a gaslight. "A gentleman wouldn't even own such a thing!"

Ritchie snagged his lower lip in his white teeth for an instant, still fondling the edge of the card. There were stars in his dark blue eyes that seemed to dance in time to the waltz playing in the ballroom beyond them.

"A lady wouldn't have posed for it in the first place."

True, but she wasn't going to admit that to him. A lady wouldn't have behaved like an incautious ninny and given in to her fiancé's importuning, champagne or otherwise.

"Touché, Mr. Ritchie." Beatrice tried to imagine a steel bar down her spine to match the busk down the front of her corset. Rigid corseting was the only way to stand up to Ritchie without dissolving in the heat from his eyes. "But I'm afraid those photographs represent an unfortunate and misguided incident. An error of judgment on my part that I'm trying to put behind me." She paused, readying herself for flight at a dignified pace. "And I hope that

members of society will also find it in themselves to rel-
egate my indiscretion to the past, where it belongs."

Turning, she made to walk away, but a hand prevented
her. A hand on her upper arm, right in the vulnerable
space between the top of her long opera glove and the
wisp of French faille that constituted the abbreviated
sleeve of her gown.

Bare skin on bare skin. Some time between their first
meeting and this moment, Ritchie had removed his white
evening gloves and his fingertips were hot as points of
fire on her naked upper arm.

"Kindly let me go, Mr. Ritchie!"

Oh, too shrill, far too shrill. But immediately he released her. Or did he? The imprint of his fingers still held
her immobilized. As did the dark fire in his eyes.

"You'll never put the photographs behind you, Beatrice. They *are* you." His voice was quiet, yet seemed to
ring through the halls of the Southerns' vast mansion. "I
suspected as much when I first saw this." He drew out
the photograph he'd been taunting her with, and it was
the most shameful one of them all, the tableau where she
appeared to be touching herself between her legs.

Appeared? Is it just that? Did I actually do it? She still
couldn't quite remember, but a shudder ran through her.
Ritchie's eyes licked over her, following its progress.

"And now that I've met you, my dear, now that I've
seen you in the flesh, I *know*." His red tongue flicked out,
touching the center of his lower lip. "You're a goddess of
sensuality, Miss Weatherly, truly a siren. And the sooner
you admit it, the happier you'll become." The fans of his
eyelashes beat down, all provocation and seduction. How
could a man have lashes as long and thick as his and still
be so uncompromisingly masculine? They were disturbingly beautiful and sensuous. "As will I."

"I'm afraid my sensuality…or lack of it…is none of your affair, sir." She tried to picture the steel bar again, but it was hopeless. She hated this taunting creature who was famous for getting any woman he wanted, but her traitorous body was yearning toward him as if it wanted to bend and mold itself to every contour of his. And trying to tell it not to yearn was wearing her out. She was close to breaking point. "Now, if you would kindly let me go, I'd like to return to my brother."

"But I'm not holding you." He laughed softly, the husky sound dancing along her nerves and teasing her most tender parts. "Except here." He ran his thumb slowly over the cabinet card, letting it linger at her breasts and her thighs.

Aghast, Beatrice almost lifted her hand to strike him, but common sense stopped her. The man was an insulting blackguard, and lingering here was just giving him exactly what he wanted. The best thing to do was to leave, and leave immediately.

"Good evening, Mr. Ritchie." Beatrice took a step away from him, but somehow it was like wading through molasses. How could she not be running yet?

"Wait a moment, Miss Weatherly, aren't you at least going to allow me to mark your dance card?"

Beatrice glanced down at the little card dangling on its ribbon from her wrist. "I'm afraid not. As far as you're concerned, it's full already."

And with that, to her surprise, the spell was broken, and as fast as she could without charging like a madwoman, she sped away from him.

She didn't look back. No, she wouldn't give him the satisfaction!

Yet she could still see him stroking her photograph as she fled.

Edmund Ellsworth Ritchie didn't follow Beatrice Weatherly. He couldn't. He could only watch her as she stalked away from him, her shoulders almost vibrating with antagonism. Every swish of her pale skirts was like a wash of flame across his body as she wended her stiff-backed path through the groups of convivially chatting guests, leaving a faint aura of lily of the valley in her wake.

Even if he could have moved, he probably wouldn't have. His cock had hardened like a ramrod the moment he'd set eyes on her, and was now a considerable bulge in his trousers. He had a reputation to be sure, but to be seen sporting a prominent erection at a society ball was a bit too risqué, even for him.

Had Beatrice seen the way he'd come up for her? She hadn't glanced in that direction, but then, what well-bred young woman would?

All of which confirmed his instincts. Despite the fact that he possessed photographs of her lolling naked on an animal skin with her dainty hand pressed between her thighs, he still couldn't shake off the notion that she wasn't quite as licentious and free thinking as such a pose suggested.

What are you, my Beatrice? A hedonistic voluptuary or an untouched Vestal? Either way, you're everything I dreamed of...and more.

It was impossible to decide which role excited him the most, but what he did know for sure was that Beatrice Weatherly had bewitched him. His ensorcellment had begun the first instant he'd set eyes on the card now back in his pocket, but meeting her in the living, vibrant flesh had increased it a thousandfold.

The collection of photographs had been circulating sub

rosa at his club for a while, a minor sensation, and bored one day, he'd asked a friend to pass him one.

The sense of shock had been like a blow to his head, heart and gut all in the same moment. He'd been stunned to silence by a young woman's exquisite, naked beauty, and he still couldn't entirely deduce why that was so when he'd seen many gorgeous nudes in his adult life. But shock had turned to arousal, and arousal to a worrying obsession. He'd meant to meet Beatrice Weatherly in order to free himself, but now, instead, everything he'd felt seeing the photographs was validated.

Her face, in animation, didn't possess the classic perfection of some of the society lovelies he'd courted. Miss Weatherly wasn't even as delicate as the photographic rendering had suggested. There was a wild, untamed quality about her, something he couldn't quite define and which she didn't seem to be aware of herself. Her complexion had a creamy, almost animal vigor and her hair was so savage a red that the photograph's hand tinting had merely hinted at it. He wouldn't go so far as to say she was coarse or uncouth, quite the reverse, but she seemed to overflow with health and energy, and perhaps appetites that more delicate hothouse paragons sadly lacked.

And her body, oh God, her scented body.

How could she possibly appear as erotic and alluring in her outdated and obviously painstakingly made-over evening gown as she did out of it? It wasn't attributable to any amount of corsetry or sundry feminine mechanicals, even though Ritchie was well acquainted with what women wore beneath their costumes.

No, with Beatrice Weatherly, every attraction came from the woman herself. Her dark green eyes, her fierce Amazonian expression, the way her head came up and she gasped as he challenged her.

I'll make you gasp, Miss Weatherly. You can be sure of that. And even if you're still angry with me, you'll be glad you let me.

A footman appeared at his elbow with a tray of champagne, and about to reach for a glass, Ritchie paused. He'd been knocked far too far off-kilter in the past few moments to be satisfied by frothy French wine.

"Bring me a glass of whiskey, if you would?" His own voice sounded strange to him, as if he really had suffered an almighty blow. But the servant seemed to notice nothing amiss and stepped away smartly on his errand.

Gazing out into the glittering throng of bejeweled women and immaculately dressed men, it seemed to Ritchie as if they were projections floating on a screen. They weren't real, just flickering, moving images such as he'd seen at a demonstration by Monsieur Le Prince in Leeds a couple of years ago.

Only the now-hidden Beatrice Weatherly was real to him, and discreetly, so as to avoid attention, he slid her photograph out of his pocket again and savored the contrast between it and the living woman.

Both were sublime to behold.

In the image, Beatrice was unstudied, dreamy and natural, her eyes averted from the camera in a private moment, so unlike the brazen stares of most naked models.

In the flesh, she met his gaze with fire and mettle and challenge.

Both incarnations stirred his loins to an alarming degree. And much, he admitted uncomfortably, in the manner they'd once stirred for his lost, beloved Clara. His first marriage had been fully and mutually satisfying in that department, as well as happy in every other way.

As the efficient footman approached, weaving his way

through the chattering, preening guests, Ritchie slipped the photograph safely back into his pocket.

The whiskey was fire and peat on his tongue, and it settled him.

Yes, he could view the photograph, and the others like it, and take pleasure in them whenever he wanted.

But they, and the ministrations of his own hand, weren't nearly enough now. He had to touch and admire the woman herself. From that isolated moment of contact, his fingers still tingled, feeling the warmth of her skin, and its softness where he'd held her upper arm. His entire body still felt the aftershocks of that singular instant, and his stiff cock jerked anew from simply reliving it.

I'll feast on you, divine Beatrice. I'll draw from you every last ounce of sensuality that's in you. Because I know it's there, even though you might deny it now. I'll taste and stroke every last inch of your flesh, and I'll feel your exquisite fingertips on my cock returning that pleasure.

And I'll do it soon, because if I don't, I might go mad.

Mad? God no… The most unfortunate choice of word. Raising his glass to his lips again, he shuddered as if an icy specter had drifted across his grave.

No! No dark thoughts now. Beatrice Weatherly was light. Heat. Passion. Everything positive and full of glorious, abundant life.

And, thanks to her imprudent brother's bad investments, and his foolhardy days at the racetrack and nights at the card table, The Siren of South Mulberry Street was now Ritchie's for the taking.

CHAPTER TWO

Creatures of the Tropics

BEATRICE FELT AS if her head was on a spring, it swiveled about so often during the dancing.

She wanted to freeze stock-still in the middle of the ballroom, turn around, and angrily demand that Edmund Ellsworth Ritchie stop staring at her!

But the trouble was, every time she was convinced he was watching her, the aggravating beast wasn't there. Had he become invisible all of a sudden? Was he watching her by some arcane, remote means, like a medium?

And if wasn't watching her, why not? Absurdly, his lack of scrutiny now annoyed her even more than being watched had.

With a supreme effort, she maintained a courteous interest in her partners, of which, surprisingly, there were quite a few. Obviously, her notoriety as the Siren was attracting most of the men, but it was still a pleasant relief not to be a wallflower, as a twenty-four-year-old spinster with no money and a besmirched reputation should expect to be.

She danced with Charlie, of course, who lectured her throughout, and stumbled once or twice, too. Brandy on his breath told a clear story, but Beatrice made a point of being especially patient and agreeable. It wasn't all her fault that her brother's life was difficult, but she certainly hadn't helped matters by being so gullible in her dealings with Eustace Lloyd, and by leaving it so long to entertain a new suitor at all.

She shared a waltz with Monsieur Chamfleur, tall and bluff and jolly, as well as a cotillion with Lord Southern himself, and several other whirls about the floor with the charming Mr. Enderby, and one or two other husbands of the ladies in her Sewing Circle.

Ah yes, the Ladies' Sewing Circle. Beatrice smiled wryly. Not much of a stitcher, she would never have joined such a group in the normal course of events, but when a card had arrived out of the blue, inviting her, she'd fallen upon it gladly. In the weeks since those accursed cabinet cards had begun circulating, along with a fruity exposé about them in *Marriott's Monde,* all other social avenues had dried up to a state of desiccation. Backs had turned on her at church, the Ladies' Charitable Guild had requested she not attend anymore, and likewise a ladies' reading group she'd not long joined but had been enjoying immensely. In the face of this universal discouragement it was worth a few pricked thumbs and a nasty hole-ridden mat or two for the chance of feminine conversation with someone other than Polly or Enid or Cook.

And the talk over the crochet, cross-stitch and teacups had turned out to be unexpectedly racy.

Until Ritchie's disclosure, Beatrice had believed the Circle to be the primary source of tonight's invitation. Both Sofia Chamfleur and her friend Lady Arabella Southern had been especially amenable at the weekly meetings.

Now, however, Beatrice had been disabused of that notion.

Either one or the other of those two ladies had acted as a pander, and had expedited her appearance here to serve her up to the infuriating Ritchie. A man who apparently had the power to haunt her when he was nowhere to be seen.

What's the matter with me? I'm having a perfectly delightful time, a much better one than I ever expected. Why do I keep wishing that every partner was that monster?

It was true. Good company as her dance partners had been, somehow they all seemed like shadows. Even Monsieur Chamfleur, who towered well over a stocky six feet tall. Only the wild, hot feelings she'd experienced in Ritchie's presence had any verisimilitude. Her arm still prickled where he'd touched her, and when she relived that touch, her thighs trembled and a betraying liquid heat welled between them.

No! He's a rogue and a womanizer and he's even less respectable than I am!

Drifting away toward the periphery of the supper room, she looked for Charlie, but he too was nowhere to be seen now. One of his lecture topics on the dance floor had been a stern homily to her on the importance of *not* being seen in conversation with Edmund Ellsworth Ritchie.

"I didn't realize it was him until he swanned up to us. The nerve of the man! If the papers are anything to go by, he's a bad lot. Just stay away from him or he'll compromise you even further."

Beatrice had nodded, for once in perfect agreement with her sibling.

Yet she was disappointed. The ball was a dazzling, fairy-tale affair, and all the more so for the remarkable and revolutionary electrical lighting system that the Southerns had recently had laid on in their principal rooms. This new light illuminated the proceedings in a harder and more brittle manner somehow. It was unforgiving, yet it caused the women's jewels to flash and sparkle and their gowns appear iridescent and vivid. But despite this modern miracle, all seemed lackluster just because she was missing a certain sharply beautiful man with navy-blue eyes, shiny, barely tamed blond hair and a mouth that could have as easily belonged to the devil as to an Adonis.

Lacking appetite, Beatrice sidled out of the supper room and across the broad, gilded reception salon. Glass doors to her right led out of the house proper into a conservatory, a vast and spacious jungle that seemed to have been shipped home from darkest Africa. Within it, the air was moist and hot, as she imagined it might be in the tropics, but it made her shudder, recalling the smaller, far less grand conservatory where Eustace had taken his photographs of her.

"To the devil with you, Eustace!" Muttering, she shook her head as if to dislodge his handsome but now hated countenance. How could she ever have believed she cared for him? Much less pose naked for him?

Loneliness, she supposed, and fear for the future. It'd been so long since she'd been courted—since the loss of Tommy, her first fiancé—and she'd been flattered by Eustace's attentions. Practical issues had influenced her, too. Engagement to an eligible and apparently affluent bachelor had promised desperately needed security for herself and Charlie, and to her chagrin, she'd bamboozled herself into believing love could grow.

Regrettably, Eustace had been as mistaken in his assumptions as she'd been in hers, although far more deceitful. His affluence was all a facade and the moment he'd discovered the parlous state of the Weatherlys' own finances, he'd made plans to drop her. But not before wringing a form of income from her in the most despicable way.

"You'll get your comeuppance, one of these days, you beast. I just hope that I get the chance to witness it!"

Dismissing the weasel who'd shattered her reputation, she forged forward into the greenery. With the sound of a German polka fading in the distance, other sounds came more sharply to her ears. Trickling, tumbling water made the huge conservatory seem more than ever like a wild kingdom, and the cries of birds, and a flash of color right up in the highest edge of her vision suggested there might even be a parrot or two loose in the upper regions. Beatrice pressed on, her footsteps silent on the tiled path in her light dancing slippers.

The source of the water was a playing fountain, fed by an artificial stream. Large, colorful fish swam and wafted their fins in the central pond, and its cool freshness cut through the mulchy, vegetable aromas of the plant life.

What an incredible place. It was like having a patch of the foreign and the exotic in your own home. Unlikely a prospect as it was, Beatrice decided not to let the specter of Eustace deter her. If she ever came into a bit of money again, she'd have a conservatory of her own once more. Something modeled after the garden room at Westerlynne though, and relatively modest.

In the Southerns' grand enclosure, however, narrow pathways wended away through the aromatic flora, and their promise called to her far more than the superficial world of dancing, chitchat, and social one-upmanship. The mystery of the place reminded her of the dark, troubling attentions of Mr. Ritchie. This wild and steaming jungle would be the perfect setting for his savage male persona.

As she explored further, holding up the hem of her

gown to prevent it picking up soil and scraps of leaf matter, another sound, more familiar than tumbling water and parrot calls, caught her ear. Faint voices, both male and female, emanated from a little way ahead of her. She heard laughter and low, intimate tones.

Goodness, an assignation!

Perspiration popped and gathered beneath her corset and between her breasts, feeling sticky. It felt as if someone had suddenly adjusted the furnace that maintained the conservatory's equatorial heat.

I should turn back…pretend I never heard them…respect their privacy.

But her days of polite, respectable and discreet behavior were over. Inching forward, Beatrice acknowledged a darker, more insatiably curious nature. Creeping like a native amongst the ferns, she followed the sounds.

And came upon a little grotto, right in the heart of Lady Arabella Southern's metropolitan jungle, where two hungry creatures were cavorting, *in flagrante.*

Sofia and Ambrose Chamfleur were sitting on a bench, both pink in the face and gasping. She, with the bodice of her dress and her corset loosened so that her milky-white breasts overspilled the top of them. He with… dear heaven…his trousers unfastened and his masculine parts…his *cock*…fully out on view.

Beatrice's jaw dropped. She couldn't breathe. Her heart throbbed like a drum. And low in the pit of her belly, a serpent stirred.

So this was what a gentleman looked like when he was aroused? It wasn't quite as she'd imagined, but then, what *had* she imagined? Women weren't supposed to dwell on this particular part of a man at all until they were married, and respectable wives not even then. But having seen certain medical illustrations, Beatrice had often speculated about it. Long ago, she'd felt Tommy's loins harden against her thigh when they'd managed to snatch a secret embrace in the rose arbor at Westerlynne, and Eustace too had become agitated and short of breath after a stolen kiss or two.

Beatrice had no idea whether Monsieur Ambrose Chamfleur was a typical fellow, or an especially fine example, but unbidden she wondered if a certain Mr. Ritchie might be even bigger. Sofia, however, appeared to be more than delighted with the size of her husband's appendage, because she was stroking it in a clever, rhythmic action.

"Dear me, *monsieur,* what on earth is this?" she murmured, her slender hand apparently untiring as it rode her husband's gleaming, ruddy length. "I swear it's quite a monster and I don't have the first idea what to do with it."

Ambrose Chamfleur's broad face looked strained, but almost angelically beautiful for such a large, bluff man. His mouth worked and his hips moved and shuffled where he sat on the bench. Pulling his wife closer to him, and cupping one of her rounded breasts, he whispered something guttural in her ear.

Sofia's eyes shot wide, but she licked her lips. "Sir, you are scandalous, and a lecherous, low-minded rogue!" The words should have been an expression of outrage, but she was chuckling and smiling. And still licking her lips.

"And if I do that for you, Monsieur Chamfleur—" the clever hand twisted, and Sofia's thumb seemed to be doing something most dexterous underneath the tip of her husband's cock "—what will you do for me, in return?"

Again, a husky whisper that Beatrice couldn't catch, even though she strained her ears to hear it.

"That seems most equitable." Sofia's smile was slow

and fond, and for a moment, she closed her husband's hand tightly around her breast, swaying as if the pleasure of it was so acute she was about to expire. Then, in a swift, sudden move, she sprang to her feet, and sank to the ground, her beautiful emerald-green skirts, so at one with her environs, spreading around her as she settled gracefully on her knees.

As she descended, her husband opened his thighs to let her in close.

Botheration! I can't see!

It suddenly seemed the most important thing on earth to observe the proceedings, and despite branches and fronds of various dripping plants and shrubs almost slapping her in the face, Beatrice edged stealthily around the grotto for a better perspective.

When she achieved it, she clasped her gloved fist to her lips.

Sofia Chamfleur was sucking her husband's shaft! And thoroughly enjoying it if all her little "mmms" and slithery-liquid sounds of appreciation were to be believed.

Beatrice watched. And watched. And the first shock turned to utter fascination.

I wonder what he tastes like? Is he sweet? Or salty? And what's his texture? He looks smooth and silky and shiny, even on the length she can't take in....

Beatrice's knowledge of men's bodies and their sexual workings came only from certain volumes she'd studied in the library at Westerlynne, after attacking the lock on the secured cabinet with hairpin. There hadn't been time to peruse them in as much depth as she would have liked to, but even with only that rudimentary information, it was easy to deduce how much a man like Monsieur Chamfleur enjoyed this act. It must be seventh heaven for any man, pressing the most sensitive part of his anatomy into such a well of heat and moisture and being kissed and licked and sucked by his beloved.

Sofia Chamfleur seemed to be having a fine time of it, too. Despite the fact that her smooth and pretty face was deformed around her husband's prodigious member, she was attempting a smile and her handsome eyes were sparkling.

She loves to please him.

Reluctant to even think about him now, Beatrice realized that even at her most self-deluded moments, she would never have wanted to kiss Eustace this way. Tommy, probably yes, but Eustace, *never!* The very idea made her shudder and her skin crawl.

But I'd kiss you, Mr. Ritchie...I'd kiss you.

The idea was preposterous. Ridiculous. Unthinkable. But before she could prevent it, another image sprang into her mind, clearer by far than any risqué photograph.

Instead of the happy Sofia Chamfleur on her knees in front of her beloved Ambrose, Beatrice saw herself, kneeling and sucking enthusiastically, her lips stretched and shiny around the even bigger organ of Edmund Ellsworth Ritchie.

This time her fist didn't go to her mouth. This time, she couldn't do anything and was in no danger of uttering a sound. It was as if a giant hand had pushed her sideways, not physically but psychically somehow. The thoughts and images were too shocking for her numbed brain to process, and yet at the same time, she seemed to feel Ritchie's cock against her tongue.

Licking her lips compulsively, and still half observing the Chamfleurs, Beatrice suddenly experienced the strangest phenomenon. It was as if time itself were slowed down and all thoughts and actions were taking place at a snail's pace. Her arms fell limp to her sides, and glancing lower inch by inch, she watched the cords and ribbons retaining her fan, her tiny evening reticule and her dance card begin to slide inexorably down the satin slope of her gloved arm and hand.

They're going to clatter when they land and the Chamfleurs will know I'm here.

In the midst of that thought, she felt less worried about being discovered than she did about disturbing her friends' pleasure.

What a shame if he doesn't reach his peak inside her mouth.

But even as these weird observations passed through her mind, and her belongings proceeded at their attenuated pace toward the tiles, another hand, not hers, swept down and caught them.

Who was this prestidigitator, this illusionist? This person who snatched her around the waist at the same time, securing her against him with his other strong hand.

She hadn't even realized she was falling.

"Hush."

It was hardly more than a sigh, but she knew the voice, the strength, and the scent of his exquisite shaving lotion. As she breathed it in, her knees were jelly. She couldn't stand.

The arm around her middle tightened as she sagged, pressing her corset against her body, restricting and controlling her.

"Come along."

Again, the low voice hummed through her flesh, making the entire length of her torso vibrate where it pressed tight against him. There was no question who it was. It was as if she'd been waiting for him to join her. Somehow waiting since before she'd ever even met him.

Half carrying, half guiding, he began backing her away

from the little scene on the bench. The Chamfleurs were completely absorbed in their pleasure, but as Beatrice's fan swung on its cord, it brushed a palm frond and made it swish and rustle audibly.

Beatrice's last impression of the jungle grotto was Ambrose Chamfleur glancing her way, smiling briefly, then moaning like a wild animal as his eyes rolled up in crisis.

As soon as they reached a safe distance away from the daring husband and wife, Beatrice tried to struggle against Ritchie's grip on her then stopped fighting him again, just as quickly. Why give the creature the satisfaction of knowing how much he infuriated her? Especially when there was another distraction it was impossible to ignore.

Against the side of her hip, a sturdy knot of hardness poked at her through the layers of their clothing. And judging by what she'd just seen, back in the hidden grotto, there wasn't the slightest bit of doubt what it was.

Randy beast!

"Let go of me, Mr. Ritchie," Beatrice hissed as he manhandled her through a French door and back into the house. They were in another part of the vast Southern mansion now, one some distance from doors by which she'd entered the conservatory.

I'm lost. Lost in a big, strange house with a man who probably has far worse designs on me than Eustace Lloyd ever did.

So why wasn't she struggling harder? She was a healthy girl with sound limbs, and if a man's nether regions were as sensitive as Monsieur Chamfleur's reactions led her to believe, a well-place knee delivered sharply should easily free her.

But you don't want to be free, do you? proposed a sly, inner voice.

"No, Beatrice. If I let you go, you'll run away again, and I want to talk to you." Swiveling her around in his grip, Ritchie's arms were still unyielding. They held her like iron bands, keeping her jammed up against the hardness at his groin. His cock felt warm and lively against her belly despite the layers and layers of her petticoats.

"It seems to me that you want to do considerably more than talk to me!"

The words came out without her bidding, and worse, her body seemed to have acquired a mind of its own now, too. Her hips jerked and rocked, bumping her abdomen against Ritchie's loins as if deliberately massaging and caressing him.

What in heaven's name am I doing?

Her thoughts whirled as he growled. Not quite as loudly and plaintively as Ambrose Chamfleur had done, but still in a way that recognized her desire.

But I don't want you! No! No! I don't!

Everything she'd ever read and been taught about ladylike behavior suddenly became nonsense. Stern words that had once tolled in her head were fading, fading. And there was no champagne or other intoxicant to lay the blame on this time. Not even the affection she'd felt for Tommy or misplaced feelings of fondness such as she'd experienced for Eustace.

No, with this man there was nothing more than instinctive antipathy at very first sight, and a low animal reaction to his maleness.

And yet still her hips churned and circled, rubbing her groin against Ritchie's.

"I can't deny that, Miss Weatherly. I want to see if that beautiful body of yours is really as luscious as the photographs suggest. I want to touch your skin, stroke you between your legs…taste you there."

His tongue…oh, his tongue…

Had the ceiling above them opened? It seemed so. From the summer night sky itself, there shot down a bolt of lightning that struck Beatrice and took her breath away. Her legs, the very ones that Ritchie seemed so eager to put his face between, turned as weak as wet wool, making her sway wildly.

No! No! No! she railed again as his arms tightened around her, *I am not a fainting miss who has the vapors just because this barbarian is trying to shock me!*

"I'll thank you not to make such crude remarks, Mr. Ritchie." She stiffened her spine and fought his grip, but it simply became more robust. "They may impress a certain type of woman, but I actually find them boring, even juvenile."

"Oh Beatrice, you're such a little liar." His breath against her cheek was as sweet and clean as his utterances were impure. He smelled a little of whiskey, and that only made her want to taste *him*. His mouth…his skin…oh, his cock.

Yes, his cock…I like calling it that!

Wicked thoughts, radical thoughts. But they didn't linger, because at that moment Ritchie's mouth came down on hers, devilish and hard.

The kiss wasn't a bit like Tommy's or Eustace's. It was dry at first, hot and firm and purposeful. No tentative, boyish explorations. No messy meanderings with lips that were sloppy and vaguely slack. Ritchie's mouth was strong and businesslike, and totally controlled. And when at last things did get wet, that was different, too. His tongue was a dart of power, pushing into her mouth and subduing her. Down between her legs, she seemed to feel it too, just as he'd described.

Sometime in their flight from the conservatory, she'd

snatched her belongings from him, but now, as she tasted his tongue and her own flicked and played around it, her bag, her fan and her dance card tumbled forgotten to the carpet. She needed her hands. She needed them so she could explore his back and his shoulders through the fine dark cloth of his coat, and cling on to him when her knees went weak again.

She needed them so she could cling on when her hips started to press against him of their own accord, driven by a divine madness and a desperate hunger for the same intimate sharing the Chamfleurs enjoyed.

Her body was electric, as if filled with the same radical force that lit the glittering mansion around them, its Promethean power channeled into her every nerve and cell. She felt alight, aflame, filled with yearning and longing and an unstoppable compulsion to press her skin against Ritchie's skin, cleaving to every last square inch of it.

When she'd had the mad urge to take her clothes off and pose for Eustace's camera, it'd been nothing more than an anemic whim compared to this. The need to be naked for Ritchie and with Ritchie was a primal drive. An instinct in her blood, pumping and surging.

Aha, this "female hysteria" they write about so coyly in certain advertisements at the back of the Lady's Weekly Journal. *Why on earth do they imply that it's unpleasant, and to be avoided? Because they're wrong, so wrong! Completely wrong!*

Her breasts felt sore and strange, and yet the sensation was delicious somehow, and far more than pleasant. They chafed against her fine chemise and the inside of her corset and she surged against the solid wall of Ritchie's body, trying to increase the effect and rub her aching nipples against him.

"Oh, you're a hot one, Beatrice," gasped Ritchie as they

broke apart to get more breath. Beatrice wasn't sure she'd taken one for at least two minutes. She was light-headed, but it wasn't through lack of oxygen…it was Ritchie. "You're more than I ever dreamed, beautiful girl," he went on, his mouth against her cheek, then her hair, his jaw brushing the side of her throat. As he spoke, his breath fanned against her, and below his hand pulled deftly at her skirts, with the skill of much practice, no doubt. Up and up they came, and then his fingers slid skillfully amongst the layers, pushing them up so he could clasp the rounded cheek of her bottom through her drawers.

Beatrice shot up in the air and started to struggle again. But just as before, without effort, Ritchie quelled her with his hands on her body and his mouth possessing hers. Conflicting urges battled. Every tenet of good behavior she'd ever had drilled into her waged war with delicious new desires—the craving to touch, taste, rub against and lay herself open to everything this man had to offer.

Her struggle died almost before it had begun, and she softened to the kiss like warmed honey. When he clasped her bottom this time, she almost purred into his mouth like a plump and lazy kitten accepting his affection, wickedly pleased that large, elaborate bustles were no longer *en vogue* and Ritchie could effect a firm hold on her without that extra hindrance to negotiate.

That's outrageous! How can I think such things? Her mind raced. *How can a kiss affect me this way?*

The thought disappeared, drenched in oceans of sensation.

How can a kiss affect me this way?

On a wave of shock and desire, Ritchie plunged his tongue into Beatrice Weatherly's mouth. He'd wanted her,

yes, the moment he'd seen the first photograph, but this…
this reality exceeded his every fevered fantasy.

Every part of her stirred him. Her soft mouth he imagined wrapped around his cock. Her delicious body he
imagined writhing in uncontrolled ecstasy as he plied her
with fingers and tongue, driving her to heights of sensation again and again and again. He imagined fondling the
firm, rounded bottom that wriggled so exquisitely against
his palm. She was a natural, unstudied sensualist and a
little perversity would only spice her ultimate pleasure.

And oh, he wanted that, her ultimate pleasure. He
wanted her orgasms. Her complete surrender. Her nakedness, his to enjoy in all ways, open to hand and mouth
and a dozen wicked sexual contrivances. He wanted her
secured to a bed so he could plunge into her, lose himself
in the scent of lily of the valley and woman's musk and
forget every sad thing that had ever troubled him. In the
oblivion of her flesh, there might be peace.

He had to have her.

How could he get her?

What could he offer?

A quick tumble with her simply wouldn't suffice. So
would Beatrice Weatherly be amenable to a *grande af-
faire?* A bohemian, worldly arrangement, between two
adults? A woman of her age and class would normally be
on the lookout for marriage, but posing naked for photographs meant she was far from conventional.

But still, the sense that there was more to her than
simply a rather licentious young woman plagued him.
What if she wouldn't accept his proposition? The thought
of her refusing him and the idea of never having and enjoying every last delicious part of her provoked a sensation like despair in his heart.

There was no alternative. He had power, resources,

money in colossal amounts, and he'd use whatever tactics he had to in order to get her. At the back of his mind, guilt—and a distaste for his own self-serving motives—pricked him, but the jabs were faint and fast fading against the hard ache in his loins and the strangely indefinable longing that racked his chest.

Even as sweet lust gouged him, he began to make his plans. Oh, how convenient it was that her brother was such a ne'er do well.

CHAPTER THREE

A Gentlewoman's Temptation

It was exactly as she imagined drowning might be. Expiring in a well of lush sensation. Transformed into a houri within the space of a few minutes, she gasped in disappointment when Ritchie broke the kiss.

She tried to resume it. Digging her fingers into his thick, curly hair, she attempted to draw his lips back down to hers. Only his hands and mouth seemed real in a world transparent.

"No, no, Miss Weatherly." His laugh was taunting, soft. "Unless you want me to compromise you even more than you've already been, right here on this runner."

He nodded toward the narrow strip of Turkish carpet adorning the corridor in which they found themselves. Beatrice blinked. How had they got here? She was so disorientated that words temporarily escaped her. She could only stare at Edmund Ellsworth Ritchie, and blink like a nincompoop.

His smile brought her to her senses. It was hard, possessive, hungry, mocking. He was highly amused by the way she'd turned into a willing trollop in his arms with barely a fight. And yet still the twist of his mouth excited her and made her want it on hers again.

And elsewhere.

Between your legs...taste you there...

Dear God in heaven, what would that feel like? His tongue in her mouth had addled her senses. If it touched her *there,* if it stroked her *there,* she might go mad.

But still she ached and melted, wanting things that had been unthinkable an hour ago.

What in heaven's name am I doing? I'm letting him turn my head again.

"Please let go of me, Mr. Ritchie. I've got to go back to the ballroom and find my brother." As she wiggled out of his grasp, her skirts fell back into place like the curtain at the end of an operetta.

A farce, most definitely...

Free and covered again, Beatrice swooped low to scoop up her belongings. "I still have dances on my card and gentlemen waiting."

"Fuck them!"

The card was whipped out of her hand, and with its tiny pencil grasped between his long, nimble fingers, Ritchie scratched out every name and scribbled his in each place.

"Mr. Ritchie, there's no need to be so high-handed. Or so profane, for that matter."

"There's every reason to be high-handed. When I see you...when I touch you, I want to have you to myself." As he hesitated, Beatrice made a move but he grasped her arm again, firmly yet gently. "But we need more time together, so we don't have to be so hasty. The pleasures of sensuality should be savored like a slow, unhurried feast." His fingers tightened and he tugged her toward a half-open door, a little farther along the passage.

"I'm not going in there for a...a feast with you. I've got to go back. Charlie will be worried."

The tug became irresistible. She started to follow, her teeth gritted, more vexed with herself than with the strong, insufferable man who was leading her along. Enlightened by the lessons of Eustace, she was not going to be bamboozled by a male of the species ever again.

"Your brother is either too busy drinking or gambling or engaged in some other pursuit to worry about you for the moment. Unless of course *you're* the precious item he's wagering."

"Don't be grotesque!"

Beatrice went hot and cold. Might it actually be true? Charlie had gone on and on about the loss of her reputation damaging her chances of the marriage that would save both their fortunes. What might he be driven to when his judgment was clouded by brandy?

Her moment of hesitation was fatal, and Ritchie whisked her along just as he'd done in the conservatory. Within seconds, he'd plunged the pair of them into a small study or smoking room, a masculine retreat, lined with books. With an air of triumph about him, he locked the door behind them.

Beatrice stepped back and back, away from her captor. Fear surged, but swirled with a delicious longing in her belly. She was a person of supposedly bad reputation, so why not be worthy of it? Why suffer the disadvantages of being a scarlet woman without tasting any of its advantages?

But maidenly fantasies on a drowsy afternoon were one thing. Facing a powerful man in his lust was quite another.

"Don't look at me like a terrified mouse, Beatrice." Ritchie frowned, his broad brow puzzled. "A girl of your experience isn't afraid of being alone with a man, surely?"

But I have no experience. I was tricked into posing for those photographs. I don't even know for sure whether I was touched while I slept or not.

So, indeed, some variety of a mouse. But she wasn't going to admit to being a fool and a gullible ninny, or Ritchie would laugh. And he'd know he could cozen her into any brand of debauchery that took his fancy.

"No, I'm not afraid of you, Mr. Ritchie." She stared at him, her eyes steady. Then, feeling the edge of a chair just behind her knees, she sank into it, feigning a composure that was far from her true state. "I'm just not particularly fond of your company and I don't see why I should grant you any further liberties. Even with my *experience*."

Ritchie shook his head. He was smiling, but he looked impressed in a vaguely perplexed sort of way. "What would it take for you to grant me a few more of those liberties, Beatrice?" He swaggered over to her and stood looking downwards. He was like a giant, a colossus, looming over her, and he seemed to own the very air around them. "I've got a lot to offer."

Beatrice swallowed. Right in front of her, he was still aroused and he did indeed have a lot to offer. She stared at his groin from beneath lowered lashes, then back up at his face.

"You're a tempting woman. Far too tempting." He reached down and cupped her face, and for a moment she thought he was going to draw her lips to him. Perhaps rapidly unbutton his trousers and offer his cock to her, as Ambrose Chamfleur had done to his Sofia.

"And *that* tempts me too, Miss Weatherly." Ritchie laughed softly as if he'd read the lewd visions in her mind. Was he some kind of mentalist, with supernatural powers?

Shaking, Beatrice turned away. If he could read her visions, he could read her desires too. And know that she'd wanted to caress him in that way, and that she'd almost reached out to unfasten his trousers.

I'm going completely mad. I've known the man barely

*more than an hour…and he's turned me into a jezebel and
a slave to carnal appetites.*

His fingers curved around her cheek. The touch was as
soft as thistledown, but no force was needed. Like a cat
hungry for affection again, she rubbed her face against
his palm, and when he pressed a little more firmly, it was
the simplest matter in the world to follow his urgings.

Beatrice laid her face against the front of his trousers,
blindly seeking tangible evidence of his maleness.

Through the fine cloth, he felt hard, warm, alive. His
penis throbbed as if it had a sentience all of its own. Beatrice's mouth watered, remembering Sofia Chamfleur's
enthusiasm, and she rubbed her cheek against him, the
response purely instinctive. She had no idea precisely how
her action would feel to him, but his low gasp of pleasure
was educational

"My dear…my dear…" Ritchie's voice was ragged,
not that of the man who taunted her and who seemed to
control her so effortlessly. Now he was teetering on the
edge of his own precipice, and the idea of that was both
thrilling and alarming.

Ritchie had so much power he could simply throw her
on the carpet and ravish her, and even though the throbbing ache between her thighs told her she wanted that,
and wanted it badly, some self-preserving thread told a
different story.

*Don't give yourself away quite so easily. Always,
always remember how Eustace duped you. From now
on, you must not let a man take the upper hand.*

With one last buss of her cheek against his groin, she
broke his hold on her, and wriggling like an eel, she slid
sideways and out of the chair. Shooting to her feet, she
skipped across the room. Out of his reach.

"I'm afraid that nothing you have is sufficient to tempt

me, Mr. Ritchie." With a twist of her lips, she stared pointedly at the lingering bulge in his trousers.

"I wonder." He didn't look down, but his imperious brows quirked.

"I'm quite certain." It was dangerous to be here with him. She had to get out. "Now, if you have nothing more to say to me, I'll return to the ballroom."

Whirling, she sped for the door, not waiting for an answer. She was close. Escape was in sight. She almost had her fingers on the key in its lock.

Ritchie's hand closed around hers, enveloping it.

How had he moved so fast? And with no sound? Was the wretched man possessed of strange occult powers of bilocation or blink-of-an-eye speed?

"Stay, Beatrice. Let me make you an offer." He turned her, his ungloved hand on her bare upper arm again. The hot feel of it sent strange sparks rushing through her veins, heading for her deepest, most responsive zones. She opened her mouth to say there was nothing he could offer, to lie in effect, but before she could, he went on in a low, hard voice. "If I can't tempt you solely with my amenable personality or my prowess as a lover, perhaps I can offer you a more businesslike arrangement?"

It was difficult to breathe. And when she did, the gasps made her breasts rise and fall alarmingly in the low, newly stitched neckline of her dress. Ritchie flashed a glance downwards, and his lips parted on a gasp of his own.

"Please let me go, Mr. Ritchie. There is nothing you can offer that I want."

"You're a liar, my dear. Your eyes and your blushing face and the way you're panting all tell me otherwise. But that's by the by." He narrowed his eyes at her, suddenly all ruthlessness, "I'm offering to pay your and your brother's debts. Which are considerable and far more than you realize, by the way. I'll also settle an annual sum of money on you both that will keep you comfortable for the rest of your lives."

Beatrice's mouth opened and closed, like one of the fish in the conservatory pond. She knew she looked foolish, but there were no words she could utter.

The debts were perilous, she knew that. Many were inherited from their late father, a dear man but a poor manager, who'd caused them to lose Westerlynne on his demise.

But other debts were more recently incurred. Charlie liked to think he was keeping things from her, but he was as good as using a lace handkerchief to mop up a swamp. Her offers of help in planning a stratagem were always brushed aside with mutters of "gentlemen's business."

There was no hiding what Ritchie wanted in return for his assistance. She knew it. And she knew he knew she knew. It was a transaction as old as time, and one could either shudder over it or accept it with pragmatism. Well-bred young women weren't supposed to even be aware of such negotiations, but they could easily be discovered in sensational fiction and the rags like *Marriott's Monde* were full of them. The ladies of the Sewing Circle whispered and giggled and chewed over such scandals of the demimonde with relish.

I'm standing at the edge a cliff top. One step and I'll tumble over. Unable to prevent herself, Beatrice pressed her hand to her bosom. Surely her heart was thundering so much the palpitations were visible? *But if I don't plunge, it's utter ruin for Charlie and me anyway.*

How much worse could this be than losing everything? She knew she could survive somehow, get lodgings, and obtain some kind of modest employment. The idea of the typewriting machine ever intrigued her. But Charlie? For all his bravado he was more helpless and without a clue than she'd ever been.

"For how long?" She drew in a breath, narrowed her eyes and looked Ritchie in his eyes. "For how long would you…you *require* me?"

"Require you?" Behind those dark blue eyes, Beatrice imagined she saw the whirring cogs of some infernal calculating machine.

"Come, Mr. Ritchie, we both know that it's nothing so noble as an engagement or marriage that you're offering in return for your largesse. If it were, you'd be all kisses on the hand and tender words and a request to present yourself to my brother and I for tea."

"You're very astute, Beatrice. I like that. I see we can proceed." His hand loosened on her arm, and with a twist of the wrist, he drew the back of it across her chest, his knuckle trailing across one breast and lingering lovingly against her nipple through her dress and corsetry.

Even through the layers, the way he circled the little crest of flesh was demonic. Her nipple puckered, though he was barely touching it, and again, ripples of sensation surged through her body, centering between her thighs. Was she such a sensualist, a woman so easy that even the tiniest of caresses could work her into a frenzy?

Is that really such a very bad thing?

The question was relevant. The boundaries of her beliefs and her values were shifting and metamorphosing. She was no longer the woman who'd arrived here tonight.

It was time to call the arrangement by its name.

"For how long do you require me as your *whore,* Mr. Ritchie? I'll enter into an agreement with you, but I insist on a finite period of time. After that, I'll simply forget you ever laid a finger on me."

Still stroking her breast, he laughed. It was a strangely young, happy sound and as he threw back his head, his white teeth glinted in the lamplight.

"You're very wise to set conditions, Beatrice. If I was selling my body for money, I'd do exactly the same." Then he lunged closer, his breath on her neck as he whispered in her ear, the scent of his shaving lotion coiling in her brain. "But I'm not sure you'll be able to forget my fingers quite so easily. Would you like a little demonstration?" It didn't seem that he needed an answer. Reaching for the fullness of her skirts, he began hauling the heavy mass of them upward again. "A little sample of what we might expect…for you *and* for me."

He planted a hard, hungry kiss on the side of her neck, and then went at her skirts with his whole attention, lifting all the layers of petticoats so he could get both hands under them. French faille and lace, cotton and linen, all rumpled like an ocean of haberdashery, but Edmund Ellsworth Ritchie was clearly a master mariner in those waters.

I should stop him. It's too soon. Too great a liberty.

He intended yet more than he'd already achieved, she knew that, but within moments, she was holding up her skirts to help him while he slid his fingers into the vent of her drawers.

Thanking providence she'd chosen an open undergarment this evening, for ease when wearing a multiplicity of petticoats, Beatrice bumped backward against the door. It was hard and uncomfortable against her upper spine, but she barely felt it.

All she could think about, all she could feel, every last thought and notion in her head—all were subsumed to the demands of her aching sex. She moaned out loud when Ritchie found her with his fingertips, effortlessly parting the silky curls and reaching the heart of the matter. Her hips churned when he settled on the little button of flesh there and began to manipulate it in a slow, lazy rhythm.

Her petticoats fell over his arm as he touched her. Beatrice could no longer hold on to them, only on to him. She flung her arms around his neck, gripping hard, as if he were her rock in a wild sea and she would drown if she didn't maintain her purchase. Her legs worked and kicked, her hips rocked and jerked and circled. But still Ritchie fondled her, not missing a single beat.

One long groan issued from her throat, the sound so bizarre and unusual to her own ears that it could have been the cry of a ghoul or some other phantom.

"Do you touch yourself often, Beatrice?"

No! No gently bred woman should admit to that!

But she did do it—yes, she did—in her quiet, lonely bed.

"Answer me! If you admit to stroking your own clitoris, I'll double that annuity."

Beatrice bit her lips, trying to stifle the uncouth sounds she couldn't stop making. He might command her flesh, but he couldn't make her utter such personal revelations. Not even for ten times the allowance!

"Don't fight me, my sweet girl. Don't fight me. I only want to pleasure you and to hear you describe your private games." He kissed her neck again, his hot tongue gliding over her skin as his finger slid around and around below.

Beatrice started to whimper again, tossing her head. She might cry and shriek and wail like an animal, but she would not speak the revealing words he wanted.

"So that's how it is, eh?" He laughed, his husky voice seeming to dance where his fingers flicked and played. "Perhaps another time then? For the moment, I'll simply make you spend."

He circled faster. And as she latched on harder to him, with both arms clasped around his neck, he burrowed beneath her skirts with his other hand, sneaking it into her drawers at the back.

Oh no! Oh no! Please, no!

The thoughts were nonsense. Her whole mind was nonsense. But her body knew what it wanted, what it enjoyed.

When he stroked the rounds of her bottom, and the tender groove between them, she arched like a steel bow and reached her pinnacle. Waves of pleasure pulsed through her belly, and her clitoris beat like a little heart, jumping and throbbing beneath Ritchie's clever fingertip.

Half out of her senses, Beatrice thrashed and jerked about, holding on hard, and when the pleasure crested again, she buried her face in Ritchie's neck, her mouth against his collar, her teeth closing and nipping at his skin. He let out a curse, but he laughed, still working on her.

"Enough, oh, I beg you…please, enough," gasped Beatrice. Perspiration was soaking her chemise, her skin felt like fire, and she was sure that any moment she was going to faint clean away. Her own cautious experimental touches had yielded some delicious little flurries of fulfillment, but nothing like this, oh no, nothing like this. And exquisite as it was, she wasn't sure if she could survive much more right now.

"Are you sure? Are you really sure?" Ritchie was gasping too, his voice broken as if he'd run a dozen miles without breaking his stride, "A woman like you must be capable of infinite sensuality."

A woman like you?

As his hands withdrew with a last affectionate pat or two, Beatrice was deposited rudely back into the world of actions and their consequences with a ringing thud. She was angry with Ritchie, but angrier by far with both Eustace and herself.

Mostly with herself. For her own gullibility, and her incautious pursuit of a little affection. If she'd been more prudent, she wouldn't even have got herself into the start of this trouble.

Finding her feet, she wriggled away, and as her skirts swished down into place again she smoothed them compulsively with her hands. But no amount of smoothing and patting could wipe away what had just happened underneath them.

"You can't behave as if that didn't just happen, you know." He looked at her, long and hard, his eyes dancing. "I have the evidence." In a slow, lascivious action, he raised his right hand to his lips, and licked the very fingertips that had stroked her so thoroughly. "Mmm... delicious. I could become addicted."

"You're disgusting, Mr. Ritchie." Beatrice strode across to the sideboard, where a silver tray bore decanters and crystal glasses. It was the first time she'd ever helped herself to alcohol in the way men customarily did, but the aromatic bite of a fine brandy might calm her nerves. She stared at Ritchie over the crystal rim of the vessel, and what she noticed made her grin before she took a revivifying sip.

A vivid red bite mark adorned his neck, just above his crisp high collar, and he still sported a prodigious erection.

Serves you right! I hope it's exceedingly uncomfortable. Because I'm not going to do anything about it.

"You could help with this." He glanced down, following her look, his long lashes flicking. "I'm sure you know what to do."

"Of course I do, Mr. Ritchie, but I'm afraid I'm not

going to oblige you at the moment." Clopping down the glass on the tray, Beatrice swept across the room and retrieved her forgotten fan, reticule and dance card. She half anticipated that her antagonist would intercept her with one of his preternatural bursts of speed, but he remained where he was, and when she reached the door, he even stepped aside. "You've had your sample, and there'll be nothing further until I see an…an offer in writing. With no assets and no good reputation, I've got to be sure of what I'm getting before I give anything more in return."

Ritchie shook his head, but the expression on his face was as much about admiration as it was of thwarted lust. "You're a shrewd businesswoman, Beatrice." He rubbed his neck where she'd bitten him as if silently adding a few other choice descriptors. "In your place, I'd do exactly the same. You'll have a letter tomorrow."

So easy? Yes, she supposed so. The formal particulars were the least of it. The very least.

"Excellent. Good. I'll look forward to it." She turned the key, grabbed the doorknob and swung open the door, her heart thudding. A few moments ago, this wretched man had gasped as if he'd been running, now she felt as if she'd done the fabled run from Marathon too. And probably back again. "I'll bid you good-night, Mr. Ritchie. I think it's time I went home. I'm feeling rather fatigued and need to rest."

Barely pausing to accept his elaborate bow, and not wanting to see his mocking smile, Beatrice rushed out into the corridor, pulling the door closed behind her with a loud slam. Impolite behavior, she admitted, but after what had happened in that room just now, the natural boundaries of polite, acceptable behavior were redefined forever.

Would he follow? She hesitated just a second or two, but the door remained closed. Much for the best, she supposed, but in that case why did her heart sink inside her with crushing disappointment?

What have I done? Oh dear God in heaven, what have I done?

Between her thighs, right at her core, she felt his touch.

The corridor was silent, but in her head, she heard Edmund Ellsworth Ritchie laughing.

CHAPTER FOUR

In the Pale Moonlight

CHARLIE WEATHERLY BREATHED deep as he exited onto the moonlit terrace and made his way, somewhat shakily, down the broad steps that led to the garden.

His head was whirling, and his heart beating. This evening was not turning out to be satisfactory at all. Not at all. He'd spent a large part of his time avoiding a couple of fellows from his club to whom he owed a considerable amount of money, and to cap it all, instead of behaving with suitable decorum, and attempting to mend her shattered reputation and conduct herself as a suitable young lady for marriage, Bea had been quite clearly seen in conversation with that wretched ladies' man, Edmund Ellsworth Ritchie.

The man was as disreputable as he was rich and Charlie would have been prepared to overlook the former for the sake of the latter, if Ritchie wasn't known to be sworn against further marriages. There were mutterings about not one, but two wives lost already. Hints of mysterious circumstances and nefariousness, but all no doubt hushed up due to the blackguard's obscene wealth.

Charlie frowned, longing for the taste of brandy, even though he was unsteady enough on his feet already. A card game would be a nice distraction too, even if he was likely to lose again.

All that remained was a cigarette. A mild vice, but it calmed his nerves all the same. Pausing to extract his silver case and light a gasper, he turned briefly and realized that, mired in his troubles, he'd walked a considerable way from the terrace and had ended up almost lost amongst a stand of laburnum bushes.

I should be looking out for Bea. I should be protecting her and sheltering her and steering her away from the likes of Ritchie, and that viper Eustace Lloyd before him. She needs a good man with a bit of money, and a proper home and children. It's no good we two rattling around at South Mulberry Street together. The house is far too costly to maintain, and we're getting on each other's nerves.

Poor Bea. He loved her dearly, and his own guilt made him impatient with her. His sister's nature was warm and wild, and he loved her for that. But it didn't make her marriageable. Even her undeniable beauty couldn't offset the trouble she'd got herself into, posing for those photographs. If only she'd named Lloyd in public as the photographer, they might have had some redress. But she wouldn't do that, claiming that what was done was done. And because the pair had never been officially engaged, there was no question of breach of promise either.

And now a new set of rumors about her and Ritchie would be circulating. Charlie had seen the eyes of the gossips following the two of them, and the whispered exchanges. Women would be fluttering furiously over the china tea and shortbread during their at-homes in the next few days, and men in clubs all over London would pick over the story while they shuffled cards and consumed brandy and roast beef, weaving salacious fantasies of his sister being debauched by that whoreson Ritchie. He'd already heard murmured asides this very evening about her "moving on to pose in another bed."

If I'd any guts I'd have shot Eustace Lloyd! One minute he's as good as proposed to Bea, the next minute she's not good enough because she posed naked for his camera. Goddammit, he's the one who sold the photographs anonymously, even if he claims otherwise, and now poor old Bea's the one who's ended up alone and ruined.

Charlie's cigarette tip glowed red as he stood in the shadows, dragging on the thing as if he could suck in good fortune with each breath, and then exhale his self-loathing for not defending his sister better.

After a few moments, the nicotine and the moonlight settled him, and as vague plans and resolutions circled in his head, his senses reached out into the garden.

There was someone else here, just feet away.

"Got a light, friend?" The soft, rough voice reminded Charlie of Westerlynne, and a handsome gamekeeper's lad he'd known as a curious youth. A man stepped out of the deeper shadows, the white tube of a cigarette poised in his fingers. Powerful fingers, steady yet relaxed.

"Yes, of course." Charlie drew out his matches again, astonished to be shaking. The sturdy, powerful man seemed much closer than before, even though he hadn't taken another step yet.

The light from the match showed a strong face too, not coarse, but a little rough-hewn, not a gentleman. What was the man doing out here? Was he a servant? A groom? He wasn't dressed for the ball, but looked well in a plain dark walking suit, and a striped shirt sans collar. His thick brown hair was as straight as wheat, and might have benefited from the comb.

Charlie shuddered, his blood turned to fire. Dark urges

welled in his gut. Another reason to be nervous, and yet excited.

They smoked in silence for a spell, the garden air tranquil apart from Charlie's heart, thumping in the night.

I shouldn't do this.

And yet senses he barely understood told him the man smoking in the shadows was of the same persuasion as he. Well, if Charlie could be sure what his own persuasion was half the time.

Charles Weatherly was attracted to his own sex. He was an unnatural, an invert. But the fact that he also eagerly desired women too only added to his confusion.

"So, friend," said the stranger after a long quiet while, "what brings you out here when the rest of the nobs are in there enjoying themselves? You look like a man weighed down by troubles."

The Charles Weatherly of polite society bristled. He should rebuke this overly familiar fellow for asking personal questions of his betters. But *Charlie,* perplexed and out of his depth, wanted to spill all…both metaphorically and physically. Orgasm was a path to oblivious forgetfulness of problems, just as drink and the thrill of the card table were.

"You could say that, *friend,*" he compromised, taking a drag on his cigarette. "I have my fair share of concerns. But what business are they of yours?"

"Just a sympathetic individual, *sir.*" It wasn't uttered with deference. "It seems like you're looking for diversion on a fine night like this…the pleasures of the moment and to the devil with tomorrow."

Oh, you're sharp!

Charlie puffed furiously. He couldn't speak, silenced by the forbidden, dark excitement, and a new emotion, almost unmanning him. Woes of his own making bore down on him like a heavy yoke, and the sudden sympathy of this stranger strummed his nerves.

His new friend laughed softly, the sound drifting low as he reached out, took Charlie's cigarette right from his lips, and tossed it with his own, end over end, onto the gravel. "You don't need that, friend," he murmured, drawing Charlie by the arm, deeper into the shadows and the moist vegetable secrecy of the bushes.

"What are you doing?" It should have come out as righteous outrage, male and stentorian. But instead, his voice seemed light and insubstantial as the moonlight. He opened his mouth again, but the shaggy-haired stranger covered it with his own, suddenly kissing him with firm warm lips and backing him up against what appeared to be the kitchen garden wall.

Charlie's head reeled, even as the last vestiges of fight made him press against the stranger's lapels with his fists. But it was an empty gesture. Just as quickly, his hands relaxed against the muscular, well-shaped chest beneath the layers of wool and flannel of his companion's clothing. In the blink of an eye, he was clutching the very same lapels, his mouth yielding as he silently begged the man not to withdraw.

Or stop kissing him.

A potpourri of tobacco and whiskey on his companion's lips was intoxicating, and Charlie wondered momentarily where he'd drunk the latter. Was it purloined from his master's supply? Stolen like these moments of forbidden pleasure?

But when a warm, wet tongue plunged deep into his mouth, Charlie wanted to weep like a girl, deliciously subdued. The man's large, confident hand closed round his genitals, at the same time, cupping and squeezing with just enough force.

Squeeze. Release. Squeeze. Release. Hardened to iron, his cock leaped with each tightening.

"Oh good Lord…good Lord," he gasped when his mouth was suddenly free, then he moaned when deft fingertips found his glans through his linen and squeezed that sensitive tip with particular skill.

"No, friend, not our Lord, just 'Jamie.'" His new friend laughed, still continuing his divine ministrations.

Charlie was overcome. Still grasping Jamie's lapels, he threw back his head, bumping it on the rough masonry of the wall yet barely registering the momentary pain. His knees buckled, and he slumped, his back pressed to the damp brickwork. Biting his lips, he fought to suppress his cries, his hips flaunting forward following Jamie's teasing, tugging fingers.

"Do you like that, sir?" A redundant question, the impudent honorific, and Jamie's low laughter only added to the sweet sensations.

"Yes, oh God, yes I do!" Charlie tossed his head against the bricks, aware of the ever-present sooty grime of the city soiling his hair. "My name is Charles…Charlie…oh hell and damnation man, that's wonderful…oh God!"

"But we've only just begun, Charlie," breathed Jamie, then he stabbed in with another deep kiss, before nibbling on Charlie's lower lip. "Shall we let the rampant beast see the air now?"

Reality suddenly pierced the hot, sensual haze. Charlie struggled for sanity, for sobriety, and tried to pull away, even though the denying words still eluded him.

But Jamie would not be gainsaid. He squeezed yet harder on the tip of Charlie's organ, the fleeting moment of cruelty like heaven to a man of Charlie's sensibilities.

"Oh no, you don't, sir." The husky voice was playful yet menacing, "I want a good look at this nice little toy."

"Not so little, I'll thank you," growled Charlie, finding his backbone from somewhere.

"Indeed," said Jamie, his deft fingers working on the buttons of Charlie's trousers…and then his linens.

Charlie gasped as the cooler air of the garden night hit his cock. Jamie eased him out of the aperture in his clothing, and he could almost imagine his flesh steaming, hot and hard as an iron bar.

"Fine…very fine indeed," murmured Jamie, his hand settling upon it.

At first he just held Charlie, his large yet nimble fingers lightly curled as he kissed Charlie's face in little nips and dabs and busses. It was a delicate exploration, all the more stirring for the intimate hold down below. Charlie wanted to scream at Jamie to pump him.

"Steady, Charlie my boy, steady on." Jamie's smile was saturnine as he pulled back a little, staring into Charlie's eyes, his own hooded and sultry as a finger drummed hither and thither, light and taunting. "I'm not ready for you to spend all over me…at least not yet. You have to earn your satisfaction, my fine lad."

Luscious fear coiled in Charlie's gut. He thought of practices performed in certain discreet houses and his organ stiffened harder at the thought, jumping in his lover's hand.

"You're a naughty fellow, aren't you?" purred Jamie, his raw tone revealing his country origins. Despite his desperate state, Charlie felt a rush of warmth, remembering happy times at Westerlynne. "But I'm not doing it all for you, Charlie my lad. Not tonight…" He reached for Charlie's hand and folded it around his very own flesh.

Blood burned in Charlie's face and in the hard rod between his fingers. Dark pleasure surged at the thought of exhibiting his private technique. His fingers shook as they fumbled and slid, and his head felt as light as if he'd supped a quart of brandy on top of the several snifters he'd already consumed in addition to champagne.

But the thought of his debts and troubles was all but forgotten, and when Jamie's hands finally strayed to his own trouser buttons, Charlie didn't have a remaining care in the whole wide world.

CHAPTER FIVE

The Indecent Proposal

"MISS BEA! MISS BEA! Wake up!"

Sleep had Beatrice in its grip. Holding her down deep, it wouldn't be shaken off and she was drowning. But not in the sea or the grimy Thames or even the lake at Westerlynne. No, she was lost in a pair of dark blue eyes.

There was no escaping them. And she didn't want to. Swathed in her dream, and enveloped in heat and sensation, she pressed her soft body to the hard muscled form of a man.

Beatrice's eyes snapped open as two things impressed themselves upon her.

One was that her maid Polly was leaning over her and shaking her shoulder with far more vigor than most employers would tolerate from their servants.

The second realization brought a furnace of blush to her already warm cheeks. Beneath the covers, her flannel nightgown was bundled around her hips in a twisted, tangled bunch and her right hand was pressed firmly between her thighs.

Damn the man. All his fault. He was debauching her in her dreams now. Heaven help her when...

"Miss Bea! Come on! Please wake up, there's men in the kitchen!"

"Men in the kitchen? What in goodness' name do you

mean? What men?" Beatrice snatched her fingers from where they'd strayed. Thank heavens for the mound of bedclothes, tucked high up to her chin. She struggled to wake up properly, still blinking at her maid.

"Two men, Miss Beatrice. They just arrived at the area door and Enid let them in. You know how daffy she can be when she's half-asleep."

Polly looked flushed, almost as pink in the face as Beatrice imagined herself to be. The young woman's plain morning cap was sliding awry, as it often did, and one or two wisps of her flaxen hair were already tumbling.

"Arrived for what? What kind of men, Polly?"

A succession of horrid possibilities, all alarming, presented themselves.

When the photographs had first appeared and her notoriety as the Siren had begun, a variety of gentlemen of the lower press had hung around, hoping for a sight of her, or a statement. For a while it had been quite impossible to go out. But then a new sensation had arisen, as they always did, and her journalistic followers had thankfully drifted away, only to be replaced by a threat of another flavor.

Bailiffs!

Oh no, it hadn't come to this, had it? Just when a solution, however imperfect and insalubrious, had presented itself. And even if it wasn't the dreaded bailiffs, there'd been some decidedly shady and tough-looking coves loitering in their street the past few days. They didn't approach in the way the journalists had, but just looked menacing, and Beatrice sorely feared they might be the hirelings of Charlie's many creditors.

Thoroughly rattled now, Beatrice wriggled her way into a sitting position while at the same time surreptitiously pushing down her nightgown. Erotic fancies must be set aside for the moment in order to deal with hard, cold realities. She just hoped these men could be reasoned with, and persuaded to wait until Ritchie presented his indecent proposal and some money was forthcoming. Reaching for her shawl, though, she was embarrassingly aware that her fingers were somewhat fragrant, and with a scent that Polly would no doubt recognize.

"Have you woken Mr. Charles? I think he'll want to deal with this."

He wouldn't, actually. Charlie would be worse than useless in this situation, and Polly had actually done the sensible thing coming to her first. But she didn't want to insult her brother's manhood by coming out and saying he was hopeless.

"No, actually…they…should I say *he* said to speak to you, Miss Beatrice. The one in charge, that is. He's brought a letter for you, and he says a reply is expected by return."

"The one in charge? In charge of whom? What letter?"

Dear heaven, the offer was here already?

And there was only one "man in charge" whose face sprang readily to mind. She could have drawn it in perfect line-for-line detail this very moment. Complete with the narrow wicked smile he'd worn as he dallied with her. The same demonic yet beautiful expression that had been on his face while he'd touched her.

Polly snatched up the tiny silver correspondence tray from the chair beside the bed and presented it as a moment-by-moment memory of all that had occurred last night washed like a waterfall into Beatrice's mind.

Ritchie's face. His smile. His hands.

His deep blue eyes, burning like dark coals. The devil!

But even though Edmund Ellsworth Ritchie was only a gentleman of sorts, she couldn't imagine him being content to wait in the kitchen for her answer to his own letter. Especially not with Cook blathering on at Enid, and the smoky range, and dish cloths and tea cloths all hung up to dry, and the general state of disorder that pervaded a house with not enough servants.

Beatrice grabbed the letter. She had absolutely no shred of doubt it was from him. He was just the type to demand an instant reply. The arrogance of him, all hurry, hurry, hurry, dance to his tune. He wanted to buy her body, on terms to suit him alone, and he wanted the agreement signed, sealed and delivered before she'd had time to entertain first thoughts, never mind second ones. It was a wonder he hadn't sent a solicitor to notarize the agreement. Maybe one of these men was a lawyer? It wouldn't surprise her.

Yet now that she had the momentous missive in her hand, she hardly dared crack open its seal, despite the fact that Polly was nearly dancing with curiosity beside the bed. To read the proposal was to make it real. Last night, at the glittering ball, she'd consorted with Ritchie, but now all that seemed like a voluptuous magic-lantern show, as phantasmagorical as the erotic dream from which she'd woken.

This letter represented the cold, sordid fact that she was selling her own flesh to get out of debt. She was an "unfortunate" who was fortunate enough to be desired by a man as rich as Croesus. And the fact that he *still* excited her was the most disturbing thing of all.

"These men, Poll…how long have they been here? I assume they're servants, not gentlemen? And if they *are* gentlemen, what were you thinking not showing them into the parlor?"

"They arrived about five minutes ago, Miss Beatrice. Knocking on the kitchen door… Gave Cook a bit of a start, and before I could stop her, Enid had opened to them. I was going to run round next door for Fred, but it didn't seem worth it. Either one of them would make ten of him." Mangling her apron in her hand, Polly seemed to be struck by the same mix of excitement and anxiety that gripped Beatrice. "The fair-haired one said he wouldn't leave until he had a reply, from your own hand!"

Fair haired? Domineering and bombastic? As the master, so the man…or perhaps one and the same?

But then again, Ritchie wasn't exactly bombastic. More clever than that, he was a subtle, persuasive libertine, and he'd swept her into scandalous and sensual behavior by dint of making her believe that was what *she* wanted.

Making her accept, nay, admit that it was what she wanted.

Beatrice set the envelope down on the counterpane and tried to concentrate. What exactly had she said last night?

What did I lead him to expect? Why can't I remember the precise words?

But it was actions she remembered clearly…and re-actions. All else was a delicious, slightly alarming haze. Surely she'd not partaken of all that much champagne? Even the glass of brandy she'd so boldly dashed down had been modest.

It wasn't the alcohol. If she'd become inebriated, surely she wouldn't have been able to recall the physical details. His touch. What she'd done, and had done to her. It all still lingered in her memory, every second perfect and crystal clear.

"This man, the blond one. Did he say who sent him? Does he look as if he's in service with a gentleman?"

Polly's eyes narrowed and her full mouth took on a sultry expression. Beatrice didn't need telling that the mysterious message carrier and his associate had made an impression, and stirred up her maid's frisky side.

"Well, he's a smart sort of chap. He doesn't look like a toff, but he's well set up. Very well set up." Polly cocked her head on one side, and licked her lips. "They both are, Miss Bea. If I was in the position to get a letter, I wouldn't mind getting one from either of them, I must admit." Did Polly wink? Beatrice could swear she had done. She gave the girl an old-fashioned look, and Polly, used to being absurdly indulged, replied with a shrug.

"Did he say who sent him, this spokesman of the pair, who the letter is from?"

"It's from a gentleman of your recent acquaintance, he said. Said you'd be expecting it too." Polly nodded at the envelope, where it lay on the bedcover like an incendiary device clad in heavy cream bond. "Aren't you going to open it now, miss?"

"All in good time, all in good time." She didn't look up. Clever Polly had instincts like a razor. Especially when she scented something juicy going on. "You can go back down and inform this man in charge of yours that I'll reply when I'm good and ready. He and his friend can wait if they so desire, but they might be here all day, and I'm sure whoever sent them has other duties for them."

"Yes, miss. I'll tell him that exactly." Polly's eyes twinkled when Beatrice finally lifted her gaze, and she adjusted her cap and straightened her apron. "But I don't really think he's *my* man in charge at all, miss. In fact I think his mate is much more my fancy. A bit rough and ready and I like them that way."

"Polly!"

Beatrice was well aware of what the other woman liked, and it wasn't always as rough and ready as she'd just claimed.

"Would you like some tea, miss? For while you read your letter?"

Beatrice quelled a smile. Incorrigible as she was, Polly's heart was kind. The two of them had been together a long time, and circumstances had forged a bond between them far beyond a conventional mistress and servant status. Beatrice was tempted to confide. But she really had to read the letter on her own first, and absorb its import without even Polly to distract her.

"Yes, thank you, Polly. And you might as well give your men some tea too."

Polly bobbed a curtsy and retrieved the silver tray. "Shall I wake Mr. Charles then?" She paused, her eyes shrewd. "Or will you deal with it, miss?"

To involve Charlie now would only cause a disturbance. He'd want to play his "man of the house" role, as any brother guardian quite naturally would. But it would be easier to present this to him as a fait accompli, with all the financial advantage it entailed already in place. He'd been strangely distracted last night in the carriage, and had barely spoken, his face relaxed and dreamy. It was probably much kinder to leave him in the dark for the moment and let him enjoy whatever it'd been that had put him in such a gentle good humor. He'd only get cross if he knew a certain person had come calling, and be both outraged and enraged—with perfect justification—on learning exactly what that person had come calling about.

"No, let him sleep, Polly. And don't mention our visitors until I've seen him." Polly's nod spoke volumes about her understanding of her employers, and Beatrice nodded back with a resigned little shrug.

But as her maid reached the door, Beatrice called out. "This man…the one who seems to be in charge. Does his fair hair have a bit of curl about it?" Her hands shook as she studied her own name, written in strong, energetic script on the heavy, expensive-looking envelope.

"Why yes, Miss Beatrice, how did you guess? That's him to a tee."

Beatrice picked at the seal on the back of the envelope with the edge of her nail. "And his eyes, did you by any chance catch a glimpse of them? They wouldn't happen to be blue, would they?"

Polly's smile was sly, even more speculative than before. "Yes indeed. Dark as night they are, almost black, a bit like India ink, Miss."

Beatrice ripped open the envelope, tearing the single sheet inside in the process, and when the faint but distinctive scent of a most particular cologne rose up from the paper, her body quivered as if its wearer was reading over her shoulder.

THE OFFER WAS utterly ridiculous.

You're buying my body for a month, Mr. Ritchie, not my immortal soul in perpetuity!

Not that Ritchie's largesse wasn't tempting. Although she tried not to be a greedy and acquisitive woman, Beatrice was honest enough to admit she enjoyed life's comforts: books and journals; a pleasantly appointed home and tasty food; the occasional new gown or pair of shoes, and outings or at-homes at which to wear them. Yes, she liked all those very much. But the blinding, almost obscene luxury of the high aristocracy wasn't her particular aspiration. She just wanted to live a middling life without any debts, and the fear of bailiffs and moneylenders' toughs she would gladly say goodbye to.

But this many thousands? On top of their outstanding debt paid and an annuity apiece for life for her and Charlie? That was absurd. A woman would have to be a combination of Cleopatra, Delilah, Madame de Pompadour and the famous Mrs. Langtry in order to merit such bounty, and Beatrice hadn't got time to learn but a thousandth of their tricks. She'd need access to all the under-the-counter books in Holywell Street and more for an education to match Ritchie's extravagance.

I wonder if Sofia can provide me with a few tips?

It would be rather embarrassing quizzing her friend on such intimate topics, and even more so, revealing why she needed the knowledge, but after seeing Sofia's performance last night in the conservatory, it was clear that the older woman was well versed in the sexual arts.

And then there was always Polly, who seemed to know everything about everything.

Despite these potential wells of wisdom, it was still going to be hard providing Ritchie with value for money. Especially when she was still technically a virgin—despite what had happened with Eustace—and her cavortings with Ritchie last night were the furthest extent of her amatory experience.

No, she'd have to insist on a lesser sum. Edmund Ellsworth Ritchie was a lecherous manipulative rogue, but she still couldn't bring herself to cheat him. She'd take only enough to pay off the debts that she and Charlie had incurred, and a modest sum to cover their needs while her brother found some kind of sensible paying employment that didn't offend his gentlemanly sensibilities and where he couldn't effect any further financial chaos. After that, a little extra to set herself up in a typewriting and secretarial concern for persons of quality.

Good. That's a decision smartly made. How cool-headed I am in a crisis.

Beatrice narrowed her eyes. There was no doubt who the taller man was, but why on earth would he choose to resort to such subterfuge? Was he trying to discover secrets about her from the servants? Some further skeleton in her closet with which to exert additional leverage over her? That seemed very much his modus operandi.

But even if there was a skeleton, Polly wouldn't reveal it. And neither would Cook nor Enid, she hoped, at least not deliberately. Unlike some ladies of her acquaintance, Beatrice always endeavored to treat the servants as well as she would like to have been treated herself in their situation. She even helped out with domestic chores as best she could now that the household was much reduced, and she hoped that her efforts to lighten the load offset Charlie's occasional airs and graces.

So, Mr. Edmund Ellsworth Ritchie, you'll be disappointed if you're hoping to find any scandalous morsels about me around the kitchen hearth. I've done nothing more wicked than I did with you last night! All my scandalous morsels are already fairly common knowledge.

"AND THEN SHOW the gentleman who seems to be in charge into the morning room, will you, Polly? And tell him I'll be down presently."

Fortified by tea, Beatrice prepared for the forthcoming confrontation. Part of her was nervous, part filled with a perverse and delicious longing. She'd soon have a lover, and by all accounts, one as skilled as he was handsome.

"The morning room, not the parlor?"

"The morning room will do. The parlor needs bottoming and it's only for persons of quality anyway."

That would show him. If it *was* him.

"And then shall I return to help you dress, miss?"

Beatrice groaned inside. The corset, the layers of petticoats, her hair…it would all take an age.

To the devil with it! And with him! He'll see me in dis-

*habille soon enough, and after last night, it's far too late
to stand on ceremony.*

Those blue eyes, so well remembered, seemed to taunt
her, and between her thighs, she imagined she felt his fingers. A sweet ache coiled and tightened in her belly.

"No, that won't be necessary, Polly. I'll receive him in
my dressing gown. You just keep an eye on the friend.
Have Cook and Enid gone out to the market yet?"

Polly nodded, her eyes popped wide, and Beatrice
laughed inside. Her maid was usually unflappable, hard
to shock.

"But, miss, it's not seemly to receive a gentleman in
your night attire. What would people say?"

"People? Pah! They already think I'm a hussy and a
fallen women, so what difference does it make now? And
I'll be dismissing this fellow again within a few minutes. He won't have time to be scandalized." She tossed
her hair, wondering what Mr. Edmund Ellsworth Ritchie
would think of so much curly redness. Polite society considered such hair savage, too wild and abandoned, but
she considered it her very best feature. "Now, about your
business, Polly!"

The other woman lingered. She gave a pointed cough.

"Now what is it?" Beatrice hid another smile.

"Won't you need chaperone, miss? I mean, an unmarried lady receiving a gent on her own…without her
corset." Polly's eyes twinkled with the spark of a conspir-
ator. "There's some that might say that's rather fast."

"Ah, well, as I said, thanks to Mr. Eustace Lloyd, that
famously loathsome and despicable cad, I *am* fast, Polly.
Positively a Derby winner!" Beatrice shrugged. Her damaged reputation still should be considered a calamity, but
all she felt was a delicious liberation. "So I might as well

enjoy the freedom my speedy status affords me, eh? Now, off you go."

"Yes, miss!" Hiding a smirk behind her hand, Polly darted from the room.

Now, as to her dressing gown? The old brown woolen one just wouldn't do. Time to bring out the fine blue one, one of the last new things she'd purchased before their fortunes had turned to dust.

If a man was prepared to pay twenty thousand guineas for the use of her body for a month, the least a girl could do was wear her nicest dressing gown.

RITCHIE COULDN'T RELAX in the damask-upholstered wing chair. It was comfortable enough, and not the usual delicate ladies' morning-room chair; but waiting, waiting, waiting, he couldn't find ease in it.

What's the matter with me? Why am I here like this, sneaking around and behaving like a youth in rut with his brains all addled by his first-ever sniff of a real, live woman?

What was it about Beatrice Weatherly that made him act this way? Despite the licentiousness of the photographs she'd posed for, his gut feeling was still that she was no jaded sophisticate. The women he kept company with were mainly society beauties with inattentive husbands, women eager to share his bed discreetly in return for pleasure and a release from the inherent boredom of the ever repeating Season.

But Beatrice Weatherly wasn't jaded or bored or married, or even particularly sophisticated, and perhaps because of that, his yearning for her was out of all proportion. She had an elusive quality that spoke to his soul and tantalized his cock. Yet for the life of him he was hard-pressed to define it.

And as for pitching up here in mufti rather than gentlemanly finery? To show her he wasn't really a toff at heart, he supposed. A self-made man who'd worked hard, like his father before him.

It was also easier to circumvent Beatrice's ineffectual brother this way too. He'd nothing against the man, but his sister was worth twenty of him.

You're a sly weasel, Ritchie my lad. Especially when it's your cock that's running the show.

Restless, he sprang to his feet, his body humming like an electrical dynamo. The room he'd been shown into by the shrewd-looking maid was pleasing enough, if a little faded and old-fashioned looking, due no doubt the Weatherly's lack of funds to pay for elaborate furnishings and a sufficiency of servants. Prowling around, he sensed instinctively that this was Beatrice's domestic domain, the room she spent most of her time in. He studied a number of bookshelves, which were less dusty than some of the furniture, and their eclectic contents surprised and inordinately pleased him. History, the classics, Mr. Darwin's treatise and other scientific tomes—all these rubbed shoulders with a broad array of novels of high and low style, and notably, issues of the literary publication, *Lippincott's,* all well thumbed. He had a feeling that Beatrice read across the entire spectrum of the arts and knowledge represented. He sensed a mind in her as curious as it was sharp.

The mantelpiece was crammed with photographs.

Experiencing a twist of guilt, he sought out the life of the quiet, sweet girl Beatrice must once have been before she'd taken to posing for pornographic images. Almost reluctantly, he scanned the frames, his heart athud.

Even in stiff formal poses, Beatrice exuded the same energetic sensuality that informed her nude studies.

Perched on a chaise longue beside her brother, and in the company of an older couple, presumably the now deceased elder Weatherlys, she lit the composition with life and vitality. Even with a perfectly straight face, to Ritchie's eyes, she seemed to smile.

He passed hungrily from image to image, devouring each glimpse of her. Here in a country house garden, in a white dress, hair down, breathtaking in her purity. Here, with enormous daring, in fancy dress and revealing her sleek thighs in what looked like her brother's breeches.

And here…oh, here…with another man, in what looked like an engagement photograph. This time it was the lucky fellow who seemed barely able to hide his smiles, while Beatrice was a poem of fond affection.

Ritchie set the frame down with thump; his teeth were gritted and his chest tight. Why such irrational anger? Why so jealous of this lost fiancé? There had been men in her life since, surely, and yet he couldn't seem to summon up much interest in them, or antipathy toward them. Even Eustace Lloyd, who was her most recent admirer, according to his sources, and a man with whom he was vaguely acquainted and for whom he didn't much care.

Beatrice had been seen in public with Lloyd on one or two occasions before the photographs had surfaced, but not since. All very decorous, an exhibition or two, once at the theater. There was no sign of any lasting affection for him here though, no image amongst this collection, so whatever had passed between them was obviously over.

Frowning, Ritchie tapped his fingers on the shelf, thinking, thinking.

Gut instinct told him there'd been no intimacy with Lloyd. The man was personable enough, but there was something not quite pleasant about him, and he'd been suspected of theft at the Plenderley's house party Ritchie had attended last year. Even though he barely knew her yet, Ritchie already credited Beatrice Weatherly with a discerning taste in the men to whom she gave herself.

And yet…who'd taken the nude photographs? He hadn't asked Beatrice, and she'd offered no information of her own volition. Could it have been Lloyd? The man had certainly shown an unusually avid interest in cameras at the Plenderley shindig.

It was something Ritchie would have to look into, as a priority. He had agents and resources aplenty; it wouldn't take long. There must be a good reason why a refined and spirited woman like Beatrice Weatherly had exposed her beautiful naked body to a nonentity like Eustace Lloyd.

Filing that thought away, he moved to the small piano in order to distract himself from uneasy speculation. It seemed odd that the instrument was in here, rather than one of the more formal rooms, but there was Chopin on the music stand, and various selections from Messrs. Gilbert and Sullivan tucked beneath it, along with the sentimental "The Lost Chord." Did Beatrice play? Most well-bred young women of her class did; it was one of the traditional accomplishments of marriageable young fillies. He pictured her slender, delicate fingers flowing over the ivories and jerked with raw desire, imagining the same dexterity on his cock.

Soon.

He was confident that she'd accept his offer. Not because he believed himself irresistible, but because he'd sensed pragmatism in her, and desire, and the hot spark of something less definable, but still intense. For his part, he'd suffered a *coup de foudre,* one might say, although emanating mainly, he owned, from regions far more southerly than the heart.

His cock ached as he rubbed his thumb and fingertip

together compulsively. She'd been so wet and silky last night. Exquisitely responsive. Right there with him. No grim, tight, resisting miss she. No bitter disappointment to him after the promise of her beauty.

A familiar cloud nudged its way into his consciousness, but he shook his head, dislodging it. He would not think of *that* now—or of *her*—just when Beatrice Weatherly was about to appear. The only woman of his recent acquaintance who could truly make him forget.

As if answering his prayers, the doorknob rattled as it turned, and he spun around.

"Good morning, Mr. Ritchie. I didn't anticipate seeing you again quite so soon."

She was a vision, everything he remembered from last night, and much, much more.

"Good morning, Miss Weatherly." Moving swiftly amongst the furniture, he strode toward her and snatched up her hand. The touch of her skin, so smooth and warm, expunged all darkness. "And why wouldn't you expect me? Didn't I say I'd have an offer for you this morning?" Like a voracious schoolboy let loose in a sweet shop, he let his eyes rove over her, unable to hide his sudden, surging desire.

Beatrice Weatherly took his breath away just as easily as she stiffened his cock.

His mouth pressed to the fingertips of her raised hand, Ritchie stared at her over her knuckles. Her brilliant hair was unbound save for a few constraining strands caught in a white ribbon at the back of her head, and she looked a fair demoiselle or an enchanted queen in a painting from the hand of Mr. Rossetti. Her magical curls tumbled and drifted like flame, heating his blood.

"Gentlemen...*and* those not quite so gentle...say a lot

of things, Mr. Ritchie. And regrettably or otherwise, they don't often mean them."

At another moment, he might have frowned over her words and demanded to know who'd misled her—whether it be Lloyd or some other fellow—in order to thrash the living daylights out of him. But right now, his mental processes were too derailed by the need to catalogue her beauty, from head to toe, every dreamlike inch.

Daringly, Beatrice was wearing her dressing gown rather than her day clothes, and she was clearly uncorseted. Fabric of a rich blue shade lay closely against her delicate curves, hinting at the glorious form enclosed and compelling Ritchie to speculate on what was underneath the robe.

Was she wearing undergarments? Or a nightgown? Maybe a chemise? Or perhaps stockings only, with lacy froufrou garters and a flower garland embroidered down the seam?

Or perhaps she was naked, warm and velvety, his for the taking.

"Mr. Ritchie, may I have my hand back, please?"

Ritchie straightened in surprise, then laughed as he released her. She'd bewitched him so completely he'd fallen into a lust-drenched stupor of speculation, just from kissing the tips of her fingers.

"Of course, Miss Weatherly…or may I call you Beatrice, now we're to be close? I see that we've dispensed with the customary chaperone for an unmarried lady."

She stood away from him, gripping her fingertips at the exact place he'd kissed her. For a moment, he saw an image of feminine hands, nervous and agitated, attempting to rub away his touch, but Beatrice didn't do that. Instead, it was as if she was folding her fingers around the kiss to seal it in.

"After last night, I'd say that the issue of my chaperon-age where you're concerned has become redundant, Mr. Ritchie." Her eyes flashed, and he couldn't tell whether it was from anger or from desire. Perhaps it was both. "But even so, that doesn't automatically indicate our continued closeness. I haven't agreed to your proposal yet."

Beatrice was a woman of medium height, but she had a towering quality about her as she stared at him. Her sharp eyes surveyed him as if he were a petitioning worm wrig-gling on the carpet at her slipper-clad feet. Fresh desire gouged Ritchie's belly so hard he felt the urge to double over.

"But my friends call me Bea, so I suppose you can too."

The concession came out of the blue, rocking him harder than the lust did.

"Bea," he murmured. "I like that. Does it mean *we* might be friends?"

"It's hard to know that yet, Mr. Ritchie. Or should I call you Edmund?"

"*My* friends generally just call me Ritchie..." He paused, watching patterns of assessment cross her face, sharp and wary, but bizarrely stimulating too. "So I suppose you can too."

Then she laughed—a free, rich sound—and the ten-sion between them snapped like an India rubber band. It didn't dissipate entirely. No, there was still an edge in the air. But the atmosphere in the room was distinctly lighter.

"Touché, Mr...touché, Ritchie. So shall we sit down and discuss this ridiculous proposition of yours?" With a graceful gesture, she indicated the damask-covered chair he'd been sitting in, and its mate, facing it before the small, cheerful fire set against the early morning chill. "That is when you've first explained to me why you've arrived in this rather unorthodox manner. Sneaking around the tradesman's entrance and dressing like a bookmaker or a pieman, rather than wealthy man of business."

"I wanted you to see another side of me." He plucked at the lapels of his commonplace houndstooth-checked suit. "See the blunt, plain man rather than the facade of Savile Row tailoring and society manners."

She gave him a wry look, as if she did indeed see straight through him and any manner of subterfuge he chose to erect. "It must be a very peculiar society that encourages manners like yours, Ritchie." She acknowledged his shrug with one of her own. "And I still consider your offer quite absurd."

"Why so?"

Though he took care not to show it, Ritchie felt irrational disappointment. He understood her qualms, but still, the idea of not having her after all hit him like a rabbit punch. "I believe that it's a generous offer, Bea, but I daresay I could be persuaded to parlay it a little further if you decree it insufficient."

He watched as she slid her hand into a pocket in her dressing gown and pulled out both his letter, and another envelope, presumably her reply. It was a simple, artless, everyday action, completely without airs, but still his cock throbbed harder at the sight of it. In his imagination, he saw that same pale, beautiful hand sliding elsewhere; slipping inside the unbuttoned fly of his trousers, seeking his flesh.

What would her fingers feel like on his cock? Would they be cool and soothing? Or warm and tantalizingly heated?

Lord, I don't care! I just want her to touch me!

"It's absurd simply because it *is* so generous. Twenty thousand guineas is a disproportionate sum. Not to mention the debts covered, and the annual payment thereafter." She looked away, sideways, a soft blush gathering on the apples of her cheeks. "I have no illusions as to my own value, Ritchie. I consider myself a gentlewoman, and I'm quite pretty, I think. But I'm just a woman like any other woman, when it comes down to it, with face and limbs and shape…and other parts—" the roses deepened "—and a month of my time is worth far less than twenty thousand."

Was she toying with him? Angling like a practiced courtesan in a game of advance and retreat? Somehow, he thought not. Despite her recent notoriety and her avid response last night, the impression came again that the Siren of South Mulberry Street was relatively inexperienced. Was that the root of his obsession with her? A yearning to educate an eager acolyte into a new world of exotic bedroom games?

And she had been willing. It hadn't been a mask, worn as some did, until it was too late.

Compressing his lips, he expunged the dark thoughts again and sought the light instead.

Beatrice Weatherly of the crimson hair, intelligent green eyes and sweet, uncorseted curves. Irresistible temptation in a softly fitted dressing gown.

"Let me be the judge of your value, Bea. I'm usually fairly shrewd in these matters and I always get my money's worth."

Those eyes widened into brilliant pools of jungle green, snapping with outrage. It was all he could do not to throw himself bodily at her and begin cashing in his investment right here in this pleasant little morning room. But instead, he held his hand out for the letters. "So, let's see your counteroffer, shall we?"

CHAPTER SIX

Counteroffer

BEATRICE'S HAND SHOOK as she passed the letters over. Would her sweaty palms have smudged the ink? It was impossible to stay calm and cool around Ritchie. His masculinity was brilliant, as hard and bright as Lady Southern's newfangled electric lighting, with a heat that singed the unwary woman who got too close. As he studied her swiftly penned response, she had to prevent herself from wrapping her arms around her middle. She felt as if she'd fly apart in pieces any moment.

Either that, or throw herself bodily at this handsome, atrocious man who proposed to buy her.

Ritchie was quite a different fellow this morning, yet fundamentally the same. His suit was a soft, well-worn, workaday checked thing, not the tailored, beautifully cut miracle he'd worn last night. With his curling undressed hair, and the suspicion of unbarbered whiskers, he looked almost the ruffian—piratical, wild and strong. He wore no collar, and the top of his striped shirt lay unbuttoned, baring not only a tantalizing triangle of his throat and chest, but, oh goodness, a few curling wayward wisps of sandy-colored body hair. He might as well have been a Gypsy rover in her morning room, and he certainly didn't look like the sort of plutocrat who could casually toss away twenty thousand guineas in pursuit of a paramour.

No, you're more the sort of buck a certain class of woman might lavish twenty thousand on for a month of your bedroom services!

Pressing her hands against the skirt of her robe, Beatrice calmed herself as best she could. She had to remain in control, no matter how intimate matters became. There was pleasure ahead, in the weeks, days and even hours, perhaps. But she still had to keep her wits about her and steer clear of any softer feelings toward Ritchie, for her own safety. Just look what had happened last time she'd thought herself sweet on a man. And yet somehow, Eustace Lloyd had drifted out of focus, like one of his own photographs, completely eclipsed by the man now sitting so calmly reading.

"This is nonsense, Bea. I can't accept it."

His voice was impatient, steely. Beatrice's head shot up, and when she looked him in the eye, her heart sank. His glittering blue eyes were rigorous.

When Edmund Ellsworth Ritchie fixed a price, he fixed a price. Even when whoever it was he was doing business with wanted *less!*

How could anybody be so contrary?

"But two thousand is more than plenty, surely? It'll pay mine and Charlie's immediate bills…I think…with a little left over for me to purchase a typewriting machine and then take some lessons at the Moncrief Street Ladies Secretarial Academy. I saw it advertised in *The Modern Woman* just the other day, with splendid testimonials."

"It's twenty thousand, the debts paid, *and* the annuity, or nothing," growled Ritchie, and to her horror, he tore her hastily penned offer into tiny fragments and dropped them like snowflakes into a little china dish that stood on a Malay mahogany side table. "And I'll throw in a dozen typewriters and a course at your blessed academy and then you can set up a secretarial agency all of your own, if you want." He smoothed out his own letter and glanced around the room until his gaze finally settled on the leather-topped secretaire in the corner. Striding over to it, he took a reservoir pen from his inner pocket, uncapped it, then held it out to her.

Beatrice gritted her teeth, every independent fiber in her body twanging taut. Ritchie was trying to take over her entire life, and her brother's, with his obscene, seemingly limitless wealth. It was a prison sentence just as onerous as their debts were.

She stared at him, suddenly wishing for a different life and a different meeting. In his own way, Ritchie was quite beautiful, and she knew he could do wonderful things for her body. If there were no money and no debt and no buying or selling involved, who knew what there might be between them.

But hell and damnation, all those things were involved! Life was a knotty tangle and not easily resolved except in the sweetly idealized daydreams of idle ladies of comfortable means.

"It's far too much, Mr. Ritchie." She retreated to formality, as a shield. "Far too much. I think that unless you reduce it, Charles and I will have to resort to our own devices and manage some other way."

"This is my final offer, Bea, and I urge you to take it." His midnight eyes narrowed. He didn't actually scowl, but his elegantly molded mouth hardened. "But bear in mind that even though I've bought up a large part of your foolish brother's debt, he's taken out additional loans from certain characters that you'll find are even more despicable than you obviously believe me to be." He twirled his pen at her. "And I saw a couple of very disreputable fellows lurking around across the road just now when my associate and I arrived, and they're precisely the kind of ruffians a shylock might employ."

A cold hand seemed to grip Beatrice's vitals. Ritchie owned some of their debts? Just how determined was he to get her? It hardly bore thinking about, but the alternative was as frightful as it was true. There'd been some unpleasant scenes on the doorstep in the past few days, and it was getting harder and harder for Charlie or indeed anybody in the house to fob them off. The household was primarily an establishment of women, apart from her brother and Fred, a yard boy whose services they shared with their next-door neighbors. Charlie had no pugilistic skills, and tended to hide out at his club most of the time. They had no big, substantial male like Ritchie around to deal with any awkwardness...or worse.

Trapped. No choice. She had to sign. And hope that when it came to it she had enough natural bedroom skills. It wouldn't do not to give Edmund Ellsworth Ritchie good value.

"Very well then, I'll sign." She marched over to the secretaire, snatched the pen out of his hand and scribbled her signature before she could give way to further doubts or the device could leak ink on her fingers. Charlie had purchased one a while back and made a terrible mess with it. "But I doubt if even the most experienced courtesan in the demimonde could give you a tumble worth that amount of money. No woman on earth could be as exotic as all that!"

The moment the words left her lips, the pen was out of her hand, capped and tossed aside. Ritchie grasped her fingers and bore them again to his mouth, pressing his lips first to her knuckles and then turning her entire hand over and pressing his mouth against her palm like a hot sweet brand. His tongue touched her skin, and he murmured, "Ah, but a tumble's the very least of what I want from you, my beautiful Bea. Don't you know that?"

Beatrice couldn't speak. Her mind circled like a carousel, fragmentary notions dancing in her brain while physical sensations cavorted around her body. She'd posed for Eustace, yes, but she was quite certain he hadn't debauched her even though he'd had the chance. He'd been more interested in developing his precious plates than disporting himself with his laudanum-dosed model.

Which left her a virgin, even if not completely naive. Like many women, she suspected, she'd picked up a variety of hints and whispers. Polly liked nothing better than to chatter about scandal and sexual antics, Charlie was sometimes careless with certain items of clandestine literature, and even the Ladies' Sewing Circle was unexpectedly educational. Beatrice was well aware that games were played, diverse pleasures indulged in, and that in the privacy of their bedchambers, cosmopolitan men and women savored a whole cornucopia of outré entanglements that had little or nothing to do with procreation.

And this was exactly what Ritchie wanted from her. This was what he'd paid twenty thousand guineas for.

"Indeed I do, Mr. Ritchie, indeed I do." Tentatively, she reached out and touched his thick fair hair. It felt like silk and, without benefit of Macassar oil or lotion, it curled waywardly.

"Ritchie," he reminded her, straightening up, his teeth white in a wolfish smile, his dark eyes glistening. He was so far from the polished gentleman of last night that he might as well be a different species of creature entirely. Perhaps a perverse and very masculine angel had tumbled to earth in order to tantalize and goad her?

"Very well, Ritchie." He was still holding her hand

as if he owned her. Which he did, of course, now she'd signed the paper.

I'm a whore now. A fallen woman. I'll never be respectable again and I'll probably never marry. I'll be an unmaidenly old maid, typing for others for the rest of my days if Charlie spends all the money.

Sobering thoughts.

"What are you pondering about, Bea?" Ritchie's eyes were narrowed again, but his expression was paradoxically gentle. "Not having second thoughts, are you?"

"Not at all. I was merely reflecting on my new status." She looked down at their hands. Ritchie's was big, but elegantly shaped, and capable, as she knew from experience, of the most delicate mastery. Just thinking about how those fingers had felt between her legs made her anticipate them anew.

"And that is?" He lifted her fingers to his mouth again, the kiss more formal and courtly this time, before releasing her.

Beatrice stiffened her back, trying to ignore the melting, yearning, embarrassingly moist sensation he induced with every simple action. She cast her mind back to their conversation in the study at Lady Southern's last night. It seemed like an aeon ago. "Well, Ritchie, as of now, I *am* the wicked woman that everybody believes me to be. I'm a whore."

The declaration was exhilarating. Liberating. Like a huge rush of pleasure at Ritchie's hand. Of course, the sensations weren't quite the same but the excitement was comparable. She'd thrown off a set of metaphysical shackles and could now float free, do anything, feel anything, enjoy anything. Her month with Ritchie could be the grand adventure of a lifetime, if she so chose, not a shameful state into which she'd been maneuvered.

And after that? Who could tell what life might hold with twenty thousand in the bank and an annuity? She certainly wasn't going to let Charlie get them into a horrible mess this time, that was assured.

She held Ritchie's gaze throughout the entire revelation. Allowing him the freedom to observe her feelings was a facet of her new understanding, a new kind of power. His slow smile told her he recognized it too.

"Not a whore, Bea. I'd never say that and I'd never believe it." He stroked his chin for a moment, and fascinated by even his smallest gesture, Beatrice admired the strong line of his jaw. "No, ours is a rational arrangement between two free-thinking adults who recognize a mutually pleasurable and advantageous situation when presented with it." Such modern talk as he pushed back his jacket and reached into the inner pocket of his rustic jacket. "But if you must label yourself, I suggest you consider 'courtesan.'"

Courtesan? Infinitely better!

Even to Beatrice's relatively untutored ears, courtesanship conjured up images of luxury, decadence, sophistication and a state of willingness to be drenched in breathless, sumptuous pleasure.

Her eyes popped wide when Ritchie withdrew his hand from his pocket—revealing a thick bundle of folded white banknotes. For all her new resolve, the sight still shocked her.

But she willed her hand steady as Ritchie held out a portion of her remuneration on account.

Yes, she'd be a courtesan…and revel in it.

CHAPTER SEVEN

Below Stairs

GRITTING HER TEETH, Polly Jenkins stared up at the ceiling beyond the old airing rack.

I should have bloody well stayed up there. Made some excuse. I shouldn't have left Miss Bea all alone with that sweet-talking bastard.

Concerned about her mistress, Polly was distracted. In other circumstances, she'd have been flirting by now. She was alone with the nice-looking brown-haired fellow who was loitering by the range, drinking tea and eating the slice of fruit cake with which Cook had plied him, and he was normally just the type she'd set her cap at. Especially as, with coast clear outside Cook and Enid had set off together for the market. Miss Bea didn't like anyone to go out alone, so Cook went in person to haggle with stall-holders for bargains now that tradesmen would no longer deliver, and Enid, who was a strapping lass, helped carry the bags.

With the coast clear inside too, Polly should have been making good headway with her handsome guest. But instead she was fretting about Miss Bea, and in danger of braining herself with the airing rack.

"Stupid thing," growled Polly, grappling with the swinging monstrosity and getting slapped in the face by a dangling chemise for her trouble. The household was too hard up to send out its laundry but the rack was heavy and one of these days, it was going to collapse on their heads and bring the kitchen ceiling down with it.

That's all I need. Miss Bea ravished or murdered by some high-handed stranger, and me out cold on the kitchen floor, with not even a grope from his mate for compensation.

It would never have been like this back in the happy old days at Westerlynne—a proper establishment, everyone seemingly comfortably off. Miss Bea happily engaged to her childhood sweetheart, the Honorable Tommy Hastings, and Polly herself courting his manservant, Sam. Even Mr. Charlie behaving with a bit of sense.

But here in London every new day bordered on chaos and most arrangements were topsy-turvy. Hence the shopping and washing at odd hours, and breakfast not served until Mr. Charlie rose from his bed, somewhere around lunchtime.

Polly tried to will herself into the morning room. She was a servant and should know her place, but still. Should she have insisted on waking up Mr. Charlie now? Even though she'd been told expressly not to by Miss Bea?

Not that Charlie would be any help. He was a sweet man when you knew him, but not the slightest bit of use in defending his sister's honor. In fact he'd helped her lose it in a roundabout way. If he'd only introduced her to a decent, respectable chap with a bit of money, instead of that sod Eustace Lloyd, they might all have been nicely set up by now instead of fearing the bailiffs and worse at any moment.

Reaching for another chemise, she eyed her silent, watchful companion out of the corner of her eye.

And who the hell are you, *when you're all at home?*

Was he a bailiff? A moneylender's thug? Him and his

mate had arrived together half an hour ago, with a letter for Miss Bea, and now the other fellow was upstairs, getting the answer. What a cheek, expecting that Miss Bea jump to it and reply straight away? And then insisting on going up to get the letter from her hand.

"If your mate doesn't come down soon, I'm going up there to sort him out! It's not right him bothering Miss Beatrice. She's got enough to contend with as it is." She turned on the man by the fire, who was the younger and had seemed to defer to his cohort. There was something decidedly fishy about the pair of them, and Polly had a feeling she knew the older one from somewhere. If only she'd never let Enid open the area door in the first place.

Even if she did fancy Mr. Quiet and Watchful over there.

"I wouldn't do that, if I were you. Mr. Ritchie doesn't like to be disturbed when he's conducting business with a lady."

Polly's blood boiled. How dare he threaten her, the scallywag? He was no better than she was, and neither was his mate. She didn't trust the pair of them further than she could throw them.

"Mr. Ritchie, eh? Who the hell is he? Who the hell are the pair of you? Marching in here, laying down the law and getting Miss Bea up at an early hour when she was out late last night." She glared at him, meeting his bold stare head-on. He might be a wiry, strong-looking type, just how she liked them, but she knew a trick or two herself, in a tussle. "She could easily have sent her answer round to your boss with Fred, the next-door's boy. That is if we were allowed to know who your mysterious boss is?"

The man unwound himself from Cook's chair by the hearth and joined her at the airing rack. Without speaking, he reached into the basket, took out a pair of Miss Beatrice's drawers and, with a salacious grin, hung them up along with the rest of the washing. As he reached for another item, Polly grabbed him by the arm.

"I asked you a question, Mr. Whoever you are. What's your real business here and who do you work for?" She held on tight to the solid muscle beneath the wool of his work jacket. He felt good, despite the danger he presented. "If I don't get a straight answer, I'll have to fetch Mr. Charles and then we'll see."

The brown-haired man laughed suddenly, as if he knew what she knew. Handsome Charlie meant well, despite his many faults, and he loved his sister. But he couldn't knock the skin off a rice pudding, much less deal with a couple of toughs on his own.

A warm hand effortlessly removed hers from his arm.

"Well, *I* work for Mr. Ritchie, who's the gent upstairs. And *he* works for no one but himself." He held on to her hand, not in a cruel way but with no sign of yielding. Despite her crossness, Polly trembled with excitement. "And don't worry, your lady won't come to any harm. Quite the reverse, he's here to do her—and this entire household— a lot of good."

"What the dickens do you mean?"

"I'm not at liberty to reveal the particulars, but my Mr. Ritchie thinks very highly of your Miss Beatrice, and only wants the best for her. You needn't have any concerns on that score."

But she was concerned. She couldn't help it.

Mr. Ritchie was a handsome bastard, that was a fact, even though for her own taste his friend here was more toothsome. But Miss Bea had been betrayed and exploited already by one despicable, smooth-talking beau, and she didn't need it happening with another.

"It's still not right," she muttered. "Who knows what that blackguard is doing to her. And even if he isn't doing anything, she shouldn't be alone with him without a chaperone. It's just not right!"

"Don't worry, gorgeous, your mistress will be safe with Mr. Ritchie. He never forces women into doing anything they don't want. He doesn't have to. They lift their skirts without him even having to ask."

"You wicked bastard!" Polly attempted to shake her hand free, and this time her antagonist relaxed his fingers and let her go. "Miss Bea isn't like that. She wouldn't lift her skirt for any man except if she were married to him, never mind your pal up there."

The man laughed. Obviously he'd seen the cabinet cards.

"Look, I know what you're thinking and you're bloody well wrong! She's a respectable gentlewoman, I'll have you know. Posing for artistic photographs is just posing for artistic photographs, nothing more!"

"I don't doubt that. But like I said, my Mr. Ritchie is a gentleman, and he's very taken with your mistress, so there's no need for you to make a fuss." He reached down, took the last chemise from the basket and draped it over the drying rack. "There we go. I'll haul it up for you, if you like."

Polly eyed him up. Despite his cheeky smirks and his cockiness, he seemed an honest sort. And easy on the eye too. Despite everything, Polly had a peculiar urge to trust what he said. And he certainly seemed unshakably loyal to his boss.

"Thank you. That'd be very kind. It's a heavy old bugger, and that's a fact."

He laughed, then looped his hand in the cord and effortlessly hauled the rack up to the ceiling. Polly imagined him being just as sure and effortless in his dealings with a woman, and beneath her skirts, her belly tightened with sudden desire.

"Thanks again, Mr… What is your name, by the way? Would you like some more tea?"

"Yes, I'll take a drop, thanks," her new friend said easily as he secured the cord with a competent-looking twist and turned to face her. "And the name's Brownlow. But you can call me Jamie, if that suits you."

Jamie. Such an easy, quiet, innocuous name, yet he looked very far from that. Jamie Brownlow was a man of the world, clearly, and tough. And he had a tricky, clever quality that was exciting.

"Jamie, eh? I expect I could call you that." Polly reached for a cloth to push the heavy kettle onto the hottest part of the range. Jamie Brownlow was at her side in the blink of an eye, and before she could protest, he had the cloth and was doing the honors for her. "Thank you, Jamie… My name's Polly Jenkins, but you can call me Polly, I suppose."

"Polly it is then." Laughing, Jamie reached for the teapot. "Let me make the tea. You maids are always worked to a standstill. Take the weight off your feet, and have a breather for a change."

How very modern. Men almost always expected women to do the serving, even if they were belowstairs types like Jamie. Not even Mr. Charlie, when he wanted some comfort, was so courteous.

"That's very decent of you, I must say." Polly settled on the old, ill-stuffed sofa that was set to one side of the fire, opposite from the armchair. "Although I'm not sure that Cook will be so pleased with you handling her pots and suchlike."

Jamie grinned over his shoulder as he set about his

task. "Oh, don't you worry, my Polly. I'm fully accustomed to handling a female's pots and suchlike. In fact I've been told I'm quite an expert in these matters." He winked, and Polly was struck by his provoking, wicked eyes. They were green, quite light, but with an unusual slate-colored cast, and they twinkled with intelligence and guile.

"Don't be so saucy, Mr. Brownlow. We've only just met, and I don't hold with overfamiliarity with men I don't know anything about."

"Ah well, we'll have to rectify that, won't we? What do you want to know about me?" He was moving about the kitchen as he spoke, working efficiently through the ritual of making the tea.

"I…I don't know." Polly felt flummoxed. As he neared the stove again, he unbuttoned his jacket and tossed it over the back of a chair, then rolled up his sleeves to show strong, well-shaped forearms. "Who are you, really? Why are you here? And who's your Mr. Ritchie when he's all at home?"

"So many questions… Let's have our tea, eh? And then maybe I'll answer some of them." He waggled his eyebrows at her in a way that made her belly tingle. "When's your Cook coming back, by the way? Will she be long?"

"Oh, she'll be a while. I think one of the stallholders is sweet on her, so who knows when she'll be back. I don't like to think of what they're up to, an old bird like her… and Enid will just wander around willy-nilly if there's nobody to supervise her." Polly grimaced. "We're not a very well-run household, are we?"

"There's worse about, Polly. I wouldn't worry." He shrugged.

She barely knew him, and yet, suddenly, she loved the way he moved, so loose and so easy. He was originally a country man, she guessed, and he still had a free way about his body as if only yesterday he'd been out trudging fields and copses with broken gun over his arm. For a moment, she frowned at the piercing pang of yearning, remembering her lost Sam, who'd always loved the outdoors. It was cruel how he and Mr. Tommy had died in the same boating accident, leaving both her and her beautiful mistress lost and distraught.

"Wake up, Polly!"

She blinked, finding Jamie before her with a steaming cup of tea.

"Sorry, I was miles away."

"In a happy place?"

Yes, it had been. But dwelling morbidly on the past wasn't her habit, and like Miss Bea, she always tried to make the best of life and look forward rather than backward.

"It was once," she said, "but me, I like to make every place I pitch up in the best I can."

"Me too. Hitch up." Taking his own cup, Jamie edged his way onto the narrow sofa beside her, and Polly's last wisps of melancholy dissolved in the sudden excitement of his proximity.

Lord, but he was a forward so-and-so!

Polly wasn't complaining though. He was handsome and he smelled lovely. She gave him an arch look and he waggled his eyebrows at her again as if he knew she thought he was forward but didn't care.

"It's a good philosophy is live for the moment." He took a sip of his tea, then put the cup down on the floor beside him. "I like to take advantage of every opportunity. You never know what's around the corner, do you, sweetheart?"

"True, very true." Polly sipped her own tea, barely tasting it, then placed the cup on the shelf next to the sofa.

She did like to seize any opportunity. For happiness. For pleasure. Since she'd lost her Sam. She was a careful girl and didn't take silly risks, but there were ways to enjoy oneself without treading the road to ruin.

And you know that, don't you, Jamie?

She looked into his lambent eyes and knew he understood her without having to spell it out.

"You're still worrying about your mistress, aren't you?" he said unexpectedly. "But you shouldn't. The boss admires your Miss Beatrice…and he wants her…but he'll take care of her too. He's like that."

Polly opened her mouth to quiz him as to what exactly Mr. Ritchie's intentions were, but no words came out, because Jamie lunged forward—and kissed her fair and square.

It was so sudden that her lips remained soft and pliant, quiescent with surprise. She blinked furiously, aware he was looking into her eyes as he kissed her, his own unwavering, but all thought of resisting him dissolved like steam from the kettle.

His mouth tasted of tea, and his tongue was bold, diving around and teasing hers without hesitation. When he pushed her back against the shabby upholstery, he settled his hand on her breast as if he'd been making free with her for months with her full agreement.

"Mr. Brownlow!" she protested, laughing, as those nimble fingers of his slid beneath her apron, searching for the buttons of her plain morning uniform.

"Miss Jenkins!" he mocked, getting a forefinger inside, probing, "Don't you wear a corset, you naughty girl?" The exploratory digit wiggled its way to the buttoned front of her chemise and slipped inside there too.

"You try spending a day doing housework, all trussed up. Even Miss Beatrice leaves hers off when she lends a hand doing chores, and she's a lady!"

His hand still inside her clothing, Jamie pulled back. "Miss Beatrice does housework? Now there's a turn-up. These genteel misses usually spend their days reading and sketching and doing good works, don't they?" With a determined push, he shoved his whole hand inside her dress, and Polly felt buttons pop and give.

"You're pulling off my buttons, you rogue," Polly gasped as that whole hand cupped her breast and squeezed, and Jamie pressed her back tighter against the sofa. "And yes, Miss Bea helps. This is a big house, and there isn't a full staff. Enid's a bit clueless, even if she means well. Cook's got a bad back and does nothing but her kitchen duties anyway. If Miss Bea didn't pitch in it'd be just me. And I'm her lady's maid too, as well as answering the door and such."

"Well, fancy that. Mr. Ritchie will be impressed. He likes a woman with a bit of backbone instead of the usual pampered beauties all the time."

Alarm made Polly stiffen, even though the rhythmic way Jamie massaged her breast and rocked against her was making her giddy.

"So, he's a regular ladies' man, is he? Does he get through a lot of these pampered beauties and backboned women?"

She frowned. Jamie was kissing her again, covering her face with wicked little busses. Something had been nagging her, ever since they'd begun talking. The name *Ritchie*…

And then she twigged it, the thing that had been bothering her.

"Bloody hell, Jamie, your boss isn't Edmund Ellsworth

Ritchie, is he? I read about him in *Marriott's Monde*. He's a flipping degenerate, always seen out with the fastest women around the town. Isn't he supposed to be tupping the Duchess of Ambleside, with her husband's say-so, because the old fellow can't get it up?"

So, it wasn't marriage or anything straight that devil upstairs was proposing. Edmund Ellsworth Ritchie was notorious in the scandal papers for his amours but there had never, not once, been any hint of a finer pursuit.

Jamie laughed. "It's all exaggeration and damned lies." He started pulling at her skirt. "Although I think he likes having a wicked reputation, Mr. Ritchie does."

"So he's not servicing the Duchess of Ambleside then?" Polly placed her hand over Jamie's and to her surprise, he halted immediately. In her experience men often weren't so easily swayed from their purpose when there was a sniff of a bit of sauce in the air.

"Good grief, no! He wouldn't go within a country mile of a raddled old hag like her. He's very particular and careful, is Mr. Ritchie. It's just that the purple press like to write juicy stories about successful men like him. And if there aren't any truthful ones, they just make them up."

"Don't they just," muttered Polly, not cross with him but with that purple press. They'd made out Miss Bea to be a loose-living strumpet, just because of those photographs. None of them would've been interested in the true facts of the matter and Miss Bea was too well-bred to parade them.

"Don't you like a bit of juicy scandal, Polly?" His green eyes were sharp and shrewd, and Polly wondered how much she could trust him. Or his master. Better not say anything. Miss Bea had enough problems already, and loose talk could get her into more trouble than ever.

"Oh, I like it well enough…but how about you, Mr.

Jamie Brownlow? Do you have a scandalous reputation, like your boss?" She relaxed her hand on his, a subtle signal.

"Oh worse, much worse," he murmured, his mouth close to her neck again. "I have proclivities of my own, dear Polly. Degenerate quirks that Mr. Ritchie chooses to turn a blind eye to."

Polly wondered. This fellow could probably charm anyone into anything if he wanted, and there was a dangerous steeliness about him too. She opened her mouth to quiz him about his quirks, but suddenly he kissed her again, hard and sweet and bossy.

When they broke apart, she was breathless and dizzy-headed, but Jamie seemed in possession of every faculty.

"Oh, I'd love to have some fun with you right now." His hand moved on her thigh, rucking up her dress and her petticoat beneath it. "I've been cursed, or some might say blessed, with the devil of an appetite for pleasure, and I can't resist a beautiful girl like you."

"You're an outrageous dog, that's what you are!" Polly wanted to resist. She knew she *should* resist. But she had that devil of an appetite too—and a fumble here and there with Mr. Charlie went nowhere toward slaking it.

"I know. But like I said, life's short. You've got to snatch happiness when you can." For a moment he looked serious, and glanced upwards, giving Polly the strangest feeling he was thinking about his master rather than himself. "What say you, Polly?"

Indeed, indeed. After the loss of her Sam, "live for the day" was Polly's credo too. But Cook and Enid could be back at any moment, or Jamie's Mr. Ritchie might conclude his dealings with Miss Bea and come back downstairs.

She took a deep breath. "Right. I might spare you a

minute. But not here. Anyone could come in. Your boss, Miss Bea, or Cook and Enid. Even Mr. Charlie knows where the kitchen is, though he's not usually awake at this hour." Sliding off the sofa, she stood up and grabbed Jamie's hand. "Come with me. If you don't mind the cupboard under the stairs, we can be private there."

"The cupboard under the stairs? How bohemian," Jamie purred, following her lead out into the passage. "It's been a while since I frisked with a woman in a cupboard."

CHAPTER EIGHT

Something on Account

"TAKE IT. A little something on account. I think your, shall we say, less established creditors are only going to get more and more insistent, and less and less likely to listen to unsubstantiated promises of restitution."

Her hand didn't seem to have any grip in it, and she couldn't get a hold on the bundle of money. Ritchie folded his strong hand around her fingers, and then conducted them to her pocket, so she could slip the notes inside it.

"Thank you, th-that's most generous of you."

Ritchie's hand glided from her pocket to the curve of her hip where it settled, sly and confident, containing her where she stood. "This is the reality of our arrangement, Bea." The fingers moved on, slipping over the soft cloth of her dressing gown. She wore only her nightgown beneath, and he would soon know that. "I give you my money, and you give me yourself, freely and unreservedly." She felt him probing, searching for telltales, trying to work out what lay underneath the blue silk. "And perhaps now I can have a little on account?"

Beatrice's heart thudded. She was bought and paid for. She couldn't prevaricate now. Her breath came in short little gasps, even though she tried to steady it. A sensation like being on a calliope made her dizzy and excited. She had to give Ritchie what he wanted. *She* wanted it too. It was lucky she wasn't respectable anymore, because being a courtesan gave her *carte blanche* to indulge herself. The gates were open and delicious sensations beckoned.

And yet her head whipped around just as Ritchie's big, warm hand cupped her bottom.

The morning-room door was unlocked and anyone could come in. Polly or Enid… Good God, what if Charlie got up early for the first time in living memory and blundered in on his sister being ravished?

"Oh, please, no…not here! Not now!"

Ritchie laughed, a rich complex sound, half benevolent, half mocking, all provocative.

"Afraid of discovery, Bea?"

"Of course I am!"

In which case, why was she pressing herself into his hold, rubbing her bottom against his fingers like a wicked little cat?

"You weren't afraid last night when you were cavorting with me at Arabella Southern's pile." His grip on her changed, his fingertips curving like an arc of the devil, pressing in to make indecent contact with her through the cloth of her dressing gown and nightdress. She squeaked out loud when he rubbed to and fro, to and fro.

"This is different. This is my home and someone might come looking for me…the servants… For God's sake, Ritchie, my brother might stroll in at any second." It wasn't likely, but her luck lately had been fickle. "Even you can see how unthinkable it is for him to catch sight of you making free with me. Even if I am doing it to save him from his debtors!"

"Only for that?" he whispered in her ear. He sounded amused, but she sensed asperity too. What did he want her to say? The receipt of a small fortune didn't automatically lead to her falling madly in love with him.

But couldn't you love such a man for nothing at all?

Where had that come from? No woman in her right mind would fall in love with Ritchie. He was only suited to wild affairs, scandal and, yes indeed, lust. His looks and his virile magnetism made that inevitable.

But the finer, more delicate feelings? No. He was a sophisticated animal, not a creature of sentiment.

But like a splinter in her thumb, the notion was embedded now, no matter how much she mentally shook herself. Ritchie wasn't for fidelity, conventionality, hearth and home, children, a respectable union. And the sooner she disabused herself of all that, the better for all concerned.

"You know what I mean, you devil," she said when he increased his subversive attentions to the groove between her buttocks. "Ritchie, please stop!"

His fingers stilled but didn't retreat. "What's wrong, don't you like it?" he mocked. "Be honest. You owe me the truth."

Beatrice gasped, her chest heaving, her uncorseted breasts rising, pressing against her daring tormentor. "Of course I like it!" she cried. "But I'd enjoy it much more if you'd do me the courtesy of at least locking the door."

Ritchie's finely marked brows lifted and he seemed to consider the idea. "You're right, my dear, of course," he said softly, giving her bottom one last light squeeze. "I'd much rather have you relaxed. We'd both enjoy that more." As if unwilling to release her, he led her by the hand to the door, where he turned the key with a firm little click. "There, that's better. Now come and sit on my lap for a while, you delicious woman, and let's both make ourselves at our ease."

They took the larger of the two wing chairs. It was

wide and commodious, and Ritchie flung himself down into it as if he owned the place. Which actually, he did, Beatrice supposed, as he'd no doubt paid the outstanding lease payments too. Bracing his strong thighs, Ritchie nodded at his lap, pulling teasingly on her hand.

Beatrice swallowed. There was a pronounced bulge in his trousers. The sort that a refined woman wouldn't remark on, but which she found utterly fascinating. When she settled down onto it, it felt quite hot even through the sturdy fabric and whatever he wore beneath.

Maybe he doesn't wear anything underneath?

This startling thought made her heart beat even faster. Edmund Ellsworth Ritchie was just the sort to brook societal rules about undergarments, simply for the devilment of it. Beatrice nudged herself along his lap, trying to tell whether he was wearing drawers or not. The action produced a husky, heartfelt groan.

"That's it, torment me with your beautiful bottom, minx. Drive me wild." He sat back in the chair, shifting her sideways, with one arm around her waist while the other took possession of her thigh. His fingers felt just as warm as the naughty bulge beneath her did.

"I was simply adjusting my position for comfort," she shot back at him. Pressed under her haunch, she felt the beast in his trousers stir.

"But not for mine, dear. Not for mine."

Beatrice wriggled again. Let him suffer. The idea of tormenting him thus brought an intoxicating surge of power.

"I thought a gentleman rather liked it when a woman rubs herself against him."

"Gentlemen do like it," he murmured, rubbing his face against her hair, "but not when there's no opportunity forthcoming for their relief, my sweet."

Beatrice frowned. What was he talking about? He could have her now, if he wanted. Now that she had the notes in her pocket, he wasn't obliged to wait, no matter how much more comfortable and opportune a bed might be. He could pluck the full flower of his new purchase whenever he wanted.

"But…um…you can have relief, can't you?" Blood rushed furiously into her face, and into the parts of her body closely adjacent to his body. Suddenly, *she* wanted *him,* because *she* didn't have to wait either. There was no saving her irrelevant virginity for marriage now.

I'm a fallen woman, Ritchie. Let's get on with it. There's no fun in being a sullied rose if I don't get to enjoy the pleasurable parts of the sullying!

"Not today, Bea. Not today."

Beatrice blinked and stared at him. What on earth was he about now, the insufferable man?

She pushed herself a little way away from him, searching for explanation in his face. But Ritchie gave her a brief, terse look and then glanced away, the action strangely final. *Don't question me,* he seemed to say, his profile so hard and cool it forbade persistence.

You are a strange man, Ritchie. A very strange man indeed. You hand over a queen's ransom for me, but now you're in no rush to sample the goods.

But even as she pondered, she sensed yet another change in him. His body relaxed beneath her, tension releasing. When he turned back to her, he was smiling, his dark eyes playful. "I'm more interested in *your* relief at the moment, delicious one, so why don't you tell me about it?" His warm hand cupped her chin, holding her face, so she couldn't look away. "I know you pleasure yourself. Don't deny it. Be forthright."

Beatrice felt as if her face were pulsing like a beacon.

Bizarre as it seemed, she felt far more embarrassed by talking about carnal acts than the prospect of performing them. How could she possibly reveal her nocturnal practices? Yet how could she not? The money…the money…

Defiantly, she met his gaze, mesmerized by the unusual blue of his eyes. It was so dense, so inky yet vibrant, with a flame deep inside. Her dilemma dried her mouth, and when she licked her lips, Ritchie sighed, and his long eyelashes fluttered, dark as his hair was fair. Against her thigh, his cock kicked again, as if she'd suddenly stroked it.

"Yes…yes, I do pleasure myself. And I know it's not exactly the sort of thing a well brought up young woman should do, but obviously I'm a bad person. A wrong 'un, with an overly sensual nature. Which is what put me in this predicament in the first place."

Ritchie leaned forward and dropped a single kiss on the tip of her nose, almost affectionately. "Not a predicament, remember, just a mutually beneficial arrangement, with many advantages for both parties. Now, come on, Bea, tell all. I'm agog to hear it." His hand slid up and down her thigh, ruffling silk, and then lifted, to cup her breast through the unfortified bodice of her dressing gown. "What do you do? And what prompts you to it?"

Now *there* was a question.

"I…I don't really know. I suppose sometimes, when I read a novel of romance, I can't help thinking what comes after the kisses and the marriage. Or if I read of a notorious scandal in a magazine, it just pops into my head, the question. What have these people done to instigate such a sensational report? It must be something desperately sensual and addictive, for them to risk discovery and shame."

The moment was pregnant with other questions. Ones Beatrice feared. Was he going to ask her why she'd posed

for the photographic images? It was a natural enough enquiry...but there was far less shame in frolicking with him
than there was in admitting she'd been duped and made
a fool of by a man who'd turned out to be a horrid sneak
and liar.

But he didn't ask. Instead, as if sensing her dilemma,
Ritchie pursued his point. "So you lie in bed thinking
about books and articles in magazines?" He chuckled, and
as the husky sound rang out, his hand closed around Beatrice's breast, gentle, yet affirmative. His thumb flicked
back and forth across her nipple, to and fro, to and fro,
making her gasp. "How very quaint... Anything else?"

It was hard to think straight with that wicked little
action repeating and repeating. He was barely moving, but
the effect on her constitution was colossal. She wanted to
move, even more than before, to grind her bottom against
his thighs and his cock, and part her own thighs so she
could press herself, her very self, against him.

"Yes...there is...there are certain other magazines,
magazines of Charlie's..." She buried her furiously pink
face against Ritchie's neck, but it didn't help. His spicy
masculine lotion only made her feel hotter and more excited than ever. "He's a bit careless sometimes. He doesn't
always put away things he should put away... I've seen...
um...gentlemen's journals, and also albums...cabinet
cards..." She paused, wanting to tear open Ritchie's shirt
and taste him, she felt so wild. "Far ruder and more salacious than the ones I posed for, by a country mile!"

There, she'd broached the issue, even if he hadn't.

"Ah, so you're a connoisseur of pornography, my dear
Bea." Ritchie's arm tightened around her, almost protec-
tively. "Nothing wrong with that, I am myself. That's how
I found you and decided I had to have you."

That fact should crush me. Why doesn't it?

But she felt only relief, almost thankfulness. She would never have met this man if it hadn't been for Eustace and his sly, persuasive compliments, his talk about creating art, and his neat way with laudanum-laced Champagne cocktails. In a bizarre twist of fate, she suddenly felt grateful to her nemesis.

"That's all well and good. But there was hell to pay when Charlie happened to obtain one of my cards in his latest selection. I don't know what appalled him most—the fact that his sister was a naked model, or that he was forced to confront me about it and admit to his fondness for such pictures."

"That must have been very difficult for you, Bea." Ritchie's voice was soft. He sounded sympathetic now, rather than teasing.

"It wasn't exactly the most pleasant revelation of my life, but one just has to deal with these things as best one can."

Suddenly, it almost seemed as if the pair of them were set in amber, detached from their sensual game of back and forth. "And what does he think of my indecent proposal to you? Have you told him about it? Perhaps there's another way I could explain the money, if you'd prefer me to."

Beatrice stared at him, round eyed. Edmund Ellsworth Ritchie was the most peculiar man, and stranger with every second that passed. One minute he was a ruthless libertine, hell-bent on shocking her and breaching every decent standard. The next, he was considerate, sensitive, and as eager to please her as a bona fide suitor.

"I haven't told him yet, but I will do today. I doubt if he'll like it, but he's not quite so proud and stupid that he won't see it as the logical answer to our problems. Poor lad, though, he's mortified that he's failed as the man of the house."

"Indeed, he *has* failed. He's failed you, my dear," said Ritchie. He sounded solemn but his eyes were twinkling. "But fortunately he has a sister who's much cleverer than he is. One who's unafraid to use her peerless assets." Visibly amused by his own analysis, he dove forward for a kiss, and took it before Beatrice could draw breath, or reflect on the darker aspect of "using assets."

Within moments, she was almost swooning with pleasure. Just from the kiss. How could the simple pressure of lips against lips, and the exploration of a tongue, seem so spectacular with this one particular man? He used the same anatomy as Eustace had, and dear Tommy before him, yet created an entirely new experience, like an angel or a god.

While his tongue played in her mouth, Ritchie's hand moved just as deftly, squeezing first one of her breasts, then the other, in a light and teasing action as if his fingers were saying good-morning to her nipples. With the introductions over, he turned his attention to the frogged fastenings down the front of her dressing gown, and dispatched them with ease before moving with purpose to the defensive line of mother-of-pearl buttons that fastened the front of her nightdress.

He negotiated those little discs blindly too, his fingers whipping down the tight row, pop, pop, pop, right down to her waist. Beatrice moaned and clasped at the edge of his waistcoat as cooler air inveigled its way into the newly opened gap, and she was compelled to wriggle again as he prized apart the bodice of her nightgown.

"Oh yes...oh yes," he whispered, pulling the opening wide in a ruthless gesture. "Tut-tut, my dear, your nipples are hard. How very scandalous." His warm palm settled over her breast, enclosing it gently. "Although I must say, I'm far from complaining."

Even after only one previous encounter, Ritchie's touch was as familiar as if he'd fondled her a thousand times, yet just as thrilling as the first time, last night. The sensation of bare skin on bare skin took her breath away even more than his kiss did.

Beatrice trembled like a filly at the gallops. A man had pulled open her nightdress. He was handling her. Caressing her, and exerting the rights he'd just purchased. A miss more cognizant of life's proprieties would have been gritting her teeth to endure it. But instead, she was loving every second. Moving excitedly in his lap, she edged forward, pushing her breast into the curve of his hand.

"Ah, my sweet, sweet Bea," Ritchie murmured, the breath of the words right inside her mouth. "So willing. So eager. I adore a woman who's honest about what she wants." His tongue pushed in, the action unmistakable. Like the raw thrust of a man into a woman. Beatrice hadn't felt that yet, but she had the instincts of every woman down the ages. Ritchie's muscular tongue made her quiver between her legs. "You must never hide how you're feeling from me, dearest. I want no hypocrisy. I've paid for the truth."

Another reminder of money. But it still didn't repulse her.

How modern I am. Smiling inside, Beatrice essayed a thrust with her own tongue and garnered a grunt of approval from Ritchie. *Not long ago, I'd have been frantically trying to pretend to myself that this was a pretty relationship, with an ardent but respectable suitor. But now...well...the truth is more exciting.*

Ritchie's tongue was relentless, dueling with hers, pushing in and possessing her mouth like an explorer in a foreign land claiming territory for the Crown. And all the time that he was kissing her, his hand was moving with the same sure confidence on her breast, squeezing and stroking, cup and release, cup and release. His other hand was at her waist, his grip unyielding.

A few breaths later she understood why he constrained her. With the tips of his finger and thumb, he took hold of her nipple and pinched it lightly until she squeaked against his lips.

Oh, that was piquant. It hurt quite a bit. But between her legs, her sex jumped and clenched, tingling with a rush of liquid heat. At his second pinch, her flesh rippled in a wave of sublime sensation and she jerked so hard on his waistcoat that she could swear she heard a seam burst.

"You like that, don't you?" His mouth moved across her face and settled against her neck, beneath her ear. He licked her skin there as he tugged at her nipple again.

Beatrice felt as if she might ignite, explode. Wild energy filled her, an excitement and amazement that made it impossible to keep still. Her legs moved of their own accord, her thighs rubbing and scissoring, trying to bring ease to the delicious heavy aching right inside her.

Longing to reach down and enclose her sex in her own hand, she prayed that Ritchie wouldn't squeeze the tip of her breast again, because she wasn't sure she could bear it much more. Silently, she begged him to stop…and the same time to go on and on, because if he didn't, she would die, she was convinced of it.

"*Do* you like that?" His voice was stern, insistent. It could have been mock sternness, but she wasn't entirely sure. Either way, it excited her more than ever. She grabbed at a fold of her dressing gown, her fingers on fire with the need to touch herself, or to reach down beneath herself, search for Ritchie's cock, and touch that instead. "Answer me."

"Yes! Yes, I do!" She swallowed, drowning in a sweet maelstrom, yet coming up for air and the light of revelation. The dawning of the libido's complexity. "I don't know why, but I like it very much."

"What does it make you want to do?"

Wriggle. Touch herself. Press herself against him. Do all those things and more. Much more.

But her throat seemed to have closed up. She couldn't form the words, only move uneasily on his lap, jerking and pulling at his clothing and hers, while the infernal tugging on her nipple continued.

"Tell me, Beatrice. I will have an answer from you." He tweaked harder, with a demonic twisting action.

"Ah! Oh my goodness!"

In a cooler moment, she would have acknowledged that really the pain was minimal, but the jolt of it made her sex ripple like a pond in a summer breeze. Was she spending? It was difficult to tell, the careening messages along her nerves were so confusing.

"I…it…it makes me want to touch myself," she gasped. "It makes me want to rub myself…the way I do when I'm alone in bed at night."

"Good, Bea, very good." He carried on, relentless. She squirmed faster, clenching muscles she was almost afraid to clench. "Is this more stimulating than looking at those photographs and journals?"

"Of course it is, you idiot!" she cried, driven mad with impatience for more, more, more.

Ritchie laughed loud, kissing her neck again and again, muttering her name in a broken, husky voice. "You're a treasure, Beatrice Weatherly, an utter delight. I knew you would be the moment I saw that photograph."

"And I knew *you* would be a dangerous, unprincipled voluptuary the moment I saw you across the ballroom last night."

"Very astute, Bea. Very astute." He nipped her neck, then the lobe of her ear, tugging on that with his teeth as he carried on with his infernal manipulation of her nipple.

She was almost bouncing on his lap now, the entire cradle of her belly in ferment, racked by the grinding ache in her sex. She had to have relief. She *must* have relief!

"If you need to spend, my darling, you really need to do something about it."

Suddenly, shockingly, he abandoned her breast and relaxed back in the chair, still holding her around her middle and pulling her with him. Beatrice could feel her face burning. She wanted to look down at herself, but she hardly dared. Her nipples felt like little stones, painfully hard, and she knew that where he'd tormented her, that one would be cherry-red.

"The solution is in your hands, Bea," he whispered, his tongue flicking out again, tickling her ear, teasing the lobe and darting inside as if faking the act of sex. "If you want to have an orgasm, you must reach between your legs and stroke your own clitoris."

Orgasm? Clitoris? How stimulating those words sounded aloud.

Against her will, Beatrice whimpered. She'd read about orgasms and clitorises, but to hear Ritchie speak of them thus in his warm, roughened voice was like performing the very act that he'd described.

She wanted to do it. Her body ached for it. But still she balked. The act was taboo, private, somehow more intimate even than letting Ritchie touch her. She imagined his eyes on her, devouring the way her fingers moved, how they glistened when she paused. Screwing up her eyes, she turned away from him, her heart thudding.

"I…I'm not sure I can…please don't ask me to."

"But you're mine, Beatrice. You *must* do what I want."

Again, his voice rang with that hint of stern, thrilling domination. She trembled, wanting to obey. Wanting it so very much, but somehow still not quite able to push through that invisible barrier and put on a show for him.

"I wasn't expecting us to begin this very morning, Ritchie."

There was a long pause. Would he insist? She almost wanted him to, really.

"You're not a coward or a prude, Bea. We both know that, don't we?" He kissed her neck again, very softly. "You're a young woman with hot blood in her veins. I think you can do anything at any time. If it pleases you." His lips brushed her skin again, an inch below her ear, as delicately as the wing of a tropical hummingbird. "And what pleases you, pleases me. Always know that."

"Is that so?" Beatrice trembled. The kiss was so delicate, yet infinitely stirring. It excited her as much, in its small quiet way, as his attention to her nipple had.

"Yes, indeed." He continued to kiss, as if it helped him think.

"So, have you pleased hundreds of women before me, simply in order to receive pleasure in return?"

He laughed, sending heated air fanning over her throat. "Nowhere near that many…Not by a long way. Certainly, far fewer than the scandalmongers would have you believe."

She twisted, turning toward him, searching his face. There had been an odd, almost sad note in his voice. He gave a little shrug, as if shaking it off, then smiled at her, as greedy as a pirate.

"Come now, Bea, have mercy on me." He reached up and brushed her hair from her brow, tucking a long red strand behind her ear. "Just show me a little of what you do, just for a few moments. You don't have to persevere to completion. I'll do that for you, if you're shy. Just show me a morsel."

He plucked at a fold in her skirt, tweaking encouragement.

Beatrice bit her lip and looked down at her blushing chest, and the curves of her bare breasts. Her nipple, where he'd fondled it was as vivid as a cherry and the other almost as pink and as pert.

A moment or two wouldn't be so difficult, would it? Lord alone knew she wanted to be touched. What was the difference between his hand and her own?

Quite a bit actually, but she'd endeavor to try. Sliding her hand against Ritchie's, she took hold of her fine cotton nightgown, and began edging it upward.

CHAPTER NINE

Playing in the Grove

"Beautiful...beautiful," murmured Ritchie.

Beatrice Weatherly's thighs were just as sweet and sleek in the flesh as they were in his most fevered imaginings, her skin as smooth as the surface of a bowl of cream. When she hesitated in the process of pulling up her nightgown, the hem still guarding her modesty, it was almost enough to be simply able to gaze on her.

Almost.

Still uncertain, she tensed and moved on his lap, the rounds of her bottom cruelly jostling his aching erection.

"Hush, nothing to worry about. You know you can do it." He ran his hand up and down the immaculate expanse, exploring the texture of her skin, imagining blood flowing wild beneath, and nerves sending messages of excitement. Fraction by fraction of an inch, he let his fingertips slide higher with every stroke, edging ever closer to her center.

Last night she'd been delicious and responsive and he knew she could and *would* be just as willing soon. Yet still she seemed nervous about exposing herself.

How strangely contrary. You'll pose unclothed for photographs that are circulated to hundreds of avid men, yet you won't show your naked puss to me in private. You're a conundrum, Beatrice Weatherly, a veritable mystery.

Again came that bizarre notion. That she was pure, somehow, despite her willingness to take her clothes off for the camera.

The possibility shook him hard. He'd thought her games of advance and retreat were just that, the feminine wiles of a woman whipping up a prospective lover with the thrill of the chase. Perhaps a woman who hadn't had all that many lovers…but certainly some.

Now he wasn't so sure.

He'd made it a rule never again to be intimate with a woman who didn't know exactly what she was doing. His few very carefully chosen mistresses had all been accomplished married women or experienced luminaries of the higher demimonde.

And now here he was. With Beatrice Weatherly. A creature who had the face and body of a Pre-Raphaelite love goddess, but who was wriggling on his lap like a country virgin on her first tryst with the plow boy.

"Don't you want to show me your puss, Bea?" He slid a fingertip higher, beneath her stalled nightdress. "I'm going to have to see it sooner or later, you know." The light cloth rumpled, and he swore he could almost feel the brush of soft hair against the pad of his finger. "And if it looks as sublime as it felt last night, I know I'm in for a treat."

"Very well. I'm sorry to keep you waiting. How remiss of me to shortchange you so soon, Mr. Ritchie." Her voice was tart, but had a hollow ring of nervousness that only added to his doubts.

On the point of asking if she wanted to call a halt, he groaned out loud. Somehow in the churning of her thighs and buttocks, she'd managed to trap his cock beneath her in a confinement of delicious pleasure-pain. A rod of torment, it was a hair away from ecstasy.

What if she made him come, beneath her, inside his clothing? The perversity of it made him shudder, edging closer.

She was a minx. A beautiful minx. And he'd see her touch herself or he'd expire from lust in the process.

"There you are. Satisfied now?" she cried, hauling at her voluminous nightgown in one final wrench, her face and chest as pink as a garden peony.

"Well, not completely, Bea," he gasped, almost undone by her, floored as much by the fire in her expression as the feel of her bottom against his thighs and the sight of the anticipated prize, her brilliant bush.

Red. Crimson. A dozen shades of sweet and fecund autumn.

The hair at the base of Beatrice's belly was as bright, dense and lustrous as the startlingly vivid hair that streamed from her scalp. The photographer's poor attempt at hand tinting had been a pale intimation of the vibrant curly cluster.

"What a divine little fleece you have, my sweet," he blurted out, aware that he sounded almost like callow lad, as if he'd never seen a woman before. But she stunned him and she moved him, out of all proportion.

"I'm so glad you like it," she shot back at him. "I'm sorry that the forestry down there is probably somewhat more untamed than you're accustomed to. If I'd anticipated your call, I would have done a little pruning." A second later they were both laughing out loud like fools.

"It *is* spectacular though," he said at last, straightening his expression and pulling her toward him. Kissing the side of her face at the same time, he took the opportunity to cup the untamed treasure. The hair felt just as soft as it'd seemed last night, silky but with a spring to it.

He couldn't wait to part the waves and dive in deep. Fingers or tongue, he didn't care, he had to be there.

But first he had to coax her into touching herself.

"I'm waiting, Bea," he purred against her temple.

She breathed heavily, and he could see and feel her biting her lip. He gave her a little squeeze, then sought her hand and drew it gently but firmly between her thighs. Just as he'd hoped, she lifted her hips toward the contact, rather than retreating.

"Well, here we are once more, my beautiful Bea, playing in the grove again." He slid his fingers over hers, matching digit for digit, then pressed her middle one through the soft hair, and into her fluidity to settle on her simmering clitoris. She groaned and stiffened, her legs kicking when he found it.

"Ritchie…oh…" she gasped as he bore down on her finger. It slipped and skated around, she was so wet.

"Do it, Bea! Take your pleasure."

She nibbled her lip, passed her tongue across it, first screwing up her eyes, then relaxing. But finally, her finger flexed of its own accord and began to work. Ritchie withdrew and let his whole hand rest lightly over hers.

Tiny liquid sounds seemed to fill the room, a counterpoint to her broken gasps and moans. Every adjustment of her jostling buttocks terrorized his cock in the most exquisite way possible.

"You like that, don't you?" His voice was hoarse as he felt her flicking and flicking, working in a pattern no doubt long practiced. Her finger moved then in a circular motion and her efforts made her growl like a tigress, the fierce sound shocking in his ear.

Dear God, had he ever been with a woman so responsive? Whatever she might lack in terms of artistry and sophistication, she more than made up for in unfettered, animal enthusiasm.

Her entire nervous system and her luscious puss were created for sex.

He knew it. She knew it. Listening to her labored breath and her little moans, the desire to see her climax swelled and gripped his senses. The desire to come himself made him almost cross-eyed.

"Spend, Bea…do it…come for me."

She tossed her head, making a little murmur of resistance, then buried her face in his shoulder. Even now, she was defying him.

"Do it for me, Bea," he repeated, flexing his hand over hers. "Do it for me, and I swear you'll unman me, woman. I'm so close, I'll come in my drawers when I feel you spend."

"Really?" A sly, beautiful face looked up at him, eyes almost calculating above her pink cheeks.

"Yes. There's no doubt about it. You'd like that, wouldn't you? To know you'd driven me so far to distraction that I disgrace myself in my undergarments in your honor."

With a slow smile, she closed her eyes, lay back in his arms and began to rub in earnest.

IT TOOK BUT A FEW MOMENTS, intoxicated as she was by Ritchie's kisses and his rude, explicit words. He was hard beneath her, almost like a separate living entity with a life of its own, and the excitement of having power over it was as potent as wine.

She circled and played, with her fingers and bottom both, then cried out with pleasure as the hard white glow of fulfillment burst inside her. Wave after blissful wave rippled through her, cresting in her sex but radiating out as far as her fingers and her toes and the very curling ends of her hair.

As she groaned and wriggled, she felt Ritchie tense, his neck arching back as he let out an oath. She tried to squirm more, and grind down upon him, but he gripped her hard, almost roughly by the waist, and held her immobile.

"Stay still," he growled, fingers digging into her as his hips bucked once, twice, three times, and then with a long, broken breath, he subsided. "Don't move," he said, more softly now, his lips against her face then settling on her skin in a sudden kiss.

Beatrice didn't move. She just lay and trembled, her body vibrating with a low, incessant energy. It was like being washed overboard in a storm, then suddenly finding oneself safe again and stunned, on a wide soft beach.

As the cyclone subsided, Beatrice grinned, unable to stop her lips from forming a smirk. Ritchie's eyes were closed, still a mystery to her, but she could barely contain her private bubble of glee.

I made you spend, you devil. I did that. You might think you've got control of me, with all your money, but I've got powers too.

He'd told her to stay still, and she did for the moment, but that didn't stop her dwelling on the masculine organ nestled beneath her bottom. It was softer now, and didn't feel as big, but it still had presence. Beatrice tried to imagine it, quiet and sated and sticky, presumably, with the seminal fluid it'd just ejected.

She had to bite her lip to stop herself laughing.

"That was rather pleasant. Did you enjoy yourself, Bea?"

How could he know she was watching him if he had his eyes closed? Was he the Great Mesmero, reading her mind? His eyes fluttered open now, as if he'd heard that thought too, and their depths of midnight-blue were hazed and sultry.

"Yes, of course I did." Why lie? For a month she was committed to revealing things to him she'd never believed she'd have to expose to anyone. Not even a husband, although chances of securing one of those now were rapidly diminishing.

"Splendid. I'm really glad, Bea. Pleasure is tonic for the constitution. It relaxes the body and eases the mind." As if demonstrating his theory, he grabbed her by the waist and urged her onto her feet. As her nightgown and dressing gown slithered back down again to cover her, she felt almost disappointed, and in an act of defiance, she didn't immediately fasten the buttons up top.

Ritchie's lips parted. Had he gasped? Did he admire her daring? It seemed so. Snatching up her hand, he kissed her fingers like an adoring swain. "I want you to have as much pleasure as possible, my dear," he went on, his nostrils flaring over her hand. Beatrice blushed—again—knowing he could smell her odor. "I have to go away on business for a few days now, but I want you to promise me that you'll play with your pretty little puss often while I'm absent. And perhaps think of *me,* instead of some fictional cove in a book."

How could she suddenly feel so hollow? They'd barely started the month he'd paid for and now he was going. Oh, men were so contrary! They accused women of fickleness and flightiness, but they were just as unreliable themselves, if not a good deal more so.

She drew away her hand, trying not to snatch. "So, these 'few days' of yours? Do they count as part of the month? Or does the calendar resume its forward motion when you return?"

Ritchie's eyes narrowed, but his expression was more admiring again than hostile.

"You're quite a businesswoman, Bea, aren't you? It's a shame you weren't put in charge of your family fortunes. I'm sure you and your brother would have prospered very nicely if you'd held the purse strings." He shrugged, his fine shoulders lifting beneath the common cloth of his jacket. "But then again, perhaps it's a good thing after all. How else would we have arrived at our arrangement? Unless I could have coaxed you into a month of sin purely on the merits of my dazzling personality and my legendary amorous skills?"

Beatrice narrowed her eyes back at him.

"Perhaps not," Ritchie observed lightly, "but in respect of those days, perhaps they can tally toward the total if you promise to give me a good account of your private pleasures in my absence and my imaginary role in them?"

"I'll attempt to do so, Ritchie, but it's not always possible to order the imagination. It does as it will. Mine certainly does." She watched the tiny intricate shift of muscles in his face as he absorbed this, still holding her hand, and found herself again wondering exactly what he was thinking. "It may not be possible to avoid fancies of being ravished by a Knight of the Round Table or a dashing Prince of Araby."

"Try, Bea, try," he murmured, his voice fierce as he drew the tips of her fingers to his lips again and kissed them with a slow, meticulous pressure. She imagined she felt the passage of air against her skin as he also inhaled again.

"Very well. I will," she whispered, shaken anew as his tongue slipped out to taste her.

It only took but a moment, then he released her, reached into the pocket of his waistcoat and took out his fob watch. With compressed lips and a frown he studied it.

"Time to go, dearest Bea. Though I really don't want to." He glanced to one side, and she could almost see the cogs of his intelligence whirring as he marked out a series of tasks in his mind. Had he separated himself from her already? Was he all the man of business now, not the lover?

"Use those funds I've given you on yourself, Bea. Buy gowns, shoes, whatever you want and need." He smirked, and the lover reappeared. "Some new items of lingerie would be nice. But nothing woolen by Dr. Jaeger, please, or other unbecoming stuff. I want to see you and feel you in silk and lace from now on, although you're perfectly at liberty to wear more rational items in your own time."

"Why, that's most accommodating of you. I'd hate to have to give up my woolen combinations all together. I'm extremely fond of them."

"Of course you are." Ritchie pursed his lips, obviously trying not to grin.

"But seriously, Ritchie, what about these creatures who occasionally lurk outside? Charlie might have debts in some very obscure quarters that even you might not have tracked down. Goodness knows who's likely to turn up looking for payment. Surely I can use some of this money you've left for that purpose?" She patted her pocket, thinking what a relief it would be to actually have funds to silence any threats.

"Don't be alarmed, Bea. I'm leaving an associate of mine in charge of the greater financial affairs. He's an expert in dealing with difficult types. Mainly because he used to be one himself." Ritchie nodded, as if mentally ticking off his list again. "But Jamie is an astute and intelligent fellow, loyal and honest in my service. Consider him the steward of your household, if you like. Clearly your brother can't be trusted with money matters, and even though I know you've a sharp, intelligent mind, my dear, I don't want you distracted by mundane matters during our month."

Beatrice opened her mouth to protest. Of all the high-handed arrogance! But then, she thought better of it. In some ways, Ritchie was right. Charlie was worse than useless at being master of a household, and at keeping hold of money. And how could she make a good fist of being a pleasure-loving courtesan if she was worrying about the price of chops and cabbage and whether to air the carpets or not? Ritchie's precious steward could take over all that if his master insisted on installing him. She smiled, suddenly picturing some big brawny type in an apron, sweeping the front step. If she was hors de combat servicing Ritchie's sexual whims, Polly and Enid would need an extra pair of hands.

"That's extremely thoughtful of you," she murmured, still finding it difficult to keep her face straight.

"Oh, I think of everything, my dear. You'll soon discover that."

"I don't doubt it, Ritchie. I don't doubt it."

Just what else lay in the depths of his labyrinthine intelligence? A finger of icy doubt tickled her spine as she watched his dark eyes. She had a whole month of discovery ahead of her.

But as she shivered, he took her in his arms and kissed her. Hard.

It was indeed almost as if he'd reached in and read her mind.

CHAPTER TEN

Cupboard Love

POLLY SWUNG OPEN the door to the cupboard. The passage itself was dim, lit only by a small stained-glass skylight over the back door, but the cupboard offered a black hazard of cleaning paraphernalia—mops and brooms, and galvanized buckets to bark the unwary shin.

Yet somehow, the dusty little niche still had a clandestine allure and its close darkness was her sometime venue for trysts with Charlie. Not that she planned to let that get in the way of her seducing her handsome new friend. Jamie followed her willingly as she drew him along by the hand, and a dense darkness enveloped them both as he pulled the door shut.

"Are you sure we won't suffocate in here?" he whispered, his hands already upon her, searching for the curves of her breasts and buttocks.

Polly leaned against the wall, nudging a sweeping brush out of the way. "We'll be all right. I think there's a ventilation brick somewhere, and it doesn't usually take that long anyway."

The moment the words left her lips, it was as if she'd dropped that ventilation brick right into the middle of their conversation.

"Now, now, now, Miss Polly, what other lucky fellows have you lured into your Stygian lair?" He grabbed her by her right bottom cheek and pulled her up hard against him, and Polly's sex leaped when she felt the sturdy bulge of his erection.

Should she tell him? Could she trust him? The Weatherly household had scandals enough, but then again, the tale of a young master poking a parlor maid was hardly news, was it? The same thing probably happened in most Belgravia houses on a regular basis, and Polly knew of at least two similar arrangements in South Mulberry Street alone.

She wound her arms around his neck and put her lips against his ear. "It's not always a roast beef sandwich that Mr. Charles comes down here for, you know."

There was a long pause, and even though Polly couldn't see Jamie's face, in her mind's eye, she saw a considering expression on it. Had her revelations given him pause for thought after all?

"So, Charlie Weatherly likes the girls too, eh?"

Too?

Now it was Polly's turn to consider. She'd long had a suspicion that Charlie liked his bread buttered on either side, but she had no absolute proof.

"What do you mean?"

"Do you mean to say that you didn't know the young master likes to bat for both teams?" Jamie chuckled, hauling steadily at her skirts until he had them up, and his hand inside the vent of her drawers at the back.

"Well, I've had that notion." His knuckle brushed her anus and she let out a breath. "But I'd like to know how… how *you* know," she stuttered as he rubbed her there softly but with authority.

"Oh, a man like me recognizes certain characteristics." He plunged in for a kiss as his fingers rode the wicked groove.

Polly gasped into his mouth. It was as if someone had lit a lamp.

"When did you meet Charlie? What do you mean 'recognize'?" she demanded when he freed her lips and leaned down to kiss her neck above the collar of her frock. "Are you an invert too?"

"Would it revolt you if I said yes?" His mouth opened against her skin, his tongue sweeping hot over it. The way he kissed her throat showed her he liked a woman's taste.

"Not in the slightest, Mr. Brownlow. It takes all sorts," she gasped as his fingertips curved around her sex from behind and dabbled in a tantalizing rhythm against her entrance. Of their own volition, it seemed, her hips tilted, trying to nudge him in the direction of her most sensitive part. "I'm a country girl at heart and you'd be amazed what goes on out of town. Sophisticated London folk think we don't know anything, but we do, you know, we do."

"Amen to that, Polly. I'm country myself originally. I can vouch for all those high jinks in the meadows and the barns and the potting sheds." Jamie's other hand began its voyage into the convoluted hinterland of her petticoat now, and after some fishing about achieved its goal—the vent of her drawers from the front. "And now it seems that both me and your Mr. Charlie like a bit of a fumble with *you,* as well as each other."

Polly opened her mouth, but whether to protest or proclaim her delight, she didn't quite know. But there was no chance for either, because Jamie plunged in and kissed her hard and long, over and over again. And as his tongue worked inside her mouth, his finger found her clitty.

As he fondled her there, wicked images filled her head. Charlie rubbing her. Her rubbing Charlie. Charlie and Jamie rubbing her, *and* rubbing each other. Between her legs, her sex leaped and fluttered, and grew stickier and stickier with each thought. Something Jamie seemed to appreciate as he doubled his efforts to arouse her.

You're so selfish, Polly Jenkins, she castigated herself suddenly, still rocking and wriggling against Jamie and his fingers. *You should think of others, not your own entertainment.*

Here she was having a lovely, fruity time with a handsome and personable man, and she'd completely forgotten all about Miss Bea and the dangers upstairs.

"What is it, Polly?" Jamie's fingers still moved, but there was concern in his voice.

"I'm still worried about Miss Bea and your Mr. Ritchie."

"Don't, my love. Don't worry," he breathed, fingertip swirling, "He likes the ladies, yes, but he's a good man too. He once saved my life, and he's saved my hide in other ways too."

Polly caught her breath as the finger pushed inside her, but Jamie went on. "He'll not hurt your lady, believe me. He knows far too much about pain and anguish to hurt another."

Questions churned in Polly's mind, but Jamie's touch was too clever for her. She wriggled and bore down, her thoughts in a whirl, her worries forgotten.

As were Jamie's, it seemed. "Oh, I wish I could fuck you here and now, Polly," he gasped, "You're the most toothsome young woman I've met in an age, and I'd love to plunge into your puss and make us both happy."

Polly wished it too, but she was cautious. So-called sophistication wasn't all that "town" was notorious for. Country girl or not, she knew about the consequences of pleasure, and that sometimes falling with child was the lesser misfortune.

"I never go the whole way, I'll have you know, Mr. Jamie Brownlow. Nothing goes inside anywhere, if you take my meaning, and there's no exceptions."

"Very wise, Miss Polly, very wise. You're a very progressive young woman." He squeezed her breast teasingly, clearly taking advantage of whatever she *was* willing to permit. "Very forward thinking, as I happen to be myself. There's no pleasure in sex if you're worrying all the time, is there? Personally, I'm a great believer in the efficacy of French letters, when fucking either sex. But alas, I wasn't expecting to meet a goddess in a broom cupboard this morning, so I don't happen to have one about my person."

French letters, eh? Now here was a man she *might* be able to go all the way with. Especially if Miss Bea took up with the apparently saintly and lifesaving Mr. Ritchie.

"Well, that's a shame, Jamie," she said softly, working back against him, "because despite our very brief acquaintance, your avowed perversions, and the peculiar circumstances of our meeting, I do believe that I like you very much, and as I said, I'm of a mind to take my pleasure where I may."

"Oh, Polly," he murmured back to her, "a man doesn't meet a peach like you every day. And it'd be a shame to waste this opportunity." He began pulling at her skirts again. Polly pushed them back down just as determinedly, but he soothed her with another silky kiss. "So I think we ought to try and improvise without taking undue risks. What do you think?"

Polly laughed. Could she trust him? She certainly wanted to. "I'm game if you are."

"Good girl, I knew you were a sport." There was a laugh in his voice, unadulterated happiness. He was a straightforward pleasure-lover, untrammeled by guilt and tiresome peregrinations on what was moral and what was sinful. As she responded to him, her hands sneaking beneath his jacket to stroke his back, Polly recognized a match for her own persuasions.

While Jamie grappled with buttons and petticoat, Polly fought skirmishes of her own with layers of gentlemen's clothing. But it wasn't long before she finally drew out a solid, sturdy cock into the dusty darkness.

He was thick and hard, the tip silky with the fluid of his excitement. It felt exquisite as she ran her fingers over him, slick and warm and inviting. She wanted to taste it but clearly Jamie had other ideas.

"Turn around, sweetheart, brace yourself against the wall," he gasped, his hands relaxing their hold on her breast and her pussy. But not before he bestowed the latter with a wicked parting squeeze.

"What an omnivorous fellow you are, Jamie Brownlow," Polly observed, turning as per his instructions. "You enjoy the gentlemen, yet you handle the ladies like a pro."

"That's the truth, Poll, the honest truth." Positioning her, and renegotiating her under-things, he pressed his hot and sticky cock against her bottom, then clasped himself against her. Hand against drawers, drawers against cock, cock against the rounded curve of her bottom. With his other hand, he reached around and found her clitty again.

"Now, there we are. Something for everybody," he remarked roundly. "Now let's get to it, lass, before my boss comes back again." Positioning his finger, he started to swing his hips and rock.

Polly thought fleetingly about Beatrice again, wondering how far her dealings with Mr. Ritchie had progressed. The toffs were just the same under the skin as their servants. Would it take them any longer than she and Jamie to get to business?

A moment later all thoughts of the world beyond the

broom cupboard evaporated. What Jamie was doing wasn't quite like having a man inside her—nothing felt like that—but it was certainly a particularly delicious substitute. The friction between her legs soon had her adjusting the position of her hands and elbows against the wall so she could bite her knuckle. It was either that, or bay like a she-hound when she spent.

Which she did. Again and again, in quick succession, her empty channel clenching the air in luscious waves.

"Do you like that, my Polly?" growled Jamie, his voice low and ragged and full of mirth. "Are you spending? Are you spending now? Answer me!" he demanded, beating on her clit in a way that made her soar. "Tell me you're spending, you wicked little trollop."

The words were harsh and exciting, but the way he said them mellowed, then grew soft and full of warmth. His tender quality made her suddenly think of Sam.

And it was that, the sweetness and the nostalgia, that filled her eyes with tears as she rocked and swooned. Pleasure overcame her again as Jamie jerked and anointed her. His essence was slippery and unctuous, warming her thigh.

Squashed against the boarded wall of the cupboard, it was hard to breathe. Both their chests heaved as they slumped, gasping, hot and thunderstruck. But after a moment or two, Polly struggled, feeling suffocated by Jamie's bigger body still pinning her to the wall.

"Oh, I'm sorry, lass," he said, lifting himself away in the darkness. "Have I squashed you? You're not injured, are you?"

There was such honest solicitude in his voice that Polly laughed. Bless him, he really seemed to care.

"I'm perfectly well, thank you, Jamie. It'll take more

than that to hurt common clay like me, you know. I'm no delicate drawing-room lady."

Her own words caught her on the raw.

Miss Bea! Was she safe? As yet unmolested by the randy Mr. Ritchie? If the master was anything like his handsome, opportunistic servant, who could tell?

"What's wrong, Polly? Have I upset you?" Jamie grabbed her arm as she fumbled with the buttons of her bodice in the dark, hampered by her twisted-about apron. With no fuss, and a good deal of skill, he fastened them up, working blind, and set the bib of her apron neat and straight.

"No, I'm not upset. Just concerned about Miss Bea. It just occurred to me that if your master is anything like you, she might already be compromised."

Listening to the small movements of Jamie doing up his fly buttons, Polly could also almost hear his keen brain ticking too.

"Your mistress is safe with Ritchie. It doesn't matter whether a woman's had a thousand lovers or is as pure as the Virgin Mary, he never forces himself where he knows he's not wanted." His hand settled reassuringly on Polly's shoulder. "If anything has happened, it's because your lady wanted it to."

"If you say so, Jamie. If you say so."

"I do, pretty girl. Don't fret."

Evading Jamie's searching hands, she slid out into the passage, with him following.

"I still think I might go up and knock. As if they want tea or something."

"No! You're doing nobody any favors by interfering, Poll. Least of all your mistress." Jamie's hand clamped around her arm, firm but unyielding. "Just bide your time until you're rung for, there's a good girl."

"Get off me." She tried to shake him free. "I don't trust you and I trust *him* even less."

She pulled and tugged, but got nowhere, and was just about to kick his shins when the morning-room bell trilled out clearly from the kitchen.

"See. I told you to wait, and now they're ready, and no harm done."

"That's what you say," shot Polly at him, straightening her apron and cap in the little mirror at the foot of the stairs. "But just look what you've been able to get away with in the same amount of time."

"He means her nothing but good," persisted Jamie. "Believe me."

Polly wished she *could* believe him. She *wanted* to believe him. But all the same, she'd keep a lookout for her mistress.

And maybe for her master too, the way things were.

CHAPTER ELEVEN

Dark Thoughts and Whiskey

I should have had you when I had the chance.

Eustace Lloyd splashed whiskey into crystal and then cursed when droplets of it flew out onto the cards spread on the table. Dabbing furiously with his pocket handkerchief he managed to repair the damage, which was just as well—they were the last set he possessed until he used the plates again.

He knew he shouldn't drink this early, but still he took a heavy jolt of the smoky amber fluid and stared down at the image in his hand. His favorite composition. Beatrice Weatherly on a tiger skin with her hand between her legs.

Eustace's cock kicked heavily in his drawers, even though neither his own hand, nor any other part of him had ever managed to get anywhere near that peerless body.

"Siren of South Mulberry Street, my arse."

Apart from that one afternoon, when he'd plied her with champagne and laudanum, the beautiful Miss Weatherly had been tediously virtuous, granting him only the occasional mild, stolen kiss. Eustace knew now he should have pressed her for more favors, but he'd been canny, or so he thought. Believing that the sale of Westerlynne had left her and that fool brother of hers well set up, he'd bided his time, hoping to snare her as a blushing, willing bride bringing with her a sorely needed fortune.

Ah, the plans of mice and men. The Weatherly parents had been as imprudent and spendthrift as his own, and their offspring were as penniless as he. Worse, Charles Weatherly was a loser at cards, at the races and on the stock market. So much so that the insolent pup had been looking to tap Eustace for funds once they were brothers in law.

But that was all water under the bridge now.

At least I got these. Poor as a church mouse you are, Beatrice my dear, but you've still made me a tidy pile of money.

Indeed, even though his hobby of photography had proved extravagant, useless and expensive at first, it was now turning him a nice little profit; all garnered from the anonymous sale of racy, erotic cabinet cards. And bizarrely, his libidinous customers seemed to be able to tell the difference between a whore brought in off the street to pose for a shilling or two, and a refined gentlewoman who'd been tricked out of her clothes.

The cards featuring the exquisite Beatrice Weatherly, the newly dubbed Siren, brought in twenty times as much coin as any others. If only he'd been more circumspect with Beatrice and ladled on the honey a bit longer, notwithstanding the fact that she wouldn't open her legs for him, and she didn't have a bean. The demanding connoisseurs who frequented the private pornography shops in Holywell Street were crying out for new and more daring poses from their luscious Titian-haired favorite.

But it wasn't the loss of potential income that cut Eustace now. Nor even the fact that his desire to attend to his photographic plates had allowed the drugged girl to struggle into her clothing and quit the studio in his mother's summer house before he'd returned to round out the occasion by fucking her.

No, it was something else, not entirely unrelated, that drove Eustace to reach for the whiskey decanter and slop another enormous measure into his glass.

Edmund bloody fucking Ellsworth Ritchie.

That bastard. Why him? Now he's started pawing her, I'll never be able to effect a reconciliation and get a few more juicy poses out of her.

Eustace hated Ritchie. Resented him probably even more than any other wealthy man in London who seemed to have all the right assets and financial connections that Eustace himself didn't possess. Why should a man like Ritchie have all the advantages? Eustace had more right to them. He had minor aristocratic associations, and that cur Ritchie was just "trade" or worse dressed up in the glad rags of fine tailoring.

It had started last year at the Earl of Plenderley's house party. If the accursed Ritchie hadn't been so fond of that clod of a servant of his, well, Eustace knew that he might have got away with a certain matter.

Yes, a gentleman would have taken another gentleman's word, and dismissed the man out of hand. Valets, footmen, maids, they were always swiping the odd bit of cash and blaming each other, and that ass Johnny Brayford had been a fool to leave so much of it lying about in his room, unattended and apparently uncounted. Having lost heavily at cards, and with no way to cover the debt, Eustace had taken a chance, slipped in and stolen fifty quid. No loss to someone who was heir to an Earldom.

But alas, Johnny *had* counted his money, and had raised a mild kerfuffle about the theft, leaving Eustace having to think fast lest suspicion fall on him because his room had been next door to Brayford's. As luck would have it though, Eustace's man had picked up a useful titbit of gossip in the servants' hall. Ritchie's own rather dubious-looking manservant had been in trouble with the law at one time. Which should have made him the prime candidate for this bit of thieving.

It all should have worked out so neatly. But it hadn't. Eustace's discreet accusation against Brownlow had been dismissed out of hand. Not only had Johnny Brayford accepted Ritchie's defence of his servant without question, it seemed that some sly housemaid or other had seen Eustace sliding out the young viscount's room, so suspicion had indeed fallen his way.

Nothing had been said, at least not overtly, but his blood still boiled at the memory of Ritchie and Johnny Brayford, laughing over brandy, eyeing him slyly, both so assured and untouchable and blasé about the loss of fifty pounds while he was suddenly out in the cold. It was the fact that the whole affair had really meant nothing to them that rankled the most.

Eustace detested them all, these confident men, but Ritchie most of all, with his obscene millions and his ideas above his station and his friendships with the great and the good.

And now, to cap it all, the filthy upstart had apparently been invited to Lord and Lady Southern's Summer Ball as an honored guest too, when no invitation had been forthcoming for more worthy members of society.

Eustace ground his teeth. Late last night, a couple of fellows at an after-hours drinking establishment he frequented had described to him how they'd seen the bastard *en tête à tête* with the beautiful Beatrice, then later they'd observed him whisking the now notorious beauty away to God alone knew where. The man had a dog's reputation with the women, and the fact that wealthy society belles threw themselves at Ritchie with their drawers wide open made Eustace resent him all the more.

"Fuck you, Ritchie! Fuck you!"

Eustace slammed his glass down on the desk. It didn't break, and he didn't even spill whiskey on the cabinet cards, because it was already empty. As he filled it up again, he took that as a favorable omen.

He'd bloody well get his own back on Ritchie, and then he'd lure Beatrice Weatherly back as well somehow too, and find a way to maneuver her into modeling for him again.

And he'd fuck her bandy-legged into next week in the bargain.

Eustace smiled at last, sipping his third large measure of the morning more slowly as he considered whether to take himself in hand as a celebration.

There was a way to do it all.

He had connections of his own, although far less salubrious than those of the likes of Ritchie.

And he'd heard rumors, delicious rumors, priceless rumors that lifted his spirits and lightened his dark thoughts.

If what had been intimated were true, he couldn't have asked for Edmund Ellsworth Ritchie to have a more priceless and ironic Achilles' heel.

CHAPTER TWELVE

Madame Chamfleur Recommends

"YOU CAN TALK TO ME, my dear. About anything. It won't go further than the two of us, and believe me, you won't shock me at all."

Well, that *I can certainly believe.*

Itching to smile, Beatrice kept her face straight. No, she probably couldn't shock Sofia Chamfleur in the slightest. Not after that performance she'd witnessed last night.

How nice it was to do something normal like taking afternoon tea with a woman friend. With so many outré events taking place in the past twenty-four hours, Beatrice was beginning to wonder if she'd accidentally stumbled into a strange, debauched dreamworld, perhaps a very grown-up version of Mr. Lewis Carroll's "Alice" adventures, where Ritchie and herself were the only two characters.

But if I'm Alice, who are you, Ritchie? Surely not the Mad Hatter or the anxious White Rabbit…in fact, that entire confection seems a bit whimsical for you.

Hungry, she reached for a slice of cake before rising to Sofia's encouragement. Unsettled by what had transpired with Ritchie this morning, and by a traumatic confrontation with Charlie later, she hadn't been able to eat her lunch. But now she was starving, and Cook's seed cake was one of her more successful offerings.

"I've done something, Sofia. Something scandalous." Beatrice paused to chew, and the other woman's fine eyes widened, the ostrich feather on her smart chapeau bobbing as she leaned forward. "It's even more daring than posing for those dratted photographs. *Much* more so...*I* can't believe I've done it myself, but I have."

Sofia Chamfleur sipped her tea, not once taking her eyes off Beatrice. She was clearly dying to know what the scandalous thing was, but she wasn't a woman to press. Unlike some of the other members of the Ladies Sewing Circle, Sofia always waited patiently for the choicest items of gossip.

"I expect you know Mr. Edmund Ellsworth Ritchie?"

Sofia's mouth curved. "Indeed I do, Beatrice. He's a good friend to Monsieur Chamfleur and I. A fine man indeed." Her eyes narrowed and took on a knowing cast. "I saw you talking to him last night at Arabella's do. What did you think of him? He's very handsome, isn't he?"

Beatrice took another bite of cake and chewed it quickly. Anything to fortify her. "Mr. Ritchie propositioned me last night. He offered me a large sum of money, and proposed to pay off all our debts provided I'd become his mistress for a month...and...um...do anything he wanted me to...in the bedroom."

There. It was out. And she felt so much better. Laughter bubbled up and she couldn't help but let it out. Sofia laughed too and reached out to pat Beatrice's hand.

"Goodness, that is rather scandalous, isn't it?" Her brown eyes were merry, and not in the slightest bit disapproving. Not that Beatrice had expected them to be. "And you said yes, I'm assuming? I do hope so, because he's really a decent, generous man despite his reputation, and he'll certainly honor his word in respect of the money."

"I did say yes." Beatrice shrugged. "After all, what have I got to lose? Those photographs have ruined my reputation and my standing in society, so I might as well be hung for a sheep as for a lamb. And we do so need the money. I simply couldn't refuse it."

Sofia nodded sagely. "Well, I shouldn't worry about society, my dear. I have a large number of friends who are much more interesting than the usual cliques of nincompoops, and I can assure you'll get plenty of invitations." The older woman reached for the teapot as she spoke, and played mother, topping up both their cups. "The important thing is that you like Mr. Ritchie. You do like him, don't you?"

Do I?

"I'm not sure what I feel about him, to be honest, Sofia. He's…he's not like anyone I've ever met before. He's very forceful. He…well, he somehow bowls one over. It's impossible to say no to him, regardless of one's intentions and one's misgivings."

Sofia Chamfleur's eyes glittered knowingly. "Ah, you *do* like him. I can tell. And who can blame you. He's very handsome and virile, isn't he?" She winked. "If I'd never met Monsieur Chamfleur, I might be tempted to set my cap at Ritchie myself."

If Beatrice hadn't been wearing her corset, she would have slumped like a badly set jelly. Sofia's warm opinion of Ritchie was a relief. She was a shrewd woman and if she approved, he couldn't be all that bad.

Sofia's brown eyes narrowed and she pursed her lips. "Seriously though, Bea. I knew that Ritchie was interested in you. He has been since he saw your photograph." Her chin came up and she gave Beatrice a very level glance. "Who do you think urged Arabella to invite you and Charles to the ball. You were asked to attend specifically in order for Ritchie to look you over."

Beatrice frowned and took a gulp of tea. It was a bit too hot, and she felt as if she was burning up inside her layers of linen and whalebone and black silk foulard.

"You could have warned me, Sofia, although I imagine it wouldn't have made any difference. Mr. Ritchie clearly always gets what he wants." She paused for more tea. "But I do feel like a prize heifer that's been paraded before the stud bull." She put her cup aside and returned Sofia's frank stare. "And I don't know whether to feel insulted…or rather pleased with myself because I passed Mr. Ritchie's inspection!"

"The London season is a cattle market even for the most prim and proper misses, Beatrice." Sofia sat back a little, cocking her head on one side, her expression unapologetic. "At least your transaction with Ritchie is based on honesty. You both know what you're getting out of it, with no subterfuge."

Ah, the pragmatic view. Beatrice felt a flutter of guilt. Ritchie probably wasn't getting exactly what he was expecting. So much for honesty.

She drew in a breath, wishing the Oolong was actually a rather large glass of sherry or Madeira.

"Ah, but I'm afraid Mr. Ritchie probably isn't getting quite what he expected. I'm sure he thinks I'm brazen and experienced, posing like that…when in fact I'm not."

Sofia frowned, then tapped her fingers together. "Ah, I had my suspicions. There's a certain languid, somnolent quality about those postcards. Were you drugged? Tricked into posing?"

In another world, Beatrice might have collapsed onto Sofia's bosom, sobbing uncontrollably and admitting all.

But somehow, since last night, she wasn't in that world and she was a very different person. Ritchie had changed her utterly. Much more so than anything Eustace Lloyd could have done to her, or even the loss of dear Tommy, when she'd lived back at Westerlynne.

The moment she'd set eyes on Edmund Ellsworth Ritchie she'd *become* the Siren of South Mulberry Street. Passion, and his fingers, had tempered her, made her strong and daring. The small matter of her virginity wasn't going to prevent her from making the best of their arrangement and she certainly wasn't about to admit she'd been drugged by Eustace Lloyd.

"Not drugged. Just a little champagne, to relax me. It was such a lovely afternoon, I think I may have nodded off." Sofia looked dubious, so Beatrice hurried on. "But I'm still a virgin…well, technically. I've never had congress with a man, but I've had…um…feelings. And as a young woman, in the country, I rode astride a good deal, and I think that may have, well, *affected* me. If you get my meaning?"

Beatrice's face flamed to what she guessed was approximately the color of Sofia's deep rose pink walking dress.

The other woman's smooth forehead puckered. "Well, thank goodness for that! At least you're better prepared than most young women." The pucker became a frown. "But this photographer… You're absolutely sure he didn't interfere with you?"

"No, I'm quite sure he didn't, he didn't have the time. He seemed more interested in his precious plates…and—" she tripped on the words "—I certainly didn't *feel* different afterward and I'm sure I would have been able to tell."

"Good…that's good." Sofia leaned forward, patting Beatrice's hand again. "You mustn't associate the sensual act with shame and misfortune. Take it from me, it's a source of exquisite pleasure and happiness, especially in the hands of an experienced lover like Ritchie. There's nothing to fear. You must simply relax and keep a very open mind."

An open mind, eh? Just what she'd deduced.

"Yes, that's exactly what I plan to do, Sofia." Still blushing, she felt oddly confident. "It seems to me that Mr. Ritchie is an imaginative man. Not one to confine himself to the more conventional…um…pastimes." She fixed her friend with what she hoped was a knowledge-able look.

Sofia laughed. "He is indeed, but I'll wager he's met his match in you, Beatrice. I think you and he will do very well together." The older woman nodded her head, as if making a decision. "But I think you need a little help. A little guidance. And fortunately I'm just the woman you need for that. Now let's have another cup of tea and while we drink it, we'll make some plans."

Over the next thirty minutes, Beatrice's jaw dropped a dozen times.

Madame Chamfleur, it seemed, ran an establishment for ladies who wished to learn more about all matters erotic. Furthermore, it also catered to wives who weren't receiving adequate fulfillment in their marriage beds and were looking to obtain it elsewhere. And a good many of the Sewing Circle members were amongst Sofia's regular patrons.

No wonder the talk there is so frisky! You sly old devil, Sofia. I do believe you run something very like a brothel for ladies. And yet you look so demure and just like a respectable married woman. Who would ever have guessed?

"You must come to our house in Hampstead for a little

tuition, my dear." Sofia beamed. "Don't look so alarmed. I'm merely suggesting you study certain publications we have there, and perhaps view a demonstration or two."

Demonstrations? Good grief!

"But you live in Belgravia, round the corner."

"Ah, but I mean our *other* house. The one my husband owned before our marriage. It has always been his place of business since he took over the establishment from his mother."

"It's a family business?" Whatever next?

"Indeed, the original Madame Chamfleur, God rest her soul, was most progressive." Sofia took out a small leather-covered notebook from her capacious handbag. "Yes, you must come on Wednesday. We'll make a day of it. I'll take you to my modiste and my cosmetician and we'll have a tour of all the best stores, then retire to Hampstead for spot of late lunch and a little education." She jotted in her book, then snapped it shut with a satisfied smile.

But when she slid the book back into her bag, she looked more solemn and pursed her lips.

"Now, that's all settled. But I must ask you something more serious. Does your brother know what's occurring? He will have to know sometime, otherwise how will you explain your sudden good fortune?"

Beatrice's heart sank. This was something she'd been trying not to think about. The confrontation with Charlie over her "arrangements" had not been pleasant, but she'd been compelled into it almost immediately, because her brother had seen Ritchie leaving this morning.

"He knows. And alas, having to tell him wasn't very nice."

Charlie's face had been a picture of outrage when she'd blurted out the reason for Ritchie's visit and what she'd agreed to. He'd shouted and stormed about, looking pale and flushed by turns as Beatrice had revealed the reality of the situation to him.

"I think it was having to accept the fact that *he's* let me down that hurts him the most, rather than me letting him down with such a brazen act of impropriety." Beatrice pleated the silk of her skirt between her fingers, still seeing the bleak resignation dawning in Charlie's eyes as she'd staunchly pressed home the fact that her solution to their terrible debts was probably the only one available. "In an ideal world, it would be kinder to him if there was some other way to salvage our finances. But alas there isn't and he's got to accept a more radical solution."

"And did he?" said Sofia quietly.

"Yes, I believe so. He seems resigned. He knows he's failed as my guardian and protector and provider, but at least he seems to have the wisdom not to resist."

Poor Charlie, he'd looked like the survivor of a storm at sea by the time she'd finished with him, but he'd hugged her and, despite tears in his eyes, he'd thanked her for her courage.

Beatrice bit her lip. "I hadn't the heart to tell him that I was planning to *enjoy* my scandalous month. It didn't seem appropriate. He'd be even more upset. He'd probably think I've descended into the pit."

"Well, he's to blame for your financial embarrassments, Beatrice. He must accept that responsibility."

"Oh, he does...he does. And I think he's learned his lesson." Beatrice let out a breath, a sigh. "And I think in a strange way, he does feel better that we've faced our problems. In fact, I expected him to start over again when I told him about Ritchie's disposition of our household arrangements, but instead he seemed positively perky. Especially when I told him we'd be getting a new domestic steward for a while. There's a lot to be said for losing the weight of responsibility and the chains of all our debts."

"Indeed there is, indeed there is," Sophia concurred. "It'll all work out for the best for both of you, I'm sure. And in the meantime, my dear, you *should* enjoy your scandalous month. It's the chance of a lifetime. A daring, delicious adventure with a daring, delicious man." The older woman smiled creamily. "And you should start out by preparing yourself for Ritchie's return…anticipating him, and the pleasure he'll give you." Sophia gave a broad wink. "I recommend you spend some time thinking about him at night while you're falling asleep, if you take my meaning?"

For the second time in their tea party, Beatrice couldn't help laughing out loud.

She *did* take Sofia's meaning and she was determined to "anticipate" Ritchie in exactly the way she'd suggested.

After all, it was precisely what the man himself wanted her to do.

RITCHIE THREW HIMSELF down into the armchair in his private sitting room. The Royal Northern Hotel in Leeds was well-appointed, almost a home away from home, but after a long day, it was difficult to relax. He'd exerted iron discipline over himself during his trip. Compelled himself to focus on his business affairs. It'd been a challenge, but the negotiations had gone smoothly, with exactly the outcome he'd planned for. With some investment in better conditions for the workers, the newly purchased mill would make him a considerable amount of money. He always found that people labored more productively and were more loyal when they were well paid, well fed and kept safer.

The irony of that made him laugh out loud.

Oh Beatrice, I wish you were here. Maybe I should have requested you travel with me?

Perhaps not, though. It would have been difficult to hold his own amongst hard-bargaining Yorkshire men, knowing that temptation was back at his hotel, warm and waiting. As it was, he'd had a capital expedition and achieved his goal in less time than anticipated. And tomorrow, he'd take the railway back south again to his reward.

But he hadn't left Beatrice behind entirely. He'd charged Jamie to manage her household, and Sofia Chamfleur to amuse and entertain her in his absence; and he'd brought with him the nearest approximation to her company.

The album containing her naked poses.

With a twist of the lips, he drew it toward him on the mahogany table next to his chair. Very well, he was obsessed with her, but he wasn't ashamed of that. Flipping open the leather-bound cover, he exposed the pages with the same reverent finger that had stroked Beatrice the other morning. It tingled as he flipped up the translucent protective sheet and displayed his new mistress in all her luscious unclothed glory.

Mine, was his immediate thought. All mine.

But that was absurd. Nobody really belonged to anybody, and if they did, Beatrice was the least likely candidate for possession. That was what stimulated him about her, now that he knew her, as much if not more than her physical beauty.

He did want pleasure in her though. Everything. Every variation from heights of sophisticated perversion to the lusty depths of animal coupling.

The anticipation was almost too much for him, and the book of images lay unstudied. Instead, he saw Beatrice spread against a white-covered bed, her creamy body flushed with pleasure, her incendiary hair spread in a sea of wild waves across the pillow. As he plowed her, she was growling his name and gouging at his back with her sharp, hard nails. The points of pain only excited him all the more.

"You *are* a siren, you are, my beautiful girl," he growled himself, throwing open his quilted robe and grabbing his cock. The heat from the well-tended fire was warm on his skin, but it wouldn't have mattered if he'd been sitting in an icehouse. All that was important was his fantasy, and his hand.

His fingers curled around his length and he began to pump, struggling to keep the strokes long and even and not to snatch at pleasure and it be over in a moment. If only it were her delicate hand handling his flesh. He imagined the dainty touch of her slender fingertips, her hold, so light and yet so tantalizing, gliding over him. She'd find the sweetest spots, and explore and tease them as she kissed him. Her mouth would taste of champagne… or maybe tea.

Like a boy in a confectionery shop, he switched to another delicacy—her exquisite back and bottom presented to him, as she knelt, her face pressed against the pillow.

What to do? Fuck her? Spank her? Tease her?

All, in good time.

He imagined handling himself as he loomed over her just as he was handling himself, supine, now. Working his fierce reddened flesh until he spent, copiously and in bliss, across her buttocks.

"Beatrice…Beatrice," he gasped, broken by her beauty, rendered a frenzied, moaning animal merely from the power of imagination, memory…and hope. His spine seemed to melt along the length of his back as he arched in orgasm. He barely contained the burst of his seed in his clutching fingers. The way it jetted forth nearly sent it flying toward Beatrice's picture—to anoint her in her absence as he'd anointed her, in his mind.

Afterward, as he lay back, sticky and shattered, another sweet illusion presented itself to him. Raising heavy, tired eyelids, he looked at the large and comfortable hotel bed across the room, and a twisting, plangent yearning gripped his heart and seemed to toss it around inside his chest.

He wanted her to be in that bed. Beatrice Weatherly, lying there sleeping. And he wanted to climb in between the sheets and sleep beside her.

The thought shocked him awake and he sat up, rubbing his fingers on his own thigh, to get rid of the drying semen.

I said never again. I said I'd never sleep the night with a woman, no matter how fond I am of her, or how shattering the pleasure has been.

The last time he'd slept in a woman's presence he'd woken to blood and the smell of smoke and a strange, quiet raving. His own blood, and the low hypnotic raving of the woman who'd just killed his son.

That wouldn't happen again. It couldn't happen again. He knew that. But in the recesses of his mind it still remained a haunting fear.

CHAPTER THIRTEEN

The Shopping Doll Learns a Few Tricks

BEATRICE COLLAPSED ON the bed at Sofia Chamfleur's establishment in Hampstead, as limp as a dish rag.

Whoever knew that shopping and the acquisition of knowledge could be so exhausting? Her head was whirling, her thoughts dashed hither and thither, from the shopping to the instruction and back to the shopping, round and round again.

They'd spent a delightful morning, touring the most fashionable West End stores, and several more exclusive establishments that Beatrice had never heard of, but where Sofia was clearly a cherished patron. Not all that many years ago, the Weatherly family had enjoyed at least the facade of being well set up, and in consequence, Beatrice hadn't quite forgotten what it'd been like to be a "shopping doll." But now, somehow, even as she lavished Ritchie's wealth on gowns and shoes and lingerie, and the expensive products of Sofia's favorite cosmetician, a still, small voice admonished her for wasting money that could have been spent more worthily. She resolved to make some charitable donations—if the various worthy matrons who administered such missions would accept funds from an apprentice demimondaine such as she—and lavish bonuses and new uniforms and even some personal treats on Polly, Cook and Enid.

Banishing thoughts of finance, Beatrice stared up at the ceiling…and her mouth dropped open.

Naked nymphs and satyrs cavorted in outrageous positions and caressed one another's bodies shamelessly. The decorations in Sofia's Hampstead house were eccentric throughout, but this guest room in particular seemed designed to stir the senses, and all that frisky fondling high above returned Beatrice's thoughts to what she'd done with Ritchie.

Why do I feel far guiltier about spending money than I do over having a handsome man touch my intimate parts?

It was bizarre but true, like guarding a delicious secret. A daring indulgence that thrilled her anew every time she took it out to examine it. And frustrated her, too. How typical of Ritchie to prime her mechanism with an hour of dalliance, then disappear abruptly on business, leaving her marking time, gathering momentum, yearning for him.

Her own fingers had helped, but now that she'd tasted shared pleasure, she wanted to sample what some of the nymphs and satyrs were doing, particularly the ones engaged in full sexual congress.

Goodness, this is an outrageous place, Sofia!

Restless despite her fatigue, Beatrice sat up again and looked around.

Everywhere was luxury and sensuality. Rich furnishings. Flowers. Paintings and sculptures all designed to rouse the senses. And this was only one room of many in the large house. What lay behind other closed doors? The hall had been as hushed as a Harley Street waiting room when she and Sofia had arrived, but there was a sense of discreet energy in the air.

The books and artifacts Sofia had shown her were astounding. Illustrated volumes on eroticism from the Far

East and the Continent. Prints and photographs far more explicit than her own accidental venture into pornography. And…things…objects…devices intended to be used as part of love play and sexual games, all shown to her by Sofia with a knowing attention to detail.

Did the Chamfleurs employ these toys in their frolics? Did Ritchie, with his more sophisticated mistresses?

Sofia had left a few examples for private examination while Beatrice took a rest before tea, and then her eventual return home. The items resided in a small but beautiful intaglio-work mahogany chest on a dressing table, but as yet Beatrice hadn't summoned the nerve to get them out and fiddle with them.

As she debated, there came the sound of a faint commotion somewhere in the house. Voices raised in welcome and conviviality, for the second time since she'd retired, but much as she strained to hear, both times Beatrice hadn't been able make them out. Tightening her red Japanese silk kimono about her—a new purchase, and a reminder of a fine night out at the Savoy Theatre in happier times, to see *The Mikado*—she sprang to her feet and padded to the door, opening it a crack. Unnerving as it was to sneak around a strange house in just the silken robe, her chemise and her drawers, curiosity drew her out onto the landing.

From a couple of floors below, the light, cheerful sound of Sofia's voice drifted up, then a man's tones, lower, not so distinguishable. Beatrice listened hard, heart thudding, but just as she ran to the banister and looked down, the door to Sofia's sitting room closed, cutting her off.

Don't be silly. What would he be doing here? He's up in the North on business.

Unsettled nevertheless, Beatrice picked up the little chest from the dressing-table tray and took it with her to the bed. Taking a sip from the glass of spiced Madeira that Sofia had left her, Beatrice savored the rich flavor and set about her box of treasures.

The chest had little velvet-lined drawers that could be lifted out, and on the first lay an object shaped exactly like a man's erect penis. So exactly shaped, that Beatrice expected it to twitch and swell, just as Ritchie's as yet unseen member had done when she'd touched it. Extending a forefinger, she gave the item a cautious poke.

No pulsation of life, but instead of the cold, inert consistency she'd expected, the ivory phallus seemed warm and felt organic and enticing to the fingers. It was hard in the way an aroused man might be hard, and its smooth surface invited a lingering inspection.

As I'm sure your cock does too, Ritchie.

Beatrice lifted it out. Sofia had explained that this thing—a *godemiche*—was also called a "widow's comforter." And the feel of it was indeed peculiarly comforting.

Or perhaps I'm just a natural fondler of men's organs?

She giggled, imagining how much that would please Ritchie. If only he was here right now to receive the benefits of her native inclinations.

Was he as big as this charming monster? Or even bigger? Judging by the bulge she'd seen in his trousers, and *felt* beneath her bottom when she was sitting in his lap, he certainly couldn't be smaller.

With her own finger, she traced the groove around the head of the phallus. It was a most particular shape and seemed to coax an examination by the smaller fingertip of a woman. Or perhaps a thumb in the little indentation beneath? Closing her eyes, she saw Ritchie's face, contorted in pleasure as she explored his topography.

Of course, the general use of such an item as this was
to put it inside one.

Beatrice tipped the *godemiche* this way and that.
Goodness gracious, it was thick. Would it even go inside?
And more to the point, would the organ it represented go
inside? She supposed there was one way to find out, but
her heart bounced at the thought of it. Circling her finger
and thumb around the thing's girth, she puffed out her
lips, doubtful.

Evading the issue, she set the faux phallus aside and
lifted out another drawer to examine more unnerving
wonders on the next level.

More ivory items, but this time a selection of spheres
and ovoids of a thoughtful size, with fine cords attached.
Some were singles, others doubles. One specimen seemed
to be curiously weighted, and on closer inspection, she
detected a very fine seam around the circumference, as if
it was hollow, and contained another, smaller ball which
rolled around.

Remembering Sofia's instructional lecture, Beatrice quivered. It would jiggle, wouldn't it? Jiggle and
wiggle inside as one walked around. Involuntarily, her
sex clenched as if grabbing at a phantom weighted ball
rocking inside it.

Down in the further depths of the chest were a couple
of small pots of balm or ointment. Sofia had explained
these too. Beatrice unscrewed the lid of the first, labeled
Lubrifiant de Cythère, and examined its contents; a silky
smooth unguent, very slick and bland, almost silvery between her fingers. She knew what it felt like, but it still
took an effort of will to admit it. The glistening stuff was
almost exactly the consistency of her own fluid, the moisture that welled between her thighs when she stroked herself…or was stroked by Ritchie.

The next pot, *épice Divine,* yielded up a thicker, more viscous substance, with a more pronounced scent. It reminded Beatrice of something.

Ah, the spiced Madeira!

It didn't take a medical genius to work out how one might use a warming ointment.

Taking up a tiny amount on her little finger, she rubbed it on the back of her hand, and as expected, the skin there glowed with a gentle but exciting heat.

Beatrice considered trying it, then thought better. Thrilling as it probably felt, it wouldn't do to provoke herself too much. She couldn't pass the rest of the afternoon in company, longing to stroke her private parts. It would probably require a bath to remove the stuff once applied.

The temptation still piqued her though, and when she'd sipped a little more wine she lay back on the bed, thinking of Ritchie and imagining him rubbing the stuff on her, then smiling devilishly when she writhed, helplessly aroused. Tantalizing fantasies danced in her head. What would happen if she rubbed the *épice Divine* on him, for example? The thought was as provocative as the effect of the ointment, and she mused on it languorously as she drifted toward a doze.

But right on the point of sleep, Beatrice heard a sound. An utterance that could have come straight from her dreams.

A woman's voice gasped then whimpered in breathy excitement.

Just like me in the morning room with Ritchie.

But where was the sound coming from? Sofia's villa was large and solidly built, with many well-appointed rooms. The noise must be coming from nearby for Beatrice to hear it.

When the noise came again, more of a moan this time, Beatrice sat up and cocked her head on one side, to better locate its source. It seemed to be emanating from the direction of a rather beautiful painting of a reclining nymph, which hung on the wall, adjacent to a well-upholstered chaise longue. An odd juxtaposition, but Beatrice hadn't investigated too closely as the image had a disturbing likeness to her own, as photographed by the wretched Eustace.

But now she drew close, to focus on the girl's voluptuous body, and found something odd about her navel. It looked very distinct, almost like a jewel set in her white belly.

Then it seemed to wink.

Oh, my goodness, it's a peephole!

And peepholes were made to be peeped through, especially when such naughty noises were issuing from beyond them.

Beatrice almost laughed out loud when she pressed her eye to the aperture and she had to press her knuckle between her teeth to keep herself quiet.

The moaning, whimpering lady was a person of her acquaintance, almost a friend. It was her hostess from the ball where she'd first met Ritchie—Lady Arabella Southern.

Standing in her drawers and corset, the famed society hostess was kissing a naked young man with an exotic tawny complexion, black curly hair and a very shapely posterior. He had his hand between her legs, and the way the muscles of his well-shaped arm were moving suggested that he was frisking the good lady Arabella with deft enthusiasm.

Oh, Lady S., you are a wicked woman! Does His Lord-

ship know that you attend the House of Madame Chamfleur?

The handsome aristocrat was a woman of middle years, a little thin and brittle looking, but the way she was kissing her naked lover and handling his body was nothing short of voracious. Beatrice fought desperately not to giggle. Arabella Southern was stately and refined in public, known for her gracious gestures and perfect deportment, but right at this moment, she seemed to have more in common with a Whitechapel streetwalker than a member of fashionable high society.

Her hands were everywhere. Sliding over the honeyed skin of her handsome young lover, fingertips curving to grab and squeeze. Beatrice let out a gasp when Lady Arabella grasped her paramour's sturdy penis and started working it vigorously, up and down, up and down.

Have a care, Arabella, he'll spend on your fingers if you don't moderate your actions.

But it seemed Lady Southern was well aware of the hair-trigger nature of the gentlemanly appendage, and as her comely friend's hips began to jerk, she let him go.

"Oh, Yuri, you're adorable! I can't get enough of you," the older woman purred, kissing her virile young companion. "I love your cock. It's such a beautiful monster. I can't wait to get it in me."

And Beatrice could see why her friend was enamored. The lad certainly was big in the gentlemanly department. His shaft was long and thick, with a rosy, rounded head.

Not as big as my Ritchie though, I'll be bound.

Not that Ritchie was *hers* as such, but she'd still wager her protector was the bigger man and her eyes popped wide as the risqué performance continued.

Goodness me, she mouthed silently, blood surging. *That again!*

Dropping to her knees in a way that was far from stately, Lady Arabella Southern applied her patrician lips to the task of sucking her youthful friend's penis.

First Sofia and her Ambrose, now Arabella and her unknown beau. Everybody seemed to indulge.

Beatrice licked her lips, trying to imagine the taste of Ritchie. Would he be sweet? Or salty? Delicate…or robust? Her mouth watered in anticipation. There was no doubt he'd want her to do it, and suddenly she wished with all her heart that he were here so she could begin her education.

Arabella's friend Yuri was certainly enjoying the experience, and that was a fact. His dark head tipped back as the countess made a meal of him, the mouth that instructed servants and chitchatted with royalty on occasion, stretched around his sturdy organ. Grabbing her head to direct the caress himself, he jerked his hips, and nearly knocked Arabella over, growling and snarling in some unknown foreign tongue that sounded vaguely Balkan. The fact that he seemed to be using the countess so casually should have been demeaning, but every line of Arabella's lean body cried out her enjoyment.

She really loved being on her knees and sucking a man's cock, and she reached around and grabbed his bottom to effect her own direction.

Beatrice watched for a few moments more, anticipating Yuri's crisis, but just when it looked all but inevitable, he suddenly pushed Arabella away, holding her from him and grinning down at her. As she gazed back up at him, he leaned over and murmured in her ear.

"Oh yes, oh yes," gasped the titled lady, clambering to her feet and climbing onto an upholstered divan adjacent to where they were standing. How handily placed that item of furniture was. So obviously positioned exactly in front of the peephole for viewing convenience.

Instead of lying on her back, as Beatrice had expected, Arabella came up on her hands and knees on the divan. Dishing her back, she looked over her shoulders invitingly, wiggling her bottom and licking her lips to entice her lover.

Yuri growled something in his mother tongue, and Arabella whimpered and undulated, a smile of pure happiness on her face. Beatrice hadn't the faintest idea whether her friend understood the young man or not, but the harmony of their bodies seemed to breach the language barrier.

Arabella certainly understood him when he suddenly and shockingly thrust a stiff finger inside her. She cooed like a dove and thrust back against the intrusion with enthusiasm.

Beatrice almost cooed too. Or more accurately, moaned in fierce frustration.

She wanted to be the woman on the divan with a man's finger inside her.

She wanted to be the one groaning and swaying, her body breached.

Ritchie, she mouthed in silence, watching the show.

"A VIRGIN? Are you absolutely sure?"

Ritchie sat down heavily in the chair, his thoughts wheeling. There was a profound difference between his own suspicions, coupled with secondhand servants' talk conveyed to him by Jamie, and this, the confirmation of a fact. Beatrice's status was pure, and she'd admitted so, frankly, to her friend Sofia.

He didn't know whether to be elated or horrified by the news.

Margarita had been a virgin. Her bold, flirtatious behavior had led him to believe otherwise, and consequently when the moment of truth had come, his attempt to embrace her had been disastrous, leading to a horror that even now he could hardly bear to think about and could not discuss.

"Beatrice, a virgin?" he repeated, fixing on the here and now, his lifeline.

"Yes, I believe she's telling the truth," said Sofia Chamfleur quietly, "unlikely as it seems, given the photographs. But after the story she told me, it seems to be the case."

Ritchie wanted a brandy. He wanted to rush out into the garden and walk round and round, turning Sofia's revelation over in his head until he could make sense of how he felt about it. But instead, he reached for the cup of tea she'd just poured for him and sipped it.

He'd arrived at his London home to find a note from Sofia, sent round by hand in answer to his wire; then climbed straight back into his carriage to Hampstead because he simply couldn't wait any longer to see Beatrice.

And now this. His new mistress was virgin. Which was both problematical and in his deepest, most atavistic male soul, a joy too.

He sipped the tea, not tasting it, staring at the cup as if it were a dug-up object, the product of a long-dead civilization. Sofia waited silently, and he sensed she was aware of his layered dilemma.

"Maybe I should just give her the money and leave her as she is? That way she's marriageable again, at least from the financial point of view." He put the cup down with a clatter on the side table, and almost smiled at the way Sofia didn't even flinch for her beautiful china. "I'm sure some decent enough fellow could be persuaded to set aside his scruples in respect of the nude photographs and marry her. As a country wife, at least."

"You must have already become fond of her to even consider that, Edmund."

Had he? He tried to consult his heart, but it was a battered organ, much out of use lately. Sticking to the satisfaction of his baser parts caused much less pain.

"I do like her. I like her very much." Within his bruised heart, a little seed started to unfurl and in his mind, he pictured a boot, stomping down on it. "But we both know that it can't go further than the bedroom. Not really."

Sofia, usually so wise, showed perplexity in her handsome face. "I don't know what to say to you, Edmund, or what to suggest." Her fingers pleated the sash of her day gown. "Except perhaps, to talk to her. See how she feels. I do believe that she's already conceived a great fondness for you too, and a desire." She gave him a very level glance. "I sense that Beatrice accepts that nobody expects her to be a virgin now, so she might as well sample the pleasures of the flesh with an experienced man she finds extremely attractive."

Ritchie smiled at his friend. "You make it sound simple, Sofia."

"I know it isn't, Edmund. But after what you've been through, perhaps you should be kind to yourself, and to Beatrice?" She shrugged, a fond look in her eyes. "I know not everyone is as lucky in life as I am, in finding Ambrose when I did, and then being in a position to do something about it."

A position to do something about it.

Despite its firm squashing, the little shoot fought to unfurl again and Ritchie reached for his tea, wishing for whiskey to calm the maelstrom of his dangerous emotions. To distract himself, he turned his mind to other matters. Ones that he knew he *could* do something about.

"This enterprising photographer… Has Beatrice revealed his identity to you?"

"I'm not sure. She wouldn't name him. She simply said he was a sweetheart."

Sofia reached for the teapot, ready to recharge their cups. "She doesn't seem like the sort of young woman to pose in the buff for just anybody, so my money's on Eustace Lloyd. He was paying court to her not all that long ago…and, well, I'm not sure I like that young man very much. Too much false charm, as if he's hiding a less-than-honest nature."

"I agree." Ritchie stared into his teacup, imagining the bitter brew of retribution rather than the delicate Indian infusion. "On all counts. Lloyd is an unsavory character. He projects a veneer of amiability, and perhaps sensitivity toward women, but he's a bad lot. Beatrice will say nothing of the circumstances of those photographs, but I suspect their revelation was not of her doing."

"Yes! Yes!" Sofia Chamfleur leaned forward, her expression earnest. "That's my belief too. That she was tricked somehow, either coerced or cajoled, I don't know which. And now, she's both too proud to admit her lapse of judgment, and yet too decent to lay blame where it's due."

"I believe you're right, Sofia. And I plan to find out for certain. This creature can't be allowed to take advantage of Beatrice's sweet, adventurous nature, and simply get away with it."

Sofia laid her hand on his arm, a brief touch. "You won't badger her about him, though, will you? If she doesn't wish to talk about it, it'll do no good to insist on the details."

Ritchie smiled. "Of course not. The last thing I want to do is cause her distress. She puts on a brave act, but I sense she's had her share of grief."

Eyes narrowed, deep in thought, Ritchie sipped his tea yet barely tasted it as the two of them lapsed for a moment into silence. With the resources at his disposal it would an easy matter to reveal the true provenance of the photographs. And when he did confirm his suspicions, he'd make that damned swine Lloyd's life a perfect misery.

CHAPTER FOURTEEN

After the Show

BEATRICE HAD WATCHED for a while, then whirled away from the spy hole, too excited to watch any more of Arabella's antics with her handsome young man. Her brain was like a galloper, images circling and circling around while her body simmered.

If only I could go back. Back to before all this happened and I knew nothing. Being an ignorant girl was so much easier.

But she hadn't been that girl for many a year. Her constitution was innately sensual and she'd be the first to admit to it. She'd enjoyed heated kisses with Tommy and strangely innocent explorations that would have flowered into the fulfillment of mutual pleasure if his life hadn't been cut short so cruelly. She'd even been drawn to Eustace, against her better judgment, because marriage offered an outlet for her natural inclinations and needs.

And now there was Ritchie. Perhaps the pinnacle of a long climb toward something she'd always yearned for, despite the stark transactional facts of his indecent proposal.

The little ormolu clock on the mantelpiece struck the hour. How many had passed since she'd arrived here? Barely sixty minutes or so, yet it seemed an eternity. She'd attempted to cool herself down with a splash of water in the very modern bathroom adjoining, but maybe she should dress now, and go down and find Sofia? The heated cries next door were done now. The room might be empty, or the lovers might be embracing, quiet and tender, their frolic over.

Beatrice's corset lay over the back of an armchair. Could she lace without Polly, or should she ring for the maid whose assistance Sofia had offered? She'd managed it on her own before, after a fashion. It had been a necessity, that time behind the dressing screen in Eustace's makeshift studio, even though her lingering drowsiness had meant she'd ended up much like a badly tied bundle of washing rather than a well-corseted young lady.

But now, just as she was about to start grappling with the laces, a sharp knock came at the door, making her jump. A familiar voice followed. "Beatrice? Can I come in?"

The corset slipped through her fingers and fell a tangle on the floor at her feet. She'd wondered earlier, but seriously, how could *he* really be here? Had her fevered imagination conjured him up?

Whirling around to grab her robe from the bed, she caught her foot in the lacing and tumbled to the carpet to join the corset, shouting "Ouch!" instead of "Wait a moment!" as she'd intended.

Like some fierce, defending angel, Ritchie burst into the room and strode over to her.

"Beatrice! Are you injured? I heard you cry out."

He was clad for business, in dark, sober gray, with perfect neck linen and a quiet diamond stickpin. He looked utterly splendid to her eyes. How she'd missed him.

Don't be absurd, Bea. He's barely been gone a couple of days!

"Beatrice, are you all right?" Concern filled Ritchie's

blue eyes, and he crouched down, frowning. Beatrice wanted to shake herself. She was goggling like a maid adoring a prince.

"I'm perfectly well, thank you, Ritchie." Impatient, she thrust away the corset and sprang to her feet. Rather too fast it seemed. Her head spun and she swayed again, hands flying out.

Even swifter than she, Ritchie stood up too, slinging a strong, immaculately suited arm around her waist.

"Clearly you are," he replied as she tried to wriggle away, and taking no nonsense, he manhandled her over to the bed, his demeanor half stern, half tender as he set her down to sit on its edge.

"What on earth were you doing rolling around on the floor?" Looming over her, he put out a hand and smoothed red strands of her hair back from her face. Her coiffure was collapsing, but he seemed not to notice, his eyes on hers, searching, worried. Beatrice was impressed that he continued to study her features for signs of faintness or enervation, despite the fact she was still wearing only drawers and chemise

"It's nothing. Thank you. Just a trip… I got tangled up in the laces of my corset when I heard your voice." It sounded farcical. It *was* farcical. She couldn't help but grin at him, and as if accepting her explanation, he grinned back at her, as handsome as the sun.

Oh Ritchie, I can see how society belles fall at your feet so easily.

"Well, Bea, usually I have the cream of society womanhood falling over themselves to get *out* of their corsets when I'm around. You're the first beauty who's gone arse over tit trying to get *into* hers."

Curses, it was as if he'd read her mind again. She could swear the wretched man *was* a mentalist.

"I'm not a society beauty. I'm just your courtesan, and I was about to dress anyway." His hand lingered at her face, and the compulsion to turn and press her cheek into his palm was almost unbearable.

"You're not 'just' anything, Bea." Sitting alongside her, he turned his hand and ran the backs of his fingers down over her cheek, her neck, her shoulder and her arm until he reached her hand. "You're a special and unusual woman, believe me." With a flick of his wrist, he took her hand and held it lightly.

How could such a slight caress have such an intense effect on her? She was trembling already, and she was sure he could feel it. Why on earth did she give herself away so easily?

"You're a flatterer, Ritchie," she replied lightly, giving him what she hoped was a nonchalant smile. He was the very thing she'd been wanting since the moment he'd left South Mulberry Street to depart on his business trip, but it wouldn't do to appear so obviously besotted. "But it's very pleasant to be flattered, so I'll accept it."

"Good," he murmured, then leaned over to kiss the inside of her elbow, the move so unexpected and so sensual it almost shattered her composure. Once again, that devilish exploratory tongue of his swept over her naked skin. Once again, it felt as if he were licking her between her legs. Something she'd recently seen Arabella's exotic swain do.

But how was Ritchie here so soon and so unexpectedly?

"I thought you were due to be in Yorkshire on business for some days to come." Her voice wavered as he began to suck the tender flesh in the crook of her elbow, like some predatory beast assaying her flavor. "I...I wasn't expecting you back so soon."

"Business went well. And I couldn't stay away any longer." His words were muffled against her skin. "I sent wires to both here and Mulberry Street on my arrival, and Sofia replied with a note to say you were here."

When he straightened up, Ritchie searched her face, his own slightly smiling and mysterious, as if reading her again, then his gaze dropped to the small pearl buttons down the front of her chemise, and the delicate ribbons.

"We've been shopping. Spending some of your money, as you suggested." His gaze felt as hot as limelight, warming the slopes of her breasts and her nipples through the muslin. "Then we came back here and Sofia suggested an afternoon rest."

Ritchie's mouth quirked with amusement, and his eyes flickered around, moving from her, to the peephole—with which he was obviously acquainted—and back to the bed where sat the open intaglio-work box and its contents, still strewn about.

Beatrice's face flamed. If it wasn't bad enough being found sprawled on the floor in her frillies, now she'd been revealed in her secret examination of Sofia's erotic playthings.

"Rest, eh?" His long, dark eyelashes flashed provocatively. "I should have known what sort of entertainment Sofia had in mind for you."

"I find such items to be interesting curiosities…but I'm not completely ignorant of their purposes." She reached for the *godemiche,* intending to return it and its friends to the box and slam the lid. Yet somehow her fingers lingered over the smooth, evocative surface and, as if governed by some infernal clockwork device beyond her control, her glance tilted downward toward Ritchie's genital area, so respectably covered by charcoal-gray fine worsted.

She looked. And she knew he was looking at her looking. But still she couldn't stop, and her fingers curved instinctively around the phallus.

When Ritchie laughed, she flung it away across the bed.

"Don't you care for your toy?" Still grinning, he retrieved it, his fingers curling around it just as thoughtfully as hers had done. "It seems quite a fine example of its kind to me."

Beatrice's heart thudded in time to the pulsing of blood in her veins and in between her legs. The phallus *was* a fine example, and it was easy to imagine it real, Ritchie's own flesh. Did he handle himself the way he handled the toy? Slowly, sensuously, and with lavish, loving care.

"Yes, I must admit it's well made," she said. How strange and feathery her own voice sounded.

Ritchie continued to fondle the cylinder of ivory, his tapered fingertips coasting over the faux veins, the thoughtfully fashioned head. Beatrice's eyes skittered from his hands to his face and back again, and from the way his long lashes fluttered once more, he might as well have been stroking his own cock. When he let out a faint breath, she glanced downward. She couldn't stop herself.

Good Lord, he *was* aroused, and sporting an enormous stand beneath his sublimely tailored trousers.

"So how do you think it compares to the real thing, Bea?" His voice was urbane, but his midnight-blue eyes were dark, hard and burning. "They call these a widow's comforter, but I'd imagine they're just as much a consolation to unmarried women."

"I—"

Have a care, Beatrice. He doesn't expect that you're a virgin. He imagines you at least modestly experienced.

"Well, I haven't had time to assess the efficacy of this particular example."

And still he stroked the carefully fashioned replica with all the relish he might apply to the real thing. Or have her apply. But who knew with a perverse man like Ritchie? He might derive a strange enjoyment out of touching the facsimile.

"Perhaps we could do that now? Assess it's efficacy, I mean." His eyes held hers, even though she was still peripherally aware of his fingers, moving, moving.

Beatrice felt enormously hot and agitated, unsure of herself, yet at the same time more sure of this than anything ever in her life before. It was a singular state, clear, yet bordering on madness.

"We could, I suppose." She glanced at the *godemiche,* and at Ritchie's thumb pressed into the groove beneath its smooth ivory head. "But wouldn't you prefer to…well… just *have* me? It is what you've paid so handsomely for, after all."

For her own part, Beatrice wanted anything that involved Ritchie's hands, his mouth or his living phallus.

And oh, his naked body…would she see him unclothed at last? Surely he was just as beautiful, if not more by far than Yuri beyond the peephole.

Indeed, I am going quite barking mad.

But her state didn't alarm her. She felt only excited, as if soaring toward a long-sought goal.

"All in good time, Bea. All in good time."

He seemed to be juggling with the *godemiche* now, holding the wicked thing between his two thumbs and forefingers and slowly turning it. She half expected him to produce his pocket handkerchief, envelop the faux penis in it, then make it disappear with a cry of "Abracadabra!"

Beatrice eyed him with impatience. What was his game? The man had spent a fortune getting her, and now that he'd got her, he seemed in no hurry to cash in his investment.

Despite his enormous arousal.

"But you want me, surely?" She flipped a pointed glance at the evidence. "Even *I* can tell that."

It was Ritchie's turn to narrow his eyes. Slowly, he assessed her, while still engaged in his prestidigitation with the ivory phallus. "Even *you?* Why would you say that, Bea? The notorious Siren of South Mulberry Street should be thoroughly experienced in the various nuances of male desire."

He does know. I'll wager he does...and if it's not mind reading, it's Sofia. I could box her ears!

"Well, even the most experienced of courtesans refrain from ogling men in public, so familiarity with their parts is usually confined to the bedchamber...I'd say." She gave him a firm look, wishing she could quell questions and manipulate conversations as easily as he seemed to be able to. "And as I've yet to view you naked, Ritchie, that remains to be seen."

Stop babbling, Beatrice!

His beautiful lips quirked, and she imagined him notching a point reluctantly to her. He opened his mouth to speak, then seemed to hesitate again, and she almost imagined him repeating *"All in good time..."*

"You seem very anxious to fuck me, my sweet," he purred, swiveling the *godemiche* again and running it through his fingers in a slow, evocative action. "And I can't say I'm not flattered. What man wouldn't be? But there's pleasure in anticipation, Bea. And games...and experimentation. And *I* enjoy those things at least as much as rutting."

Infuriating man!

Here she was, all ready to make a woman's greatest leap, and Ritchie was toying with her, running rings around her. And the more he held back, the more she wanted to take that critical bound.

She wanted to yell at him, *For heaven's sake fuck me, you contrary beast!*

But she managed to resist.

"Well, then, let's get to experimenting, shall we?" she said, her head coming up as she offered him a smile as challenging as his own. She hoped.

"Oh Beatrice, Beatrice, Beatrice, you're adorable. What more could a red-blooded man want?" He stared at her, smirking broadly. Yet suddenly, even in the very midst of his good humor and obvious desire, Beatrice saw the strangest twist of sadness. Something in his eyes... just for a moment—the shadows of unbearable pain, softening her heart.

And then the moment was gone again, and there was only mirth—and lust—in those dark ocean-blue depths.

"Why don't you undress, Bea?" said Ritchie, still twizzling the ivory cock idly between his fingers. "I've yet to see *your* beautiful body in the flesh, and you will insist on reminding me I've paid handsomely for the privilege."

Tingles of apprehension raced through her. The moment of truth. She'd undressed for Eustace, of course, but only behind a screen, and then floating on a tranquil sea of intoxication. Now, despite the excellence of Sofia's spiced Madeira, she was stone-cold sober and in full possession of her faculties. For a moment, she wished she'd drunk another warming glass, then realized that despite her nerves, she wanted to be fully aware, all senses acute. She had less than a month now with Ritchie, too short a time to spend in insensibility.

"Very well." She plucked at the ribbon on her chemise, trying to steady her shaking fingers.

"Wait!"

Her fingers froze again. What now?

"You're not cold, are you, Bea?" Ritchie dropped the *godemiche* on the bed and sprang up, heading for the fireplace, where a small fire puttered against an unseasonable chill in the air. Had Ritchie seen her shivering?

"Maybe a little."

Ritchie built the fire a bit, then strode to the window. Sofia's villa was secluded, and set in extensive gardens, but the distant windows of another residence were visible. Ritchie pulled the thick velvet curtains together, cocooning them in total privacy.

"There, that's better. Nobody to pry on us now, Bea." He turned up the lamps. "We can be simply ourselves."

Whoever you *are, Edmund Ellsworth Ritchie?*

"Yes, that is better, thank you, Ritchie," she said.

But to be sequestered in their own secret realm was intoxicating. Here, she could do anything, be anybody; whatever and whoever Ritchie wanted her to be. A great and very sweet sense of lightness and freedom enveloped her senses.

Her nervousness a strange pleasure now, she returned to the task of unfastening her chemise.

CHAPTER FIFTEEN

The Secret Realm

HE FOLLOWED THE small manipulations of those slender fingers as if his life depended on it. His heart thudded. His cock thudded too. It was the first time all over again, anticipating the sight of a beautiful woman's body. He'd felt like this with Clara, and yes, even with Margarita, though less so with his more experienced paramours. But right now, he couldn't for the life of him bring to mind the particulars of any other woman's form.

Was Beatrice nervous? If so, she was making a very good fist of feigning nonchalance. Was she afraid? No, not that. He'd seen that, and the bright anticipation in Beatrice's eyes was not the same.

He wanted to plunge across the gap between them and assist her unveiling, but he had to let her take her own time, her own pace. Her fingertips were so beautiful and delicate, the way they moved, and he imagined her handling the *godemiche,* and handling him. His cock bucked hard in his drawers and his heart lurched wildly.

At last the ribbons and buttons were undone, yet the fabric remained tantalizingly unparted. In a graceful yet primal gesture, she plucked at the hem of the soft garment, pausing just a second. Her breasts lifted beneath the cloth as she sucked in a deep breath, then with a tug and a twist and wiggle, she dragged the chemise off over her head. As the white muslin came away, it appeared to dislodge a hairpin or two as well, and her casually formed coiffeur tumbled around her shoulders in a cape of haphazard fire. Unable to stop himself, Ritchie shot forward, and retrieved the pins, his head full of lily of the valley and his eyes dazzled by desire.

"Dangerous," he muttered, tossing the pins onto the small chest at the side of the bed. He wasn't sure what he meant—them, or her.

As a virgin, she should have been shrinking, covering herself with her hands. As a natural enchantress, she drew in another breath, her breasts lifting and her head coming up, her eyes so bright and proud they almost struck sparks.

"Oh, Bea…you're perfection."

His fingers flexed, ready to reach out and cup the soft, sweet orbs, but he couldn't move. He was afraid to, in case he fell apart in shattered fragments of awe and lust. The other day, at South Mulberry Street, he'd seen a little of this beauty and it had all but floored him. Now he had a better view and he felt light-headed.

The jewel-green eyes seared him with questions. How could she possibly not think he found her to be the acme of all loveliness? But it seemed she did, and her falter of self-doubt nearly felled him completely.

"Here, let me help you." Amazed he could still speak at all, and completely incapable of holding back further, he reached for the fastenings on her drawers. His usually deft fingers fumbled, but he sent up a prayer of thanks that she'd taken heed and wasn't wearing woolen combinations. They were a hindrance to fashion, but Beatrice would still have looked exquisite bundled up in the sanitary creations of Dr. Jaeger, he was sure.

Their hands bumped at her waist, and they worked at

cross-purposes until Beatrice gave an exasperated sigh and left him to it.

"Lie back." Ritchie swept aside the box and all the playthings on the bed, his impatience scattering everything hither and thither. "Hup!" he urged, pulling lightly on the billowing muslin drawers as Beatrice subsided amongst the pillows.

Her eyes widened, but she didn't hesitate. Resting on her elbows, she wafted up her hips so he could divest her of the last of her garments.

Still holding the bundled drawers in his hands, Ritchie gazed.

So this was it. The sight he'd longed for, the vision that had made upwards of twenty thousand guineas into small change.

Worth every last farthing.

His fingers twisted in the fragile cloth and he felt it tear. She was beautiful. Supreme. Breathtaking. Yet not in the way of some earthy and voluptuous love goddess. Beatrice Weatherly was gentle of figure, neat and trim and softly curved, almost girlish despite her twenty-four years. He saw faint marks on her waist and thighs where not too long ago she'd been corseted and gartered, and he wanted to rub his face along each one, kissing and soothing.

Her dainty puss was a crimson bloom, dazzling and seductive against the snowy contrast of her skin.

"What's wrong?" Sitting up again, she frowned but didn't cover herself. "Not what you were expecting from the cabinet cards?"

"Far better than the cabinet cards. Infinitely better." He tossed aside the drawers, realizing he must have been sitting there like a foolish youth, still mangling them.

"Well, thank goodness for that! I thought I was going

to have to give you your money back, and return all the new frocks and fripperies I bought this morning."

Her talk was bold, but her skin gave her away. A pearly pink blush had stolen over the skin of her cheeks, her chest, and the slopes of her breasts. She was enacting the bold sangfroid of a high courtesan, but inside she was a bashful, modest girl.

"No refund necessary, Bea. You're everything I anticipated." He fought to keep his voice calm but inside he was a tempest. Leaning over her, he stole a kiss because he could no longer bear not to.

For a moment, she lay inert, her mouth soft beneath his. Then, as if animated by the power of electricity, she came to life, winding her arms around him and pressing her bare body to his clothed one. Ritchie twisted where he sat, to hold her better.

He'd told himself he wouldn't fuck her today, but now he wasn't sure he could contain himself. How could he hold out against her, the sweetest concoction of enthusiasm and innocence? Boldness and a divine, essential purity?

She created an ache in him that had never ached before. Not even when he'd loved and married twice.

I'm naked and I'm kissing a man. I'm naked and I'm kissing Edmund Ellsworth Ritchie.

Who would have thought she would have come to this? Yet, as Ritchie's firm, delicious mouth dominated hers, Beatrice felt for the first time in her life that she was truly where she'd always been meant to be.

She loved Ritchie's lips. Their texture was velvety and their muscular mobility was both dominating and tender. She couldn't help but respond in ways that seemed opposed to each other. Defy, yet yield. Govern, yet submit.

How could a mouth, a pair of flesh-and-blood lips, create such artistry?

Squirming and wriggling, she rubbed her skin against his clothing, the texture of the fine worsted a caress in itself. She wanted to see him as naked as she was, but this stark contrast was excitingly provocative.

His hands began to rove, as she'd known they would. Another texture. Another provocation. Warm, caressing flesh against her flesh. Strong fingers floating over her skin, leashed power contained. She could feel the tumult in him humming like a spinning top, yet his touch was measured, not greedy, not licentious.

If anybody was licentious, it was she, unable to stop herself from rubbing, rubbing, almost undulating against him like a purring cat in ecstasy. But she made a sharp sound of displeasure when he sat up, withdrawing from her.

"I *do* wish you'd get on with it," she said, then cried, *"Oh!"* and laughed at her own absurdity.

"I'd love to, sweet thing. Just let me take my coat off, and kick off my boots." Ritchie didn't laugh at her, but his face was full of smiles and sudden, happy youth. It had never really occurred to her how old he was before, but he had at least a decade on her, perhaps a bit more. And when he was sad, which she'd seen once or twice, he looked his years.

But now...now he looked joyous, almost angelic. Like a young god with his thick fair hair and his wicked smile.

The well-cut coat was flung across the room in the general direction of a wing chair, and in a flash, he'd un-laced his polished boots and kicked them away. Then, with barely any more care, he whipped out his elegant stickpin, and tossed it amongst the little heap of her own hairpins, before tugging at his neckwear and wrenching it free.

The beautiful foulard sailed through the air to join his coat, and as it floated, he unfastened his high, stiff collar and pulled that off too. Then, about to plunge forward again, he paused and unhitched his watch and chain and set those aside, too.

He doesn't want them to dig into me.

This small act of consideration twisted her heart and doubled her longing for him. A longing for his touch, his lips, his skin. Everything. They had but a month and she wanted him now.

The finite nature of their relationship made every sensation more intense, more luminous. Tugging at his shirt and waistcoat, she drew him to her again, searching for his mouth and finding it. When he surrendered his lips to her, she wound her arms around him, loving again the sensation of cloth on skin, the piquant rub. She parted her legs, pressing her pelvis against him. It was so easy. So natural. So strangely apposite.

Ritchie's kiss was hungry but measured, and her heart leaped when he stroked her body as he devoured her. His hands were warm, and they smoothed over her, leaving a glow, a tingle in their wake, almost as if they'd been coated in *épice Divine*. The more he touched, the more she moved. Was compelled to move. His tea-scented mouth consumed her soft, anxious cries.

"Let me pleasure you," he murmured, blending the words into the kiss. "Let me concern myself solely with *you* for the moment. I want to see your face, the way you move, the sound of your voice as you spend. I don't want to get lost in my own desire."

Beatrice stared at him in puzzlement as he drew back and looked down on her, his face alight with a near zealous glow. He wasn't at all what she'd expected of a man, especially one who purchased a woman to satisfy him. Were all men like this, or was Ritchie very special and rare?

"But—"

He stopped the words with his fingers on her mouth. She could smell the scent of her lily of the valley toilet water on his skin, and other odors, also hers, but more exciting.

"Your pleasure is my pleasure. Indulge me. There'll be time enough for us to fuck. To see a woman *in extremis* is a rare and wonderful thing. It needs to be savored."

His hand slid from her mouth, down over her chin and neck and settled lightly on her shoulder. He stared at her, his indigo eyes intense as if he were still speaking with them, and she understood. At least a little.

Watching her respond to him, watching her squirm and struggle with an excess of sensation, then spend helplessly, meant as much to him, if not more, than the act of congress.

So be it. Who was she to argue? How many hundreds of disappointed wives, used quickly and without thought by clumsy husbands, would give anything to be in her place?

"I'm yours, Ritchie," she said simply, and meaning it. On a far deeper level than the terms of their monetary transaction, so deep and sudden it alarmed her. "My pleasure is yours." She paused, her heart floating. "I'm happy to give it."

"You're a treasure, Bea." His face was complex tapestry of emotions; some clear, like satisfaction and desire, others more fleeting and inchoate. But joy and erotic fervor won the day. "Now lie back and be my odalisque. Let me serve you. I promise you'll enjoy it."

"I don't doubt that. You seem to have a considerable degree of flair in that department." Beatrice smiled up at him in what she hoped was a sultry manner, lowering her eyelids, aware of a great irony yet feeling no distress in it.

This was *exactly* how she'd posed in the photographs Eustace had taken of her. Languid. A creature of the senses. A goddess or houri, her body draped on a couch, offered and available. But that had been facade for the camera, and this was real. Real like breath and life and blood and desire.

Ritchie loomed over her, kneeling on the bed at her side, his own eyes hooded, his mouth curved and knowing. His fingertips coasted over her shoulder, her collarbone, then skated down to her breast, settling on the nipple and plucking it provocatively between finger and thumb.

Beatrice's hips jerked. Her body loved this, though she knew not why. She remembered the way he'd tormented her like this in the morning room, back at South Mulberry Street, and between her legs, her sex fluttered, hungry and suddenly slick.

Ritchie's smile broadened and he switched to the other teat, teasing and tweaking. Then back again, to and fro until her nipples were pink and hard and crinkled, exquisitely sensitive, and almost with a life of their own, silently calling to his fingers, begging for more. Without warning, he plunged down, took one between his muscular lips and sucked on it.

"Oh! Oh, my goodness!"

Between her legs there came a grind of pleasure, intense and keen, almost painful. Not a crisis, but close to it, and she cried out again. She wanted to grab Ritchie's hand and conduct it to the fierce little bud of her clitoris, but somehow, he constrained her, forbade her to move, through sheer force of will.

"Yes. Good." His breath was hot against her breast, and he paused only for a second, to utter the words. Then he was sucking again, tugging hard and flicking with his tongue. As if he'd read her mind, and deduced the exact way to plague her most, he settled the flat of his hand on her belly, fingertips touching the edge of her intimate hair but going no further.

Beatrice thrashed her head on the pillow, grabbed knots of the bedding and twisted them, her hips lifting in silent plea for touch, for contact. But still Ritchie held back, concentrating on her breasts, his hand still and tantalizing on her abdomen.

"What do you want, Beatrice? Tell me what you want."

"I…I want you to touch me." Her pelvis lifted and rocked, lifting his hand with it. She imagined some kind of arcane machine inside her, working her muscles and sinews without her control.

"Where? Tell me where?"

"You know where!" she cried, compelled to assert herself, an incomplete submissive, "You're a very perverse man, Ritchie, and you ask the most foolish questions."

He laughed, his voice light and untrammeled, perfectly happy as he slid his fingers into her sex.

She couldn't hold back any longer; couldn't just lie there and accept. Grabbing his head, she dove her fingers into his thick, fair hair and below, squashed her hand over his where he touched her. She felt him laughing again, right against the skin of her breast, but he complied, pressing more firmly against her clitoris with his fingers and circling wickedly in the way now so familiar.

Beatrice thrashed and squirmed, gripping on hard, not caring if her nails dug into his scalp or the back of his hand. The things he did, with tongue and finger, made a madwoman of her, bent only on taking as fully as he was giving. She let out a harsh cry as her body clenched, and clenched again in surging waves. Pleasure seemed to make every hair on her head stand on end as the crisis took her and shook her.

Ritchie, as she might have expected, was relentless. He gave no quarter, driving her to peak after peak with his artistry. Only when she could take no more did he seem to sense that, and let her catch her breath. A gentle kiss replaced his sucking and licking at her breast, and between her legs his fingers relaxed, leaving his hand cupped around her in a featherlight hold.

In a daze, Beatrice almost laughed herself. Absurd thoughts filled her mind, floating on a wave of Ritchie's cologne.

How can I be an insatiable voluptuary and still a virgin? And if I were a rich, rich woman, how much would I pay for Ritchie if he was one of Sofia's "gentlemen"?

"Thirty thousand at least…" she murmured, and then it was her turn to laugh, "Maybe sixty…"

"What are you burbling about, my siren? What's so amusing to you?" Ritchie sat up and stared down at her, grinning and curious. He reached out and tenderly brushed back wayward tendrils of red hair from her brow. The gesture was so gracious and natural that Beatrice almost grabbed his hand and kissed it.

"I was just thinking… If you were one of Sofia's stallions, how much would I pay you for *your* services?" She sat up, very aware that she was still naked and he clothed. She wasn't afraid or embarrassed—never that, now, with him—but the contrast of skin and cloth remained. "You give so much, you're worth a princely sum."

His smile broadened. "I'll bear that in mind, Bea. One never knows when one might fall on hard times, and if one has assets, one should employ them."

"Indeed." A cool realization drenched Beatrice's happy glow. Hard times had driven her to exploiting her assets. It was too easy, lost in a haze of sensuality and pleasure, to forget that she and Ritchie were not engaged in a romance, but a business deal of flesh for hire.

"Now don't look like that," he said. His uncanny senses had detected her sudden dark thoughts. "Yes, we've been brought together in unusual circumstances. But there's no reason why we shouldn't enjoy our time together as more conventional lovers would." He took both her hands, and held them firmly. "It'll be a much pleasanter experience for us both."

"Yes, of course. But…well… It's all been a little bit one-sided thus far. I'm not exactly giving you what you paid for, Ritchie."

Ritchie shook his head, the lamplight glinting on his curls and making a halo of them. "Ah, that," he intoned. "The carnal act. The coup de grâce. The fuck." He raised one of her hands to his lips and dusted a kiss on its back. "It's not the be-all and end-all of sensuality, my darling."

"But it does seem rather important. Most men set the greatest store by it, and you barely seem interested."

"Oh, I am interested. Believe me, I am. But there are certain considerations to be borne in mind." His blue eyes bored into her like darts of midnight.

Beatrice ground her teeth. Her girlhood riding habits might have made things somewhat easier for her than for many women, but the…the actual ingress was still going to come as a shock and perhaps it was better to admit to the fact before the critical moment.

"And what might those considerations be? Do tell," she prevaricated.

"The fact that you're a virgin, my dearest Beatrice, and you've never fucked a man before."

CHAPTER SIXTEEN

Those Considerations

THERE, IT WAS OUT. But how did one tell a man that your virginity didn't matter that much to you? Except that you were quite glad he was the one to take it.

"So what if I am?"

Ritchie's face was a picture. A masterpiece of amusement, mild exasperation and a dozen other emotions, some not quite so easily deciphered.

"Well, the surrender of her virginity is generally considered to be a major event in a woman's life, and usually reserved for marriage." For the very tiniest part of a second he glanced away, as if hiding himself from her. "And as our arrangement is not of the marrying variety, the disposal of your virginity raises questions."

Oh, for heaven's sake, not a debate!

Beatrice wished her robe was in easy reach. She didn't wish to enter into a great big discussion regarding virginity while she was bare naked and Ritchie wore the shield and armor of his Savile Row tailoring.

Still, what could she do? "It's mine to dispose of, Ritchie." She matched his steady stare with one of her own. "And I choose to dispose of it with you. Shouldn't you be pleased about that?"

"I am, Beatrice, I am." His hands tightened around hers as if he sensed she might try and shake herself free. "But that doesn't stop me being concerned about you. I'm not sure you should waste such a precious gem on a man like me. When I saw the photographs, I believed that you were experienced. They are the very acme of sensual beauty. They suggest abandonment. Satiation. A familiarity with fleshly pleasures."

"Appearances can be deceptive." Yes, not least of all those of Eustace, who had seemed a sincere admirer and a decent man.

"Not entirely," countered Ritchie, his thumbs smoothing across her knuckles as if to calm her. "You *are* an exquisitely sensual and responsive woman, Beatrice, a natural libertine... But you do still have your maidenhead; you can't ignore that."

"Well, it's a damned nuisance to me now, and I want rid of it," she said, speaking the utter truth. "Since my reputation is sullied beyond repair, and nobody would ever believe I was untouched even if I am, what's the use of hanging on to something that's meaningless." His piercing gaze bored into her, almost emitting light yet as dark as it was brilliant. "I thought you would have been glad to oblige me, Ritchie, really I did."

Especially as I'm sitting here naked and you have sight of all my charms.

"I shall oblige, my dear. But I must be sure that you don't want to save it for your husband, as his natural entitlement."

"Fiddlesticks! No man is entitled to anything in that fashion. A woman's body is hers to dispose of."

"Ah, what a radical you are, Bea. A veritable suffragist. Would you laugh in my face if I told you I'm in favor of your views?"

It didn't surprise her at all. Ritchie was an unusual man, and though she barely knew him, he seemed forward thinking. That he should espouse the rights of women was *exactly* what she might have expected of him.

She smiled rather than laughed. "No, your views don't surprise me, Ritchie. I'm rapidly coming to the conclusion that you're a very rare and rum sort of fellow, as my brother would say."

Ritchie made a soft, wry sound. "Indeed I am, Beatrice. Indeed I am." He drew her hands to his lips again and kissed the back of each one in a swift, decisive gesture. "And I shall be happy and honored to be your first lover."

Beatrice opened her mouth to remind him he'd paid for that honor, but held back. He'd paid for a month of sensual pleasure and indulgence, not a month of somebody constantly *reminding* him he'd paid.

"Shall we do it now then?" she suggested, shocked at how exciting the mere suggestion was. Just when she'd thought he'd sated her, the hunger boiled again.

"Let's work up to it, Bea. There's no rush, and the more gradual the approach, the sweeter the prize. I don't want to…to sour your memories." He frowned again, and Beatrice sensed him going away from her somehow, as if revisiting dark anguish. If he hadn't been holding her hands, she would have reached out and smoothed his pleated brow with her fingertips.

"Don't worry, I'm sure I'll be perfectly all right. Perhaps I could have a glass of Madeira, to relax me?"

"Yes, that's a capital idea. You're a very sensible girl." He released her and padded over to the side table where the decanter stood. "A very beautiful and naked sensible girl," he added, returning and putting the glass into her hand and conducting it to her lips. "But you need to trust me completely in this. A roundabout approach will be the gentlest and least painful, believe me."

What on earth did he mean? Beatrice sipped a little wine as Ritchie turned from her, rifling amongst the contents of the intaglio-work box still strewn across the bed.

"Oh, I'm sure it won't be painful. I'm probably not an actual virgin anyway. I used to ride astride as a girl, wearing a pair of Charlie's breeches. Mama had the vapors when she first found out, but she knew she couldn't stop me." Watching Ritchie, she nearly choked on her Madeira when he retrieved the ivory *godemiche* from the haul and ran his fingers over it again.

"I think we'll employ this fellow in the first instance," he announced, looking at her from beneath his lush lashes. "He's much easier to control than the somewhat intractable male appendage. That organ has a mind of its own, especially when gloved in the silky heat of a beautiful woman's puss."

"But what about you? Shouldn't your...um...appendage be in receipt of some pleasure, too?" She swigged down a little more wine, then set the glass aside firmly to stop herself downing the whole lot in one. "Speaking of which, I should like to examine yours before too long."

Ritchie barked with laughter. "And so you shall, so you shall. But first let's introduce you to our thoughtfully designed ivory friend, shall we?" His thumb moved provocatively along the ivory length, invoking the same shivers of fascination as before. "Lie back, Beatrice. Relax and let us pleasure you."

Beatrice slid onto her back, shuffling along the counterpane, unsure how to dispose of her limbs, until Ritchie dropped the ivory phallus and laid his hands upon her. Grasping her by the hips, he edged her down further, then slid the palms of his hands flat against her inner thighs and parted them.

It was impossible to look. She closed her eyes, turned

her head on the pillow. Restless, she laid her arms back and grasped the bars of the brass bedstead, bracing herself.

"Relax, my darling. You're as stiff as a wooden doll. Let your limbs go loose. Don't be afraid."

Difficult. But then Ritchie leaned over her, and she could feel the brush of his waistcoat against her breasts as he placed his face against her ear and murmured sweet nothings into it. She couldn't have said what they were, but the words were mellifluous and soothing, nonsense talk about how beautiful and clever she was. The syllables flowed from Ritchie's lips like a honeyed elixir and propelled Beatrice into exactly the state of relaxation he'd prescribed.

As her body followed her consciousness, all tension ebbed away and she felt light and completely at her ease.

Ritchie's hand slid along her arm where it lay on the pillow, her own hand no longer clinging to the bedstead for dear life. His fingertips hovered at her wrist, light as the kiss of a exotic hummingbird. How bizarre, was he taking her pulse?

She could almost believe he might have hypnotized her, her state was so euphoric. And even more so when he kissed first her brow, then her cheekbone, then the corner of her mouth.

Lulled and dreamy, she felt the touch of something firm and slightly cool against the skin of her belly. The *godemiche.* Ritchie circled it lightly over her abdomen, dipping it into her navel and making her giggle it felt so strange and so provocative. Then, gradually, it began to move, and the circles to migrate downward until they were brushing against her mons.

Slowly, slowly, he approached the heart of the matter, sweeping the ivory phallus over the insides of her thighs

and the creases of her groin. Beatrice gave a little squeak
of surprise when he slipped it into her cleft and let it rest
on her clitoris. She could almost imagine it was Ritchie's
own cock now that it was warmed by her skin.

Like a mermaid floating in a warm, benevolent ocean,
she felt completely calm, utterly at home. Even when
Ritchie began circling the tip of the phallus very con-
certedly around her clitoris, she still felt only a delicious,
harmonious gathering of desire and pleasure. When a
crisis came, it was almost gentle, like a breaking wave in
a lake of warm syrup.

"Lovely…lovely…" he murmured, letting the *godemiche* rest between the lips of her sex while he turned
away for a moment. Instinct told Beatrice what he was
about, and her suspicions were confirmed when she heard
a soft, liquid, slicking sound.

He was heating the *Lubrifiant de Cythère* with his fingers. He'd dipped them in the jar and caught up some
of the potion. And now he was about to apply it to her
flesh…or to the phallus…probably both.

A long ripple swept the entire length of her body, and
even the tips of her hair seemed to flutter.

Ritchie leaned over her again, nudging aside the phallus to anoint her. The silken gelée was at skin heat now,
blood heat, and it felt delicious where he painted it on
her sex with generous strokes. He slid it over her clitoris, and her swollen folds, then down deeper, circling her
entrance. When he'd done that, he repeated the process,
warming more of the clear, slippery ointment and rubbing it lightly again and again where a man would enter.
Where *he* would enter…in his own good time.

Coasting on the pleasure still glowing there, Beatrice
lifted her hips, pushed against him, impatient now. Eager

to feel what possession was like, whether it be his fingers or the *godemiche* or him.

"I wish you wouldn't keep me waiting," she murmured, reaching down and pressing on his hand. "I want to know what all the fuss is about." Her eyes flashed open and met Ritchie's staring down at her. He was smiling, but he looked impressed.

"Very well then, courtesan, so you shall." He leaned forward and kissed her lips, then spoke against them, his breath warm on her face. "But if it hurts…if you don't like it…stop me. No suffering nobly in silence, promise me."

"Promise," she replied, shuddering in anticipation as his middle finger pressed lightly at her entrance. "Believe me, if I want you to stop I'll tell you so in no uncertain terms, Mr. Ritchie."

"That, I can believe."

He pressed firmly and his finger slid with ease, skating on the *lubrifiant* and her own silkiness, right up to the knuckle.

"Ooh!"

What a strange sensation. Particular, yet exciting. Two bodies joined. Not congress yet, but still intimate. Beatrice wriggled, pressing her hand over Ritchie's.

"How does that feel, Bea?" he whispered. "Not unpleasant, I hope?"

"No, not in the slightest… It's…it's unusual. I don't know what to say."

Ritchie kissed the corner of her mouth and crooked his finger inside her.

Beatrice squeaked and thrashed, shocked by an intense bolt of pleasure as the pad of his fingertip found a sensitive spot she'd had no idea even existed. He was stroking inside her, yet she felt it in her clitoris, and it was so astonishing she almost spent again.

"Hush...hush..." His words flowed over her, a gentle balm while down below he tantalized her with lush new sensations. Within a heartbeat, he was pressing again, massaging and making her squirm. Her own silky moisture flowed and blended with the *lubrifiant* and before she had time to think about it, Ritchie withdrew his finger, only to press again...with *two*.

This was different. There was tension, more pressure, some accommodation required. Beatrice gasped, finding herself suddenly panting. The stretching sensation taxed her but still felt good. Better than good.

"Beatrice? Am I hurting you?" Concern roughened Ritchie's voice. But why so? He must have caressed dozens of women this way, maybe even other virgins.

"No! A little...maybe...I don't know..." She drew in a deep breath, arched up, her senses on fire from the strangeness of it all. It was wonderful and dangerous and heady. "Please don't stop!"

Urges, intense and shocking, raced through her body, making her want to do things. Things that the feel of his fingers pressed inside her seemed to demand. She wanted to touch herself as well as be touched, and she plucked at her nipples, as if driven by an arcane instinct. Wriggling her bottom against the counterpane, she was just about to move one hand lower, to join Ritchie's in her cleft, when he did it for her, pressing the tiny bud of her clitoris with the flat of his thumb.

"Ah! Oh my goodness!"

Pleasure came again in an enormous burst, and she bent like a bow, up from the bed, almost lifted by Ritchie's hand at her sex. Her heels gouged the coverlet and she tugged at her nipples, the tiny pain there a counterpoint to the sweet sensations in her belly.

"My dear, beautiful Beatrice," said Ritchie, his voice broken as if awed.

And then, even as she rode the crisis, he tested her further. His fingers slid from her body, and in the blink of an eye, the *godemiche* replaced them, mutely requesting entrance. Poised to penetrate it felt cool now, having no life of its own, and hard, so unlike the resilient quality of the skin and muscle and tendons that constituted a human finger.

But what it shared with a living man, within a certain approximation, was its size.

"Relax," he murmured again, kissing, stroking with his free hand, gently encouraging with what seemed like the sheer power of his will. "Relax, dear one, relax. All will be well."

Beatrice fell back, bewitched by the low, sweet huskiness of his voice. Her flesh felt mellow and loose, still glowing with pleasure, but the ivory phallus was an unyielding, inanimate object against her. She understood the reasoning of employing it thus. It had no rampant lust-crazed male driving it…but still, she wished it was Ritchie's cock, not a faux one.

"Soon…don't worry…soon," he crooned, astounding again her with the strange way she seemed to be able to read her. "This way is better…I promise. You'll enjoy me more, when the time comes, for accommodating our friend here." He pushed more purposefully with the *godemiche,* edging the very tip of its carved shape just inside her.

"If you say so, Ritchie. If you say so."

"Trust me."

Should she? Could she? After Eustace Lloyd, she should never ever have trusted a man again, but somehow she knew that if she wanted Ritchie to stop right now, he would do so. And not even be angry with her. And it was because he *would* stop that she didn't want him to.

As he pushed, Beatrice suddenly experienced a yielding of her flesh, a sense of give that wasn't really painful but quite distinct. It lasted barely an instant then the phallus slid in with a measured glide. A gasp escaped her lips, and a tear slid from the corner of her eye, but not from pain, or even relief. No, the emotion seemed jumbled and new, past understanding. She could only slide her arms around Ritchie and hold him close, as touched and moved as if it had been him inside her.

"Good girl…good girl," he purred, his voice velvet as he murmured more nonsense encouragements in her ear. Slowly, he withdrew the *godemiche,* then slid it in again, repeating in a soft, easy rhythm, each stroke feeling more familiar than the last.

So this is what it feels like to be fucked?

It wasn't quite what she'd expected, but then, she wasn't sure what she *had* expected. This delightful friction seemed to work upon her like a magical mechanism, building up exquisite tension. Would a real man inside feel this way, too? She supposed so, but Ritchie's cock would be warm, and hard in a more pliable way. Feeling the rhythmic stroke of the faux phallus, she longed for the coming hour when it would be him.

"How does it feel? Do you like it?"

Beatrice opened her eyes to see Ritchie watching her face, monitoring her like some magical doctor of love with his patient. She blushed, knowing her pleasure must be written large across her features.

"It…it feels most particular, and really quite pleasant." She bore down on the thing, trying to quantify with a part of herself that had never quantified anything before. She groaned and moved her thighs, gripping the thing with interior muscles. The deliciousness mounted and tension gathered in her belly.

"Touch yourself, Bea…while I fuck you with it."

Of course, that was it…the perfect thing. Her fingers were moving toward her center before he said it.

Oh, how luscious. How delightful.

The *godemiche*. Her own hand. Ritchie still kissing her, his free arm sliding around her and clasping her to him. As her fingertip circled, pleasure crested again in a yet bigger wave.

Beatrice cried out and surrendered, perfectly happy, her body rippling and flexing around ivory.

"YOU'RE NOT GOING, are you? I thought…well, I thought we might…um…perhaps, do it? Or I might at least see your masculine appendage."

When Beatrice returned from the bathroom, the sight of Ritchie donning his coat, with his necktie already perfectly restored and his boots firmly laced, was like a body blow. She'd been sure that their delightful interlude with the *godemiche* was just an appetizer.

Ritchie stared at her, his face a picture, and Beatrice almost laughed despite her disappointment. She was beginning to enjoy shocking him.

"Sweet Beatrice, I would love to stay," he said, his voice a mixture of amusement and regret. "More than anything. But I have business to attend to, and they are matters rather pressing." Smoothing his lapels, he came toward her and when he reached her, he cupped her face between his hands. They felt as warm and gentle as when he'd been handling her body. "I'll make it up to you, dearest, mark my words." His finely marked sandy eyebrows quirked. "And I promise you an entirely free hand with my masculine appendage next time we meet. He will be at your service, in any capacity you require."

"I should think so!" Beatrice had to laugh this time. He was absurd, but strangely loveable for all that. The most peculiar man she'd ever met, and yet somehow, she could no longer imagine giving her virginity to any other. Even dearest Tommy was becoming fainter and fainter in her imagination, like a beautiful image finally faded by the sun.

And by the brilliant radiance of Edmund Ellsworth Ritchie's sensuality.

"Do you forgive me though?" he demanded, pressing a kiss first to her brow, and then to her lips, touching delicately as if he feared a loss of control. "I'm sure you must think me the most perverse of men."

"I do. I do indeed, Ritchie," she responded, her mouth barely a whisper away from his, "but I think I'm rapidly developing a taste for all things perverse. Which is convenient for the pair of us, wouldn't you say?"

Ritchie stared at her, his eyes serious. Once again, she got the impression that she'd exceeded some kind of expectation he'd formed of her.

She'd exceeded her own expectations, too. Her plan had been to dispatch her obligation to him and, at the same time, take some pleasure in him, and learn the ways of men—before returning to a quiet, unremarkable life away from society.

But now, the plan and her expectations were changing by the moment. And the prospect of a future pounding out letters on a typewriting machine did not seem as satisfactory as it had once done.

"We'll do very well together, you and I, Bea," said Ritchie at length, smoothing his fingers over the finely patterned satin of his waistcoat. "I shall be occupied for the rest of this day with matters arising from my trip up North, but I promise you that tomorrow we will spend time getting to know each other." His long, sooty lashes, so thrillingly dark in one so fair, swept down in pure provocation. "And I'll introduce you to those parts of me you so fervently desire to explore."

Impetuously, Beatrice reached down and cupped the part in which she was chiefly interested. His cock was hard in the fine dark worsted of his trousers, and when she squeezed him, he let out a laughing oath.

"Beatrice. Beatrice. Beatrice. You plague me." His hips jerked forward as if they had a mind of their own and were intent on forcing his cock into her fingers. "If it weren't for the fact I'd wired several important investment brokers to meet me at my club, I'd gladly stay here and let you play with my cock to your heart's content." The beast stirred, hot and hard within his clothing. "But alas, the appointment is made now and it would be injudicious to let them down."

She was disappointed, but she was also worldly now, and felt strangely philosophical. Giving him a last, light caress and a kiss on the cheek, she drew back with a smile on her face as she adjusted the sash on her new Oriental robe. "Yes, a gentleman with your extravagant tastes must ensure that his business prospers enough to sustain them." Dropping him a wink, she wound the strip of satin around her fingers. "And you and I *will* have a lovely time together tomorrow. I insist on it."

"You can wager your life on that, Lady Yum-Yum, I assure you." He looked her up and down, the kimono clearly meeting with his approval. Beatrice wondered if he'd ever attended *The Mikado*. Unlikely though it was, with such a long run, perhaps he'd been in a box that night with some society beauty, while she'd been in the stalls with Charlie and her parents. If the performance hadn't been quite so wonderful, she might even have looked up and seen him. "Now, you take a rest, frisky miss, then you and Sofia can enjoy a long, intent dissection of my many quirks and foibles."

"Your *very* many foibles," averred Beatrice, arching her eyebrows at him.

"Indeed." He was brisk now, already drawing away from her if not yet physically gone. "I'll send a carriage around to South Mulberry Street for you tomorrow at seven. We'll take an early supper at a place I know. Very quiet and discreet, but I think you'll find it diverting."

The desire to grab him, rip open the silken robe and press her body against his was so intense that Beatrice could almost taste it. But instead, she reached up, stroked his face and bestowed a light kiss on his lips.

"That will be wonderful. I look forward to being diverted, Ritchie," she murmured, stiff with the tension of not demanding more. "It's something at which you excel."

"As do you, Beatrice. As do you." Ritchie's voice was a growl, and his kiss almost savage though it was only a moment before he put her from him, turned on his heel and strode to the door. Once there, he turned for a last look at her, his face fierce yet so tender her heart turned over.

And then he was gone, the door closing behind him with a quiet thud that seemed to reverberate like a thunderclap.

The pretty room, so filled with things, felt suddenly empty.

CHAPTER SEVENTEEN

The Not so Secret Secret

"AND YOU'RE QUITE CERTAIN this woman is Edmund Ritchie's wife?" demanded Eustace Lloyd of the rather disreputable character who sat across from him in the Ten Stars pub in Clerkenwell. Len was an acquaintance of an acquaintance of a friend, and Eustace had been put on to him because he was a known winkler-out of the kind of personal information that figures in public life almost invariably didn't want winkled out.

"That's correct, guv. She's his missus all right, and they don't make much of a secret of it."

"I see." Eustace took a sip of his ale and grimaced. It wasn't what he was used to, but one had to blend in when one met in places like this. "And how did you find out all this?"

"They's having some renovations done to the place, and I managed to get myself on the work crew for a day or two...then struck up a conversation with one of the maids. Like you do."

Renovations?

Eustace frowned. When he'd heard idle talk in a less salubrious gaming club than he normally frequented, he'd assumed that if Edmund Ellsworth Ritchie *did* have an insane wife, she'd be locked away in some horrible Bedlam, as many such creatures conveniently were. But an establishment that was well maintained didn't suggested that.

"What are the conditions? I take it the place is an asylum."

Len paused to take a long swallow of his own ale, then signaled to the barmaid for another. "Well, suh, if Willow Lodge is an asylum, I wouldn't mind being a loony myself. It's a cushy number, it is. Good grub, comfy rooms, and the staff on instant dismissal if they don't treat the inmates soft and sweet. It's more like a private rest cure for the nobs than a madhouse."

This wasn't what Eustace wanted to hear. What prospects for blackmail were there if Ritchie's wife were being well cared for in comfortable surroundings? Good God, the accursed man was more likely to garner sympathy than censure.

But perhaps not...

"And Mrs. Ritchie? What of her, what is her condition? Sometimes these wives are shut away simply due to some disagreement with their spouses, cruelly incarcerated when in fact they're quite sane. I suspect that's the case in this instance?"

Len accepted his new pint of beer, laughing and winking at the barmaid in the process. Eustace wished that the man would get on with it. He disliked this place intensely, with its smells of body odor and cheap gin, and tobacco smoke one could cut with a knife almost.

"Oh no, Mr. Lloyd, she's a bedlamite all right. Quite demented, so my friend Maisie says. Has to be restrained, does Ritchie's missus, although they gets nice padded straps, with sheepskin, I believe. She's quiet on the laudanum, as a rule, but they have to give her it by the bucketful to stop her ravings...and keep any knives and other sharp stuff well out of her reach." Len drank deep. "Oh, and lucifers too…she likes to set fires. Mostly after she's had a visit from her dear hubby. That seems to set her off."

Eustace leaned forward, even though Len didn't smell a lot better than his surroundings. "So it's Ritchie's cruelty that's driven her to this condition?"

"I wouldn't say that… Maisie says Miz Margarita speaks most fondly of the fellow when she's having her good days. It's just when she's having her bad turns she raves about all men and their lewd and filthy ways."

Curious, very curious. Clearly there wasn't much hush money to be had from Ritchie in respect of his wife's treatment.

But knowledge of an insane spouse who wanted to kill Ritchie for his "filthy ways" might just be the lever that would pry Beatrice away from the bastard, at least, and lure her back into his arms—and his studio—in gratitude.

Still, though, the reason for Margarita Ritchie's incarceration piqued him.

"So, he locked away his wife because she lost her wits," he prompted, taking a tiny sip of his unappetizing beer. "As simple as that?"

"Ooh, no, guv…not just that."

"Then what?"

"She got locked up because she murdered his kiddy from his first marriage, they say…did the little lad in by smothering him in his cot, poor mite." Len shuddered, then quaffed down more ale, as if calming his nerves. "Then she went after Ritchie with a letter knife and tried to burn his house down!"

CHAPTER EIGHTEEN

The Ladies' Sewing Circle

"SO, EDMUND ELLSWORTH RITCHIE, young lady? It seems he's taken a shine to you, you lucky thing. You must tell us everything."

Having hoped to avoid the subject of Ritchie at the meeting of the Ladies' Sewing Circle the following morning, Beatrice now realized that she'd been sorely deceiving herself if she'd thought she could get away with it. Ten sets of eyes were riveted in her direction, and ten sets of eager ears were clearly waiting for all the details. Not least of all, those of Lady Arabella Southern, who'd fired the first salvo of enquiry.

Beatrice flashed a quick glance at Sofia, who gave an infinitesimal shake of the head. There was no way her discreet friend would have disclosed even the merest hint that Beatrice had shared a tryst yesterday with Ritchie at her house in Hampstead, much less their scandalous financial transaction. But this was the first meeting since Arabella's ball, where several Circle ladies had been in attendance, and now curiosity was rampant.

"There's nothing to tell." She crumbled the cake on her little plate. They were at Prudence Enderby's house today, and the Enderbys' cook was only marginally more accomplished than Beatrice's own. Prudence always served a Madeira cake that was notorious across London, possibly as a source of building material, and mostly hacked into doorstep-thick slices. "I met him, and we engaged in some conversation. He seems very personable. I found him entertaining."

"Yes, and I blush like that when I've been *entertained* by Mr. Enderby," remarked Prudence, smirking gleefully. "Please don't say that that rogue Ritchie hasn't asked to call on you. The man's a carnal renegade and you're just the kind of lush young thing who'd tempt him."

"Especially if he's seen those photographs of you," cut in Lady Arabella, clearly keen to still lead the attack. "Knowing you're such a bold young woman, he's bound to be intrigued by you."

Not quite as bold as you, it seems.

Beatrice hid her smile, but the fact that she'd seen what she'd seen gave her a degree of confidence. The fact that friends of hers were no angels themselves assuaged at least some of her disquiet about being a bought woman. She glanced at Sofia, who seemed to be suppressing a smirk of her own. Not all the women here at the Sewing Circle were voluptuous adventuresses. Some simply liked to tell tall tales about their daydreams. But Beatrice could now count herself amongst the number who were more than simply talk.

"Mr. Ritchie is very charming and good-looking. I'd be a liar if I didn't say I found him attractive."

"Attractive, that's putting it mildly," continued Lady Southern. She was one of the few ladies who was actually making an attempt at sewing today, although it appeared she was darning a woolen sock for some reason known only to herself. "He's delectable. So manly and so…so threatening. He's notoriously daring and ruthless, and ooh, one just knows he's equally dangerous in bed." The peeress rolled her eyes, as if in anticipation, then gave a little shrug. "But alas, he's never once made a play for me, much to my sorrow. You should think yourself lucky, young woman. He's reputed to be one of the best lovers in London, so if you get a chance to verify that claim, please take it."

"Lady Southern, please!"

It was mock outrage, and from the grins around the room, it was obvious most of her companions realized that. For the second time, Beatrice had to suppress her smile at Lady Southern, and hold back a pert remark to the effect that *she* had obviously found compensations aplenty. Principally in the form of her limber, dark-haired swain at Sofia's pleasure house.

"Oh, do call me Arabella, my dear," the other woman remarked, cheerfully stabbing at her eccentric needlework. "We're all friends here, and all perfectly discreet."

Discreet? Maybe. Prepared to accept a whore, albeit an expensive one in their midst? That was debatable. Some things were best not expatiated upon.

"Thank you, Arabella," replied Beatrice, accepting another cup of tea from Prudence, who was still eyeing her avidly, as if anticipating further revelations. "I must admit that Mr. Ritchie has expressed a strong desire to call on me…and I… Well, I would like to see him again."

Ever one for understatement, Bea. You can't wait to be with him again, and you're simply dying for him to do the deed and fuck you!

"In what way would you describe him as ruthless?" she continued instead. That was the perfect word for him. She'd never known a man as single-minded when it came to getting what he wanted. But at least he was openly determined, not sly and underhanded like that low rat Eustace.

"Well, he's notorious for not letting anything, or any-

body, get in his way if he's set his mind on something…
or somebody." Arabella gave her an arch look.

"He does sound excessively determined by all accounts," remarked Miss Ruffington from her seat set a
little to one side of them. "It might be wise to let him
know exactly where you stand…and not allow any liberties you're not prepared to grant."

Startled, Beatrice looked at the other woman closely.
She'd sounded vaguely bitter, as if she had perhaps her
own experience of gentlemen taking liberties, one that
had not turned out quite as amenably as Beatrice's dealings with Ritchie thus far. Adela Ruffington was another
relative newcomer to the group, and though a bit of an
oddity, a pleasant one for all that. She was a little older
than Beatrice, and quite handsome, if unusual in appearance. Her nose must have been broken at some time, and
was now very slightly kinked at the bridge, but she had a
proud, gracious bearing, intense eyes and lustrous dark
brown hair so abundant it always seemed to be right on
the point of escaping its pins. The fact that slender Adela
too wore mourning, as Beatrice herself had lately done,
only added to the serene drama of her appearance.

And to further set her apart, Adela Ruffington didn't
sew either, but instead spent her time drawing pocket
studies of the other members of the Circle in her sketchbook. When Beatrice had glimpsed them, she'd been
stunned by their seemingly effortless artistry.

"You're quite right, Adela. I will be careful, please
don't worry." She turned back to Arabella Southern,
fixing the peeress with a purposeful look. "So I would
be obliged if you could perhaps illuminate me with some
insights into Mr. Ritchie's ruthlessness. I think it would
serve me well to know his nature a little better."

"Well, a lot of what I've heard is about boring business dealings, so I don't know the precise details." Arabella pursed her lips, clearly not a keen follower of the captains of commerce and industry. "Except that he has a reputation for oh so cleverly outsmarting a rival when in pursuit of a lucrative concern or a financial advantage of some sort. His timing is amazing. When Aloysius Potter, the newspaper tycoon, was after the famous Lazard Printing Works, he turned up to sign the papers and found that Ritchie had been there two hours before him, and secured title to the entire works for a mere fifty additional guineas and a judicious ladling of entrepreneurial bonhomie."

"Didn't he outbid Sir Bentinck Gieves for a Bronzino at Christie's recently?" interjected Lucy Dawson, blinking behind her spectacles. "The old fellow was dead set on getting the painting, but Ritchie just kept on bidding and bidding until he had to give up."

"Exactly…excessively determined…" Adela Ruffington looked up from her sketchbook, her hand stilling. "Although, in this case, I commend him. Gieves is a miserable old so-and-so… He'd hide a thing of beauty like the Bronzino away, where nobody can appreciate it. Whereas Ritchie immediately donated it to the National Gallery just to annoy him."

So, Ritchie could be both brigand and philanthropist in one stroke?

"Ah, tish pooh, paintings and printing works," mocked Prudence. "As the gossip columns will attest, it's in the pursuit of amour when he's at his most audacious." Eyes gleaming, she leaned forward, confidentially.

"Is that a fact?" Beatrice gave her an old-fashioned look. Now they were getting to the heart of the matter, it seemed, and a little demon of jealousy stirred. She shouldn't have cared a jot about Ritchie's other women, given the temporary nature of her own liaison with him. But somehow she did.

"Oops, sorry," apologized their hostess, although without any apparent hint of repentance. "But didn't he once snatch Mrs. Chevington right out from under the nose of a certain Very August Personage, who also had his eye on her, and had more or less 'decreed' that she would be his latest conquest?"

Wide eyes all turned, agog, toward Prudence. Not least of all Beatrice's. Was the other woman referring to perhaps the most exalted connoisseur of women in the land?

"You don't mean…?"

Prudence nodded solemnly. "Indeed I do."

"But…goodness, it's a wonder Ritchie wasn't banished from society altogether. Wasn't the, um, August Personage angry?" The demon danced again in Beatrice's bosom. To take such risks, Ritchie really must have desired Mrs. Chevington a great deal.

"Oh no," interjected Arabella, eagerly taking up the thread. "I was at that reception myself and I saw a little of it. Apparently HRH laughed heartily, slapped Ritchie on the back, and supposedly said, 'Well done, old fellow, take her, she's yours'!"

"Good Lord!"

"Good gracious!"

All around the Circle there was fluttering and gasping and other expressions of feminine excitement. What must it be like to be desired by a man who was prepared to risk royal displeasure to get what he wanted?

Does it thrill me? Or does it terrify me?

It was both emotions at once. Excitement and apprehension. And yet none of this talk seemed to touch on the real Ritchie—it was all sensationalist, his public reputation. She wanted to ask her friends what they knew about his past, and his deeper life, but something held her back. Silent she remained, mulling over her thoughts while the rest of the ladies continued to chatter. She was grateful when the topic—perhaps driven by a sympathetic female sensibility that enough was enough—turned from her and Ritchie to the latest daring dalliances, real or imagined, of Mary Brigstock, who seemed to be enjoying an uxorious renaissance in the mature years of her marriage.

Yes, Edmund Ellsworth Ritchie was a daring and remarkable man, Beatrice acknowledged, picturing the hard blue glitter of determination in his eyes. He was bold enough to steal a woman from the clutches of the Prince of Wales himself, and then presumably relinquish her again when the novelty value of his prize inevitably faded.

That will be me when our month is over. So I'd better prepare for it and view him as a delicious adventure, nothing more.

She wasn't a valuable printing works, a famous painting, or some other lucrative asset, so there would be no need to keep her any longer when he'd got his money's worth.

CHAPTER NINETEEN

The Pact

POLLY WAS BORED, and she didn't like it. Used to being in service her entire adult life, having this much leisure was unexpectedly tedious.

Not that she'd ever been overworked by the Waverlys. In the country at Westerlynne, she'd been part of a large household, and as Miss Bea's personal maid, her duties had been far from onerous. Her mistress was a kind young woman and one of those very rare souls who treated servants like equals. She went out of her way to be as little trouble as possible.

Even here at South Mulberry Street, with just herself and Enid to do housework, Polly still hadn't been sorely overtaxed, thanks to Miss Bea again. She's pitched in where she could, and done a fair share of the chores, something unknown in the best houses.

But now, everything had changed. The household had transformed. Thanks to Edmund Ellsworth Ritchie, there was money aplenty to pay bills, buy goods and employ staff. And his right-hand man, Jamie, was around to keep order and steward the establishment.

In the space of a single day, Polly had been returned to her duties as Miss Bea's lady's maid, and the housework was to be done by a trio of maids from an agency, with

Simon, a rather serious but amenable enough footman, on hand to open doors, hail cabs and deliver messages.

Today, while Miss Bea was out visiting her friends. Polly had been occupied sewing, for which she had a fine hand, and also unpacking, pressing and putting away her mistress's beautiful new purchases, all the items that had been sent around from various shops and stores. It had been a pleasure to handle the lovely gowns and shoes, and also a great deal of exquisite lingerie. The latter essential, Polly supposed, when one was the mistress of as rich and notoriously randy man as Mr. Ritchie.

Polly frowned.

Don't hurt her, you rogue, or I'll be after you and have your guts for garters!

This was the way things had to be, she accepted that, but Polly always hoped to go with Miss Bea to a good marriage to a kind, rich man who'd love her and take care of her. A home where there might also arise some well-found coachman, or perhaps a handsome tradesman with a bob or two that she could take up with herself.

She'd never once anticipated her mistress becoming a whore.

"Stop it, Poll, no sense in brooding." Muttering, she trudged up the back stairs to the small sewing room on the second floor, carrying an armful of Miss Bea's less exotic underwear and several of Mr. Charlie's mended shirts. "Make the best of the situation."

That brought a smile to her lips. There was plenty to make the best of, in fact even *more* now. Not only was she still enjoying the occasional frisk with Mr. Charlie when he was at home, there was now the mysterious Jamie to canoodle with, too.

Pity neither of them were around at the moment, she

could just fancy a little male company and a kiss or fondle or two.

Still smiling, she nudged open the door to Mr. Charlie's room with her hip and sidled inside. When she'd put away the sewing, she'd skip off up to her room for a little while and entertain herself with her latest wicked daydream, one that had been plaguing her since Mr. Ritchie's handsome associate had first appeared.

"Well blow me!"

The shirts and the underwear went tumbling to the carpet as Polly gaped at the scene that met her eyes. It seemed that Mr. Charlie wasn't at his club as the staff had been led to believe, and neither had Jamie Brownlow left for Mr. Ritchie's house.

The both of them were here. In bed together and apparently naked.

It would appear that her daydream had come true.

"Well, here's a how-de-do indeed," observed Jamie mildly, ruffling Charlie's hair as he sat up and faced Polly, who stood openmouthed in the doorway. "Do you mind shutting that door, Polly? I know you're a broad-minded girl, but some of the others might get a bit of shock if they looked in."

"Sorry, sir...I'll just pick these up and be on my way. Sorry to have disturbed you." She swooped down and grabbed for the clothing, somehow managing not to take her eyes off the two entwined men, and their hips only just covered by the sheet. Jamie grinned at her, his expression unperturbed, and even though Charlie's face was pink and wild-eyed, he didn't entirely look displeased to see her. In fact when he turned again to Jamie he seemed quite smug.

What have you been plotting, you horny rogues?

The shirts and underwear seemed to have minds of

their own, and no sooner had Polly retrieved one item than she dropped it reaching for another. "Sorry about this," she repeated, her own face turning twice as pink as Charlie's as the sheet rustled in the general area of his groin and Jamie's hand.

The two men held each other's gazes, and even though she was attempting to fold a pair of drawers at the time, Polly saw a flash of understanding pass between them.

"No need to rush away, Polly." Charlie's voice was gruff and excited as he glanced from Jamie, to her, and back to Jamie. "Er…if you don't have any pressing duties, perhaps you'd…you'd like to stay awhile?"

The final item of her bundle retrieved, Polly stood there, mangling the layers of cotton and linen and undoing every bit of pressing she'd worked so hard at.

Was Charlie asking what she *hoped* he might be asking?

It seemed from Jamie's broad smile that it was.

"Yes, Polly, why don't you join us?" He withdrew his hand from beneath the sheet, and what she suspected he might have been fondling, and held it out to her in a gesture of invitation. "You're a bold girl. You might enjoy our fun."

Polly hesitated, tempted. She'd never seriously believed she'd see these two together, no matter how much the idea had teased her imagination. What were the odds of two men who liked both fish and fowl in the same household?

"Come on, Polly," encouraged Charlie, shuffling and causing the sheet to slip and reveal a glimpse of his shiny, roused cock.

Polly took a step forward, eyes narrowed, brain ticking. This was an illegal act the men were engaged in. Would her complicity be actionable?

But on the other hand, they were offering their trust, taking a risk, a chance on her.

"If I get into bed with you, I want both your words, in writing, that I won't get into trouble for lewd behavior." She placed her hands on her hips and studied their faces, almost laughing at the identical looks of astonishment.

Charlie blinked. But Jamie gave a grin and nodded his head. "You're a shrewd girl, Polly. I don't blame you." For a moment, he looked thoughtful, then almost cross as if a memory perplexed him. "The word of a servant is most often ignored. I know that to my cost. You're wise to be cautious." He turned to Charlie and gave him a very firm look.

Charlie blushed, and at the same time seemed to realize his member was on show. Tweaking the covers, he looked flushed. "I do give you my word to you, Polly, as a gentleman. You know how fond of you I am. You've always been nice to me just when I needed it. Cheered me up when I've been feeling down in the mouth."

Polly held firm, not moving.

"There's a notebook in my coat, Polly," said Jamie with a grin, "and a pencil. Bring them across and we'll make our words. And then maybe we can have our jolly time together."

Polly retrieved the coat and fished in the pocket, inhaling a whiff of a very nice gentleman's toilet water in the process. Jamie was an odd cove. Neither master nor servant. But his clothing was well made and as gentlemanly as Charlie's. It was only that first day that he'd turned up dressed as a working man.

She handed him the little black back notebook she found, its pencil secured by an elastic strap, and his fingertip managed to stroke hers as he took the book from her.

Jamie wrote quickly, decisively, then passed the book to Charlie, who nodded. He still had a bit of nerves about him, but he managed a quick smile.

Polly watched the two of them and felt an odd twist in her heart, as if a bond had already been forged among the three of them. Both men attracted her, and when she tried to set a balance between them, they kept coming up even-stevens.

Jamie passed her the book, and she scanned the brief note written in it.

We, the undersigned, promise to share the pleasure of our bodies and treat each other fairly and honestly and with kindness, and never to speak of what passes between us to another living soul.

It was far from a legal document, but a lump formed in Polly's throat. Her hand shook. The paper's contents were of great moment, and its sincerity moved her.

"Polly? Are you unwell?" Charlie's voice was full of concern, as were Jamie's dark eyes.

"I'm capital, Mr. Charlie, thank you very much," she replied briskly, resisting the urge to rub her suddenly watery eyes. "Hand me the pencil, Mr. Brownlow."

"With pleasure. And it's Jamie, remember? No formalities in here, beautiful Polly. We're all happy libertines. All equals." He turned to Charlie with an old-fashioned look as he passed the pencil across.

Not quite equals. Polly smiled as she wrote her name neatly beneath the little declaration. Jamie was most definitely in charge of their merry little band, but she didn't mind that, and neither, it seemed, did Charlie.

When all their signatures had been appended, Jamie passed the little book around again.

Goodness. A pact. She'd never had one of those, even with Sam.

"Satisfied now, Polly?" Jamie smirked at her as he took the book and placed it on the chest of drawers at the side of the bed, alongside a small rectangular tin box with a design of roses and lilies painted tastefully upon it. Polly had a fair idea what that might contain, and a surge of excitement in her belly almost made her gasp.

How grand. To go all the way and still be safe.

"Yes, indeed M- " She grinned at him boldly, then flashed a wink at Charlie, beyond him. "Very satisfied, Jamie. Or at least, I soon hope to be."

"In that case, pretty as you look in your uniform, my poppet, why not strip off and join us in bed?" In a sudden sleek movement, Jamie lunged up onto his knees, and throwing back the sheet, he turned around and knelt at the bottom of the bed, patting an inviting space in the middle.

But it wasn't the rumpled bed linen that drew Polly's eyes. Both her two new conspirators of love were in a state of high arousal, and their fine organs seemed to point directly toward her. Charlie's member was relatively slender, but nice and long, while Jamie's didn't have quite the length, but was thick and sturdy to an eye-watering degree.

Spoiled for choice.

Making a show of smacking her lips, she reached for the pins that secured the lace-trimmed cap of her afternoon uniform. Tossing the pins onto the chest, she flung the cap in the general direction of the two men, and then giggled when it landed on Charlie's fine erection.

The two men laughed, and Jamie reached out and caressed Charlie with the cotton cap while Polly tackled her hair.

A look of surrender and pleasure made Charlie's face quite beautiful, and his body shook. He seemed more at ease than Polly had seen him in a long time. The fondness she felt for him welled up, and she felt happy, too. Prone to misfortune and bad judgment, Charles Weatherly still had a kind heart, and it was only anxiety, she suspected, that had sometimes made him thoughtless.

"Come on, Polly, don't keep us waiting!" he gasped, smiling at her despite Jamie's distracting ministrations.

Apron, shoes, dress, stockings; she shed them all in short order. It'd been in her mind to attempt a seductive little dance for her two swains, but she was too impatient. Maybe there'd be another chance sometime to show them a below-stairs Salome?

Glad she wasn't a lady, and strictly corseted, she flung off her chemise and drawers, too, sending the voluminous piles of white linen flying in all directions. Then, only then, and naked, did she hesitate.

She'd never shed all her clothes for Charlie. Their snatched liaisons had only really begun since the move to the smaller London house, after Westerlynne had been sold, and the moments they'd spent had always been swift and stolen.

What if, being fond of men, he found her curvaceous body repellent? What if he preferred sylphlike bed partners whose slighter hips suggested the masculine form?

But Charlie's eyes were wide, and hot, and filled with desire and eagerness.

"My God, Polly, you're a pretty girl. A real smasher." For a moment he looked wistful. "We should have got our clothes off before now, shouldn't we?"

"She is indeed a beauty," confirmed Jamie, his hand still on Charlie's cock. "And she's here now, and we're all naked…so let's get to it!" With his free hand he reached for Polly and tugged her toward them, and a place in the middle. As she moved forward, he released Charlie so she could slide in between them.

"Goodness me, I'm the meat in a sandwich, aren't I?" Polly glanced from one man to the other, still spoiled for choice. Charlie was slender and had hair of a reddish hue that echoed his sister's brilliant Titian curls, while Jamie was of stockier build with thick light brown hair that was straight and shiny. They made a delicious contrast and Polly couldn't decide which one she desired the most.

"Hard to choose, eh?" purred Jamie, coming up onto his knees, and drawing Polly up with him. Grabbing her lightly by the back of her head, he pulled her mouth to his for a kiss.

It was quick and hard and his tongue went straight in. And even as hers sought to fight back, he drew her fingers to his cock.

So it's to be you, Mr. Brownlow.

But he confounded her. After a few moments of hungry, domineering kisses, he drew back and urged her by the arm toward their companion. "Gentleman's prerogative," he said with a laugh.

Polly needed little encouragement. Just as Charlie had never seen her naked, she'd never seen his unclothed body. But now that he was on show to her, she liked what she saw.

His skin was paler than Jamie's but it had a creamy sheen to it, and boyish freckles in the most delightful places. For a gentleman of leisure, his musculature was surprising firm and well formed, and his cock was obviously as pleased to see her as it was to see Jamie. With a cheerful sigh, she threw herself into Charlie's arms, and shuddered inside when he pressed her back against the pillows. He might not be the dominant partner when paired with Jamie, but he was still a man who knew what he wanted.

Charlie's kiss was as enthusiastic as Jamie's and just as stirring. She tasted wine on his tongue, but it was merely a trace, not the marker of intoxication. Twirling her tongue around his, she sampled him like a butterfly seeking nectar.

His hands were keen too, roving over her body as if excited by the new freedom they had to explore her person. He squeezed her breasts in the vigorous way she liked, and the lovely pressure shot to the place between her legs like a message transmitted by electrical telegraphy. Responding exactly as whim took her, she rubbed her belly against his thigh, then opened her legs to press her crotch hard against him.

Hugging each other hard, they rocked and swung against each other, tingling excitement building. Polly squeaked into Charlie's mouth when other hands joined the dance, touching both their bodies. Her eyes snapped open and she saw Jamie looming over Charlie from above, kissing and nipping at his lover's pale shoulder while slipping a hand beneath Polly to squeeze and play with her bottom. Charlie's eyes were wide and he was groaning into her mouth, so she guessed that Jamie's cock was rubbing against his groove.

Polly hugged them both, sliding her hands over all the male flesh she could reach, while she massaged her puss against Charlie's hard-muscled thigh. When she reached down and grasped his cock it was a rod of iron.

Even as she touched him, other fingers explored her sex, curling around with clever deftness from the rear and making her wriggle and squirm harder, craving stimulation from whatever quarter it was presented.

"Come along, my dear pair. I'd love to see you fuck each other."

Jamie's voice was low and husky, ringing with desire. He manhandled Polly and Charlie apart with a magisterial hand.

"But first, we'd better wrap up the old man, hadn't we? We don't want lovely Polly to end up getting more from us in nine months time than she bargained for." He reached for the patterned tin on the bedside chest.

Polly's suspicions were confirmed. French letters. How grand. Now she could enjoy her bedmates to the full, and her sex surged with excitement as she watched Jamie deftly roll the prophylactic down the length of Charlie's cock.

You've done that plenty of times before, haven't you, my lad. And probably more than once with Mr. Charlie, I suspect.

Charlie's face was a picture as Jamie handled him. His eyelids fluttered and his mouth went soft and dreamy. Polly wondered why she wasn't envious of his so obvious pleasure at another lover's touch. But she couldn't seem to summon the green-eyed monster. She felt only pleasure and happy anticipation.

When Charlie was encased, Jamie sat back to admire his handiwork. Charlie's cock seemed to sway and throb as if proud to be on show in its fancy rubber coat. Jamie touched it lightly and made the sway more pronounced.

"Very fine, isn't he, Polly?" He smiled across at her, two fingers lightly supporting the other man's organ as if displaying it as a treasure for her approval.

"Absolutely smashing, but I'd rather like it inside me now, gentlemen, if I may?" Sliding down on the bed, she opened her legs, then, in a moment of naughty merriment, she slid her two hands between her thighs and parted the lips of her sex.

"You're a saucy madam, Polly Jenkins," announced Charlie, his eyes wide open now and his face alight with hunger. Polly wondered whether she'd misconstrued the exact nature of the men's relationship, because Charlie surged forward, full of confidence, reaching to touch the jewel she offered him. "One of these days, you shall have a spanking for your forwardness, young miss."

Polly hid her grin. He was barely a year or so older than her, but there was confidence in his touch. It set her writhing and wriggling again, especially when Jamie moved alongside on her other flank, and took a nipple of hers in each of his fingers and thumbs.

"Oh my Lord…oh yes…ooh! Oh, oh!"

The pleasure was intense, all-consuming. She had two men playing with her. Tugging. Tweaking. Rubbing. Above and below. Squirming, she grabbed for both of them, the rubber-clad cock and the bareback one.

"Now, now…behave yourself." But Jamie wasn't really at all stern as he abandoned her nipples, grabbed both of her hands and then held them above her head. Against the head of the bed, he snagged both of her wrists in one of his big, capable hands. "Right, go at her, Mr. Weatherly, if you will?"

"Indeed. Right ho!" cried Charlie, utterly joyful to be ordered to his task. Maneuvering himself with a grace she'd never really appreciated in him before, he hopped between her thighs and fitted his cock against her sex.

Then, as he started to push, he turned his face to Jamie, and the other man kissed his lips in a deep kiss that made Polly shiver and tremble. She moaned, her eyes glued to the sight of the men's dueling mouths as Charlie's cock surged in deep and plumbed her cunny. The visible thrust

of Jamie's tongue in Charlie's mouth echoed the thrust of
the man inside her, and somehow seemed to lend it extra
vigor. She churned her bottom against the sheets, boil-
ing with desire, and when Jamie released her hands, she
threw her arms around both of them, embracing as much
of each man as she could reach.

"Kiss *me* now," she growled after a moment or two,
but to which of her two lovers, she didn't really know.

Jamie obliged, while Charlie buried his face in the
hollow where her neck met her shoulder and rocked his
hips, fucking her deeply. His breath was hoarse against
her skin, and Jamie was gasping too as he kissed her.
Someone's clever hand crooked at an angle and slid in
between her belly and Charlie's as they slapped together,
then plunged into her sex, seeking and finding her aching
clitoris. Every time Charlie plunged in, he knocked the
fingertips against her.

Lost in each other, they slipped and slid and rocked
and bounced and ground together, the experience so intense and rambunctious that she lost account of who was
doing what to whom and with what. After a little while,
Charlie cried out wildly and mouthed profanities against
her neck, his hips beginning to hammer like the very pis-
tons of a steam engine.

But even as Polly knew her gentleman was spending,
the wicked finger on her clitty circled devilishly and she
tumbled over the edge into supreme pleasure right alongside him. She sobbed and cried, kissing Jamie's face as
her body clenched and her sex rippled in long, delicious
waves.

She was still in ecstasy as Charlie collapsed over her,
the wind knocked completely out of him.

"Come along, Mr. Weatherly, that's no way to treat a
lady," said Jamie with a soft laugh, and before Polly knew

what was happening he'd hauled Charlie right off her and plopped him down on the bed at her side.

In barely a heartbeat he'd taken his companion's place, drawing Polly's hand down to his cock as it paused for entrance, to assure her that it too wore a jacket.

"Lovely girl," he whispered, and with a strangely sweet sigh, he began to slide in and out of her in smooth, heavy strokes.

Pleasure surged again, welling up from the very depths of Polly's vitals in a way that felt new and fresh and rampant.

How can I take on two men like this? How can it seem right and sweet and natural, all the three of us together?

Yet it was right, and as Charlie roused again, and rolled onto his side, he embraced and stroked them both, he and she. Feeling his touch sliding over thigh and flank, male and female, Polly turned to him, her body jerking against Jamie's. On his face, she saw a look of befuddled happiness, as if he too wasn't sure how this had come to pass, but was joyful and grateful all the same.

And as she spent again, Polly hugged both her men to her, chanting their names, Charlie and Jamie, one after the other.

CHAPTER TWENTY

"Madame de la Tour"

NEVER HAD THE AFTERNOON hours passed more slowly. Home from the Sewing Circle, Beatrice couldn't settle any of her usual pastimes whilst waiting for her next amour with Ritchie. As she leafed through the *Illustrated London News,* the words and pictures were a blur to her, and even a rather unsettling novel, a work by Mr. Wilde in the latest *Lippincott's* that had initially provoked her interest, couldn't hold her. Abandoning *The Picture of Dorian Gray,* she thumped away at the piano for a while instead, but even attempting her favorite, "The Lost Chord," resulted in far too many chords that were indeed far better off lost. And as for her "Wand'ring Minstrel," it would have done music lovers a service by wandering as far away as possible.

Hour after hour, she struggled for composure, to no avail. Her body was sensitized and susceptible, a powder keg waiting for the spark struck by a certain challenging smile or a pair of dangerous blue eyes. She hardly dared think of him lest she ignite.

And everyone else in the household was acting oddly, too. Since the morning of Ritchie's visit, there had been a strange, latent atmosphere at South Mulberry Street.

Cap more awry than usual, Polly smiled dreamily she helped Beatrice to undress. Awry herself, Beatrice eyed the maid, recognizing a mirror to her own state. Was it anything to do with the handsome Mr. Brownlow? Beatrice suspected as much, grateful that Polly's abstraction made her less openly inquisitive about her mistress's doings.

But from where did Charlie's sudden good humor derive? For the first time in months he seemed at ease with himself, and had apparently forgotten his qualms about her and Ritchie. He'd made jokes and droll conversation over a breakfast far more substantial then he could usually manage due to post-alcoholic "delicacy," and in an unstudied moment, unaware of Beatrice's scrutiny, his smile had been almost beatific.

What on earth has happened to everybody?

Something had most definitely occurred, and at any other time Beatrice would have passed the hours mulling over it and devising clever questions from which she could deduce the answer.

But these were not other times. These were the times of Edmund Ellsworth Ritchie and the greater part of Beatrice's mulling was over him alone.

At seven, the carriage arrived as he'd specified. On the front steps, as Beatrice attempted not to shake and dither, her heart thudded in anticipation of him being in the conveyance waiting for her.

But the interior was empty.

Her spirits dipped, then rallied.

Only a little longer, Bea. You'll soon see him.

The quiet, efficient coachman had specified their destination as Belanger's, a discreet and much muttered-about dining establishment in the heart of St. James. It was the haunt of the rich and the famous, and oft alluded to in *Marriott's Monde* with hints of scandal and outrageous activities.

But will I be able to eat?

The prospect of Dover sole or guinea fowl à la russe didn't excite Beatrice one bit; her hunger was for Ritchie and his touch…and his skills.

The well-maintained carriage was smoother ride than most, but still it trundled on the uneven surfaces of the streets and swerved hither and thither amongst the sheer press of cabs, carts and other coaches out even at night. Rocked in her seat, Beatrice barely noticed the throng of London's humanity outside the comfortable interior. The sounds of street vendors and newsboys came to her as if from a distance, beyond the border of her secret, sensual realm. It was a country inhabited only by Ritchie, and herself, and the movement of the carriage seemed to mimic his caress, as did her clothing, sliding over her body with every sway.

Beatrice had never worn silk underwear before.

Back home at Westerlynne, serviceable cotton and muslin had always sufficed, and since her arrival in London there hadn't been money to spend on extravagance. Finally out of mourning for her parents, Beatrice had relied on Polly's skills with the needle to make over some older outfits, and all her meager clothing allowance had gone on one or two reasonably presentable new gowns, deemed essential purchases if she were to stand any chance of snaring a husband.

A husband!

Glad she was alone, Beatrice snorted in derision. How ironic that now she had plenty of money for spouse-luring finery, she no longer had a reputation suitable for matrimony.

But that didn't reduce her pleasure in the clothing for which Ritchie had paid. The delicate fabric that whispered over her skin like a zephyr, and the carefully fitted che-

mise, and lace-and-ribbon-trimmed drawers sat beneath
a featherweight and equally fancy corset designed by Sofia's modiste. It was the most comfortable corset Beatrice
had ever owned, and it barely felt as if she were wearing
one at all.

Her petticoats were silk too, and they swished and
slithered as she walked, or even just shifted on the carriage seat, recalling the magical drift of Ritchie's fingertips.

*All for you, my dear sponsor and protector. All for you,
having purchased my virginity, too.*

Perhaps she'd lose that particular asset today? She sincerely hoped so. What was the point of being a scandalous mistress if you didn't get a good seeing-to for your
efforts?

At last, the carriage pulled up outside Belanger's, and
Beatrice snapped out of her reverie. On stepping down, a
doorman escorted her across the pavement like a visiting
empress, and when she turned to thank the coachman, he
was already atop his vehicle and pulling away.

Was the threshold to Belanger's quiet, luxurious foyer
another Rubicon? Her heart thudded as she advanced,
head held high. Nerves would settle, she knew, as they
always did. But they'd twang in an entirely different way
when she set eyes on Ritchie. The prospect of seeing him
again made the hushed atmosphere and the eyes of a smat-
tering of fashionably dressed people—men, women and
couples—in the restaurant's reception lounge far less
daunting.

A rather stout maître d'hôtel sprang forward to greet
her. "Ah, good evening, Madame de la Tour, may I welcome you to Belanger's. How gracious of you to patron-
ize our establishment." He bowed his head, then indicated
the way ahead with an expansive, theatrical gesture.

Madame de la Tour?

Beatrice blinked. Surely he'd mistaken her for someone else? But seeing her hesitation, the maître d' gave her a kind, twinkly look, his face both friendly and somewhat conspiratorial.

Ah, that was it. At Belanger's people often didn't use their real names and "Madame de la Tour" was a *nom de voyage* that Ritchie had fancifully bestowed on her.

Well, it would've been nice of you to inform me, you infuriating wretch! If I'm to have a high courtesan's name, I really ought to know it in advance.

Smiling at the maître d', she silently maligned Ritchie in an unladylike fashion as she followed her new friend into another sumptuous room.

It wasn't like any restaurant Beatrice had ever visited. Not that she'd visited all that many. The large area was discreetly lit, the lamps imparting a gentle glow on the handkerchief of open space in the center of the room. For dancing, Beatrice wondered? Or some other entertainment? A musical quintet played softly on a small dais adjacent to the window. Selections from *The Mikado,* if she wasn't mistaken. She smiled, wondering if Ritchie had influenced the program.

The dining tables themselves were not to be seen at first, but then Beatrice realized that they were all set in deep alcoves around the perimeter of the room. Each of these niches was hung with ruby-colored velvet curtains, and while some were caught back with gilded cords allowing the diners to view the room and enjoy the music, other alcoves were enclosed in a cocoon of tantalizing privacy.

As she followed the maître d' around the edge of the pocket-size dance floor, Beatrice couldn't help speculating on what might be going on within the closed alcoves.

Assignations like hers and Ritchie's? Risqué activities in a semipublic place? Men aroused. Women, with bodices unbuttoned, panting as their paramours toyed with them. Skirts raised, and even sly fingers exploring the apertures in silk drawers just like hers.

Suddenly the light corset didn't seem quite so light and an unbecoming sweat broke out beneath it. Heat filled Beatrice's face, and between her legs a familiar heaviness gathered. In the space of a few heartbeats, *she* was the woman with the raised skirt, and Ritchie the man with the deft, exploring fingers.

"Here we are, Madame de la Tour."

The maître d' stepped back and allowed her to precede him as they reached what appeared to be the most spacious yet secluded of all the alcoves.

Trust Ritchie to secure the premier table, nothing but the best for him.

Am I the best, too?

Her qualms evaporated when Ritchie rose from his seat to greet her. His smile quelled all doubts and left only delicious anticipation. Every time anew he looked more handsome. Every time anew, he turned her head, made her heart race and her body quicken.

"Beatrice, you look wonderful!" Ritchie took both her hands, making her little bag swing wildly as he raised first one then the other to his lips, kissing them hard through the kid leather of her gloves.

"I must say that's a very fine ensemble." As he straightened, his blue gaze traveled from her toes of her new glacé kid boots to the very crown of her jaunty leghorn hat. "Have you arrived directly from the typewriting school? You're looking fetchingly businesslike."

"Thank you. One aims to impress." Beatrice kept her tone light, but inside his compliment made her bubble.

She'd put a great deal of thought into choosing her clothing.

Courtesans were supposed to wear sumptuous gowns, elaborate jewels, the best and most feminine of everything, but even though she was strangely glad to be a demimondaine, Beatrice didn't want to look like the rest of her new sisterhood. To look as if her sole purpose in life was to please a man.

So Beatrice had selected garments she would still be able to wear when her month with Ritchie was over and done with. Her neatly tailored midnight-blue costume had almost masculine revers and an immaculate white underbodice cut like a man's shirt, and she'd even borrowed one of Charlie's neckties and a pin. Sofia's modiste had tut-tutted at her, *zut alors,* when she'd chosen the very serious ensemble, but Sofia had smiled and nodded, her face approving and knowing.

"With you dressed like that, Beatrice, I shall feel as if I'm corrupting the very sternest suffragette." Ritchie beamed, still holding her hands, then leaned in. "And that's a prospect I find *disturbingly* arousing."

"You said you approved of women's rights," Beatrice reminded him as he ushered her into the alcove almost before she could feast her eyes on his ensemble.

"I do. Especially yours."

Almost as if he'd anticipated her choices, Ritchie too had eschewed full evening dress. The stern cut of his attire seemed to complement her own and his dark gray frock coat, with just the merest hint of blue, made his eyes glow the color of a twilight sky. His waistcoat was the same shade, as was his neckwear, and today's pin was a subtle golden bead.

I don't think I want any dinner. I just want you, Mr. Ritchie. You're so handsome I simply want to devour you!

The thought made Beatrice's heart thud, and she felt intoxicated before wine had even been brought.

Ritchie assisted her as she slid along the plush banquette behind the exquisitely set table, then took his place beside her as she tugged off her gloves, struggling with what suddenly seemed like a surfeit of thumbs. The intimacy of sitting side by side, thighs almost touching, made Beatrice want to fidget with suppressed energy beneath the voluminous fine lawn tablecloth and wonder what activities might be concealed beneath its acreage.

If Ritchie felt the same agitation, his powers of self-control were far superior. He calmly ordered champagne, choosing a remarkable vintage, then consulted with Beatrice over the sumptuous menu, comparing dishes he liked with her preferences. He asked her opinion of the Gilbert and Sullivan, so finely played.

He even pointed out several exalted personages in the open alcoves. Personages who were dining with personages of the opposite gender with whom they really shouldn't have been dining. He smiled and winked at her, nodding at alcoves where the curtains were tightly closed.

But he didn't touch her. At least not with his hands or his strong thigh next to hers.

It was his only eyes that were attentive. He met her gaze courteously, but every now and again, his regard would drift over her, lingering at the line of her throat above her crisp white collar, or the curve of her breasts beneath the blue barathea of her jacket.

Studying her hair for a moment, his mouth curved in an unmistakable arc.

Blatant lust.

"What is it?" There was no use dissembling. "What are you thinking, Ritchie?" Anticipation bubbled in her like the delicious Veuve Clicquot they were drinking. With Ritchie, Champagne held no negative connotations.

"Your hair, Beatrice. I want to see it set loose and streaming over your shoulders. And then sweeping like a curtain of gilded crimson as you bend to suck my cock."

Beatrice quelled a sputter. Bubbles threatened to go up her nose, but she managed to control herself. She'd seen Arabella Southern perform that particular act on her handsome paramour, Yuri, and Sofia on her darling Ambrose. And she'd read a hair-raisingly naughty set of instructions on how to do it, too, in one of the many explicit books and journals she'd perused at Sofia's pleasure house.

"Well, I'm certainly looking forward to making the acquaintance of that particular portion of your anatomy, Mr. Ritchie. So far I've been denied a formal introduction."

Ritchie chuckled and reached for her hand. She thought he was going to conduct it to the very organ they were discussing, but instead he ran his thumb slowly and seductively over her knuckles, the action making her own intimate regions tingle in response.

"You're a very forward young woman, Madame de la Tour. So audacious I ought to pick you up, throw you over my shoulder, then cart you out of here and give you a spanking."

Beatrice had seen *that* in Sofia's saucy magazines, too. Ritchie beamed at her. Reading her mind again?

"Why take me to task? You're the one who started this with your talk of my hair and your thighs…and…um… sucking." His fingers explored her hand and somehow the very tip of one managed to sneak beneath the edge of her sleeve and find the very spot where a doctor would read her pulse. Her voice began to shake as it circled and massaged.

"Look here, Ritchie, it's too late for me to play the delicate, incorruptible miss with you. We both know I've revealed my true nature. So why not reveal the full extent of yours?"

Ritchie's face hardened, his eyes suddenly stricken. But the flash of dark emotion was over again as soon as it had registered, leaving Beatrice wondering if she'd imagined it.

"So what do you want, Bea?"

With her free hand, she reached for her champagne glass and took a fortifying drink of the glorious pale golden liquid.

"Everything," she said simply, then added in the lowest voice possible, "and especially, I want you to fuck me."

The forbidden word brought a flush to her cheeks, for all her resolve to be a bold, unprissy miss. Ritchie's eyes twinkled like stars, expunging all memory of their momentary darkness.

"Well then…would you like to forgo dinner? I have a private room reserved for us upstairs."

Beatrice's heart thudded. Messages sped along her nerves, conducting instructions to her thighs and the muscles in her haunches, telling them to slide along the banquette and stand so that Ritchie could lead her away to that private room upstairs. But the butterflies of anticipation needed a little something to fight with first.

"No, thank you, Ritchie, not just yet." If he was disappointed, he hid it well behind his smiling mask. "I think I'll eat a bite of dinner first. I've a feeling I might need my strength shortly."

Ritchie shook his head and winked at her, then signaled for the waiter.

But contrary to her claims, when the food came, Beatrice couldn't do much justice to the meltingly tender *filet de boeuf roti,* the buttered asparagus tips and the *pommes de terre madagasque,* even though they were all glorious. She couldn't drink much either, after the first glass of champagne. Ritchie nodded, as if approving her abstemiousness, and requested that the waiter bring her *eau Evian* instead.

Sipping the bottled water, Beatrice relished its head-clearing chill. What need was there for alcohol with Ritchie around? He was overproof himself, surging in her veins, every movement and gesture an intoxicant.

His hands fascinated her, fast becoming an obsession. She'd never seen such objects of grace, so long-fingered and strong. He used his cutlery with elegant precision, even though it was obvious he enjoyed his food. A foolish notion came to Beatrice as he laid down his knife and fork to take a drink of the water he too had chosen. Would he consent, when their month was over, to having his hands molded and a plaster model made so she could keep it and treasure it?

Don't be absurd, Bea! How on earth would a busy man like Ritchie ever have time to stay still long enough for the plaster cast to set?

"What are you thinking about, Bea?"

Luckily she wasn't holding her own glass or knife, because his voice made her jump on the banquette. "Your hands," she blurted out, off guard. "I...I like your hands. They're very elegant and strong. I find them quite beautiful."

His odd, sideways look put her in mind of a bashful boy receiving his first compliment from a girl for whom he harbored a tendre.

"Thank you, Bea." Ignoring his meal now, he lifted his

hands as if examining a pair of rare artifacts as yet undiscovered. "No one's ever praised them before…except sometimes to applaud what they can do."

His blue eyes were intense as he looked at her, not wavering one iota.

His women, they were the ones who'd praised his manual dexterity. Beatrice was no poetess, but even she could have composed a sonnet to those magical eight fingers and two thumbs.

A slow but now familiar smile spread across his handsome features, and he turned sideways on the banquette, to face her.

Reaching out, he took her hand, her right one, closest to him.

"I like your hands, too, Bea. They're delicate and slim—" his fingers slipped to and fro over her knuckles again "—yet clever and deft, capable of the finest work." He lifted her hand to his lips and kissed it quite hard. Beatrice groaned inside, wishing all their surroundings would suddenly dissolve and they'd find themselves alone. "I'll wager you're a wonderful seamstress."

Beatrice laughed out loud. "Oh no! You're completely wrong there. I'm the world's worst at needlework. I'm the dunce of the Ladies' Sewing Circle."

Slowly, but with purpose, Ritchie turned her hand over, examining the tips of her fingers as if looking for wounds wrought by her wayward embroidery needle. "Ah well, maybe you have other skills to compensate?"

"I'm not sure…" Her voice shook a little, but she covered it with a smile, her heart bounding. "But I'm always eager to master new accomplishments."

"Good girl…good girl…" Ritchie's voice seemed to vibrate with laughter, and his breath was like a warm wind from the Indies as he kissed her hand again, the palm this time, his lips barely touching her skin. The light contact stirred every inch of her body, bringing a blush to her face and a glow of pleasure to every hidden zone.

"Would you care for dessert?" he enquired as he put her hand from his lips and settled it on her thigh, barely inches from his own. "The ice cream at Belanger's is amongst the finest in London. It's brought in from an establishment in Little Italy, completely unadulterated, a masterpiece of cream and vanilla." He seemed much closer on the banquette now, and heat of his body permeated though his clothing and hers, all the layers of silk and barathea and fine worsted wool rendered insubstantial.

The luxurious dessert sounded wonderful. Another time she might have succumbed to it with childlike pleasure, but right now she wasn't sure she could handle a spoon.

"Thank you, but I've had sufficient to eat. It was all delicious." She slid out her little finger and touched his thigh with the tip of it. "But you have some. Don't let me stop you."

"I'm not hungry anymore either. At least not for ice cream." His eyes flicked down, in the direction of the tiny contact, then with a conspiratorial wink, he flicked the tablecloth over their thighs, and her hand. "But I have a fancy for a brandy. How about you, Bea? Will you take a brandy with me?"

She'd poured herself brandy the first time they'd met, the first time he'd touched her. The fiery spirit was their personal sacrament, and she yearned for what it symbolized.

Sensuality. Contact. The pleasure of touch both received and given.

But this time, Beatrice wanted to be the one touching, and the prospect of it made her blood surge and an intoxicant far more powerful than fine cognac rush through her veins. She spread out all her fingers across the surface of his trousers, then squeezed the iron-hard muscle beneath.

Ritchie's sinfully long eyelashes flickered for a moment, so shockingly dark in contrast to his fair hair. But he remained as calm as a saint when the waiter arrived with barely a summons, and brandy was ordered and plates taken away.

"Pour me a little more water while we wait, if you would?" Her voice was steady, and so were her eyes, on him.

"Of course," he said, and when he reached for the carafe, she slid her hand sideways and covered his groin.

He still didn't turn a hair, but Beatrice swore she heard the faintest of sighs. His actions were perfectly steady though as he refilled her glass and reached to set it by her left hand.

"So, Madame de la Tour, are you fond of exploration?"

To an outside observer, it would have been the most casual of enquiries, meaningless social chitchat, but Ritchie's suave tongue-in-cheek tone made Beatrice smirk. She rewarded him with a very gentle squeeze.

"Indeed I am, Mr. Ritchie, indeed I am." For a moment, she pursed her lips to stop herself laughing at the way his eyes popped wide. "I love to voyage in the darkest, murkiest undergrowths, discovering new wonders with which to entertain myself." Massaging him lightly once or twice, she turned her attention then to his fly buttons. Quite a task when she was working blind and at a somewhat awkward angle.

Ritchie pursed his lips as her knuckles knocked against his erection. "That's admirable, madame. There's nothing I respect more than an adventurous woman, and I go out of my way to assist in such endeavors."

"Really? How very philanthropic of you."

Beneath the cloth, Ritchie's hands joined hers, first one, then the other, nudging her aside as he negotiated the fastenings of his trousers and his linen.

Good Lord, I can't believe we're doing this!

Ritchie's hand took hers, drew it near him again, setting her on the most daring path of exploration she could have ever imagined. It took barely more than a heartbeat to part cloth and draw out the princely prize she sought.

Oh, he was so hot. And hard. And sturdy. Her fingers curved around him just as if they'd known his contours for a lifetime, and loved them as long. It felt perfectly appropriate to be holding him.

"Oh, Bea," murmured Ritchie, slumping against the plush upholstery of the banquette, his eyelids fluttering closed in an expression of sublime wonder. She could almost imagine it was the first time he'd been touched by a woman thus, even though that was arrant nonsense. Dozens of lucky females must have handled his trusty treasure. Women far more experienced than she.

It really was a voyage of discovery.

Fingers still lightly wrapped around him, Beatrice gnawed her lip. Did men like gentle treatment, or firm? His shape and the lovely silky feel of his skin down there invited an eager examination, but she was aware that too vigorous a handling could be disastrous. At worst, she could hurt him, and at best, precipitate a crisis far sooner than either of them wanted.

"Something wrong, Bea?" Ritchie's eyes flicked open and his expression was both smoky and sensual, and at the same time razor sharp. "Your discovery not to your liking?"

Was he mocking her? Teasing her inexperience? Back at Sofia's house, he'd seemed to delight in it. Meeting his eyes, she gave his penis a light but determined squeeze, and got the satisfaction of a gasp of indrawn breath.

"On the contrary, I find it most pleasing and not at all a disappointment."

Ritchie laughed, then gasped again as her fingers delicately tightened.

"A disappointment?"

"Well, I've been led to believe that gentlemen tend to overestimate the qualities of certain…appendages. They lead ladies to expect Corinthian monuments when in reality the item is far less mighty."

Ritchie seemed to absorb this, then his hips bucked ever so lightly, and the monument slid to and fro between Beatrice's fingers.

"And were you hoping for such a monument, Madame de la Tour?"

Remembering the *godemiche,* Beatrice slid her fingertip into the same groove that she now discovered in living flesh. "Hoping, yes," she murmured as Ritchie gasped again. "Expecting, too, in view of certain preliminary explorations." Her grip was awkward, and hampered by the tablecloth, but she settled her thumb in opposition to her fingertips and rolled his flesh lightly between them. It seemed instinctively the desired approach. "And as I say, I'm not in the slightest disappointed." A little more pressure, but not too much. "In fact, I'd go as far as to say, I'm considerably impressed."

"So am I, Beatrice…so am I." Ritchie laughed, cocking his head back again, his plush lower lip snagged in his teeth.

So this is what makes the grand demimondaines so all-conquering. This power over men, the ability to bestow or deny pleasure and sensation.

It seemed such a primitive accomplishment, yet it was

significant. It could drive the world. Here she was with a man who'd bought her, who'd handed over money for her body, her acquiescence. He could make or ruin her and her brother, just for the whims of desire. And yet right now, she had him in the palm of her hand, in the most literal of senses.

Such dominion was an aphrodisiac elixir, as was his sublime male beauty. Deep within her belly, and between her thighs, Beatrice's own flesh shivered, and what had been a gathering heaviness became a grinding ache of need.

Yes, tonight, she *must* have him. She could wait no longer. She had to learn and become whole, possess him as much as he would possess her.

Swirling her fingertips around him, Beatrice met Ritchie's hot look with one of her own.

"I've changed my mind. I don't want any brandy," she said, holding him firmly. "At least not here. I'll take it in that reserved room, upstairs, if I may."

Ritchie stared at her, his eyes luminous as if he beheld the light of the world.

"You're a wonder, Bea," he said, his voice almost vibrating. "A perfect wonder." He paused, drew in a great shuddering breath, almost as if she'd knocked it clean out of him. "But I'll need a moment…the state I'm in…to rearrange myself."

"Perhaps I can assist you with that?"

"Oh, I'm sure you can…I'm sure you can."

And with that he reached over and kissed her, full on the mouth, while she still held him.

CHAPTER TWENTY-ONE

Moments of Truth and Beauty

IT WAS A LOVELY ROOM. A beautiful, extravagant room, sumptuous with velvets, gold leaf and fine furniture. But as she wandered around it, clad in just her chemise, her drawers and her corset, it wasn't exactly the setting in which Beatrice had imagined she might lose her virginity.

Even allowing for her liaison with Ritchie, she'd anticipated the deed being done in either her own bedroom or his. But clearly that wasn't to be the case, and Beatrice stared around the handsome chamber while the man himself took his turn in the remarkably modern bathroom she'd just explored.

"Ladies first," he'd said, patting her on the rump, and she'd spun around, astonished. Not at the barely felt tap, but the sound of his voice. For a well-known Lothario he sounded unexpectedly tentative.

Perhaps what he'd said was true? Perhaps his mistresses really did number relatively few and his reputation was exaggerated? A cold shudder gripped her. Maybe he didn't normally consort with untried virgins, and he wasn't looking forward to her first bedding with much enthusiasm?

Oh no, not so. His seductive smiles were hot, and full of hunger. He did want her, she was sure of it, and the state of his flesh, down in the restaurant and at other times, couldn't lie.

But was he still concerned that he might hurt her?

But what if you do, Ritchie? I don't care! If there's pain it'll be over in a moment...and then...and then...

And then what? Judging by what she'd felt and fondled beneath the tablecloth, he was bigger than the faux phallus. He'd be over her, inside her, imposing himself upon her. They'd be together, as one, the closest two human beings could ever be together apart from a child in its mother's womb.

Oh Ritchie, do hurry up! Don't keep me waiting.

As if summoned like some mythical djinni out of the *Arabian Nights,* Ritchie appeared in the suddenly open doorway to the bathroom. He'd shed his frock coat and his neckwear already, but now his waistcoat and his shirt were unfastened, too. Strolling toward her, he flung off the waistcoat, aiming it blindly, but with surprising accuracy at a mahogany chair as he flipped his braces off his shoulders, to leave them dangling.

"Beatrice...you're such a lovely woman," he said in a low intense voice, sitting down beside her. His smile was intense too, and infinitely complicated. It flickered around his mouth like a poem of emotion, and blazed in his eyes, both light and dark. He touched her face with the tips of his fingers, setting points of heat against her skin for just a second. Then he bent down and unlaced his boots and kicked them away before pulling off his socks. As he tossed those away, Beatrice suddenly wished that he'd let her sink to her knees before him, as his handmaiden, and uncover his feet. Her fingers tingled as she imagined massaging his strong, narrow toes.

Good grief, what an absurd idea, Bea! You're a temporary concubine not some kind of slave.

Thinking on the matter, she'd never really seen herself in the conventional woman's role of support and helpmeet to a man. She wasn't that domestic paragon, it didn't sit right with her nature. Yet for just a moment, she'd understood the role's allure.

But it was only a moment, and to assert herself, she launched forward and sought his mouth with hers, reaching up to wind her hands around the back of his neck and dig her fingers into his thick, fair curls. He smelled of soap and shaving lotion and fastidious man, but she longed for the real male, the savage beneath, red-hot and wild.

Kissing him hard, she felt his smile, and was suddenly cross.

Take me seriously. I'm not a toy or a girl. I'm a woman. She kissed harder, pressing her body against him, compelling him to acknowledge the contours of her breasts where they pressed up, shaped by her corset. Almost wishing now that she'd shed every stitch of clothing and not retained her undergarments, she slid a hand down over his shoulder and along the length of his arm, then grasped his hand and drew it to the mound between her thighs. Her drawers were newly purchased from Sofia's modiste, all Parisian silk and froufrou and as pretty as a picture, and at least their traditional style retained the oh so convenient opening.

"So impatient," he murmured against her mouth, but he squeezed where she wanted him to. The pressure made her squirm and bear down, loving the pressure and wanting more, more, more of it.

"Of course I am," she growled back at him. "I've waited too long. I want to know what it's like." She rocked against the fulcrum of his hand, already halfway to pleasure. "I'm tired of having a risqué reputation without the experience that goes with it."

"Very well then, siren, let's not waste another moment."

Still caressing her sex, he pushed her back against the bed.

BLOOD SURGED around Ritchie's body, pounding in his head, his heart and his groin. Ever since it had dawned upon him that Beatrice Weatherly was still a virgin, he'd fought to maintain control and rein in his desire.

He wasn't an animal. He took no woman roughly. Now more than ever, he held himself to be a considerate lover, one who used his skills to ensure his lover's pleasure. For an instant, cold horror gripped him as he remembered the last time he'd been teased and goaded into releasing the check he'd always levied on his passions. The nightmare haunted him to this day. And yet, at the time, he'd believed his husbandly enthusiasm to be welcome.

The grimacing, blank-faced shadow hovered momentarily over the bed, but when he snapped open his eyes, Margarita disappeared.

Ceding all his attention to a creature of light and warmth.

What man could think of another woman with Beatrice Weatherly in his arms? Her smile and her scent were a healing benison. As was her sweet honesty, perhaps an even greater power.

Beautiful Bea...beautiful Bea, you really want me, don't you? This is no act, no facade, no fickle game of a mind that doesn't know itself.

The last dark shade of his insane wife fought to clutch away his happiness, even in absentia, but he shook his senses, and drove out it and her, breathing in lily of the valley and a far more earthy scent.

He kissed Beatrice. He dug his hand in her luxuriant red hair and twisted a hank of it around his wrist; not to pull, but to bind himself to her. Between her legs, he squeezed in a deep, passionate rhythm, loving the way she rocked and squirmed and locked her thighs around his hand to keep it there.

Even if Beatrice had been possessed of all the arts of the divine Madame Bernhardt herself, there were telltales that could not be simulated. His fingers had worked their way into the vent in her dainty silk drawers, and he could feel her moisture seeping onto them from her sex. She was deliciously wet, running like a river, sweet and ready. He'd planned to utilize a *lubrifiant* when the time came to penetrate her, to ensure her comfort and ease. Perhaps he still would, just to be sure…but to his hand she felt so slick that it probably wouldn't be needed.

But I'll pleasure you first, adorable one. That's a promise. A necessity.

Eager and well prepared as she was, the shock of accommodating a man for the first time might well steal away Beatrice's pleasure, even if he was gentle, so it was a point of honor that she climax first, by his hand.

Or perhaps another, just as luscious way, if she'd let him.

The thought made him smile against her mouth, and circle his tongue around the soft margins of her lips.

BEATRICE WAS SIMMERING, teetering on the brink, her body gathering itself and her clitoris throbbing beneath his hand. But as she thrust herself against him, Ritchie suddenly pulled away.

"No, please…what are you doing?" She grabbed at

him, trying to pull him back, pure instinct and basic need making her beg.

"Hush, sweetheart, don't worry."

Slowly he kissed her lips, then pressed his mouth to the hand that'd held his in place at her groin. That kissed, he moved to the swell of her cleavage where it almost spilled from the top of her corset and nestled his face there, too. "I'm going to do something for you…something nice… something I hope you'll like." His tongue snaked out, licking her curves, flickering and teasing the slope of each breast, tasting the perspiration on her skin. "But if you don't like it, you must tell me and we'll try something else. Promise me that." He paused and looked up impishly, his tongue still against her skin as he punctuated his words with more teasing licks. "But I've a feeling you will like it…very much."

Suddenly it dawned on Beatrice *exactly* what it was he might be talking about.

Oh! Goodness me!

For the moment though, his mouth continued to rove over her cleavage, and to facilitate that, he popped open a couple of the hooks at the top of her corset. Prizing aside the lacy frippery of her chemise, he bared her, bringing her nipples out into the open and then lapping at them with his tongue.

Oh, that felt so good. Warm and wet, like a soft bath of pleasure flickering over each teat, one after the other, and back again. Beatrice tossed her head where she lay, still sideways across the bed, her fingers buried deep in Ritchie's blond curls, stirring up the light but intoxicating fragrance of his hair lotion.

If his mouth felt this wonderful at her breast, what unimaginable heaven would it feel like when it wandered lower?

He seemed in no hurry though. Lingering in a leisurely fashion over her nipples, he licked and sucked them, and occasionally took each one between the edges of his teeth and worried it lightly. Beatrice moaned, loving the delicate spike of danger, the not quite discomfort that made her hips start to wiggle as if she were an automaton, and her bottom squirm and rock against the bed.

As Ritchie nipped at her and clamped down hard on her puss with his dividing fingers, her legs kicked and she shouted aloud, suddenly spending.

Waves of exquisite sensation pelted around her body, but before she could barely appreciate them, Ritchie was moving and sliding from the bed onto the floor. With a perfect grace that she was almost beyond appreciating but still somehow managed to catalogue, he settled to his knees, between her thighs, and gazed at the center of her pleasure.

"Relax, my beautiful Bea, relax," he murmured, ever his mantra, then before she could draw another breath, he plunged on in.

Beatrice knew that men did this to women. She'd seen it in the "educational" reading material at Sofia's house and in Charlie's forbidden periodicals. But those were just images, and this was a warm, real mouth. Ritchie's mouth. And it had settled between her thighs to explore her grove.

At first he just kissed lightly, petting the fleecy curls of her pubis with his closed mouth, as if her were a male animal nuzzling its mate in greeting. The contact was elusive and teasing, and devilishly calculated. He was goading her into wanting much, much more.

"Ritchie, please, I want more," she groaned. What use was it to dissemble with him? He understood her needs. He could read her sensual soul. She couldn't hide her desire from him and she didn't want to. He cherished her honesty, and it was an easy gift to give.

"And you shall have it, my sweet. As much as you like."

With his strong, flexible thumbs, Ritchie dove into her pubic hair, pressing and parting to expose her. Wet as she was, the warm air of the room still seemed to tingle on her delicate flesh. When Ritchie blew on her, she keened and rocked, grabbing his hair again.

"Do you like that, Bea?" he whispered, right against her trembling, fluttering clitoris.

"Yes, you terrible devil, yes! Don't taunt me…just do whatever it is you plan to do!"

Ritchie laughed, directly into her sex, his mirth a caress in itself. She seemed to feel his low chuckle right in the quick of her belly.

But a second later, he wasn't laughing, he was licking, his wicked tongue traversing her every fold and contour.

"Oh my Lord! Oh my goodness!" cried Beatrice, astonished even though it was what she'd been aching for since he'd hinted his intentions. She had no idea what she'd been expecting, but this was wonderful, wonderful, wonderful. As she lifted her hips, pushing herself against his hot, moist mouth, she felt Ritchie cleverly rearrange her, lifting her thighs over his shoulders to press his face in even closer.

And then he began to suck as well as lick, varying and alternating and playing heavenly games with her. He teased the delicate inner lips, lapping, tickling, slipping his tongue around, exploring and arousing.

But like the wicked tormentor and prevaricator she knew him to be, he avoided the critical zone. The little knot of flesh that ached and screamed for him.

"Ritchie, please!"

"Please what, Bea?" His voice was muffled yet still sounded devilish, the ultimate sinful tease.

"You know!"

"Yes, I do." His tongue furled to a point, swooped down and delicately probed inside her, as if supping her nectar. "But I still want to hear you say it, my glorious girl."

"Oh, for heaven's sake!" She tugged his hair, punishing him, but he didn't falter, still pressing his tongue against her entrance, scouting the territory. "Lick my clitoris, you frightful man, and stop trying to drive me to distraction."

"Very well then, I obey," he growled against her. And obeyed.

"Oh! Oh, Ritchie!"

Within a breath, within a heartbeat, within the blink of an eye, he ignited her, sending pleasure rushing through her body from the touch of his swirling, darting tongue. Gripping her hips and pressing his mouth in harder, he feasted upon her, drawing the sensitive little bud of her pleasure between his lips, and dabbing down firmly with his tongue.

Spending furiously, Beatrice grabbed at his hair and his shoulder, jamming her pelvis upward and beating on his back with her flailing heels. Beyond control, beyond shame, almost beyond her wits, she arched like a bow drawn by a master's loving hand.

There was only Ritchie, his mouth and his tongue, and his strong hands cradling her rocking, squirming bottom. He was merciless, driving her again and again to her peak.

The whole world seemed to whirl around the juncture of Ritchie's lips and her flesh. It was like being lost on the high seas, yet journeying the sweetest, most longed-for voyage. Half insensible, Beatrice bobbed and floated on tall waves of divine sensation, dashed again and again onto the rock of the man who pleasured her.

Beatrice didn't have any strength left in her limbs. They felt like India rubber and incapable of obeying any commands, even if she had the wits to give them. She just lay and panted, aware of Ritchie's curly head resting on her thigh, his warm breath still wafting across her sticky, quivering puss.

"I think I just died and ascended to heaven," she gasped, uttering the first semicoherent thought in her head. "I never realized that…*that*…would be so good."

Ritchie lifted his head and looked up at her across the plane of her corset. "I believe that those who would make a scientific study of such things have coined the term cunnilingus," he said solemnly, and Beatrice quivered again. His lips were shining wet. With her.

"Indeed, one must always know the correct term." So why was she blushing at the word after she'd just enjoyed the deed? "But it does sound rather Latin and clinical for something so delightful."

Ritchie smiled, looking very pleased with himself, and then licked his lips. Which made Beatrice's clitoris leap again, the little action was so wicked and suggestive. Especially now… "I'm glad you enjoyed it, Bea. I thought you might…although occasionally the more delicate ladies find it somewhat alarming at first."

"Ah, well, as I keep informing you, Ritchie, it's turned out that I'm even less delicate than my reputation suggested." She shrugged, wriggling a little way across the bed. With her puss still so close to Ritchie's beautiful mouth, there was a strong temptation to surge forward and demand through action rather than correct Latin word that he "service" her once more.

"Reputations are meaningless, sweet girl." Ritchie rose

to his feet, a creature of perfect elegance despite the fact
he must have been kneeling rather uncomfortably on the
carpet. "And *you* are exquisite."

So are you.

Looking up at him, her heart rolled inside her. He *was*
exquisite. Yes, dynamic and masculine, but still a rare
jewel of mature male beauty. In the opening of his shirt,
the skin on his chest gleamed, and she wanted to rub her
face against the bit of soft sandy hair there. She wanted
to kiss his throat. Touch his face. Then press her cheek
against the front of his trousers as she'd done at Lady
Arabella's ball, and feel the hard heat of his male shaft
through the cloth.

And she *still* hadn't seen the damned thing!

Ritchie's eyes twinkled and she realized he was following her appraisal, right to its inevitable destination.

"Lie back against the pillows, Bea. You'll get your
wish," he instructed, and as she started to slide into place
on the bed, he joined her, on one knee, and gripped her
by the waist to help her move.

So strong. Beatrice wanted to wind her arms around
him and pull him to her. And possibly never let him go.

Never?

The feeling was sudden, alarming, and not at all sensible, but a wiser and more perceptive part of her nature
suddenly acknowledged that it had been there all along.

*Nonsense. Don't be a fool. You can't fall like that for
a man like him.*

But it was true, and in a strange reversal it had happened. In this peculiar *Vita Nuova,* it was Beatrice that
had fallen for a rather disreputable Dante at very first
sight. The realization shook her, but it made her want to
hug him even more, for reassurance as well as pleasure.

"You're shaking, Bea. Don't be afraid." Ritchie in-

clined over her, stroking her face, that complicated pan-
oply of emotion in his eyes again. He looked intense,
dark, almost confused and, unbidden, she reached up to
stroke his face in return.

"I'm not...well, not a great deal. I'm more eager than
anything really."

The darkness flew from his eyes and he laughed softly.
Beatrice felt a great lightening inside herself, a bubble of
the spirits, comprehending the extent of her female power.

"In that case, my dear, I'd better not keep you waiting
any longer."

CHAPTER TWENTY-TWO

His

UNABLE TO LOOK AWAY, even if her life might have depended on it, Beatrice watched as Ritchie set about the buttons of his trousers. His hands were deft and clever, as always, but something about the way his fingers darted over the fastenings—and then wrenched the fine cloth aside to attack his shirttail and his undergarment—told her he was as nervous, in his own way, as she was.

But she didn't worry. He *was* experienced and she knew that with him, her first time would be the best it could possibly be. There would be no blundering and fumbling, and no being left wondering what all the fuss was about, such as she might have endured at the hand and cock of some naive notional husband.

Husband?

Ah, the lure of that dangerous line of thought again. She banished the word, along with the unwise feelings that went with it. Best to be on her guard against fancies of that order, and always remember this was a pragmatic arrangement, a deal struck for a month and for money. The fact that her fellow negotiator had turned out to be unexpectedly likable, as well as the most physically attractive man she'd ever met made no difference whatsoever.

A second later, all pangs and notions and unwary

thoughts flew clean out of her head as Ritchie prized his erect member out of his linen.

"Goodness me!"

There was a considerable difference between imagining what Ritchie's handsome masculine appendage might be like, and even touching it, to seeing it in the flesh, in all its glory. Beatrice's first response was a tingle in her fingers.

Who would have imagined that the thing would be so…so appealing?

How extraordinary. Beatrice wasn't quite sure whether she'd describe Ritchie's member as beautiful, exactly, but it was certainly fascinating, impressive and seemed to have a life of its own, almost independent of the man to whom it was attached.

"I didn't expect it to be quite so rosy…. It's…well… it's quite remarkable."

Ritchie guffawed, subsiding back against the pillows, still clutching himself as he laughed and shook his head.

"Beatrice Weatherly, you are priceless," he said after a moment, rolling back to face her. "So…now you've finally seen it, you're not feeling too alarmed to proceed, are you?"

"No, indeed not…but…well…may I touch it again first?"

"Of course, sweetheart." Reaching out, he took her hand in his bigger one, and curled her fingertips around his cock, enfolding it and them with his own fingers.

So warm, so smooth-skinned, and to her hand, so familiar, it almost felt as if it were designed specifically for her caress. Beatrice knew the Almighty had given men this state in order that they might join with their women, but even so, there was something about the feel of Ritchie's hard, hot shaft that simply invited a rhythmic movement, to and fro. It had been her natural instinct beneath the tablecloth just as it was now.

To and fro.

Ritchie made a low, murmuring, indistinct sound that might have been "Oh dear Lord" or maybe just a growl of some kind. His long lashes fluttered and his hips bumped, instinctively pushing his flesh through their linked fingers. He was enjoying himself, that much was very obvious, and that in turn made Beatrice feel deliciously powerful. Ingenue she might be, but still she seemed imbued with natural gifts.

Conscious of his sensitivity though, she kept her manipulations slow and of an even, rhythmic pace. Ritchie's lips parted, and he bared his white teeth, gasping hard.

"You have a most particular skill, darling Beatrice," he said, his chest heaving. "Particular and far too delightful. I'm sorely tempted to just lie here and let you pleasure me on and on until the natural conclusion occurs." His lashes dipped, so sultry. "But if I do that, I'll have nothing left in the barrel to make love to you with. Well, at least not for a while."

For a moment, Beatrice was tempted to take him to that limit, so she could watch him spend in her hand and see the mysterious substance men ejected. But much as that would have delighted her, she wanted him inside her even more.

Ritchie's eyes snapped open, and again, as she'd so often thought in the short time she'd known him, she could almost imagine he'd divined the thoughts in her mind.

"And I do want to make love to you, Bea, more than anything." Controlling her fingers, he drew her hand away from his shaft.

Make love.

He'd called it "make love" rather than "fuck" or "have" or "know" or "possess" or any number of lurid or fanciful terms for the act. It wouldn't actually *be* making love, because there was no love involved—at least not on his side of the balance—but to use the expression afforded the process a special grace. Impulsively, Beatrice leaned over and kissed him lightly on the forehead, then shied away again so he couldn't see her eyes.

Almost immediately, he turned her face with his hand, back to him again, and his indigo-blue eyes bored into her, testing her soul. Shaking, she continued to try and evade him. She couldn't let him see that see she was already making far too much of their liaison, even before they'd joined their bodies.

"Are you ready, Bea?" Still he probed her. "Are you really ready?"

"Yes! Yes, I am! Isn't that what we're supposed to be here for?" Aware that she sounded fractious and on edge, she gave him a crooked smile and reached to delicately stroke his cock again. "He wants it, too. Look how eager he is to get on with the business."

"Blind beast that he is, he isn't the only one," Ritchie said, with a sudden grin. "Now roll over onto your back, beautiful girl, and we can all get on with it, can't we?"

Beatrice subsided against the pillows, glad that her corset was light and flexible and she could lie back comfortably wearing it. Feeling loose and free and daring, she began to toy with her own nipples as she gazed back at Ritchie, her senses fired by silvery streaks of pleasure that darted straight to her cleft.

His eyes still managing to remain fixed on the small motions of her fingers, Ritchie searched around behind himself, one-handed, on the bedside chest. Finding what he wanted, a small decorated tin, he opened it and drew

out an item that Beatrice recognized from her afternoon
at Sofia's establishment. Arabella had been fitting one
onto her playmate Yuri, just before Beatrice had been
compelled to abandon the peep show, too overheated. She
knew what it was, from Polly's racy talk.

"So that's a French Letter, is it then?"

"Indeed it is," observed Ritchie, then proceeded enrobe
his shaft in the tube of fine rubber before Beatrice's fascinated gaze.

It looked most unusual. But then, in these, her first
really close observations, the male member looked somewhat unusual, too. It seemed a shame to cover up such a
magnificent masculine monument in what amounted to
a mackintosh, but she was grateful for Ritchie's caution
on her behalf. Especially as she'd heard also heard from
Polly that many men were quite aggressively resistant to
the idea of prophylactics, claiming that the rubber spoiled
their pleasure.

But what if he didn't use one. What then?

Deep in her soul, Beatrice was astonished to find a
well of disappointment. And an absurd longing. Whatever
scraps of her reputation that remained after her month
with Ritchie would be vaporized if he left her enceinte
and without a wedding band.

And yet, that tiny ridiculous flame of madness still
plagued her, and behind her closed eyes, she saw an image
of a gurgling infant boy with a head of bright blond curls.

"No!"

"What is it, Bea?" Ritchie's brow crumpled in concern,
even as his long fingers lingered at the root of his penis
where it emerged from his trousers. "Have you changed
your mind?"

"No, not at all," she gasped, reaching for him and at the
same time waving away the ridiculous notions. "I'm just

a little nervous…I don't know what I'm saying… Please, Ritchie, please…please make love to me."

"My lovely Bea," breathed Ritchie, moving over her and settling between her thighs. "My beautiful, beautiful Beatrice. Since the first moment I set eyes on your image, I've wanted this. Most of the time I've been able to think of little else."

Yet still his progress was measured, mindful of her. Holding his weight off her body, he reached into the vent of her drawers, between her thighs, to stroke and play with her. She could hear the small slippery sounds where he dabbled in her wetness.

"Tilt your hips, my sweet, that'll make it easier." Abandoning her puss for moment, he clasped her bottom through the silk of her underwear. Adjusting her position, his fingertips lingered on her, curving around her buttock. "There, that's better."

Then the tip of his cock touched her, right at her entrance, hot, and feeling larger there even than it had appeared to her eyes. Despite the might of him, Beatrice surged up, unable to help herself.

He was knocking for admittance and she was quivering and ready to admit him.

"Yes," urged Ritchie, his weight on one elbow as he reached under her again to pull her tight against him. His shaft was prodigious, but as he pushed—slowly and intently, yet with simmering energy—her body yielded, his entry made easy by her natural fluid, their play with the *godemiche,* and the equestrian prowess of her girlhood. What little resistance remained was slight only, and waned again almost immediately, without the faintest trace of pain.

What resulted was a peculiar but exquisite sensation, and uniquely moving.

It's him. In me. We are one.

Tears welled in Beatrice's eyes, but not from sorrow. As her body adjusted, and the sublime, familiar tremors miraculously began to gather, she could honestly say that she'd never been happier in her life.

Ritchie's lips found hers in a kiss. Light as a breath, his mouth seemed to dance on her lips, gentle and insubstantial in a way that made the thrust of his flesh below seem all the more solid. The contrast of the two stole her breath from her body.

"Are you well, Bea? I'm not hurting you, am I?" He was questioning her in a calm, responsible way, yet his voice was ragged, as if he were clinging to self-control by the merest tip of a fingernail. She could sense him fighting his own nature in order not to frighten or alarm her and that sweet solicitude made her heart turn right over. Her desire to reward him drove her just as hard as her lust for pleasure.

"No…no, you're not hurting me at all." His flesh felt strange inside her, but exciting and stirring, like the trigger of some immense, titanic process. She was teetering on a hairspring, eager and voracious. "Please, Ritchie… don't hold back…I want your pleasure. Go on…fuck me! Fuck me hard! As hard as you like!"

He laughed and she felt it inside her. Every last fiber of her body vibrated with it.

"You tempt me, siren," he growled, gathering her to him, adjusting their bodies, pressing in further, if that were humanly possible. "But if I please myself, I may not be able to please you as much." He gasped in a deep breath. "My pace might be somewhat faster than yours, my sweet. I've been anticipating this since the first moment…and I'm a man, and we men are sometimes weak when it comes to the demands of our blessed cocks."

As he kissed her face, then the side of her neck and her ear, she whispered back at him as a wanton sprite danced inside her, "Well, you don't feel weak to me, Mr. Ritchie. In fact I don't think I could ever imagine anything *less* weak than this." As if by instinct, she squeezed him with the muscles at her core. She hadn't known she could do that, but his sudden, passionate exhalation of breath told her it felt as just good for him as it did for her. Embracing him again, she pressed her whole self up against him.

"Oh Beatrice, Beatrice, Beatrice, you're a natural-born angel of seduction. When you do that, have you any idea at all how it pleasures me?" Bracing himself, he gripped her bottom hard, and thrust at her, plumbing her in short, sharp jabs. Beatrice saw stars as, with each stroke, his pubic bone knocked her clitoris.

"Well, I have an inkling," she gasped, fighting for breath. "I'm just experimenting…I really haven't a clue what I'm doing."

As Ritchie laughed again, her body seemed to assume a life of its own, moving eagerly, matching his movements. Her parted legs flexed, and it seemed the most natural thing in the world to bring up her knees, tilt her pelvis and open herself yet more to him. As she locked her ankles around his hips, he let out a sigh, and an instant later, his thrusts accelerated, becoming jerky, wild and primal.

"Oh Bea, I wanted to last," he gasped, his teeth clenched. "I wanted to be so good…for you…to hold on and endure."

"It doesn't matter. I don't care a jot…I really don't…I like it like this!"

And she did. And so much more than like. Thumping herself up against him, she whimpered at the delicious friction, the shimmering heat gathering around his fast-pumping shaft. Letting out moans so feral that they almost made her laugh at herself, despite the pleasure, she grabbed at his bottom through his trousers and at his back, wrenching at his shirt and tearing the fine cotton fabric.

All was action, straining, gasping, grabbing, reaching for the pinnacle of sensation that seemed to barrel down toward her, channeled through Ritchie's dear, surging body. Sweat poured from her, soaking her undergarments, pooling beneath her breasts, and in the creases of her groin so close to where her lover labored powerfully. She clutched at him harder, trying to climb inside his flesh just as he plunged into her. As his face pressed to the side of hers, she felt him perspiring, too.

But was it really sweat? Or was his face wet from some other fluid?

As she tried to look at him, he surged in deeper, deeper than before, his athletic hips somehow circling as he plunged.

And then it came. Her spending. Expected but still sudden.

There was no great cataclysm, no violence, no wrenching of heaven and earth. Just the sweetest, lightest, most silvery plume of sublime bliss that seemed to gently bloom and glow in the core of her body, and flow on outward.

"Oh, Ritchie," she sighed. "Oh, my darling Ritchie…"

In her heart she said other things too, but kept them quiet.

ROLLING AWAY from her, Ritchie's heart roared in protest at the parting of their bodies, but still he kept quiet.

He was elated, stunned almost to insensibility, confused and drenched bone deep in the aftermath of pleasure. The intense lust he'd conceived the moment he'd first seen Beatrice Weatherly in those beautiful and explicit cabinet cards had been fulfilled, and so much more. So much more. His limbs tingled and he felt as strong as a conquering lion and yet as weak as a kitten; more wrung out by this swift tumble with an inexperienced virgin than by any amount of protracted bouts of sophisticated love play with the most hedonistic society beauties.

The emotion he'd sworn he would never again allow into his heart had burrowed its way in there nevertheless. But for her sake and his own, he struggled to suppress it.

What's to become of me? I can't hurt you, Beatrice. I simply mustn't.

There was nothing to be done but remain as two friends who enjoyed good bed play for the rest of their month together, and afterward take matters no further than that.

Because he *couldn't* ask for more. He couldn't *expect* more. And he certainly didn't deserve more.

And to lead Beatrice Weatherly into expecting more than a temporary liaison with him was both callous and cruel.

He couldn't offer what he suddenly wanted to offer her…because the sorrowful fact was that he was already thoroughly married.

CLAWING HER WAY out of semiconsciousness, Beatrice stirred on the bed, stretching her limbs and wrinkling her nose.

Was that strange, foxy odor *her?* That tang of sweat and muskiness? She supposed it must be because her legs were still wide open and so was the vent in her drawers. Thank goodness the room was warm, or she could have caught a most inconvenient chill.

Full awareness came like the dowsing of rain from a spring storm, and snapping her eyes open, she snapped her legs shut, only to find that the sharp movement reminded her why her thighs were parted in the first place.

Ritchie!

Struggling upright, she saw him, illuminated by a turned-down lamp and the light of a small fire burning in the grate. Had he lit it himself? Beatrice sincerely hoped he had, given her state of outrageous dishabille.

But whatever had happened, Ritchie was drowsing too, just as she'd been, lounging in an easy chair, yards away across the room, his long legs stretched out before him. As she watched, he stirred as if he'd sensed her, then his eyes flicked open. Fully awake in the space of a heartbeat, he rose to his feet in a fluid, almost mammalian movement, and strode toward the bed, his gaze intent.

"How do you feel, Bea? Did you sleep?" He reached out to touch her face, and she experienced the most ridiculous urge to flinch away from him. Not because she didn't want him to touch her, but because he hadn't been lying beside her, holding her close, when she awoke.

"I'm well...thank you. And yes, I must have fallen asleep." Not succumbing to her gut reaction, she manufactured a smile for him and turned her face into his caressing palm for a moment. Perhaps she'd been snoring? Maybe he'd got a cramp and had to rise? She'd make allowances for him.

"I thought you'd be asleep beside me," murmured her lips, apparently having assumed a life of their own, independent of her reason.

Ritchie gave her an odd, strangely sad little smile.

"I don't sleep with women." He shrugged, his thumb moving lightly over her cheek, brushing her lips. "I make love to them. I fuck them. I profoundly enjoy their company. But I don't spend the night in their beds."

Beatrice frowned.

"Not ever?"

"No. Never."

"Why not?"

It was Ritchie's turn to frown, although it seemed to be at himself, rather than her.

"Just a foible of mine, Bea. Just a foible. It's not through anything lacking in women...and God knows it's not through anything lacking in *you,* my sweet. It's just...my custom."

A strange custom. And as Ritchie's hand slid down over her jaw, her neck and her shoulder, and on down her arm, Beatrice trembled, a suddenly empty place inside her irrationally yearning for what she couldn't have, rather than the many sweet gifts of pleasure with which he could still shower her.

Don't be so contrary, Bea.

"Ah well, we all have our little customs, don't we?" she said, feigning cheerfulness as he squeezed her hand and then let it loose.

"Indeed we do, don't we?" He stood up, beside the bed. "Now, it's very late, Bea, and we should get you to your home now. Unless, of course you'd like to stay here for the night?" His eyes flickered over her, making Beatrice realize that her breasts were still exposed, her nipples peeking pink and ripe above the edge of her corset and pulled-down chemise. "I'll arrange for a maid to help with your dress, and a carriage to take you home in the morning. The breakfasts here are quite splendid, I believe."

"You only *believe?* Ah, I suppose if you don't actually sleep with anyone, you don't know much about hotel breakfasts then?"

Why was she suddenly being a shrew? He owed her nothing. He was paying well over the odds already for what he was getting.

"I'm sorry. I didn't mean to be shrill."

Ritchie sat down again and reclaimed her hand, holding it in both of his, long fingers straying again over the pulse at her wrist.

"You weren't shrill, Bea. The fault is mine. I should be more mindful of your fragile state, shouldn't I?" Fingertips danced over her skin, calming somehow, almost hypnotic. "I'm used to women of the world, ladies who've been around a bedroom or two in sophisticated circumstances. They usually want to dash home to their husbands far faster than I want to leave their beds."

"I'm not fragile. Not at all. I'm a robust country bloom, really, you know."

He lifted her hand to his lips and kissed it, once, very precisely.

"But you were a virgin, Bea, and you gave me a beautiful gift. I should be more grateful."

"But—" she began, feeling compelled to remind him of their agreement, their transaction.

Before she could, though, he set his other hand, just the fingertips, across her lips.

"What you gave me was more than I transacted for, Beatrice, far more." His midnight eyes glittered. They were fierce, but their sheen looked suspiciously moist for a moment. "And you'll be rewarded. Now, come along, get that beautiful body of yours out of bed and back into the rest of your clothes. I can help you if you require it, or if you prefer we can summon a maid."

"I can manage, thank you." Oh how she wished that they'd both been naked. But they hadn't been, so she didn't need a maid.

A short while later, the two of them descended the staircase together, both as superficially immaculate as when they'd arrived, although beneath her clothing and beneath her skin, Beatrice knew she could not have felt more different.

On Ritchie's arm, she was no longer a virgin, she was a woman well bedded.

Aware of every inch of him, though barely touching his elbow, she was a woman in love.

God help me.

The foyer was silent as the grave, the lighting down low. The night porter had sent a runner to summon Ritchie's carriage, and informed them it would be but a moment, gesturing to one of the deeply upholstered sofas in the social area where they might wait in comfort and out of the night chill.

"Let's go outside and wait," said Beatrice, suddenly oppressed. She was a woman with a lover who'd paid for her services, that was the reality of things, but lurking around the foyer only made the situation seem more seedy. The night air might be rank and smoggy, but its very coldness would clear the head all the same.

"You might catch a chill, Bea," murmured Ritchie, looking doubtfully at her light costume, which had been perfectly appropriate for a balmy early evening, but now seemed insubstantial in the chilly small hours. In his topper and overcoat, he was far more adequately attired.

"Don't worry. Remember, I'm a hardy breed. I'm quite warm and I'm sure the carriage won't be but a moment." Stepping out boldly, she made for the entrance, compelling him to come along with her.

Beneath the portico, it was very cold, and Beatrice steeled herself not to show her immediate shivers. It seemed Ritchie saw them anyway, because in a sudden sweeping gesture, he divested himself of his both his long, dark coat and his fine, fringed silk scarf and draped both the garments around Beatrice's shoulders. When she opened her mouth to protest, he said, "I'm a hardier breed than you are. Don't argue, Bea."

Enveloped in Ritchie's own heat, Beatrice almost sighed with pleasure. Wearing her lover's coat was somehow, in a strange way, deeply intimate. A communion, just as their joined bodies in bed was. She allowed herself to shiver now, but not from the banished cold. Especially as Ritchie slung an arm around her shoulders, over his coat.

She looked at him. He looked at her. The strange bond was acknowledged though neither of them spoke. It felt almost peaceful to be waiting together in the foggy night.

But the quiet moment was shattered almost immediately as a trio of people descended the steps from Belanger's too, and joined them under the portico.

Beatrice tried to ignore the newcomers, but it was difficult because the man and his two rather gaudily dressed female companions were all a little worse for drink, and noisily laughing. Ritchie frowned, and seemed on the point of remonstrating with them, but Beatrice closed her hand around his arm and silently held him back.

But the man seemed vaguely familiar, and when he managed to catch Beatrice's eye, he gave her nod and a rather forward smirk, tipping his hat.

Who was he? Had she met him before? Then it dawned on her. She couldn't quite remember his name, but he was someone she'd met briefly while at a small photography exhibition, during a rather hurried public outing with Eustace. Grinding her teeth, she wondered whether he recognized her from that event or from Eustace's subsequent photographic handiwork.

"Beatrice? Is something wrong?"

She looked up into Ritchie's concerned face to see his eyes snapping from her, to Eustace's friend, and back again. "Is that man bothering you?" His jaw was tight, as if he were tensing like a coil spring to defend her.

"Not in the slightest. It's only someone I met briefly at a function." He didn't seem convinced, but luckily, at that moment, a carriage hove into view along the misty street, and to her relief, Beatrice recognized the coachman as theirs.

The short ride home was passed in silence. Ritchie seemed deep in thought, his brow furrowed beneath his fine top hat, even though he held on to Beatrice's hand as if either one of their lives depended on it. She seemed to feel every small muscle of his fingers and his palm through his glove and her own. Her body trembled, knowing what those strong fingers could do.

It wasn't long before they reached South Mulberry Street, and Ritchie leaped out of the carriage to hand her out onto the pavement and escort her to the door.

"I'll send a note tomorrow," he said, his voice edged again as if he were troubled. "I have many commitments...and I may have to go out of town during the day. But we'll see each other in the evening, at least. If only for a little while."

Beatrice nodded, feeling edged herself. She wasn't sure why he never slept with his women, but now that she knew that, she was afraid the conundrum might obsess her. Indeed, much as she longed for the familiar comfort of her own feather mattress, her mind now presented a picture of her sharing it with Ritchie, perhaps so she could ease the nag of whatever it was that was troubling him.

How sweet to sleep in those strong arms. Feel his

warmth when the fire went out and the room started to cool down, and give back her own warmth.

How sweet to reach for him, in the night, and open her legs for him.

"Take care, Ritchie," she said suddenly, not sure what hazards might face a gentleman of business, but anxious at the thought of any harm coming to him.

"You, too, beautiful Bea," he said softly, then swept his top hat off his fair head, and leaned in close to kiss her.

It lasted but a moment, yet Beatrice had to fight with her own limbs not to grab at him and attempt to haul him by every scrap of force she possessed into the house with her. As it was, the lock clicked, and the doorknob turned in answer to her knock, and the door swung ajar, opened by the quiet but efficient new footman.

"I'll send you a note," repeated Ritchie, squeezing her hand and sweeping on his hat again, then letting her go as he stepped away. "Now go inside, my dear. You'll catch a chill. I'll see you tomorrow."

Then, tipping his hat, he strode away and climbed into the carriage, pausing only to cast her one last look, strangely complicated and yearning, before the coachman clicked the horse and it sped away into the night.

It wasn't until Beatrice stood in the hall, and the footman held out his arm to receive it, that she realized she was still wearing Ritchie's astrakhan-collared overcoat.

CHAPTER TWENTY-THREE

Billets Doux

NO NOTE ARRIVED the following morning, despite all
Beatrice's exertion of wishful thinking and willing one
to. Every time a servant appeared to bring her a newspaper or a cup of tea, or consult with her on some domestic matter, her heart lifted. Every time that there was no
communication forthcoming, either Polly or Charlie or
Jamie Brownlow or any other received a bright, but se-
cretly hollow smile from Beatrice.

She was bored. Flighty. Unsettled. A new state for
her. Ever a self-sufficient individual, Beatrice had always
found ways to occupy herself, either with long hours of
reading, with duties of the house, when times had been
hard, or visiting and other social pursuits in better days.

Now there was no need for her help with housework,
and no one really but Sofia Chamfleur to visit. Beatrice
sent round a card, but got only a card in return from Sofia,
promising a visit another day.

*Too busy running her ladies' house of assignation or
whatever she calls it.*

But Beatrice squashed her disappointment. No doubt
Sofia's risqué enterprise took up a lot of her time.

The copy of *Punch* she'd been reading—usually a favorite diversion—slid from Beatrice's fingers. Its satiri-
cal mischief was as barbed and amusing as ever, but she

couldn't concentrate. She could only think of Ritchie, and his smile, his hands, his cock.

"You've ruined me, you blackguard," she muttered, and yet the epithet was fond on her tongue, and she knew that the ruin was only that he'd spoiled her for all other men, because, unless she was mistaken, she loved him.

Absurd! I barely know the man...how can this have happened?

But it had. Which was why a sensible girl like her was now mooning around the house like a lovelorn ninny, hanging on the prospect of a few scribbled words from her object of adoration.

"Fiddlesticks!"

Leaping to her feet, *Punch* forgotten, Beatrice fetched a well-studied copy of *The Modern Woman* from the sideboard, and started flicking through it, seeking an advertisement she'd noted, announcing Addlington's Patented Typewriting Machines. Better to be practical and look ahead. Be ready for...afterward.

But the advertisement didn't fire her with quite the independent zeal that it had formerly done. Beatrice frowned, almost annoyed by the soft, slyly circling thoughts of marriage, night after night in bed with Ritchie, and maybe one or two small children with curly flaxen hair.

"Absurd," she exclaimed again, and went to the bureau for a sheet of paper. She'd write to Addlington's now, and order one of their machines to be delivered. At least she had the funds now, and she could begin practicing in preparation for an industrious life after Ritchie.

Before she'd put pen to the paper though, there was a knock at the door, and in her usual precipitous manner, Polly sidled in, not having waited for a by-your-leave.

Beatrice studied the girl momentarily as she held out

the silver letter tray. What was it about her that was so different in recent days? A new confidence? No, she'd always had that. It was a glow, an air of suppressed excitement. As if Poll too was fearful of something but thrilled by it also.

I know how you feel...I know how you feel...

"Letter for you, Miss Bea," Polly announced unnecessarily.

Ritchie's letter. It must be. Beatrice's heart pounded hard, and she stopped using her musings about Polly as a diversionary tactic.

"Thank you, Polly." She took it, slightly surprised by the thinness of the paper, and its cheap quality. That didn't seem like Ritchie at all, nor did the indistinct hand. "Are...are you well, Polly? You look preoccupied somehow. You're not concerned about your place, are you? You mustn't be. It doesn't matter that Mr. Brownlow's here, and the others. You'll always be the senior servant as long as I have anything to do with the matter."

"Don't you worry, Miss Bea. It's not about my place... not really. And you shouldn't concern yourself." Polly smiled and winked. "You know me. I always have a way of making things work out right."

Quite true. Polly was intelligent and resourceful and sensible. Probably far more so than her mistress, Beatrice reflected ruefully.

"Very well, then, Poll." Beatrice turned the letter over in her fingers, a stir of disquiet rippling. "But if you should ever need to discuss anything, you will come to me, won't you?"

Polly bobbed her usual cursory curtsy. "Thank you, Miss Bea. Don't worry, you'll be the very first I'll come to, that's for sure."

That sounded ominous, but not much so as the letter

seemed. Beatrice studied the envelope, still unopened, when Polly had gone.

Not from Ritchie. Absolutely not. On closer inspection the writing bore no resemblance to the firm, decisive hand that had leaped from the page in his proposal.

And yet it was still familiar, but from a far different source, unfortunately.

> My dearest Beatrice,
> I know we did not part on the best of terms, and perhaps I was a little hasty in breaking off our engagement. The business of the photographs was unfortunate. By a stroke of bad luck, a fellow from the camera club got hold of the plates and seeing their rather titillating nature, he took it upon himself to make a bit of coin from them. They were being circulated before I could pursue the matter, and already in too many hands to save your reputation.
> But now, I feel a little guilty that I didn't stand up to Mother when she said I must break off with you. Young ladies have been the subject of far worse scandals, but have gone on to redeem themselves, so I feel that I owe it to you now to help you restore your place in society.
> I have missed you, dear Beatrice, and I'm hoping that we may once again step out together. I will certainly not be ashamed to be seen with you in polite circles, and if you would send a reply to this note, I would be more than happy to call on you so we can resume our friendship. And perhaps more?
> With fondest regards, your hopefully to be reinstated fiancé, Eustace.

Fury boiled up like white-hot magma from the heart of an Icelandic volcano, and drawing back her lips in a snarl, Beatrice rent the letter in two, letting out a mighty, wordless screech.

Flinging the pieces to the carpet, she leaped up in the air and jumped on them, pounding them with her slipper-clad foot.

"You unutterably insufferable bastard, Eustace Lloyd! How dare you!" Giving the letter pieces another hefty stamping, she then set about pacing to and fro.

The gall of the man. What outrageous lies and condescension. It was so preposterous a communication that she could hardly believe she'd received it, but when she snatched up the pieces again and read the words through a haze of red mist, there they were, imparting their unbelievable message.

I wouldn't take up with you again, Eustace Lloyd, even if Ritchie ruined me and left me half-naked and begging in the gutter and you the only offer of succor in the whole wide world.

Her gut still simmering, she swept the pieces back onto the floor and stomped across and rang the bell.

A cup of tea was in order. A familiar, comforting beverage to calm her ire and set her thinking straight, even though her immediate inclination was to specify a pint of brandy for herself and instruct that a cask of hemlock be sent to Eustace at the earliest opportunity.

Men!

She threw herself down into a chair, to seethe and think.

A WHILE LATER, Beatrice was calm again and not in the least inclined toward murder. She'd read the shredded letter several times. Eustace's motives were still a mystery to her, but somehow, when it came down to it, she couldn't find it in her heart to really hate him. In fact, as she'd already noted, if he hadn't done what he'd done, there was very little chance that her path would ever have crossed that of Edmund Ellsworth Ritchie.

"Thank you, but no thank you, Eustace," she murmured, taking up her pen again.

My dear Eustace,

Thank you for your letter and your offer of renewed friendship. I appreciate the kindness you would bestow on me, but regretfully, I have to decline, as I no longer believe we are suited to each other and I would not want you to risk your reputation on my account.

Fortunately, for my own part, I've recently made the acquaintance of a wealthy and well set up gentleman who takes no interest in reputations, good, bad or otherwise, and I hope that you too will soon meet an amenable young lady who is a much better match for you than I would ever have been.

All best wishes, Beatrice Weatherly

"And I hope you accidentally tread in a pile of horse droppings next time you're out and about too," she added to herself as she signed the note with a flourish, "and then slip and end up on your pompous hind parts in the middle of the street." With little regard for the folds, she stuffed the note into an envelope before she could think better of her braggadocio.

Perhaps it wasn't wise to mention a "wealthy and well set up gentleman", but Eustace did have an impossible degree of cheek implying that she was damaged goods and that he was doing her a monumental graciousness by being seen with her again.

There was nothing wrong with her at all. In fact Ritchie seemed to think there was quite a lot right with her!

About to ring the bell again, Beatrice was surprised by another knock on the door and the entrance of Polly with the silver salver again.

"Another letter, Miss Bea."

Now this was the one she'd been waiting for. She could tell that strong, decisive script from several feet away. She snatched the missive off the tray and asked Polly to come back in a little while for both the answers.

Ritchie's note wasn't condescending. In fact there wasn't much to it at all. Simply the time and place— *Belanger's at 7:30 p.m.*—and the words, *My carriage will collect you.*

His large, uncompromising signature followed, with a postscript.

I hunger for your beauty.

She ran her fingertip over the letters, imagining the pen held in his long, elegant hand.

As I do for yours, Ritchie. As I do for yours.

SEVEN-THIRTY FOUND HER at Belanger's and in receipt of yet another billet doux, handed to her by the maître d'hôtel, who treated "Madame de la Tour" with anxious solicitude as if she were a valued patron of many years standing.

Beatrice, forgive me, I shall be delayed a little. I've arranged for a light meal to be served in our suite. Enjoy it while you wait for me, it will bolster your strength.

She could almost see him wink at her, those indigo eyes of his twinkling with mischief. What the dickens was he planning that needed such fortification? She hardly dare anticipate, but at the same time, couldn't prevent herself.

So, no pretence of respectable public dining this time?

Having settled in, she surveyed the room they'd shared previously. It looked just as lushly appointed and welcoming as before, with fresh flowers in the vases and lamps turned low, but this time, supper was laid out on a folding rosewood table. Game pie, cold fowl, cheeses and a selection of rather exotic-looking fruit, varieties imported at great expense. There was champagne on ice, and jug of lemonade too.

The food looked delicious, and tasted splendid too, when Beatrice took slice of chicken in her fingers and nibbled it. Here on her own, there was no need to stand on ceremony, and even though she wasn't really all that hungry, she picked at items from the table, standing tapping her feet, waiting, waiting.

How long would Ritchie be delayed? What was he doing? Where was he?

Surely a courtesan would take the late arrival of her lover in her stride, paid to please when and where and how the man who'd bought her so disposed?

But increasingly, Beatrice knew she was thinking in a different fashion. Fooling herself, despite her better intentions, that she and Ritchie were engaged in a more "conventional" love affair rather than the indecent transaction it was in reality.

"Stupid, stupid, stupid," she chastised herself, taking a sip of lemonade in a champagne glass. The drink was heavenly, sweet, yet sharp and crisp, challenging the taste buds. It reminded her of Ritchie, somehow, but then, everything did.

Abandoning the supper table, she crossed to the bed and sat on the edge, her senses excited simply by the fact it was a bed. A place where she and Ritchie would make love before long, and hopefully, be naked together. She yearned to see his body, and discover if it fulfilled the promise of his clothed elegance. His bare chest the previous night had been a tantalizing preview, and now her fingertips itched to travel over the rest of him, exploring and pleasuring.

If they were to be naked, perhaps she should set a precedent by shedding her clothes before he arrived. To encourage him to abandon his quickly and join her?

Furthermore, getting undressed was at least something to do while she waited, something exciting and daring, even though unfortunately it wasn't the first time she'd stripped off her garments for a man.

Botheration! I didn't mean to think of Eustace tonight!

Shaking her head as if to dislodge him, she set about her clothing, easily summoning the handsome image of Ritchie but somehow still unsettled by the sudden thought of her former fiancé. That insulting note continued to nag at her, even though she pitied the man too.

For ease, Beatrice had chosen a moiré dinner gown, in midnight-blue, that unbuttoned down the front. Even though she had Polly to help her with dressing and undressing, sometimes, in the past few months, the maid had been so hard-pressed with her other duties in the house that Beatrice didn't like to insist on her services as a personal servant, and had often dressed and undressed on her own. She'd developed certain canny little tricks for dealing with buttons and corset lacing and the like, because even though she knew some ladies were helpless under the dominion of their draconian underpinnings, she'd never been one to let anything get the better of her. Especially the time she'd fled from Eustace.

Still, the layers of silk and flannel and whalebone, and more silk, took a while to shed, and despite the fact she'd half hoped Ritchie might arrive before the process was completed, Beatrice stood naked on the rug beside the bed with still no paramour in sight.

Ritchie! Come now!

The command was silent, and unanswered. In the pier glass across the room, her bare body mocked her, so she shook out her hair and raised her arms, striking a classical pose.

How could he resist her, the Siren of South Mulberry Street, in all her glory?

Pushing away thoughts of the photographs she'd posed for, Beatrice lifted the coverlet and slid between the sheets. She felt a fool just standing around in her birthday suit, with not even a wretched camera for company, so maybe a short nap would fill in the time until Ritchie's advent.

The bed linen was cool and fresh and felt like a chin-to-toe caress on her heated skin. Her intention to doze was derailed by the passive sensuality of the cotton as she moved her limbs beneath the sheet. She sighed, her stomach fluttering as the crisp fabric rubbed against her puckered nipples.

Still snaking around, she cupped her breast and fondled herself, seeing dark blue eyes glitter in her imagination. He liked her to touch herself, so she would do it. Regardless of the fact that he wasn't present to enjoy the show.

This is for my pleasure, Ritchie, not yours. In fact, I shall make you *a show in my mind.*

Closing her eyes, she imagined him standing where she'd stood on the rug, as naked as she was. It was easy to imagine the way his body might be formed, and in respect of his cock, she had her recent memories for reference.

Ritchie wasn't a massive man, but the way he moved, swift and light, suggested the athleticism she now pic-

tured. He was graceful too, in both larger movements and
the detailed articulation of limbs and hands. The latter
were a poem as they roved over his own body, the left,
flat against his chest, touching the nubs of his nipples, the
right extending down to grasp his sturdy reddened cock.

She bade him stroke himself, and his imagined sim-
ulacrum being far more biddable than the real man, he
obeyed her.

Now it was his turn to be a classical image, like a
god from ancient times at his self-pleasure. Limbs flexed,
back arched, throat a long taut line as he tipped back his
head and thrust with his pelvis, pushing his erect member
back and forth through the ring of his fingers.

Beatrice seemed to hear his voice too, then almost
laughed when she realized it was her own voice gasping
and murmuring. She was breathing heavily, tossing and
moaning under her breath, her own fingers at play at her
breasts and between her legs, mimicking Ritchie within
the limitations of their pleasingly different anatomy.

How easy it was to summon pleasure while imagining
him. She could almost feel the weight of his body resting upon her, pressing open her parted legs even further.
Her sex rippled, her inner channel clenching as if it were
trying to caress him inside her.

"Oh, Ritchie," she gasped, putting both hands to her
mound, flicking at her clitoris with her fingertip while
pressing two fingers of her other hand inside herself. It
wasn't a substitute for his fine shaft, but it was better than
nothing, and still delightful in itself. Working herself, she
squirmed around the bed, her mind filled with visions of
him and his avidly imagined nakedness.

The tension began to gather. Pressure. Heat. The sensation of reaching, reaching, reaching for a sweet treasure.

She rubbed furiously with her finger and, astonishing herself, pushed another inside.

"Oh…oh, goodness…oh yes!" she chanted, feeling as if the angel of sexual fulfillment was descending to her, coming ever closer, clad in blinding light.

Then the doorknob turned and the door swung open, and closed again.

Dancing on the brink, Beatrice wanted to curse. And cheer. She screwed her eyes tight shut, still straining, and at the same time fervently convincing herself that a waiter or a maid would *knock* before they entered. Neither of those would be removing an overcoat, and perhaps a top hat, and hanging them on the stand by the door—the actions suggested by small sounds of rustling cloth.

"My dear Miss Weatherly, what *are* you doing?"

Just that low, laughing voice nearly triggered her.

"What does it look like, Mr. Ritchie?" she gasped, still struggling for the exquisite prize, then slumped, relaxing her straining muscles.

"It looks to me as if you are a very naughty, impatient young woman and you didn't wait for me. Either to eat, judging by the state of this repast, or otherwise."

Beatrice snapped open her eyes, and saw Ritchie sipping lemonade from the same glass she'd used herself.

"And you are a very naughty, obtuse gentleman. You *told* me to eat without you!"

He laughed, knocked back the drink, then set aside the glass and strode forward her, unpinning his necktie as he came.

"Ah, but I didn't tell you to diddle yourself without me, did I?" His tie, a shimmering silk length of midnight blue, and gold pin dropped onto the cabinet set beside the bed. Eyes narrowing in determination, he set about his studs.

Giving him an old-fashioned look, Beatrice shuffled and started to sit up.

"Now what are you doing, Bea?" queried Ritchie, still unfastening.

"Waiting for you."

"Oh, no you don't, madam. You carry on where you left off. Don't you dare cheat me out of the rest of the show." In a dramatic gesture, he reached out and whipped the bedding away.

Exposed, Beatrice flushed pink. Almost everywhere, it felt like. Her ears were burning and her chest was rosy, as were her face, neck and shoulders. Despite that, it didn't occur to her to demur.

Sliding back against the large, plump pillows, she let her hands find their way back to their previous locations. Her clitoris throbbed beneath the pad of her forefinger, and her channel was so slippery her fingers breached it easily.

"Divine," sighed Ritchie, sitting down on the bed's edge to get a better view.

Hot and twitchy, Beatrice scowled at him. "I know I am…but it's so unfair. I've barely seen anything of you yet. I wish you'd take your clothes off too."

He gave her a long, odd look, as if assessing not just her body, but her mind and her heart, too. It should have disturbed her, interrupting her train of pleasure, but somehow it only nudged her closer.

"All in good time, Mistress Impatience. You'll get your wish. Although you might not be all that impressed when you get it."

Now she was a bit distracted. Whatever did he mean?

"Well, all looks promising from where I'm sitting." Abandoning her clitoris for a moment, she reached out boldly and gripped the muscles of his thigh through his trousers. He felt solid and well exercised, in peak condition.

"Uh-oh, get back to the business in hand." Gently but firmly, he pried her fingers off him, conducting them back to her crotch.

"I've lost my thread now."

"Well, whose fault it that?"

Beatrice studied him, especially his eyes. He'd looked troubled a moment ago, but now the familiar playfulness was back. Her heart and her sex gave a delicious lurch of anticipation.

Whatever he wanted, she was ready to perform.

CHAPTER TWENTY-FOUR

A Flawed God

Ah, she understands, she understands.

Ritchie's nerves seemed to vibrate with pleasure. Some women never truly understood eroticism, not in a hundred years, nor in a thousand fucks. But naughty Miss Beatrice Weatherly was ready willing and able to put on just the show he wanted.

"Whose fault is that?" he repeated more softly.

"Mine." She shifted her position on the bed, and the fingers that had stalled began to move. The flame of desire leaped in her glittering eyes.

"Thread found again, I see."

She didn't answer, but just continued to diddle herself, fingertip circling and hips working as she bore down on the fingers inside her and squirmed her bottom against the sheet. The very goddess incarnate of rambunctious sensuality with her sleek limbs and her rioting tumble of Titian hair, she tilted her hips as if offering a better view.

Ritchie gasped silently, not sure what tempted him most, the sight of her working fingers—beating on her clitoris and sliding in and out of her puss—or the pale arch of her throat crying out for kisses. The way she wriggled about and murmured and pleasured herself made Ritchie want to tear open his trousers and his linen and beat himself off, too. His cock ached like a bar of molten lead, and as Beatrice's eyes closed, he cupped himself through his fine suiting and squeezed.

Oh Beatrice, Beatrice...

Her beautiful bottom lifted from the bedsheet as she reached for fulfillment, gifting Ritchie with a glimpse of the sumptuous curves of her bottom.

"Oh! Oh, my goodness!" Her lovely face contorting, Beatrice bounced on the bed, her fingers working furiously as she spent in front of him. Amidst the spasms, she let out a most unladylike oath, delivered in such a refined yet animal voice that Ritchie couldn't help but laugh out loud, loving her free and uninhibited way of pleasure.

"My dear Miss Weatherly, where on earth did you learn such a word as that?" he demanded as she subsided back against the mattress, hot and gasping.

"I used to be a country girl, remember," she panted, her pale hand still cupping her blazing red bush, "and stable hands and farm boys use much worse words than that." Her coral-pink mouth curved in a smile as if she were chanting those wicked words in her head.

"Well, I'm shocked, Beatrice. I thought you were a well brought up gentlewoman, and now it turns out that you spent your young womanhood in the company of rough countrymen, learning the bluest of language and the Lord alone knows what else." Unable to stay away from her a second longer, he inclined over her prone, smirking form and looked deep into her laughing green eyes. As if she were unable to prevent herself, she licked her rosy lips, the sight of it almost unmanning him.

BEATRICE QUIVERED all over at the fire in Ritchie's eyes. "Isn't it my turn to get a treat now? It's only right...I put on a show for you."

"Really? You think so, do you, Bea? That you deserve

a treat?" He was sitting beside her, twisted at an angle, his head tipped to one side as he studied her. "After all that foul profanity and lolling about with your legs open, making free with yourself without my permission." He pursed his lips for a moment as if containing a laugh.

Beatrice huffed out a breath, then arched and stretched, her limbs languid with pleasure. "Oh, la-di-da, Ritchie, you know that you liked it. And by that token, you should grant me my reward."

Ritchie continued to stare at her, his eyes assessing her body. "Very well. Choose one thing," he said crisply, smiling a challenge at her.

She didn't need time to think. "I choose that you take your clothes off. It's only fair."

His hands stilled, and he looked resigned. Why was he so reluctant to disrobe? He was handsome as the devil and his body was lithe and strong. What had he to hide?

Ritchie didn't speak, but glancing away from her, he slid to his feet and began by flinging off his waistcoat. As trousers and dress socks followed, he moved with economy and no show of bravado. It was as if his body was just a mechanism to him, physical machinery that was fit for purpose, not a work of art to be admired...as Beatrice perceived it.

At the stage of drawers and unbuttoned shirt, he paused, giving her a long, indecipherable look. Was he bashful? Surely not. But there was a hint of apprehension in the way he looked at her.

With a shrug, he peeled his shirt off over his head.

Beatrice's heart thudded hard.

Oh, he was beautiful. Sublimely formed, indeed, but that wasn't what made her gasp.

Ritchie had scars. They'd been hidden when his shirt was just hanging open, but now they were revealed and made Beatrice wince in her tender soul, and ache with sympathy.

At some time, Ritchie had been subject to fire and it had left him with a number of burns on his arms and his shoulders. Was his back also marked, Beatrice wondered, and as if he'd heard her, Ritchie turned slowly.

Astonishingly, somebody had taken a knife to him too, and he had a couple of angry red gouges across his shoulder blades, long and deep looking.

Although she wasn't aware of flinching, Ritchie's eyes narrowed as if she'd cringed from him. "I did warn you, Bea," he said softly. "Would you prefer it if I put my shirt back on?"

"Why on earth would I want you to do that? I'm not afraid of a few trifling little scars and they…they don't repulse me, if that's what you're so concerned about?"

In a long pause, Ritchie seemed to weigh her words, her demeanor, everything about her. She knew he could detect a lie in her, but she hadn't told one. Even so, his intense scrutiny made her tremble and wish for the courage to reach out and caress the marks that must have pained him so much in their creation.

"I do believe you're telling the truth." His cautious expression dissolved into a slow, familiar smile. A sultry grin that made her tremble for a different reason.

"Of course I am, you dolt! Now please stop plaguing me with half measures and get your drawers off and show me the rest!"

Ritchie exploded in a guffaw of laughter. "You really are the living end, Beatrice Weatherly, as God is my judge!" Shoulders still shaking, he moved closer to the bed, giving Beatrice a better view of the considerable disturbance behind the flies of his drawers. There was an impressive bulge that seemed to be growing by the second.

Beatrice knew he was used to women far franker than she in his amorous exploits, but now wasn't the time play the dainty miss. "Well, you've teased me long enough as it is, Mr. Ritchie, so I'd appreciate it if you'd remove your undergarment."

"Very well," he said, deftly divesting himself of it. As he flung the garment aside, his sturdy cock bounced upward, propelled by the momentum of the throw.

Ah, here was an anatomical feature that bore no scars. It was immaculate in its strange, mammalian beauty. Beatrice's fingers prickled with the urge to reach out and touch it once more, it was becoming such a friend.

As she raised her eyes from the appendage that entranced her, she met Ritchie staring at her as if he too were entranced. She almost heard a metallic clash as their gazes locked.

"Satisfied?" He slid onto the bed beside her, and Beatrice swore she could feel the heat of him before they even touched.

"Not by a long chalk," she shot back at him. "I have a feeling I should emulate a cook or a housekeeper, and test the condition of the provisions manually first."

"Is that so?" With a low laugh, he moved against her.

"It is!" But touching without permission was a contravention of the game.

"Presently," replied Ritchie, his beautiful eyes flashing, "your treat is to *look,* but not touch, Bea. I want free run of your body, without your roving hands to distract me."

Beatrice wanted to protest, but Ritchie's words and the heat in his eyes were too exciting. There was something deep and thrilling and strange about being vulnerable to him. As if he were a god, a flawed god, and she his willing sacrifice. Her skin tingled as if soft, cool flames were racing across it, and between her legs her cleft ached, her hunger for him gathering heavy and voracious. Instinctively, she reached out toward him.

"Behave yourself," he growled, and lay against her, half over her. His thick cock pressed against her hip and thigh, and one of his own thighs lay across her, the crisp tickle of his light body hair an extra stimulation. "Behave yourself," he repeated as she stirred against him, instinctively moving and pressing. "Grip the bed rail if that will help." Laying his lips against the exposed slope of her neck, he settled his hand across her aching nipples once more.

Beatrice complied, gripping the rail, but she couldn't keep still. She was a ferment of sensation, of frustration. Twisting her hips, she opened her legs and tried to press her sex closer to him.

"Beatrice, Beatrice," he breathed, lightly toying with her, moving his lips against her skin, causing a tingle of pleasure with just a simple exhalation and the dance of his fingertips.

Her body cried for him. Screamed for him. Demanded him, and the solid bar of his penis where it butted against her. She tried to rub him with her thigh, but that was unsatisfactory. She wanted to know him with her fingers and her puss.

Or perhaps my mouth?

Her eyes shot open. What a voluptuous, daring thought. Her mind briefly sorted through images of Sofia sucking enthusiastically on her beloved Ambrose's sturdy organ, and Arabella Southern making a meal of the handsome, swarthy Yuri. Yes, those ladies had appeared to be having a perfectly splendid time with their lovers' cocks in their mouths, even though there was no apparent stimulation for them.

Oh, I should so like to sample you, Ritchie.

Still clasping the rail, she twisted to look at him, and as if he'd heard her, his long lashes flicked up and he stared into her eyes from close quarters.

"What is it, Bea?" His look was narrow and knowing, and her heart thumped. How could he read her so easily, and divine her schemes.

Almost without thinking, Beatrice ran her tongue around the edges of her lips again, and against her thigh his cock leaped as if he'd read her salacious thoughts.

"Nothing…just hungry for you, Ritchie."

His mouth curved, playful and a little smug. "Indeed. Would you care to specify *how* hungry, my delicious siren?" His hips rocked and his hard flesh slid to and from against her, hot and provocative.

"*Very* hungry," she answered firmly. "I should like to savor you, Mr. Ritchie. In fact the very thought of you makes my mouth water. Really it does…" She gave him a slow look out of the corner of her eye, hoping that he found the expression seductive. "In fact if you'll allow it, I'll show you just how much."

"Really?" His smile widened.

"Really."

He didn't answer, but kissed her very hard, his tongue pushing into her mouth as if to subdue *her* naughty tongue. Or perhaps suggest another possession, somewhat similar but more comprehensive. Beatrice accepted the intrusion, hoping it would confirm her intention to taste him.

Still kissing her, and imposing his strong body over hers, Ritchie reached above her head and unwound her fingers from the rail, as if freeing a bond. Instantly, Beatrice grabbed for him, clasping at his back and muscular flank, arching her torso against him.

After a long breathless grapple against each other, Ritchie put her face from his and looked into her eyes, his face alight with mischief. "So, Miss Weatherly, you want to *savor* me, do you?" This time it was his turn to run his tongue around the firm lines of his lips, and he did it so evocatively that between her legs, Beatrice's flesh rippled.

"Yes," she whispered, sounding less sure than she would have liked. She was no experienced Sofia or Arabella, well schooled in giving pleasure with her tongue.

Ritchie stroked her face. "Don't worry, Bea, you're a most adaptable young woman and an astonishingly quick learner. I haven't the slightest doubt in the world that to be *savored* by you will be truly sublime."

Beatrice pulled away from him and sat up, blushingly aware of the way the action presented her naked breasts to him. Sitting around like this in her birthday suit with an equally unclothed man stretched out beside her was a novel experience, and it reminded her how much of an ingenue she still was, despite having posed naked for photographs.

"I hope you're right, Ritchie," she answered simply, placing her hand on his thigh and letting it rest lightly there, an inch or two from his fine, upstanding cock. "Because I really don't have a clue what to do."

"Use your instincts, Bea." Ritchie's voice was soft and infinitely kind, which seemed incongruous in this erotic situation, and yet very much him. "Anything you do to me is beautiful." Placing his fingers over hers, he squeezed encouragement.

Where to begin?

Beatrice gazed at Ritchie's cock. A man's sexual organ was a strange thing really, but she found it intriguing. Well, she found Ritchie's intriguing, and with little in the way of comparison, she deemed him an excellent specimen, neither too small nor too large, perfectly in proportion with his general dimensions. The proper size, and both elegant and primitive.

Sweeping the thick curtain of her unbound red hair out of the way with one hand, she bent down and lowered her mouth toward him.

RITCHIE WANTED to shout, to whoop, to cheer. He wanted to reach out, cradle Beatrice's head, his fingers plunged into the sublime tresses of her extraordinary hair, and guide her tender mouth toward his cock. He wanted to jerk his hips upward and push into her mouth, find bliss in its heat and wetness, then thrust and thrust until he spent on her tongue.

But instead, he lay quiescent, showing nothing of his turmoil of pounding lust, not even clenching the bedsheets for fear he alarm or disquiet her.

He nearly moaned aloud though, feeling her breath upon his glans. Knowing she couldn't see his face for the brilliant swath of her lush hair, he bit down hard on his lower lip, battling for self-control.

When her tongue touched the very tip of him, he had to shut his eyes tight and suppress a welling tear of tense emotion.

"Ooh, salty," she whispered, her velvety lips barely brushing him yet making every last inch of his body go rigid, and the inches that were rigid already harden into heavy, aching iron. He tasted salt himself in the blood from his bitten lip.

Adjusting her position, she surveyed him this way and that, from the closest of quarters. As she did so, the cape of her Titian waves slid over her shoulders and her back, the soft ends sliding like silk along his belly and his thighs.

Forward she went again, her dainty tongue extending to caress him. Tentative, yet clearly a natural sensualist of phenomenal intuition, she flicked and flirted around the crown of his cock, exploring and tantalizing him, then parted her lips and let the swollen tip enter her mouth.

So warm, so wet, she engulfed him, still playing his flesh with her tongue as she sucked and bobbed.

He couldn't hide his pleasure now, even though for a moment, he clawed at the sheets, clinging to a last scrap of self-control. Then, with a darting thrust of her furled tongue, she sought the tender groove beneath his glans and he had to cry out loud. Questioning, she glanced up at him, her face gracious and beautiful, even with her mouth stretched around him, but when she saw him nod at her, she returned to her task.

Ritchie plunged his hands into her thick fall of hair, guiding her, holding her, yet trying not to control or constrain her. His mind was spinning as he teetered on the brink of spending long and hard.

But he mustn't do that. He shouldn't. Not to a young woman so recently a virgin, eager though she was. The temptation was huge, but he managed to resist and claw back the last vestiges of his reserve.

"Beatrice…Beatrice…enough!" he gasped, gently nudging her away from his aching cock.

Rising, she flung back her hair again, her expression perplexed. "What's amiss? Was I doing it wrong? You *seemed* to be enjoying yourself." She rocked away from him, pursing her lips and then running her tongue over them, as if still tasting him. Ritchie almost exploded there and then, it excited him so.

"I *was* enjoying it, Bea… I was enjoying it so much I

can barely describe…too much…" Hauling himself up, he reached out and cradled her cheek, his thumb stroking lightly over her moist lips. "But I didn't want to take my pleasure selfishly… I'd rather share it with you, my sweet, not come in your mouth without pleasuring you."

Beatrice smiled, slow and creamy, like a contented little cat, her lips curving beneath the pad of his thumb. "You really shouldn't worry, Ritchie. You're always far more than generous in that regard. The deficit still lies with me, by a considerable margin."

Ritchie laughed. What a spectacular and tantalizing woman she was. How uniquely she saw things. His cock throbbed as she regarded him steadily, her green eyes twinkling.

"I'm not keeping score, Miss Weatherly, and neither should you be." He bobbed forward and kissed her on the lips, his mouth almost brushing his own thumb. "At the moment, I think we should forget all checks and tallies and simply fuck each other."

RITCHIE'S HAPPY LAUGH was like a warm breeze aross Beatrice's face, and he kissed her until she was breathless, until she couldn't think of anything but having him inside her. Her hands traveled over his body as their lips and tongues grappled, and this time he seemed to have no qualms about letting her explore the marks of his scars with her fingertips. Even as Ritchie's hand slipped between her legs and found her ready again, a part of her mind was wondering what had happened to him and what or who had hurt him.

But she knew now was not the time to ask. And as he fondled her clitoris, the questions dissolved like smoke.

Excitement gathered beneath his fingertip, now familiar, but ever new and fresh. She could just have let him diddle her to her peak again. It would have been easy and sweet and without effort. But that wasn't quite what she wanted.

"Please, Ritchie," she gasped as they broke apart, even while he was still touching her. "Please, Ritchie, I want you inside me."

Ritchie muttered an oath in response, but he was laughing, smiling. "And you shall have me, beautiful Bea. Indeed you shall." He kissed her again, hard, and carried on stimulating her. Sensation tilted on the edge, like a vessel filled to the brim, almost welling.

Beatrice pulled back. "No! With you! I want us to spend together." She rolled onto her back, spreading her legs.

"A delicious offer, Bea, but let's try it another way." He reached for her shoulder, and drew her up again, then reclined back on the mattress himself. "You can plow me instead."

Beatrice blinked.

Oh! He wants me to ride him!

Glancing at his cock, where it reared up as hard and eager as it had been when she'd mouthed him, she tried to imagine that sturdy engine pushing up into her. Her puss quivered in a long silky ripple, but whether in anticipation or apprehension, she couldn't tell.

"Don't worry, sweetheart." He reached for her hand and squeezed it. "You'll be in charge…you'll have control…the upper hand."

"Indeed," she murmured, still eyeing his cock.

"But first we need to clothe this monster." He gave himself a cheerful shake, which made Beatrice want to giggle, both at the way he swayed and the fact that even a man such as Ritchie seemed prone to an inflated masculine pride in his own anatomy. Although in his case, she deemed it well justified. "You'll find a tin of French Letters in the drawer of the cabinet beside the bed."

Beatrice quickly found the prophylactics, and prized one out. It was slippery and tricky and seemed determined to wiggle in her hand, and yet Ritchie, with his hands now behind his blond head and a smug look on his handsome face, seemed equally determined that she should do the honors.

She tried. And tried. But the wretched thing would not behave, and Ritchie's splendid cock was a terrible distraction. Afraid of hurting him, Beatrice fumbled even more.

Eventually, she gave up the battle. "Look here, I'm a beginner at all this, remember." She tossed the rubber sheath onto Ritchie's bare belly. "I think you'd better deal with this device or we'll both die of frustration."

"You're probably right," murmured Ritchie, catching up the troublesome rubber sheath and in a matter of moments, deftly enrobing himself. Beatrice frowned. He'd made it look laughably simple.

"I'm sure I'd get better with practice." She reached out, touched a fingertip to his shaft in its fine protective coat and smiled inside as Ritchie gasped, baring his teeth. "But I'm afraid that requires you to be on hand."

Ritchie clasped her wrist, easing her hand from him, his finger resting against the spot where her pulse thudded. "I'll have a box of the finest imported West Indies bananas delivered to you, and you can hone your skills with those." He dropped a momentary wink. "They're rather tasty too, I think you'll find."

Not as tasty as you, no matter how fine and costly an import.

She winked back at him and he laughed, as if he'd heard the thought as clear as day.

"Now…how the dickens do we do this?" Beatrice

peered at Ritchie's member, no less imposing for being sheathed, and pointing up at a fierce, rampant angle.

"You'll have to kneel over me…position me against your puss…and then bear down."

"But…um…you're pointing up too much." She eyed his rigid cock dubiously.

"Don't worry…you can manhandle me a bit…it won't break." He squeezed her hand encouragingly where he still held it.

What followed was quite a performance, and Beatrice was convinced that her role in it was somewhat less than graceful. But Ritchie didn't seem to mind her maneuvering and crouching and huffing and, yes, manhandling him. In fact his eyes blazed bluer with hunger at the sight of her, and with his strong hands at her waist, he helped her find the perfect pose.

"That's it, my darling. Ease down…ease down," he urged huskily, still guiding her.

Her thighs burning with gathered tension, Beatrice obliged him.

Down she slid, as Ritchie reared up, holding her firm. His cock pushed upward, in, in, into her, filling her up, possessing her body, almost too much.

"Ooh," she gasped. "I…I'm not sure…"

The sensation was stunning. It took her breath. Even from his supine position, Ritchie still seemed to master her. His penetration encompassed more than just her sex. It was as if his spirit were rising up into her also, and flowing from his cock to touch her heart, her mind, her soul.

"Breathe, Bea, breathe," he urged. "Relax…let me in… let us be one."

His words were rough yet strangely sweet, like spiced

honey melting her fears and doubts. As he whispered "Relax" again, her body yielded, admitting him further.

With a shuddering sigh, she settled down upon his pelvis.

"I...I..."

The sensations rendered her speechless. Feeling his cock inside her, lodged so deep, was more dazzling even than when he'd lain on top of her and possessed her. The might of his flesh imposed itself totally on her senses. But even if her mind wouldn't work, her body knew what to do. She squeezed down on him, caressing his flesh from within.

Ritchie let out low ragged sound, halfway between a groan and a laugh. His face contorted in a grimace, his eyes fluttering closed. "Oh yes, my dearest Beatrice... oh yes..." Rearing up from the pillows, he slung an arm around her and hugged her where she sat, astride his hips, perched on the prow of his sex.

Their bodies haphazardly aligned yet profoundly joined, they rocked and wriggled against each other, Beatrice's eyes almost popping at the impact of each movement. Every time Ritchie adjusted his hold, or bucked upward with his hips, the action dragged tellingly, tugging at her clitoris from within her own body and inducing ripples and flutters of intense delight. Flinging an arm around his neck, she embraced him, her fingertips digging into scars and pristine skin alike as exquisite feelings racked her.

His chest heaving with hard gasps, Ritchie held her tight for a moment with one arm whilst his free hand cast around behind him to heap the bolster and the pillows at his back. Then he rested against them, smiling back at her from his position of greater comfort.

"You're remarkable, Bea," he breathed, still gasping,

his face flushed, eyes alight as he slid his hands back to her waist and held her firm, hard, down on his cock. "A pearl beyond price…I never realized how precious, even when I desired you from your image."

Beatrice didn't know what to say. When he spoke like that, it touched too closely on her secret, hidden, never-to-be-voiced desires. The longing she nurtured to herself because she couldn't reveal it to Ritchie, not ever. Closing her eyes, she tipped her head back, arched her body and bore down on him, squeezing his rigid flesh again with her inner muscles. If she couldn't tell him that she loved him, she could at least pleasure him to the best of her ability. And make their limited time together as supreme as she was able.

"Oh God…oh God in heaven," Ritchie snarled, arching just as she did, and rolling his head on his shoulders. "You feel too good…too wonderful…I'm too close…" He hauled in a great breath. "Stay still a moment, dearest… very still. I don't want to spend too soon and not grant you pleasure first."

I don't care! I don't care!

Her pleasure would come any instant whether or not Ritchie spent. She was balanced on the finest of hair triggers. His care for her pushed her closer and closer.

But she stayed still. Because he wanted her to.

"Yes, dear, yes," he breathed. One hand on her waist held her steady, while the other, with a deft twist of the wrist, slid down between their bodies to find her clitoris.

How good to her he was. How giving.

Beatrice gasped and whimpered as he found the very focus of her pleasure, flicking and stroking her bud with breathtaking accuracy. How focused and clever he was, considering that he too was probably only a heartbeat from his crisis.

Holding on to his shoulders, she tossed her head, her hair flying around both of them as the intense, gathering sensations pooled in her belly and circled and spiraled ever inward toward the juncture of his fingertip and her aching clitoris.

It was too much, too sublime, she could hold back no longer. Her body moved of its own volition and with a groan like a wild animal, she bore down, pressing on him, and on his strong, igniting finger.

Great, contracting pulsations beat through her. Her body grabbed at him, rippled around him, drew his own pleasure from him while her mind went white and blank, finding peace in the ferment.

As she spent and spent, barely conscious, she was still aware of every tiny physical thing passing between them.

The upwards buck of his hips, the harsh cry of his completion, the scent of his sweat. Her eyes fluttered open, and she saw Ritchie's eyes were closed. His face was almost serene, even though his teeth were clenched. His blond hair was tousled and his skin gleamed with a film of perspiration and an inner glow as if he were a saint in an icon.

He was the most beautiful sight she'd ever seen…and from the corner of his eye she could swear a single teardrop trickled.

"Oh my dearest Bea," he gasped again, then his head pitched forward and he collapsed against her, hugging her almost awkwardly against him, just as she slumped nerveless against his shoulder.

LATER, they fucked again, refreshed by a little more supper and champagne. This time, Beatrice flung herself on her back and Ritchie raised his sandy brows at her, clearly more than happy to indulge her choice of position. With a laugh, he plunged forward, between her legs.

Beatrice laughed back at him and clung to him furiously, pounding her hips at his with every bit as much vigor as he thrust into her, newly energized by deep erotic hunger.

We're a match.

The thought came again as they bounced and rocked against each other, pleasure gathering around their joined vitals.

We're a balanced pair. One completing the other. Better together than as separate individuals.

If only they could stay that way. Regret wound its way through the bright raiment of their pleasure, but Beatrice kept it safely to herself.

It surfaced again though, keen and quiet, when she and Ritchie were lying together, naked, warm and finally sated. Would he sleep here with her? He'd said he never did that, not with any woman. But he seemed so relaxed... Perhaps he'd make an exception?

No sooner had the fancy materialized than it was shattered. In a quick, light movement, Ritchie sat up, lifted the sheet and slid from the bed to cast about the room, finding and donning his clothing.

"Can't we stay and sleep awhile?"

She hadn't meant to ask. To seem like a clinging nuisance was the last thing she wanted. What *he* wanted was a convenient mistress for a month, good value for his outlay, not some miss with designs on snaring more of him.

Ritchie gave her a strange look. Perplexed, a little sad, as if he regretted his own strictures yet wasn't prepared to bend them.

"No, Beatrice, we can't," he said in a flattish voice.

"Well, at least I can't." Already putting studs in his shirt, he came and sat beside her on the bed. Was it worth flinging her naked form against him and drawing him back to her? Surely he'd not be able to resist? But the fact that he *might* was an unpleasant prospect.

"Why don't you stay, Bea," he said more gently. "I'll send a note around for Polly to come and assist you in the morning. I'm sure you'll sleep well. The bed is comfortable."

There was a smile on his lips, but his eyes were wistful, almost melancholy.

What is it, Ritchie? What's hurt you so much that you just can't allow yourself more? That you can't...can't trust me?

But she didn't voice the question.

"No, it's all right. I'm used to Cook's breakfasts, average as they are, and I'll probably sleep better in my own bed." Sliding from beneath the sheets, she followed Ritchie out of their shell of intimacy and began gathering her own scattered clothing.

But all the time, her heart mourned for what was lost. As usual, she'd hoped for far too much.

CHAPTER TWENTY-FIVE

Home Truths

BUT IN THE DAYS that followed, it was difficult not to want too much. Especially as Beatrice didn't see Ritchie as frequently as she would have liked, which made their shared trysts ever more precious.

Ritchie was addictive to her. Like opium, or some other exotic drug. The more he touched her, the more she wanted to be touched. The more they came to know each other's bodies, the more Beatrice craved to know his mind. When they weren't in bed, she pounced on any stray morsel of his background she could discover.

Over dinners and lunches at Belanger's and other discreet establishments, they discussed politics, economics and books, sometimes agreeing and sometimes quite at odds. At private art exhibits, they found a shared love of the paintings of Lord Leighton and Mr. Alma-Tadema. Lying in bed, between sweaty acts of lovemaking, they discussed the country, riding and horses, and walking. Ritchie promised her a bicycle when she expressed an interest in mastering the art of cycling.

Nevertheless, in many aspects, he still eluded her. She could sense that behind his confident, urbane, unashamedly pleasure loving mask, there lurked some plangent, almost agonizing sorrow. He let slip hints of it when she revealed some of the sadder aspects of her own past: the death of her parents, and the loss of Westerlynne where they'd been so happy as a family.

Toward the end of an afternoon of delicious perversity, wherein games with silk scarves were played, a few playful spanks were levied across her buttocks and a good deal of rocking and writhing and gasping against each other was enjoyed, Beatrice found herself dozing, while Ritchie "kept watch," as she liked to call it. He simply would not allow himself to sleep after their pleasure, but seemed to find contentment in watching her nod off and snooze.

Drifting at the edge of consciousness, she heard Ritchie's words as if they came from across a great chasm, even though he was within touching distance, his back propped up against the pillows.

"Why have you never married, Beatrice? Have you never loved?" Her eyes snapped open, sleep fast fleeing. "Surely a woman as exquisite as you must have had offers?" She turned to him, looking up. His expression was more guarded than she'd ever seen it.

Why did he ask these questions? He surely knew almost as much as it were possible to know about her. In the days and weeks of their liaison, she'd become increasingly suspicious that much of her life was an open book to him, due to talk that passed between Polly and Jamie Brownlow, and perhaps even through the conduit of Charlie, too. Those three were most definitely up to something. Something she could scarcely not condone, given her own sybaritic behavior with Ritchie.

"I was engaged once, but the young man died in a sailing accident," she admitted, almost sure that he already knew all about Tommy. "I was very fond of him."

But if he knew about Tommy, how much was he aware of her dealings with Eustace?

Had Polly or Charlie said anything? She'd never even told those two, her closest, the entire story and she'd requested they never speak of him to others. It was preferable that people believed she'd made headstrong choices rather than admit to them she'd been duped like a fool.

But, facing facts, Charlie was notoriously indiscreet, and couldn't keep a secret to save his life. Polly was fiercely loyal, but she hated Eustace with a passion. She might disclose his identity in the name of retribution.

There was always Sofia, too. Beatrice had never told her daring friend who the photographer was, but it was common knowledge Eustace had briefly courted her, so the pieces could easily be put together.

Yes, it was more than likely that Ritchie suspected Eustace as the man who'd ruined her reputation, but, unlikely as it seemed, he'd never pressed her on the origins of the cabinet cards. Was he simply biding his time? Coolly planning some kind of retribution? She feared as much. Her sincerest wish was that he'd never pursue the matter, but he was strong willed and she feared some drastic response. Eustace had drugged and tricked her, then ended their relationship almost immediately. He was a low cad, but she still couldn't bring herself to wish real harm to him. Especially as Eustace's selfish ways had indirectly brought Edmund Ellsworth Ritchie into her life.

But she doubted that her lover would see it that way.

"I'm sorry, do you prefer not to speak of him? Perhaps it's better not to stir up unhappy memories."

Confused, Beatrice frowned, then suddenly realized she must have been silent for several moments, brooding on Eustace and what Ritchie may or may not know of him.

"No, please, there's no need to worry. It doesn't hurt to think of Tommy now. I loved him, and I missed him for a long time after his death, but he would have been the last person to want me to live my life in melancholy, pining for him. He was good and kind that way, a sweet and generous man."

"He sounds worthy of you." The words were oddly neutral, almost studiously so, and his handsome face was unreadable.

"I'm not quite sure how worthy I was of him though." A pang of guilt shot through her. If she'd agreed to marriage sooner, instead of preferring to wait, she and Tommy might have wed, and he might not have gone out on the boat that day. "I was a bit flighty. I behaved like a silly girl and asked if we could wait a while before marrying. Life might have been quite different if we'd gone to the altar sooner."

Beatrice shuddered. Deep solemnity had settled over them, and yet it seemed crass to try and break the mood with an amusing remark. Her guilt deepened.

If Tommy was alive, I would never have met you, Ritchie. Well, not in the way we are now.

Those dark blue eyes sharpened, as if he'd read the thought, but he said nothing.

"And what about you?" she said on an impulse, setting her hand on his arm and letting out the query she'd been battling to suppress. "I know you've been married, even though you never speak of it. You must have loved, and loved deeply…more than once."

Shutters came down again. Ritchie's mobile, beautiful face became a mask, his eyes almost blank. Beatrice cringed at the mistake she'd made, even though it was a question she had as much right to ask as he did. Or maybe the money, which she quite forgot these days, denied her those particular rights over him?

The muscles in his arm were rigid, hard as cured wood,

but Beatrice didn't retreat from him. If only he'd let her ease his pain.

Then, after an aching silence, he seemed to relax, and in a soft voice said, "Yes, Bea, I loved." He dragged in a breath. "I loved someone good and kind too…and I'm damn sure I certainly wasn't worthy."

"But—" she began, yearning to tell him he was good and kind himself and more than worthy of the love of any woman. Most of all her.

"No…remember what your Tommy would say. No dwelling on the past. We should enjoy the present." He rolled toward her, his mouth seeking hers, and his hand roving with purpose down her body. "I find that I want you again, Beatrice my angel, and it's really rather urgent. Do you think you could find it in yourself to want me too?"

In their quiet moments of reflection, her body had calmed and cooled, but as he began to stroke her between her legs, she did indeed find that she wanted him. Wanted him urgently in the very place he was touching.

"A GENTLEMAN TO SEE YOU," said Simon the new footman a few days later.

Beatrice's heart leaped. Was it Ritchie? It must be Ritchie, back somewhat early from another of his trips to the North, to inspect a mine this time. What other gentleman would be visiting her, the infamous Siren of South Mulberry Street, a woman of dubious reputation to begin with, but now the avowed mistress of a rich and notorious man.

But then, why didn't Simon *say* it was Mr. Ritchie? And why was he holding out a card on his little silver tray?

A shudder of disquiet rippled through her, and she

tossed aside the latest novel she'd been attempting to read, with scant consideration for its binding. As it hit the upholstered chaise, she had a sudden, horrible premonition who the waiting gentleman might be—another certain someone who didn't care to take no for an answer. Her worst fears were confirmed by the small rectangle of white card.

Eustace Lloyd Esq.

Her first overpowering instinct was to instruct Simon that she was not at home to Mr. Lloyd, and that she would never be at home to Mr. Lloyd. But that was the coward's way out, and Eustace being Eustace, he might well keep on turning up at her door until she relented. Better to get this awkward and inevitable interview over now, and put the whole sorry business of her former, if unofficial, fiancé behind her.

Even if she and Ritchie went entirely separate ways once their month was over, she would never, ever in a thousand years take up with Eustace Lloyd again.

"Show him up, please, Simon," she said, already mangling the *carte de visite* between her fingers.

Beatrice sprang to her feet, not quite sure how to receive her visitor. Her nerves were jangling, and not is the pleasant, delicious way they did in anticipation of seeing Ritchie. Instead, it was like the sensation of dragging fingernails along the baize of a billiard table, or the sort of small chalkboard a child might use for its letters. The little hairs at the back of her neck stood to attention, and she took up station by the window, hand on the sideboard that stood beside it, to steady herself. For once, she was glad of her corset to keep her back straight and true.

The door swung open, and Simon ushered in Eustace.

"Mr. Lloyd, miss."

I know...unfortunately, I know.

"Thank you, Simon, that will be all."

"No, you…bring some brandy, will you? And look sharp."

Simon's eyebrows shot up at Eustace's order, but Beatrice nodded.

"What can I do for you, Eustace? Other than supply you with strong spirits at eleven o'clock in the morning?" she enquired far more tartly than she'd intended. She could have slapped herself for letting him irk her so soon.

Eustace gave her a slow, smug look that made the back of her neck prickle. He seemed to know something that she didn't and he was a man who enjoyed having the upper hand. His slippery but vaguely menacing expression spoiled what otherwise were his considerable good looks.

While he kept her waiting—for no more than a few seconds but feeling like an age—she studied him, her own eyes narrow.

In the strictest of terms, brown-haired Eustace was handsomer than Edmund Ellsworth Ritchie, and he was also somewhat younger. But his pretty looks were soft somehow, less burnished, lacking the character and gravitas that a few lines and laughter wrinkles imbued. He was also putting weight on, she saw, and his fashionable suit was snug in a way that wasn't quite as becoming to him as he obviously thought it was.

Which was fact that gave Beatrice some satisfaction, and allowed her to smile at him pleasantly.

"Eustace?" she prompted, as he continued to stare at her.

"Well, my dear Bea, I've come to suggest that you reconsider your reply to my recent offer." Flinging himself down in an armchair, he stuck out his legs and crossed them at the ankle. "I think you and I could do pretty well together, despite the obvious disadvantages. If you were to live quietly and not be seen out too much in society, I don't see that your tarnished reputation should be a difficulty."

Beatrice's jaw dropped. She didn't know where to begin, or how to count the ways she was insulted and annoyed by him. Breathing steadily to remain calm, she sat down in a chair facing Eustace's smilingly confident form. Marshalling her thoughts, she opened her mouth to answer him, but just then there was a knock and Simon entered with the brandy.

"Will there be anything further, miss?" he asked politely, on having set the decanter and glass at Eustace's elbow. His eyes narrowed a little in her guest's direction, as if indicating he was ready to eject him.

"No, that will be all, thank you, Simon." When the thoughtful young man was gone, she turned to her erstwhile sweetheart, still unsure what she was about to say.

"Well, what do you think, Bea. You'll not get another proposal now, will you?"

Beatrice leaped up and paced.

"Eustace," she said at last, rounding on him, "I'm sure, or at least I hope, that you really don't realize quite how you've insulted me with your offer. Always supposing I actually wanted to get married, I'm afraid that you're probably the last man on earth that I would choose." She paused, quelling her intense desire to growl, and ignoring the angry thud of her heart. "I'd hoped that we could be amicably parted, and agree not to refer to what is past, but your sheer effrontery forces me to impart a few home truths."

She spun on her heel, snatched up a glass from the tray, and splashed a little brandy in it. She was already a fallen woman in his eyes, so what difference did it make being a toper too.

"If you recall," she went on, brandy hot on her tongue, "you were the one who damaged my reputation in the first place. Admittedly I was foolish to pose for those photographs, but I thought we were sweethearts, and that I could trust you, and that I was helping you study classical composition. Little did I realize that before long my image would be for sale all up and down Holywell Street…and that you'd have thrown me over as your sweetheart for the very scandal *you'd* inflicted on me."

She knew there was another reason, too. He'd thought she had money, and when he'd discovered she was impoverished, she wasn't much use to him. In fact she'd presented a hindrance if he were to pursue young women more advantageously placed.

"But the plates were stolen," Eustace protested, although with little assertion. "That wasn't my fault…and I was prepared to overlook the disgrace. It was just Mother who couldn't set it aside, and she's so delicate that a scandal would make her ill."

Mrs. Lloyd had the constitution of an ox, and many of that beast's physical characteristics, but Beatrice held her tongue on the matter. The situation was unpleasant enough as it was, without her worsening it with childish insults.

She tossed down a mouthful of brandy, barely tasting it this time. "So why then has she all of a sudden decided that I'm acceptable?"

"She wants me to be happy and she accepts my fondness for you." Eustace seemed calm but he poured himself more brandy.

Your mother doesn't want anybody to be happy, Eustace. Least of all you.

In a flash of insight, Beatrice realized that his mother's unloving nature probably had a lot to do with Eustace's behavior and the course of his actions. A pang of sympathy for him twined with her crossness. It wasn't his fault his family were so horrible. She decided that conciliation was a better course than furious hostility.

"Dear Eustace, I am flattered by your…um…proposal. But we really aren't suited. I sincerely feel that. And I'm certain that you'll soon find someone with whom you'll be far happier." It sounded weak, but even if the business with the photographs had never occurred, she couldn't accept this pale shadow of a man when she'd already basked in the sun. She opened her mouth, attempting to frame some tactful mention of another "friend," when Eustace set his glass down with a clatter.

"That bastard Ritchie will never marry you, if that's what you're thinking! You won't get anything more than a bit of cash, a few trinkets and the occasional seeing-to from him, you silly girl."

Beatrice spun away from him, unable to bear the ugliness in his eyes. To think she'd once been fond of this man.

But it was his words that had rocked her. Despite the fact that she was now going to refute it utterly, every fiber of her being longed to be Ritchie's. To be his wife, so they could spend the rest of their days together. She'd tried to deny the fact to herself, but now Eustace had compelled her to accept it. For which she found her anger blowing a storm with him.

"Mr. Ritchie is a friend and he's been very kind to both me and Charlie. He's helped us out of our temporary financial difficulties."

"Edmund Ellsworth Ritchie is a whoremonger and a despicable vindictive cur." Eustace's lip curled nastily.

"He might be taking his revenge on me now on your behalf, Bea. But that's only because it amuses him. Mark my words, when he gets fed up of fucking you and he's ready to move on, he'll toss you aside like the lowest trollop in Whitechapel!"

Beatrice almost teetered on her heels, but managed to hide it. What had Ritchie been doing? How had he harmed Eustace? As she'd deduced, her lover obviously did know that Eustace was behind the photographs and, inevitably, he'd taken action somehow to "avenge" her.

"Don't be absurd. Ritchie is friend. I can't imagine why you think he's harmed you in any way. He isn't that kind of man."

But that was a lie.

She'd seen the murderous look in Ritchie's eyes when that man had looked at her salaciously outside Belanger's. Her lover was fiery and territorial, and even if it were only a temporary arrangement, she was his possession, or as good as.

"You've no idea what kind of man he is, Bea dearest. He's maneuvered me out of a dozen lucrative deals in the markets in this last week alone. Caused doors to be closed to me at certain clubs. Even rooked me out of a racehorse I had my eye on."

Beatrice's anger surged. And not solely in Eustace's direction. What was Ritchie thinking of? Eustace was a pathetic creature, she saw that now. And just because he believed he was some kind of lord of the London society jungle, Ritchie still had no business crushing lesser beasts under his heel. Especially not on her behalf. If he had done what Eustace claimed, she'd have serious words with him next time she saw him. But for now, she had to deal with the lesser beast.

"Ritchie is a shrewd businessman. I'm sure it's just a

coincidence that he's pipped you to the post on certain deals. I can't imagine in a million years that he'd try and do you down simply on account of...of his friendship with me. That's just absurd."

"Friendship? Don't make me laugh...the man's out to ruin me purely because I happened to see his mistress naked before he ever did. The man's a blackguard."

"No, he isn't! He's tender and considerate! And generous..."

And he was. Generous in goods and gifts, but more generous in spirit and emotion. Despite the fact he'd bought her, Ritchie had treated her like a queen, and barely asked for anything in return for his great bounty; certainly nothing that she wouldn't have given to him gladly.

"Ha! So generous and tender and considerate that he's got a wife he claims is insane locked up in a lunatic asylum, just because he grew tired of her!"

Eustace's face twisted in an ugly sneer, but Beatrice barely saw it. Dark splashes formed before her eyes, and she felt she might swoon, but for a supreme effort of control she managed to exert.

"Yes," her taunter went on, "that's why he'll never marry you, you silly bitch, even if he ever wanted to. He can't marry any woman because he's got a wife already!"

AFTERWARD, Beatrice could not have told anyone precisely how she concluded her interview with Eustace. But she must have managed it somehow, and completely without succumbing to a fit of the vapors. She found herself still upright when he'd gone, and no Polly or other servant hovering over her, trying to revive her.

She just felt cold. And a little numb. But also angry.

It wasn't even a surprise to her, when she thought about

it, to discover Ritchie was married. Some of Eustace's tale was no doubt perfectly true, but she hoped in her heart that a larger portion of it was exaggerated.

Ritchie just wasn't the kind of man to lock up a sane woman simply because she bored him. But then again, he was ruthless in the pursuit of what he wanted. The tales told at the Ladies' Sewing Circle were only the tip of a vast iceberg of his single-mindedness and determination, and the way he'd snared her certainly bore witness to it. As did his apparent pursuit of retribution on her behalf.

Eustace was quite unprincipled, and she'd wished ill fortune on him herself on plenty of occasions, but she knew that if it came to it, she wouldn't truly want anything terrible to befall him. Wanting his downfall wasn't a Christian attitude and despite admitting she was a sinner in any number of ways—especially lately—she still tried to cling on to a belief in charity.

Oh Ritchie, why do you have to be so extreme in every possible way?

Extreme in passion. Extreme in revenge on her behalf. Extreme in the way he'd bewitched her and compelled her to love him.

It was a measure of how besotted she'd become with him that her reaction to Eustace's visit had been so... so much *less* than extreme. She'd barely seen the man, except from a considerable distance at a public exhibition, since the afternoon of the photographs. She should *really* have been more flustered on seeing him again, or perhaps flown at him and attempted to box his ears. But in truth his presence barely seemed to have touched her.

It was Ritchie, with his evasions and omissions, his outrageous acts and, yes perhaps, even his matrimonial heartache that consumed her every thought. She had to have everything out with him. Bring into the open all the things he was concealing from her, and those that she was concealing from him.

Only then was there a chance they could satisfactorily continue their liaison.

And continue it to the very last moment of the very last hour of the very last day…because she couldn't deny herself even a second of the time she had left with the man she loved.

BACK AT HIS LONDON ROOMS, Eustace Lloyd hurled a glass against the wall. The brandy he'd had in South Mulberry Street had barely affected him, and now, rejected and furious, he needed more.

"Bitch," he growled, ignoring the splinters and the stain on the wallpaper and snatching up another tumbler which he filled, almost to the brim.

How could she still care for Ritchie, knowing what she now knew?

Eustace tossed more brandy down his throat, barely tasting it. Instead of thanking him and then warming to his overtures, Beatrice had rejected him. He'd seen the shock in her eyes, and a flare of anger, but instead of directing it at Ritchie, she'd turned it on the man she should be showering with gratitude.

It was intolerable. His innards burned in a way that had nothing to do with alcohol.

He hadn't bargained for the effect Beatrice had wielded over him, facing her in the flesh again after a little time apart.

She was more beautiful than ever. Glowing. Ripe. More erotic even in her expensive but sober gown than she'd been lying naked on a chaise longue while he'd photographed her.

Fucking. That was what had changed her. Transformed

her from a beautiful but naive and trusting young woman into a goddess. Confident and sensual, she was radiant with experience and a knowledge of passion. And the fact that his own shortsightedness had denied him the pleasure of her seared him like vitriol.

Damn you, Beatrice. Damn you.

He had to have her now, more than ever, but if he couldn't he'd spoil her pleasure with her lover and split the two of them.

It was time to put his plan into action. Time to remind Edmund Ellsworth Ritchie of his responsibilities…and introduce the lawfully wedded Mrs. Ritchie to her husband's whore.

CHAPTER TWENTY-SIX

The Lion in his Den

EVEN THOUGH IT had been difficult until now to winkle information about Edmund Ellsworth Ritchie out of his faithful man, Jamie Brownlow, Beatrice supposed her ferocity had finally done the trick.

She'd marched into the study he was using, and found the man in question and her brother poring over the document-covered desk. Carefully setting aside the fact that the two of them were unsuitably close to each other, and that Jamie's hand on Charlie's shoulder looked suspiciously affectionate, Beatrice had demanded to know Ritchie's whereabouts and an approximate time of return.

"I believe Mr. Ritchie will be home this afternoon, Miss Beatrice. He usually sends a telegram if his plans are likely to change, but as yet, I haven't received one, so I assume all has proceeded as he anticipated."

"Excellent, then I'll visit him this afternoon. Could you oblige me with his address?"

The handsome Jamie looked troubled, then surprisingly, seemed to glance to Charlie for an opinion. Charlie shrugged and gave a little grin. "Better tell her, old chap. She'll find out anyway, if she wants to. Bea has a way of wheedling out whatever information she requires."

"Thank you, Charlie. So, Mr. Brownlow, where does

your employer actually live? Despite the fact that he and I are intimate, he hasn't actually told me."

Charlie looked a bit pink, and Jamie looked even more uncomfortable, but after a moment's hesitation, he yielded up an address.

"Oh, for heaven's sake! The impossible weasel! He only lives a couple of streets away!"

Beatrice simmered, and was still simmering at two o'clock when she set out from South Mulberry Street in her walking jacket, and with her hat set at a determined angle. For more than a fortnight she'd been trysting with Ritchie at Belanger's and other neutral locations, while the wretched man only lived around the corner.

So much he was keeping from her. So many secrets.

Of course, she reminded herself for the hundredth time that he *owed* her no revelations. She was his mistress, and a temporary one at that. She had no rights over him, and could entertain no expectations beyond their arrangement.

And yet part of her knew deep inside that it was more than that.

Are you keeping me at a distance because you *want more, too? Because you care more than you should? Because your heart is engaged, just as mine is, and this liaison has become more than simply a confluence of our libidos and my debts?*

She strode out on the pavement, a woman alone, so far beyond respectable convention now that she didn't think twice about walking out unaccompanied. Jamie Brownlow had suggested he escort her to Ritchie's house, but she'd squashed his offer in no uncertain terms.

Charlie had been beetroot-red in the face when his sister had refused accompaniment and announced that she would probably end up either boxing Ritchie's ears or requesting him to fuck her until she couldn't see straight.

Because yes, despite it all, her body still yearned for him.

On reaching 17 Prudholme Place, Beatrice rapped impatiently with the knocker, not giving herself a chance for second thoughts. She was going to beard the blond lion in his den whether he wanted her to or not. Waiting patiently at home and cooling her heels like a good mistress was not for her anymore. She had to make her voice heard.

After just a few moments' wait, the door was opened by a smartly dressed middle-aged parlor maid. It seemed strange that Ritchie had a household and a life she knew nothing of, but she supposed his other paramours had never been interested in such minutiae the way she was.

"I should like to see Mr. Ritchie, if you don't mind? I'm a friend of his. Miss Beatrice Weatherly."

The maid, obviously used to protecting her employer's privacy, seemed hesitant. Was Ritchie, the married Lothario with a locked-up wife, often hounded by other women after all?

"I'll see if he's receiving visitors. May I take your card?"

Beatrice considered simply pushing her way in regardless, but years of drilled-in politeness stifled that urge. Fishing a card from her bag, she handed it to the protective servant, and then was surprised to be ushered inside into a small reception room and invited to wait.

The room was quiet and pleasant, not cluttered with a thousand things as many such rooms were, including those in her own home. There were few ornaments, only one or two unobtrusive pictures on the wall, and absolutely no photographs to be seen anywhere, on any surface.

Well, he certainly wouldn't want pictures of his wife, would he, if he'd shut her away somewhere to *avoid* seeing her?

But Beatrice didn't believe Ritchie was as callous as that, not for a minute. Bitter Eustace had every reason to exaggerate and to malign his enemy, and he'd also wanted to hurt her for rejecting him.

The moments ticked by, marked by a small lacquered clock with a decorated enamel face. It was the fanciest thing in the room, and very pretty, but Beatrice wasn't in the mood to appreciate its attractions. She just wanted the time it marked to pass, and Ritchie to appear, and she couldn't sit down in one of the comfortable but elegant chairs until he did so.

Where are you, you wretch? she thought, pacing.

As if motivated by the power of her will, the door swung open with some force.

"Good afternoon, Bea. You've anticipated me. I was about to call on you when I'd finished my toilette, but alas now you've caught me in my dressing gown."

He'd only been away a couple of days, but Beatrice's eyes feasted on her lover as if they'd been apart for years. Despite everything, it amused her that she'd caught him in his dressing gown, just as he'd ambushed her in hers what seemed like a lifetime ago, when they'd first forged their arrangement.

Clad in his rich blue robe of paisley silk velvet, Ritchie was the very picture of freshly bathed male pulchritude, his jaw just shaved, his hair wet and curling, his eyes bright with unfeigned pleasure at the sight of her.

"You've caught me in less," she answered quickly, her heart skittering, her fingertips tingling inside her glove with the need to touch him. He seemed more desirable to her every time they encountered each other, and no amount of deception and dark history could alter that.

Ritchie gave her a long look, pursing his lips. She could see him ticking off every sign she was exhibiting.

Then he tugged the sash of his robe tighter, as if he were arming himself.

"If I'm not mistaken this isn't a call to welcome me home from my travels with passionate lovemaking, is it?"

"No, I came in search of conversation, not carnality, Ritchie." She felt herself twisting at the strap of her little bag and forcibly stopped herself. Fidgeting was revealing. "My status as a mistress, bought and paid for, decrees that I should refrain from asking questions and probing the secrets of your life, I accept that. But I'm afraid my nature is to seek enlightenment and knowledge…in order to give me strength." His blue eyes flickered as she spoke. "Especially since the last time I was too trusting…well…I suffered the consequences."

Ritchie drew in a deep breath. "Your reasoning is sound, Beatrice, and I understand it. Believe me, I know full well the perils of trusting that all will be well."

Who had Ritchie trusted? Even with the clamor of her own questions and doubts, Beatrice heard the note of sorrow and bitterness in his voice. It must be his wife, his supposedly mad wife in whom he'd mistakenly put his trust.

"I don't know where to begin," she blurted out, at a loss in the face of how much she wanted and needed to know.

"Well, why not sit down, for a start." Ritchie gestured to a leather-upholstered settee, hesitated, then took a seat himself, holding out his hand to draw her down beside him. "Please?"

Beatrice sat, keeping her distance from him, fiddling with first her bag, then her gloves, making a meal of taking them off.

"Ask anything you want, Bea. Anything." She thought he was going to lean back, lounge against the upholstery, a challenge to her curiosity, but he didn't. Instead he leaned forward, took her gloves from her, dropped them on the seat, then folded his hands around hers.

Yes, make it more difficult for me, you devil! His touch tingled like a galvanic current, radiating out from the contact to every part of her body.

"Are you married, Ritchie? I know it's not my business, really, because I'm only your…your *courtesan* or whatever we choose to call it on any given day, but I've decided I would like to know."

There, it was out. Perhaps the hardest question.

"Yes, I'm married, Bea. I've been married twice. My first wife died—" so much depth of sorrow in the quietly spoken little words "—but my second wife is very much alive."

"But she doesn't live with you?"

Ritchie let out a sigh, not of exasperation but of a resigned acceptance.

"No, Margarita doesn't live with me. We haven't lived as man and wife for years. She's not in her right mind. She's been diagnosed as insane and resides in a private nursing home, in Wimbledon, where she can have as safe and comfortable a life as possible and be well cared for… and not hurt herself or anybody else."

Ritchie paused, almost as if his mouth and jaw were locked by tension. Observing him, Beatrice recalled again his naked back and shoulders, and the scars. The wounds from cutting and from fire.

Margarita's doing? It seemed the obvious explanation.

About to pursue the point, she hesitated. Ritchie looked as if a barrier had come down behind his eyes, to keep him from pain or memory. Or both. When she opened her mouth to quiz him, he broke in, his voice harder than before.

"What prompted the sudden desire to question, Beatrice? I expected gentle enquiries long ago—it's a woman's nature to want to know such things."

Beatrice gritted her teeth, torn by conflicting emotions. Sympathy. Aggravation. Curiosity. She wished she'd never come here, and yet she knew it would have been impossible not to.

She shook her hand free of him. Those hands of his made it difficult to think straight. "As I said, I didn't think it was my place…but then someone paid me a visit and apprised me of certain home truths."

"Eustace Lloyd."

If a glacier of cold disdain could be two solitary words, these were they. Ritchie's voice was flat and dismissive.

"Yes, the very man you've apparently ruined on my behalf, it seems." Beatrice snatched up one of her gloves and began to mangle it again, not sure what she would have done if her hands were free. "Although if you'd stopped to consult me on the matter, you'd realize that wasn't what I wanted at all."

Ritchie took the glove out of her hands again, and tossed it and the other and her bag all aside. Removing ammunition? "Lloyd exaggerates. I merely saw to it that he was excluded from two or three choice business arrangements in the last couple of weeks. And that his memberships at two of my clubs—where he's been repeatedly caught cheating at cards, I might add—have been rescinded." He stared at her, his blue eyes steady, challenging her to protest. "That's hardly ruin, Bea, and he's a resourceful man. Perhaps he'll find some other trusting young woman to pose nude for his camera, and recoup his fortunes in the pornography market?"

Anger bubbled like hot acid in Beatrice's chest, all the more coruscating because she didn't quite know where it was directed. At Ritchie? At Eustace? At Polly, or Charlie, or Jamie, or whomsoever had finally confirmed to Ritchie that Eustace had photographed her? Perhaps it was self-directed even, and that most of all? Bereft of her gloves to wrench at, her hands clenched into fists, and before she knew it she was pummeling Ritchie's chest, thumping the front of his blue robe and the solid muscle beneath.

"Yes, very well, I *was* trusting. I admit that! And he put a little laudanum in my champagne to loosen my sensibilities," she cried as he grabbed her wrists in a firm but not unkind grip. "But I *wanted* to do it, too. Do you know that? I wanted to do something daring and forbidden. I'm not a paragon of genteel womanhood, Ritchie, and I never was, really. Why on earth do you think I found it so easy to contemplate fucking you for money?"

Ritchie's hands tightened. "He drugged you?" The face she thought so beautiful hardened. Ritchie suddenly looked older, and furious. Murderously furious. "I'll kill him. Never mind ruin him, I'll kill the bastard!"

"Don't be absurd! He didn't hurt me." Ritchie's fury was mighty to behold and a little frightening, but inside Beatrice felt a deep atavistic thrill. What was wrong with her? She should be horrified by his threats of murder on her behalf, and yet she exulted. For her, a warrior would fight…

And there were practicalities. Before Ritchie could protest, she went on. "But, Ritchie…if he'd never taken those photographs, we would never have met. You wouldn't even have known I existed."

Ritchie looked away for a moment, his hands still holding her. "We'd have found each other. I know that. One day I'd have looked across the room at a ball or a reception, and I'd have wanted you immediately."

"And then where would we have been, might I ask? I might have been married, and then you'd never have had me." The irony made her laugh. "I might be a notorious trollop now, but if I'd married, I would never have countenanced betraying my husband."

They stared at each other. The thoughts and ramifications hurtled and circled through her head like images in a kaleidoscope, and she could almost see the same thing occurring behind Ritchie's blue eyes.

Slowly, he relaxed, releasing her. Beatrice rubbed her wrists, realizing how tightly he'd held her, and almost immediately he took hold of them again, gently soothing and massaging the little hurts.

Then he sighed. "We seem to have landed ourselves in something of a conundrum, Bea, haven't we?" There was fire in his eyes, but it was inward now.

"Yes, somewhat…I'd say."

Ritchie gave her a long, appraising look as he let go of her. It wasn't judgment, more searching, looking for something he had to face that was not entirely amenable to him.

"You want more, Bea, don't you? More than this?" His gesture was slight, and openhanded, but it seemed to encompass their entire relationship.

More? Yes, I do want more. With you I want everything.

It was true and this time she didn't suppress the notion. She did want to marry him, and be with him forever. And give him children.

And as so very often, she could tell he knew exactly what she was thinking.

"But you know I can't give you that. I'll never be able to." His voice ached with regret, with sorrow.

Beatrice wanted to hold him, kiss him, and yes, even take him to bed right now in order to ease what was troubling him. And she felt a window open inside her, a window onto a new way of considering their future.

"Maybe I don't want quite what you think I want." She held his gaze boldly. "We don't have to marry. I don't care about that." And as she said it, it dawned on her that she didn't, not the marriage part. "We could live together, just as if we were married. I don't give two pins for respectability. I said farewell to that concept quite a while ago."

"No, that's not good enough."

"How so?" Had she misread him? She didn't think so. She didn't have his clever powers, apparent as they were, but she was intuitive enough.

"You deserve the very best, Beatrice. You deserve a wedding, respectability. A comfortable, secure place in society. Not a half life."

Men! How could they be so stubborn? Whoever said that women were the more contrary sex was completely mistaken.

"I've told you. I don't care."

"But I do! I want to give you everything you lost, thanks to Lloyd." His jaw tightened and he threw back his head to stare at the ceiling, as if for inspiration. "But I can't." He lowered his gaze, to look at her. "And I think it's probably better that we conclude our relationship now, before I lead you on any further and cause you any more pain." He drew in a breath as if the very passage of oxygen was agonizing. "If you quit me now, perhaps something of your reputation will be salvageable. With a bit of money behind you, you'll soon attract another suitor. A man who can give you what I cannot. A decent man who'll love you and make a life and a home with you."

"Which you don't want to, presumably?"

The room suddenly seemed frozen in ice. Why in the

name of all that was holy had she said that? In her heart, she knew he cared for her—why had she goaded and insulted him so?

It was the madness of love. Perhaps he now had a mistress lacking in wits as well as a wife?

"Don't be absurd, Beatrice." If he was aware he was mirroring her own utterance, he didn't show it. His face was like thunder, a bright and righteous thunder. "I care for you, you stupid woman! Can't you see that?" He drew her hand to his lips and kissed it passionately. "And that's precisely why we should part now, for your own benefit. I'm done with ruining women's lives. I'll not hurt you further."

The feel of his lips against her fingers, his breath against her skin was like a dousing with pure pleasure. A reaction which she was sure worked both ways, and made her more and more infuriated at him for being so obtuse.

"I've told you. I don't care. Why must we go around in endless circles like this? And why has a notorious womanizer like you suddenly turned into such a paragon of moral decency to rival our Queen herself?"

He dropped her hands. Moved back on the settee, the slide slow and weary. And reluctant.

"I think it's best if you leave, Beatrice. The longer we go on like this, the more difficult it becomes." He reached for her gloves and her little bag and held them out to her. "But don't worry, the money is yours, free and clear, as is the annuity and the sums committed toward your family debts. That's the least I can do."

"No! I will not be paid off!" In the folds of her skirt, Beatrice clenched her fists again. She was going to do something silly, she could feel it, so the tighter she held on to herself the better. "I'll take only enough for Charlie's debts and to set me up at typewriting school…but no charity!"

She straightened her spine and glared at him, daring him to contradict her.

The gloves and the bag hit the carpet. "Don't be ab—" Ritchie stopped short, almost as if he was about to laugh, then his face seemed to mutate through a dozen changes of expression at rapid succession: anger, fear, frustration, despairing amusement.

Then something else.

"If I didn't know what insanity was truly like, Beatrice Weatherly, I'd swear you've driven me to it."

Drawing in a great sigh, almost a gasp as if she'd knocked the air out of him, he slid forward again on the settee, and before she could react, he hauled her into his arms and brought his mouth down on hers.

The kiss was hard. Harder than he'd ever kissed her. But she welcomed it. No matter what happened in the future between her and this most unhappily married man, this moment and this embrace was theirs completely.

"One last fuck, Bea…that's all I ask of you," he said against her lips.

"Don't say 'last.' We've not settled anything yet," she contradicted, against his lips. "Concentrate on the matter in hand, Mr. Ritchie. Don't start a new discussion."

Ritchie's hands threaded in her hair, beneath her hat, and both the pins that held her coiffeur and the hat itself began to slide. With his tongue in her mouth, swirling and tangling with her own, she felt him growl when he pricked himself on one of the pins' sharp points.

"Accursed, wretched things," he snarled, snatching his mouth away for a moment, and attacking her head-gear. Pins flew everywhere and her hat went sailing over the back of the settee, then his hand slid into the auburn mass of her hair again, shaking it free and loose over her shoulders.

"You're perfect, Bea," he said simply, and very fiercely, then pressed his mouth to hers again, parting her lips immediately and pushing her against the upholstery.

As are you...as are you...

Unable to speak, she let her hand converse for her, sliding over Ritchie's shoulders and upper arms and exploring the musculature beneath the velvet of his dressing gown. He was bare, beneath, exciting and naked, and the idea of one single layer of cloth between her fingertips and him was infinitely stimulating.

As he cupped her breast through the fine-woven fabric of her jacket, and all the confabulation of blouse and bodice and corset beneath, she slid her hands swiftly to the front of his robe and wrenched it open.

She felt him gasp, but pressed on, even though he was as intent on exploring as she. While he attacked the buttons of her jacket, then her blouse, she ran her hands briefly across his flat belly and took a firm hold on his cock.

"Oh dear God, yes," he panted, steadying for a moment, his hips jerking against her on instinct. "Yes, oh yes..."

Yes indeed.

Beatrice loved the sensation of Ritchie's cock in her hand. She loved to caress him and feel all that power contained in turn by her own power. Their relationship she likened to a seesaw of supremacy, and when she had her fingers wrapped around her lover's member, she had control.

But they were still tilting at each other. Even as she caressed him, her strokes daring, a little ragged, lacking in finesse, Ritchie had the presence of mind to pursue his own agenda. Buttons carefully secured by some unknown seamstress went flying around the room just as the hairpins had done before them. Ritchie wrenched and tugged and, yes, tore at her clothes, pulling everything open at the front. Furiously intent, he sat back a moment, sizing up the hooks of her corset, then unfastened some of those too, so determinedly that Beatrice could swear he bent most of the little metal shapes.

Ripping open her chemise beneath he bared her breasts.

Then he slid his hands beneath and cupped them, lifting and squeezing them even while she still squeezed him.

Slumped against the upholstery, Beatrice regarded Ritchie from beneath lowered lids, her body aflame with delicious sensations, her fingertips massaging her treasure. His face was all beauty, somehow both intent and distracted, his lips parted, his white teeth digging a little into the lower one. Where his robe was parted, his body gleamed, and his cock was large and ruddy against the pallor of her caressing hand.

Questions of money and commitments and personal freedom seemed distant in the face of this intimacy. Nothing could be wrong when they were touching each other. All was well…

Then a tread in the corridor beyond set her jerking upright on the settee, snatching at her clothes in a flutter as she abandoned her lover's hot shaft to its own devices.

"Rest easy, my darling. Nobody will enter. There's only Agatha and the cook and a footman in the house, and they know better than to disturb me when I have company." Nevertheless, Ritchie drew her close and shielded her body and his own erect nakedness.

Yes, I'll bet they're banned from even knocking on the

door when you're entertaining one of your woman, in case they put you off your stroke.

His women. She knew now that there had not been all that many, and bearing in mind the sorrow and anguish of his situation she could hardly condemn him for seeking some solace and physical comfort.

But still the footsteps had unnerved her a little. "If you say so," she murmured doubtfully, glancing at the door and edging her way further into the protection of Ritchie's body.

He stroked her face, looked into her eyes. His were still full of desire, but also tender and solicitous.

"Let's go to my bedroom. We'll be more comfortable there." Leaning down, he kissed the slope of her breast, lightly as a feather's stroke, yet still infinitely arousing. "I need to be inside you, beautiful Beatrice, and my bedroom is where the French Letters are."

As Ritchie began to fasten up her corset as best he could, and somehow restore order to garments that he'd decimated, Beatrice almost suggested that they forgo the prophylactics. But that was foolhardy, ridiculous, and he'd never agree, no matter how keenly he wanted to fuck her.

Much as she would love to have a baby of Ritchie's to love, and no matter how her every instinct yearned to give him a child, to become pregnant would destroy every last fragment of her reputation for good and ever, and Ritchie would never allow that.

"Yes, let's go to bed," she said, and helped him finish making the best of her ruined clothes.

CHAPTER TWENTY-SEVEN

To Sleep, Perchance

SHORTLY AFTERWARD, Beatrice found herself in Ritchie's bed, naked.

It was a nice bed, deep and comfortable with firm mattress and fragrant, freshly laundered linen. But it could have been a fakir's nail-studded cot and rife with fleas and lice and sundry other livestock for all she cared.

Just as long as she had Ritchie on it with her.

Her heart surged as he slid into bed at her side, reaching for her. His eyes were intent and gleaming, and his brow puckered in a slight frown.

Was this their last time? Oh, please, no! It was imperative that she find a way to persuade him that she didn't care about reputation. Assure him that she didn't care a jot about marriage. The pleasure of his company and his body would suffice for her, regardless of the dictates of church and society. This was what she wanted, and as she wound her arms tight around him and pressed her belly against his cock, the way his flesh blindly sought hers made her melt in body and spirit.

He kissed with fervor yet also tenderness, his hand sliding down her back, drawing her closer against his hard, hot shaft and cupping her buttocks. The tips of his fingers tantalized the groove between them, exactly in the wicked way that most excited her. With a little whimper she jerked her hips, rocking against him.

"Beautiful Bea," he murmured, in between kisses.

Her fingers explored too, as she twisted against him, floating over the marks on his back and caressing them as if affection might heal them. Or at least heal the more profound pain for which they stood.

She longed to cradle him in every way: heart, mind, body. Take him into herself and make him forget all past hurts and remember only happiness, and at the same time perform that process on herself. Hungering, she eased her legs wider, rubbing his sex with her own for both pleasure and invitation. Her clitoris throbbed as she rode his stiff member.

"Ritchie, I have to have you," she groaned, working against him as their bodies slid and strained, their limbs entangled. Delicious heat gathered at the most intimate point of contact, but his happy laugh, against her lips, was an equal pleasure.

"And I you, my luscious siren. I you." His fingers danced and flickered, still plaguing her for a moment, then he eased back. "But first we must take the required measures."

Ah yes, the blessed French Letter. But if it was his preference, and his wisdom, she wouldn't argue her own foolhardy case just for the sake of it.

Ritchie's muscles rippled in the lamplight as he turned, opened a small drawer in his bedside secretaire, and drew out a now familiar tin. In a flash, he had one of the small and clever rubber devices in his grasp. As he prepared to sheathe himself, Beatrice reached for the prophylactic.

"Let me this time. I think I'm sufficiently proficient by now."

"Very well, clever Miss Weatherly." With a creamy grin, he lolled back against the pillows.

Inclined over him, her long hair dangling across his body and about to do the deed, Beatrice was struck by a sudden, daring thought. Ritchie loved her auburn waves, and loved to run his fingers through them. How would he feel if she used her tresses on a very different part of him? Leaning further over, her cheek almost on his belly, she wound a thick lock of her hair around his rigid, upthrust shaft.

RITCHIE GASPED ALOUD. The audacity of her. The wicked sweet inventiveness. The clever little minx, she'd read one of his secret wishes and made it real.

Falling back against the pillows, he smiled for pure happiness. Beatrice Weatherly couldn't be real, she was so perfect, the living embodiment of all his dreams. Dark thoughts, worries, his anxiety for their future, and for her, they all faded away like wisps of smoke in a deeper mist of sensuality.

Her hair was silk against him where she slid it over his cock, up and down, sleeved in her hand, the sensation quite unlike any other caress, however skilled. Moaning and shifting his hips, he looked down at her, and found her gazing back up at him across the planes of his body and from beneath her lowered lashes. Pure devilment gleamed in her emerald eyes, and then with a grin, she adjusted her pose, and licked the tip of his cock even while she rubbed it with her hair.

"Dear God in heaven, Beatrice!" he growled, both lost in the sublime sensations, yet experiencing life with a pin-like clarity. He was both dazed with pleasure yet thinking clearly, as never before.

*I cannot lose you. I cannot survive without you. I want
only you.*

And it was true. Though he'd loved before, and deeply
and truly at the time, he could not remember experiencing love like this.

Beatrice Weatherly was far more than just a supremely
natural and enthusiastic bed partner with a rare gift for
the sensual arts. She was spirited, kind, and loyal to
others almost to a fault. And she was also good-humored,
not proud, and had the wisdom not to take herself too
seriously.

I love you, Bea.

He was sure he hadn't spoken the words aloud, but
nevertheless, Beatrice looked up at him, her green eyes
knowing as she swirled her tongue around his cock tip.

"Bea, you're a she-devil!"

This time he did cry out, because she did a wicked
clever thing with that naughty tongue of hers that made
him gouge the bed linen and nearly tear a sheet asunder.
And she went on doing it until he almost reached the end
of his tether.

"Enough! Or I'll come in your mouth!"

Reaching down, he gently prized both Beatrice and her
splendid hair from around him. She allowed him to do
so, but reached for the abandoned prophylactic. For an instant, barely more than a flash, Ritchie saw a sweet vision
of her in a white nursing gown, those lush red waves
fanned across a mountain of pillows while she cradled a
babe with similar red hair and his own blue eyes against
her bosom. The imagined child could never replace the
little son he'd lost, but he could love it just as much, in a
different way.

But then the idyllic vision was gone, and he was faced
with reality again. But not such a terrible reality, all things

considered, as he watched Beatrice lean over him, her pale brow puckered with intense concentration as she negotiated the rubber device and the process of introducing his penis into it.

He almost laughed as she unconsciously stuck out her tongue, not in sexual devilment this time, but because she was so intent on what she was doing, and doing it right.

Beautiful girl. Beautiful, clever Bea. I cannot lose you.

And as Beatrice finally sheathed him to her satisfaction, and gave him a grin to mark her pride in a job well done, Ritchie resolved to find a way to keep her on whatever terms she specified.

I can't lose you. I don't care that you have a wife. I want you and I want you on any terms.

Unable to wait longer, Beatrice grabbed Ritchie's shoulder and urged him closer, opening her legs to invite him to enter her. Every moment was precious with this married yet not really married man, and it pained her to waste a single second of it not entwined with him.

"Kindly don't keep me waiting, Mr. Ritchie," she commanded, as he moved his body over hers. Reaching between them, she grasped his cock and positioned it at her entrance.

"You're very bold, Miss Weatherly," he answered, allowing her to manipulate him, "and very demanding." He laughed and she felt the ripple of it in every inch of their contact, even where she held him between her legs. "You must be patient and allow me to service you."

"Then kindly proceed, sir!" She laughed, wondering if he could feel it, the same way.

"That I shall!"

Ritchie nudged away her hand, then worked his strong hips, pushing inside her. Pushing deep.

Ah, that sensation! Ever the same, and yet always different and new. There was no way to describe the delicious yielding that also conveyed power. Beatrice could do nothing in that moment but wind her arms around Ritchie, her lover, and be his.

What had begun in hasty passion and playfulness became more stately. Slow, measured love, their bodies rocking against each other in harmony and grace despite the raw, animal nature of the act.

Pleasure though, gathered quickly for Beatrice, her flesh quivering around Ritchie's shaft. She tried to contain herself, but reading her intimately with his amazing perceptions, the man fucking her growled in her ear.

"You mustn't resist, beautiful Beatrice...you must never resist." He paused, pressed his mouth hard against the crook of her neck and her shoulder. "Take your pleasure now, my love. Relax...spend now."

My love? My love?

Beatrice wailed. Sublime pulsations rippled through her loins, making her shake her head and grab at Ritchie's back and his bottom, digging in her nails.

He loved her. He loved her. How could she not be in heaven?

IT WAS SO DIFFICULT to stir when she felt so cozy and safe. It was almost as if she were back at Westerlynne, comfortable, secure, with not a single care in the world. Happy.

Beatrice blinked. Squeezed her eyes shut. Opened them again. The room was unfamiliar, well-appointed but spare. Very masculine. Warmth at her side, and a familiar, delicious scent instantly told her from whence that manly aura emanated.

Ritchie!

She'd been asleep in Ritchie's bed and, judging by

the low, steady breathing she could hear, so was he. She hardly dared turn and look at him for fear it was still a dream.

And there he was, slumbering just as she'd suspected, deep in the arms of Morpheus, sprawled almost like a boy, face down against the pillows. His fair hair was tousled like a fallen angel's and his lips bore a slight smile as if his dreams were pleasant.

Gooseflesh prickled Beatrice's arms and her heart galloped, but not from fear and apprehension, but simply sheer wonder. Hadn't he told her he never slept in the presence of a lover? That even if a woman slept, he stayed wakeful, on guard?

Yet here he was, sleeping like a contented babe, beside her. It was momentous, and beautiful and significant. She hadn't imagined his words of love. They had been real and true, and here was the confirmation of his trust, and the fact he felt at peace with her.

Torn between trying to return to sleep herself, and never sleeping again, so she could watch him like this until the end of her days, Beatrice felt her limbs fill with nervous energy. She didn't want to wake him when he looked so tranquil, but the urge to fidget was almost unbearable. Her fingers ached to stroke his back, tangle in his thick blond hair, follow the line of his ear, neck, shoulder. Her mouth tingled as if it were suffering some small degree of pain from not kissing him.

Slowly and with infinite care she slid from the bed and cast around for her chemise.

A few minutes later, after exploring the splendidly appointed private bathroom adjacent to the bedroom, and almost swooning when she sniffed at his bottle of shaving lotion and his fine, custom-blended soap, she crept back toward the bed. Only to have her eye caught by certain items that sat atop the elegantly fashioned chest of drawers.

A pair of Morocco leather-bound photograph albums if she was not mistaken.

The first brought a wry smile to her lips, for it contained the very photographs of herself that had brought her ultimately to this place. She had only ever actually seen one or two of them, purchased discreetly by Polly, via a third party, at her behest. Mixed feelings beset her. She was still annoyed and let down that Eustace would betray her in such a low, ungentlemanly way, and yet at the same time, she couldn't help but grin, wider and wider. For all his faults, her ex-fiancé had created a beauty for her that was far more exotic than she believed was accurate.

She could almost imagine that a man like Edmund Ellsworth Ritchie might become so besotted with her physical form on the strength of them, and proceed to set down a small fortune to possess the body depicted.

Is it just these breasts? These thighs? The mysterious grove between my legs?

Tracing her fingertip over her own form, she asked the questions, but she was aware now that they knew each other, it was more. So much more that the thought made it difficult to breathe.

Setting down the source of her notoriety, she opened the second leather-bound album and found it could not have been more different. Or astonishing.

These were family photographs…from a man who seemed to exist without family because all thought of the same clearly brought him pain.

Several of the depictions were of an oval-faced young woman with an old-fashioned coiffeur and a plain but elegant dress. Her expression was mild, but her eyes seemed bright and happy, even in the indistinct image, and there was a warmth and humor there that Beatrice found instantly appealing. She knew the woman not at all, but somehow felt that she could be a friend if life had turned out very differently. Even though she was obviously Ritchie's first spouse, *Clara,* from her name printed neatly beneath the image.

When she turned the next page though, Beatrice experienced a pang. Here were Ritchie and Clara together, looking every inch a pair of excited newlyweds, despite their formal expression for the camera.

Oh, you look so young, my darling! And so full of joy and love...

Beatrice could not have estimated Ritchie's age now. He seemed ageless. And yet here, in this small photograph, with his happy bride, he appeared little more than Beatrice's own age now. A young man, in love with his wife. Just as much as Beatrice was with him, this very moment.

Peculiar feelings surged through her bosom. Not exactly envy. No, not that. But a certain wistfulness and yearning that confused her.

The next photograph almost made her gasp, but she stayed it in time to prevent her waking him.

It was another image of Ritchie and Clara, taken a few years on, judging by the styling of their clothes, and in it the happy young woman had daringly posed whilst enceinte!

A child? Was Ritchie a father? Did the child live? And if so, where was he? Or she?

A cold hand seemed to clench in Beatrice's chest. She couldn't imagine Ritchie not being the fondest of fathers, even if his wife was lost to him, so it only remained that the child that had sprung from Clara's belly must be dead.

Oh, you poor man, you poor man.

For a moment she turned to him, watching him while he slept so beautiful and at ease, and feeling glad that she'd given him some measure of contentment. The loss of a child and a wife, both loved, then the loss to insanity of a second wife, presumably also loved, was more than one person should ever have to endure.

No wonder he'd shunned a pursuit of the more tender emotions, in favor of satisfying only his flesh.

More pages only reinforced the sadness. The first was almost unbearable. It showed Ritchie, clad in the profoundest of mourning, holding a tiny babe in a lace christening gown. The pose was formal, and Ritchie's face composed, but even so, every line of his body seemed to reveal a confused agony of fatherly love and unquenchable sorrow.

Further photographs revealed the infant was a son. As he grew, the little lad appeared in a sailor suit, clutching a humongous toy yacht, then astride a plump pony, his small face beaming with pride at his achievement. His papa stood beside the placid mount, holding the leading rein, proud too, but still with the telltale shadows in his eyes.

Beatrice touched the photograph, pondering the fate of the robust-looking little boy, so well favored with his mother's thick dark hair and his father's distinctive, handsome features. Where was he? *Was* he dead? If he still lived, she had a sudden fierce urge to meet this son of Ritchie's and become a friend to him even though she could never be a substitute mother.

"He's dead."

The words were cold and flat, yet echoed with the same pain that informed Ritchie's eyes in the photographs. Beatrice spun around to find the man himself sitting up in bed, watching her, his face hard and unreadable for one normally so full of expression.

Words of her own seemed irrelevant, redundant, but quietly she said, "I'm so sorry, Ritchie. So very sorry. What happened to him? He looks such a strong little chap." Carefully, she closed the album and crossed to the bed, settling onto the mattress, facing Ritchie, her chemise tucked around her thighs.

She could see he wanted to look away from her, to hide his eyes, but tightening his jaw, and every muscle in his face, he held her gaze. "He…he was killed." Moisture gleamed in his beautiful dark eyes, and she could see him gritting his teeth hard, fighting for control.

"I'm so sorry," she murmured again, feeling inadequate. "I shouldn't have pried into your personal things. I'm sorry if I've caused you pain by reminding you of him."

Ritchie's bare chest lifted as he drew in a deep breath. He pursed his lips. But still he faced her. "No, don't be sorry, Bea. I'm glad you know about him. His name was Josiah, after my father, but I always called him Joe."

His face seemed to crumple. He dragged in breaths again, as if he were drowning, and then seemed to collapse whilst still remaining upright. Beatrice threw herself toward him and flung her arms around his bare, shaking shoulders.

For several minutes, it was hard to tell whether he was weeping or simply gripped by some paroxysm of grief so profound that it made every muscle in his body jerk and tremble. He seemed unable to speak, so she clung on, holding him and rocking with him.

Eventually, though, he calmed, and she backed off, giving him freedom. As they faced each other again, he grabbed her hand and held it hard.

"He was a fine little fellow. Bold and brave and good-natured, and he could be unbelievably droll for one so young." A smile leavened the pain in his eyes. "Of all the achievements in my life, he was the greatest. And I know that even though she only held him once before she died, Clara felt the same way."

"Oh, Ritchie…how…how… Oh Lord, I don't know what to say."

"You don't have to say anything, my sweet girl. You're here, and that's what matters." His fingers tightened and then suddenly relaxed as he obviously realized he was hurting her. He shrugged. "For all that Clara's death devastated me, Joe was a comfort to me. He seemed to be a part of her I could keep with me and love."

"He looked a splendid little boy. So robust…" She caught her breath, not sure if she should ask, but feeling she had to know. "Was it an accident?"

Ritchie remained quiet for a few moments.

"The death certificate was marked asphyxia, due to the ingestion of fire smoke, but—" he paused, looked away for a moment, then stared at her, his eyes very level "—it was murder. A murder that will never be prosecuted. He was smothered to death in his sleep."

Sick horror engulfed Beatrice's soul. She didn't need him to say more. The explanation presented itself to her, stark and almost incomprehensible yet perfectly logical.

Edmund Ellsworth Ritchie's beautiful son by his first, dead wife had been suffocated by his insane, second one.

"Oh, Ritchie…" was all she could say, and raise his hand, entwined with hers, to her lips.

"I blame myself," he said, his voice bleak, his skin strangely cool where she kissed his knuckles. "I should never have married Margarita, but I was lonely, and her father's business had failed and she…she needed security.

It seemed an agreeable solution to both our dilemmas, and Clara had made me promise, almost in her dying words, that I should not remain alone and that I should seek new love when she was gone."

"And did you care for her? For Margarita?" It seemed important to ask.

"Yes. Yes, I did. I found her fey manner intriguing and she could be a witty companion. And of course, Margarita is very beautiful, and man that I am, I confess that swayed me." He shrugged, and for a moment, looked shamefaced. "She was pleasant to Joe, and I thought…I hoped that they would become friends."

"Was she…did she…um… Did she seem, though, to be in full possession of her wits?" Beatrice let out a nervous laugh. It sounded so absurd. "I'm sorry…I know she must have…obviously."

Ritchie gave her a sad smile. A resigned smile.

"She seemed highly strung, perhaps, but my hope was that a settled family life in comfort and security would bring her peace and calm." He shrugged again and sighed. "I suppose that will teach me never again to think of myself as an expert in the human psyche and afflictions of the nerves."

He fell silent again, and Beatrice waited.

"Our problems began almost immediately we were wed," he resumed, his voice low. "During our engagement, Margarita was flirtatious and sometimes a little forward. I was sorely tempted to precipitate matters, but I contained myself." He smiled wryly. "Something I know you will find difficult to believe now."

"I do believe it. You've been kind and patient with me." It was the perfect truth. For a man who'd paid so handsomely for her favors, he'd followed her pace and been astonishingly undemanding after their initial encounter.

His answer was to kiss her fingers now, just as she'd kissed his, then his face grew solemn again and he continued his narrative.

"In our marriage bed, she was reluctant and anxious. I didn't press the matter. I knew not all women take to the conjugal role immediately, even though Clara had been as eager and delighted to try it as any husband could hope for. I was in no particular hurry and I didn't want to force Margarita into my arms before she was ready to be there happily.

"Then one night, she seemed to invite me, winding herself around me, raising her nightgown and rubbing herself against me…" His mouth quirked. "And beautiful as she was…is…I was happy to accept. But it was a disaster. When it was too late for me to stop, she began shrieking and struggling and striking at me. I tried to pull back, but my loins got the better of me. I had to finish. Afterward, I held her and gentled her as best I could, and promised I would not trouble her again until she was sure she wished to resume…" He sighed again, closed his eyes. "I believed all was well…I really did. I believed I could make her happy, both in our bed and out of it."

Ritchie fell silent again for a long, long time. Beatrice almost thought that he'd decided he simply could not go on any longer, but at length, he began to speak…revealing horror.

He'd been woken in the small hours by shock and pain, and Margarita kneeling over him with his letter opener, an ornamental dagger he'd been given by a friend back from India. She'd struck him again and again, with crazed strength, her eyes blank and glazed as she'd repeatedly gashed his arms and back while he'd tried to turn over and restrain her. It'd only been when a pounding had come at the door and Jamie Brownlow had burst in that Ritchie had managed to grab his wife and wrest the dagger from her.

But that hadn't been the end of it. Even while he'd dripped blood so profusely he'd almost passed out on rising, Ritchie had heard the cries of servants out in the hall and smelt burning. His first thought had been Joe, and he'd rushed to the child's room, the source of a small blaze.

"I rushed to him. The fire wasn't near him, just around the door. I was able to bash my way through...but he was dead." Ritchie's voice was as raw now as if he were still fighting the inferno, his throat choked with smoke. "Dead...but not from smoke or flame. She'd put a pillow over his face and smothered the life out of him." Tears flowed freely down his face, and he seemed to sag. "Afterward, it seemed pointless to accuse her. She was fully raving by then, in a hell of her own making. All that was left to do was make sure that she was well cared for in a safe and comfortable place. A private sanatorium where she'd be treated kindly but kept securely, very securely away from society."

He lifted his head and looked again at Beatrice, his expression drained and weary.

"And now you know the full, sad story, my love. The reason why I throw myself into affairs both business and amatory with such single-minded determination." His blue eyes gleamed with a combination of utter exhaustion and wry sorrow. "I thought that I'd found a life that suited me at least, and was the best I could hope for, that I'd never *want* more. But now I know there is more that I want." He reached out and slid his hand into her hair, cradling her head. "More that I need and love and yearn for... but can never really have. At least not in the open, public way that you deserve." He leaned toward her, touched his forehead to hers, then touched his mouth to hers, in brief and tender sweetness. "To be married to you is my dearest wish, Bea, but alas I still have a wife that I cannot, in good conscience, divorce."

Beatrice's heart fluttered furiously, and the urge to laugh hysterically bubbled up. This situation, and her love for Ritchie, was layered and layered up with irony.

The last man she would ever have expected to want to marry was the man she now *wanted* to marry. But he couldn't marry her, because he was married already.

And yet...

"Marriage isn't everything, Ritchie. I've told you that I don't need it and I don't expect it. It's only love that matters." This time she was the one who brought her lips to his, offering tenderness, but also determination. "And as it seems that you love me as I love you, we have all we need."

His arms crushed her as he flung them around her and squeezed.

"You are the most splendid woman, Beatrice Weatherly," he proclaimed eventually, after he'd kissed her to within an inch of her life, and seriously disarranged her chemise in the process. "But you deserve the best, my love. You deserve your rightful place in society. Acceptance in the finest homes. The respect and admiration of all lesser mortals at every glittering ball and soirée."

"I don't care one bit for society, Ritchie. You know that. And I don't mind living quietly, out of the public eye, as your mistress. All I want is you, and to know that Charlie's position is safe, and that my servants have a good place and security."

"We shall have to discuss this, Beatrice. And most stringently, if we're to agree." His voice was stern, but his eyes were glinting. Relief sluiced through Beatrice like a refreshing wave. Thank heavens, somehow, she had managed to alleviate the sorrow that memory had brought down on him. He seemed an altogether happier man now. The sadness over his lost son, and the terrible circumstances of that death, would probably linger with him to his dying day, but if she could at least distract him from it, in the main, her job was done.

"Yes indeed, Mr. Ritchie. I'm prepared to negotiate." And much more, she thought, as his warm, clever hands slid beneath her chemise and deftly whipped it off over her head.

Sliding his fingertips down her throat and her chest and over the swell of her breast to her nipple, Ritchie surveyed her archly. "Oh, I think if we're to find some kind of accommodation over our future together, Beatrice, you might like to start calling me 'Edmund'…if that suits you?"

"Very well, *Edmund,* I will!" She almost hiccupped over the name when he squeezed her nipple, inducing delicious darts of pleasure.

CHAPTER TWENTY-EIGHT

Déjà vu

AFTER LOVE, they slept again, deeply and refreshingly, as if the awful revelations, once uncovered, had been cathartic.

It was only the thumping on the door that roused Beatrice from her slumber, and Ritchie, at her side, snapped awake too.

"Mr. Ritchie! Mr. Ritchie! There's someone here. Please can you come." The voice of the maid who'd admitted Beatrice earlier sounded anxious and confused, as if she were at the end of her tether.

Turning up the lamp, Ritchie turned to Beatrice. "Wait here, my love. I'll attend to this. Don't worry." His words were calming, but in the flickering light, his face belied his even voice, looking tense and rather pale as he was suddenly gripped by some dread premonition. He sprang from the bed and pulled on trousers and a shirt, tugging the latter over his head and haphazardly shoving in the tails before slipping his braces into place.

"Mr. Ritchie!" came the voice again, and he strode to the door, stepped out into the passage and pulled the door almost shut again behind him.

Who could it be at this time of night? Whatever dread had gripped Ritchie seemed to take a hold on Beatrice, too. Was something wrong with Charlie? Had he slipped back into his bad ways again and been beaten up by a creditor? Surely not, now that he seemed to spend so much time cloistered with Jamie Brownlow.

Voices drifted in through the small gap where the door was ajar. Low, indistinct, but intense. Ritchie sounded astonished. Horrified, even. More out of control than he'd ever seemed before. After a few moments, he stepped back inside the room, his usual confident demeanor shockingly adrift.

His handsome face was like a mask, and as white as a sheet.

"What is it?" Beatrice clutched the bedding closely around her. Somehow she felt she needed armor, yet all she had was cotton and linen and wool. "What's happened?"

Ritchie ran his hand through his hair, visibly thunderstruck yet fighting to regain his composure. It seemed that his thoughts were difficult to marshal.

"We have a visitor. I don't know how…or why…but Margarita is here. She says a messenger from the Lord called 'Mr. Smith' has liberated her from her jail."

Margarita?

For a moment, Beatrice drew a blank. Awoken in the night, in a strange bed, her mind was still disorientated, but after a second, the full significance of that name came crashing down.

"Your *wife?* She's here?" The questions were redundant, as the anguish on Ritchie's face told an eloquent tale. "How has she got here? I thought she was kept securely in the sanitarium?"

"She was. But someone has released her…I don't know how. Either by trickery, posing as an agent of mine, or by spiriting her out of there by subterfuge." His frown deepened. "I have my suspicions as to who is responsible for this, but it seems she insists this angel Smith brought her here in a carriage."

"Smith? Who is Smith?" Beatrice had her suspicions, too. There was one far less than angelic individual who wished them both harm.

Ritchie shrugged at her, his face a mask of raw frustration.

"Eustace! That despicable weevil! How can he be so hateful?" Betrayal and anger surged through Beatrice's chest like bile.

"Indeed, and it seems he's simply deposited my wife here and retreated, leaving chaos in his wake."

"Is she…is she?"

"Raving? Yes, it seems so. I must go down. Mrs. Brewer and Agatha managed to coax her into the parlor and Agatha is sitting with her, but it's me she's calling for." Ritchie reached for his waistcoat and shrugged into it as he stepped into his carpet slippers. He seemed dazed, still trying to bring order to his wits.

"Can I help? Perhaps I could speak to her?" Fear of what Ritchie's wife had done and could do was very real, but Beatrice felt helpless and compelled to offer. Her own feelings were a maelstrom, just as his must be, but perhaps together they could deal with this completely unexpected event.

"Bless you, my love, for offering." Pausing, he hugged her fiercely. "But I have a feeling that the sight of you might inflame her even further."

Even as he held her, a cacophony seemed to erupt somewhere in the house, from a lower floor. General shouting, crashes, a woman's voice eerie and high, shrieking.

"I'd better go, Bea. I think she's too much for any servant to cope with. I'll have to try and calm her and send one of the others round to my doctor's house to fetch him." With a last squeeze of her hand, he dashed to the door and turned briefly at the last moment. "Stay here, my love…please… I'd never forgive myself if she should attack you too."

Then he was gone, pounding across the landing and down the stairs, even as the sound of more shouts and crashes came floating up.

What to do? Beatrice felt powerless, completely at a loss. Sitting up in a bed, in a room, in a house she was completely unfamiliar with, while a murdering madwoman raged downstairs, with the Lord alone knew what intent in mind. If, indeed, she even had a mind.

Unable to remain inactive, Beatrice sprang out of bed and began to dress, pulling on her drawers and her chemise, and a single petticoat. Her costume was out of the question, as it would take a while to wrangle herself into her corset single-handed, so she pulled on Ritchie's luxurious dressing gown and belted it tight around her, then pushed her bare feet into her boots and buttoned them up.

More noises echoed through the house as she dressed. Other voices now, in panic. More crashing, and a sudden strange roaring sound. And crackling.

What in heaven was going on?

Despite Ritchie's instructions, Beatrice dashed out onto the landing, and immediately realized that something terrible and dangerous was occurring.

Smoke was pothering up through the stairwell, and a voice was screaming in stark fright on the floor below.

Oh dear Lord in heaven, Margarita had somehow managed to start another fire.

Ritchie's voice, harsh but in control, echoed up the stairs.

"Mrs. Brewer, Agatha, get out, get out now! Shout for

a bobby as loud as you can…get someone to summon the fire cart…. You, Oliver, run to 34 South Mulberry Street and bring Jamie here. Hurry! Go now, all of you!"

Footsteps thudded, and as a great cracking sound echoed through the house, as if wood were already shattering in the flame, two voices rang out. One Ritchie's loud, filled with anxiety, yet broken as if he were struggling with something, the other high, queer, almost musical, almost floating above the bedlam.

"Beatrice! Beatrice! Are you decent? Come down… you must get out of the house!"

"Ah yes…my dear, dear seducer…you send them away so you can do it to me. Put it in me, the way you did…and hurt me!"

Beatrice's eyes prickled from smoke rising up. She bent over the banister, trying to see the shrieking woman who had suddenly become her nemesis.

As she looked down, two faces looked up. Ritchie and his wife, locked in a struggle, he trying to restrain her, and she kicking and flailing and jerking with a strength that seemed to exceed the human norms.

"Ritchie!" Beatrice cried out in alarm. He was already smeared with soot, and she could see blood on his shirt. Oh dear Lord, what was happening? The same again as before, in some kind of horrific déjà vu?

"Beatrice! Listen carefully," called Ritchie, struggling for his words as he grappled with the woman writhing and jerking in his arms. "Go to the back stairs…see if they are clear…and get out of the house as fast as you can! Please go, my love…get to safety, for the love of God."

Before Beatrice could answer, Margarita let out a fierce screech, her face, which under normal circumstance would have been exquisitely beautiful, a mask of fury. Her features were contorted and her hair—which was golden blond and far paler that Ritchie's, already appeared to be frazzled and a little scorched in places.

"Whore! Filthy strumpet! Whore!" she bellowed up the stairs, redoubling her enraged struggles. She seemed to be clad in some kind of simple day dress and a shawl, but both were soot smeared and also a little singed. What on earth had she been doing, while she was left? Had she injured the servant bidden to watch her?

"Beatrice, please! Look for a safe way out, as quick as you can!" Ritchie cried, then he gasped in pain.

To her horror, Beatrice saw the flash of something in Margarita's hand. A small knife? Scissors? Something she'd concealed about her person? Whatever it was, she'd managed in her twisting to jam it into Ritchie's restraining arm, and in the moment of shock, he loosened his grip and she sprang free and darted away from him.

Heading up the staircase for Beatrice!

Ritchie followed, thundering after his wife, blood dripping thickly from his arm. The two of them reached Beatrice's landing almost together and Ritchie grabbed for Margarita, reestablishing his hold.

"Whore! Whore! Whore!" howled the blonde woman, tossing her head, kicking back against her husband, her slipper-clad feet hitting his shins.

"Beatrice, check the back stairs. We may be able to get down that way," cried Ritchie, between struggles, nodding vaguely in the direction of the wall at the far end of the landing. Beatrice darted toward it, just avoiding the flying feet and fists of the still defiant Margarita, and found a discreet concealed door that must lead to the servants' stairs.

But it was no good—thick black smoke was already billowing up. How the dickens had Margarita managed to create so much havoc, so fast? The cunning of the insane, no doubt, and now they were all paying for that infernal guile.

"I don't think we can get out that way, Edmund," she called, then had to stop and cough violently. Rushing back to the banister, she peered down, blinking at more smoke, only to see what she'd worst feared, down below.

The main staircase was on fire, and the cracking sound had been parts of it collapsing.

"The flames will cleanse you, dirty strumpet. Destroy your filth…and his," chanted Margarita, her eyes wild.

"Into the bedroom, Bea…now…" gasped Ritchie, his voice sounding odd, almost weak. "We'll have to try and get down by means of the window somehow. But we're very high."

Beatrice dashed into the bedroom, the scene of so much beauty, and now perhaps their path to safety. Flinging open the curtains, she looked down, and saw a sheer drop, many yards to the street below. A crowd had gathered and someone pointed up at her.

"Can anyone get a ladder?" she shouted out once she'd hauled up the sash. The night air was chilly, but blessedly fresh after the gathering smoke. "Please look for one. We can't get down. We're trapped."

"Trapped in sin and filth," screamed Margarita from behind her.

"Oh, for pity's sake, shut up!" shouted Beatrice, whirling around, horrified at the paper whiteness of Ritchie's skin as he hung on to his still fighting wife for dear life. The whole of his arm was a mass of red, blood trickling down from his wound. She wanted to run to him, help him hold Margarita, but the ferocious expression on the latter's face was truly terrifying. Beatrice sensed that if she went any closer it would incense the madwoman even more.

A commotion in the street drew her back to the window, and to her relief she saw the fire cart clattering along the cobbles, horses at a pell-mell gallop, bell jangling furiously for people to get out of their way. Uniformed firemen leaped down from the contraption almost before it pulled to a halt, their keen eyes sizing up the situation. Almost immediately they began maneuvering their long ladder into position and priming their pump.

"We're saved," Beatrice called out to Ritchie, turning to him. "They're putting up a ladder."

"Climb down, Beatrice. Go now!" he ordered. "For my sake. I'll bring her."

Beatrice flew to the window.

"Can you climb down, miss," bellowed up a brawny fireman, "or shall we come up and carry you?"

The ladder didn't look strong. In fact it looked narrow and fragile. Beatrice swallowed. She had no particular fear of heights, but still the ladder looked perilous.

And how the devil was Ritchie going to get the screaming, squirming, kicking and flailing Margarita down it? His wife seemed to have an inexhaustible well of demonic energy and she was still fighting him as hard as ever.

"I can climb down," Beatrice yelled down to the assembly of firemen, neighbors and passersby. Even as she quickly scanned the throng, she saw her brother racing up the street, with Jamie Brownlow and Polly, too. They were all three in their night attire, robes and shawls hastily thrown on.

"Bea! Bea! Are you all right?" shouted Charlie, his voice sharp with anxiety. "Can you get down? Is Ritchie with you?"

"Yes, I'm coming down now…Ritchie's here…with… with someone else. We're coming down."

Her head began to spin. It was the smoke. The fear. She

snapped around to Ritchie and thought furiously. How in heaven's name could he get this maenad down that rickety ladder? Should a fireman come up? Could even the sturdiest of them hold Margarita in her madness?

Suddenly, an idea came. Also mad, in its own way. Before she could think twice, she leaped across the room toward her lover and his battling wife and, hauling back her arm, she aimed the first-ever punch of her life at Margarita's pallid jaw.

It connected with uncanny precision and force.

Pain exploded in Beatrice's knuckles and shock thudded up her arm, but almost like a miracle, Margarita slumped in Ritchie's arms, not quite out cold, but clearly stunned and mercifully silenced.

For a moment, Ritchie was silenced too, a look of pure astonishment on his soot-smeared face. Then he laughed, in shocked, wild way, as if he too were stunned. "Wonderful! You're a genius, my love. Now we can get her out safely, and save ourselves too." Lifting the limp, murmuring form of his wife fully in his arms, he carried her to the window. Beatrice trotted at his side, her bruised knuckles smarting furiously.

"Can you climb?" demanded Ritchie again, his sharp eyes obviously noticing the way she was flexing her fingers. "Shall I carry you and then come back for her?" He nodded to Margarita, who he'd propped on the low seat by the window.

A loud bang and a fresh plume of thick black smoke coming from the landing distracted Beatrice for a second, but stiffened her mettle. "Yes, I can climb perfectly well. But shouldn't you carry your…your wife down first?"

Ritchie grabbed her hand, the blood from his sticky on her skin. "No, you first, my precious love, you first… now go!"

Plunging forward, Beatrice gave him a quick kiss, tasting smoke and blood, then, dragging in a great breath of the fresh air from the street, she readied herself, bundling her petticoats between her legs just as she'd done when wading in the stream at Westerlynne what seemed like a lifetime ago, and hauling up Ritchie's dressing gown and tucking it around her waist so it wouldn't interfere with her footing. She didn't care a fig whether half of London saw her legs now. Goodness, plenty of folk had probably seem them bare anyway, in the photographs.

"Hurry!" urged Ritchie, and Beatrice turned around and, with her heart in her mouth, and a wary foot, stepped backward onto the ladder.

Oh, it felt so narrow, so insubstantial. Fear paralyzed her for a moment, then she steeled herself. The longer she shilly-shallied about, the longer Ritchie was in danger. Slowly but steadily, trying to watch her footing but without focusing on the pavement so far below, she began to descend.

The next moments were unreal, as she stepped down and down, fearing for each step, descending through a world of noise and light, dangerously close to flame and whooshing water from the hose playing ineffectually on the lower part of the house. Once or twice, she nearly missed a rung and had to hang on tight, her heart thundering, but eventually, her foot connected with the solid ground of the pavement.

Instantly, she was enveloped in not one but two pairs of arms. Charlie, hugging her and sobbing, and Polly too, doing exactly the same.

"Oh, Bea, thank God you're safe!"

"Oh, Miss Bea, you had me worried there, really you did!"

But there was only a second to savor their relief, and

her own. Shaking off the blanket that Polly tried to wrap her in, Beatrice returned her attention to the ladder, her heart screaming silently, *Come down, my love, come down.*

Flames were belching through other windows now, and smoke was issuing from the opening through which Ritchie would emerge. It was hard to see. But at last, he appeared, with Margarita slung over his shoulder, her blond hair tumbling down around her face, and down his back. She looked mercifully inert as he began to work his way down the ladder, rung by rung, hampered by his burden.

Beatrice gnawed her lip and clenched her fist, her damaged knuckles forgotten. She wanted to cry out to him to hurry, hurry, but she didn't want to distract him at a crucial moment and cause a misstep. It felt as if she had a giant spring coiling and coiling inside her, agonizing tension gathering with every inch he traversed down the narrow ladder.

Slowly, slowly he descended. All seemed well. Beatrice's heart began to rise. They were still above the first floor, but surely it wouldn't be long now.

And then, in a blur of motion...disaster.

With a great screech, Margarita came to life. Tossing her head, she shouted out, "No! You shall not have me! You shall not!" Then, twisting and kicking, she beat Ritchie's back with her fists and wriggled furiously.

He held on, even though the ladder was rocking and sliding, then, to Beatrice's watching horror, more blood began to bloom on his shirt and trousers.

She still clutched the little knife, or pair of scissors, or whatever it was.

Ritchie held on, but letting out a great, broken cry of her own, Beatrice realized he was weakening. Loss of blood and shock were draining his strength, and, just as the firemen raised a second ladder, close to the first, in an attempt to aid him, Margarita screamed out, "No! Get away, whoremongers!" and with an immense shove of unnatural energy, she kicked out with her heels and dislodged both herself and Ritchie, still holding her, from the ladder.

Beatrice screamed, too, but the sound was frozen in her throat. She could only watch in horror as the two figures tumbled through the air toward the hard, hard pavement. As they fell and twisted, time seemed to slow down and they appeared to float strangely as if suspended between life and death while several of the firemen and a number of the stronger-looking male passersby struggled to maneuver a huge blanket beneath, to catch them.

With only partial success.

As she fell, Margarita kicked still, flailing like a demented puppet, and neither she nor her husband landed fully on the blanket. She pitched to one side, her head striking the pavement, and Ritchie tumbled between two of the blanket holders, landing awkwardly a couple of feet away from his spouse.

Shattering the column of ice that seemed to surround her, Beatrice flew to him.

"Ritchie! Ritchie!" she cried, automatically reverting to the name she was most used to as she knelt beside him, staring down into his horrifyingly blank face. "Edmund, my love…please…wake up!"

For several long seconds, his features remained mask-like, then suddenly he grimaced, his mouth twisting as he blinked and blinked again. "Bea?" Then his eyes snapped open, and filled with joy as a ragged smile lit his soot-and-bloodstained features. Struggling to sit up, he winced hard, then bit his lip.

"Thank heaven you're safe, my love."

"Thank heaven you're safe, my love."

Their words came out in a weird echo of each other, and they both laughed, hysterically and in shock. But Beatrice frowned an instant later at the expression of pain on his face.

"You're hurt. Where are you hurt?" She turned and called to the crowd. "Please, is there a doctor here?" As a tall gray-haired man with a distinguished yet compassionate face hurried forward she returned her attention to Ritchie. "My love, where are you hurt?"

The muscles of Ritchie's face seemed to be locked tight. He spoke through gritted teeth. "I fear I may have broken my leg, dearest." He gasped with pain as the friendly doctor attempted to confirm his sudden patient's diagnosis.

Beatrice peered at Ritchie's leg. The ankle looked a little odd. She grabbed his hand as he groaned under further examination.

"It could be a break, but not too serious," pronounced the gray-haired physician. "Stay very still a moment. I must look to the young woman too."

Oh Lord, Margarita. Beatrice had completely forgotten her in her concern for Ritchie. Ignoring what must have been considerable pain, her lover came up on his elbow and together they peered through the melee of firemen, passersby and concerned parties, to the prone figure stretched out a few yards away.

Still she lay. Motionless. Lifeless. Her golden hair tumbled about a face that sat atop her neck at an awkward and sickening angle, but her eyes, staring wide open, were strangely peaceful.

Beatrice looked away, horrified. She'd never known Margarita, and the woman's madness had caused anguish and physical pain to Ritchie. But nobody deserved to die in the street, their neck broken.

"I know…I know." Ritchie's voice was thin and reedy, but still possessed a quiet strength. Beatrice met his eyes, and saw in them the same confusion she was feeling. Despite his physical pain, he still felt for his lost wife, no matter how she'd damned him. "I would not have wanted this outcome either, despite everything."

Suddenly the night seemed very, very cold, and the hubbub all about them very distant. Beatrice was dimly aware of Polly and Charlie fussing around with blankets and brandy—and Jamie, more self-possessed, dealing with the firemen—and though she must have thanked them, all she was aware of was Ritchie's face and his hand, still held in hers.

He groaned as the doctor treated him, then seemed to quiet with a little morphia, only to ask Beatrice if she could find out if his servants were all safe. When she was able to report that, he managed a wan smile.

"My house is uninhabitable though," he said with a sigh. "I shall have to instruct Jamie to make alternative arrangements. I'll need somewhere to recuperate." He nodded vaguely to his leg, now in a well-fashioned temporary splint.

Beatrice stared at him, her wounded love, and suddenly seemed to come back into the world again, and the possession of her faculties and decisiveness.

"I'll speak to him. There's no need. We have room at South Mulberry Street. It might be a bit of a squeeze for everyone from both our households, but I won't hear of you, at least, being anywhere else in your condition. What better place to nurse you than in my own very comfortable bedroom?"

Ritchie's smile became considerably less wan, even

if a little drowsy, as if like she, he was suddenly making a conscious effort to throw off the darker aspects of this momentous evening and begin to embrace the future that now lay before them.

"But what about your reputation, Miss Weatherly? A man being nursed in your bedroom, what will polite society think?"

"Rats to polite society! We both know my reputation doesn't exist anymore. What difference does it make?" She squeezed his hand, and was pleased to receive a determined squeeze from him in return. "All that matters is that I'm able to supervise your recovery and do everything possible to speed it."

"Well, my dearest…" His voice was slurred now, as if the drug was taking a stronger effect. Which it would need to if he were to be moved soon, and without agony. "I'm not normally a man who takes kindly to being dictated to…but in this case, I accede to your wishes." His eyelids fluttered, but before they closed, he gave her one last glance, of pure blue fire. "I'm completely yours."

Perhaps you are now, my love. Yes indeed, I think you are.

As Ritchie's eyes closed, she raised his hand to her lips and kissed it tenderly.

"Will you marry me, Beatrice?"

His voice was faint, barely a breath, but it hit Beatrice like a thunderbolt of joy.

"Yes! Oh yes," she whispered, smothering the hand she held with a dozen more ragged kisses.

Ritchie murmured, "Good," then promptly slipped into insensibility.

CHAPTER TWENTY-NINE

At Last

"AREN'T YOU SUPPOSED to be resting, Edmund? What's all this? How on earth have you got down here?"

Despite her worry for him, Beatrice's heart lifted on seeing her fiancé up and about and looking so hale and hearty. Not to mention so deliciously handsome in a brand-new blue dressing gown. It was scarcely seven days since the fire at his house, yet ever the man of business, Ritchie was already directing his affairs again, with the help of Jamie and various clerks and secretaries who kept arriving at South Mulberry Street with documents and reports. The morning room now seemed to have become his new office.

"Don't worry, sweetheart. Jamie and your brother assisted me down the stairs a little while ago." From his place on the couch, he reached for her, hand outstretched. His bad ankle—only severely sprained after all, as it turned out—was resting on a cushion placed on a small stool in front of him. "I'm feeling very well now and I'm getting better by the day. Especially when you return to me, looking so beautiful and fresh and desirable, and yet so sanctified from your devotions at church."

"Flatterer," chided Beatrice, sitting carefully down beside him, arranging her skirts. "But I still think you shouldn't work so hard. You did sustain a concussion as well as your injured ankle too, you know. And you lost a lot of blood from your…your wounds."

Beatrice shuddered. It still pained her to think about Margarita stabbing him and trying her misguided best to kill the man she'd been wed to. The feelings were confused. Beatrice swung between regret that she'd been unable to defend her loved one against Margarita's attacks and a sensation of profound pity for a woman as crazed and unhappy as the deceased Mrs. Ritchie had been.

Pushing his papers aside and sending half of them fluttering onto the carpet, Ritchie slung a decidedly vigorous arm around her waist and pulled her close to him.

"Try not to feel sad for her, darling. There was nothing anyone could do to help her, believe me." He looked away. "There were times when I wished her dead, for what she did to Joe, but eventually I accepted it wasn't her fault and I wished she could have been happy."

They sat in silence for a moment, while the sweet consolation of a warm and comforting arm around Beatrice's waist worked a form of magic, dropping a veil over the past sorrows and tribulations and illuminating the path toward bright hopefulness ahead.

The fire had proved a catalyst, changing lives as much as it had ended Margarita's. Attending the funeral of Ritchie's deceased wife in his stead, Beatrice had been astonished to see Eustace Lloyd there, too. The ceremony had been brief, and attended by very few people, and her former sweetheart had buttonholed her for a chat, his face somber. Without fully admitting anything, he'd confirmed her suspicions that he'd been involved in removing Margarita from the sanitarium. Listening to his evasions, Beatrice had felt a strange numbness and a peculiar lack of anger. He couldn't hurt her now. In fact her only faint concern had been that Ritchie would act the avenging angel and hurt Eustace instead.

But it seemed an opportunity had come up. A position managing a rubber plantation, in the Malays. Eustace was leaving England to start afresh, and had even sold most of his photography equipment. Beatrice had a shrewd idea who'd made this advantageous far-off post available, and she was glad her new fiancé had chosen to simply remove her old one from the country rather than seek to do any more harm to Eustace than he could well do to himself.

Now, observing this man she loved, she marveled. A lesser individual would have wreaked dire vengeance on Eustace, given the resources and connections that Ritchie enjoyed. But instead, he'd chosen a more humane response, out of respect for her feelings.

"I still think you shouldn't be overtaxing yourself with all these papers and decisions," she said at length, giving him a mock frown, even though she began to melt when he gave her a shamefaced smile and the shrug of a guilty little boy.

Although not so much the boy. There was a man's body beneath that robe. A man's body in very little clothing, just drawers and undershirt, as far as she could tell. He was leaving off trousers at the moment because getting them on over his heavily bandaged ankle was troublesome.

Beatrice adored this informal Ritchie. The one she'd first seen when he'd visited her in this very room what seemed like a lifetime ago but was barely a few weeks. Had she realized then that she'd love him so profoundly and so soon? Perhaps there'd been a hint of it, already, deep in her heart but carefully hidden.

Staring at him, her fingers tingled with the urge to touch him and explore him, but she held back. The man was still recuperating. She really should not be making carnal advances just yet. There would be plenty of time for that when they married, as they would do when he was fully well again.

Well, in that case, Beatrice Weatherly, why did you just consult your friend Sofia on the walk home from church, and discuss with her how one might best pleasure a gentleman incapacitated in a lower limb? You're incorrigible, woman, really you are.

Ritchie, it seemed though, had no qualms whatsoever about advances. He cupped her face in his free hand, and drew his thumb across her mouth in a slow, teasing stroke, while with his other hand he clasped her waist more firmly.

"I'm not an invalid, darling Bea. Just a healthy man who's temporarily inconvenienced by a few minor injuries." His fingertips slid across her cheek and on around the back of her neck, beneath her hair, to draw her face to his. "All the undamaged parts of me are working perfectly, I assure you."

"That I don't doubt, Edmund," she responded pertly, only to be silenced by his warm mouth on hers and his wicked tongue slipping immediately between her lips.

Oh, how wonderful! How wonderful!

Beatrice succumbed happily, flicking her own tongue around her fiancé's in a spirited tussle. Even though they'd been sharing the same bedroom—Ritchie in the bed, and herself on a couch, to be on hand if he should be ill in the night—their dealings with each other had been platonic thus far, quietly affectionate, both of them simply grateful for the fact that they'd survived a near catastrophe and were now safe and together.

But now, she wanted more. Now, she pondered Sofia's suggestions, reviewing how it might be possible to enjoy

certain pleasures without further injuring her slightly
battered fiancé. Cautiously, she slipped her arms around
Ritchie and was rewarded by a masculine growl, low and
husky.

"Yes, Bea…yes," he murmured against her throat, his
hand moving again now, drifting down over her shoulder
and heading for her breast. When he squeezed her, she
moaned, arching herself against him.

"Are you aroused, Miss Weatherly? How scandalously
indecent." He grinned at her, his hand massaging the soft
orb, deftly managing to pleasure her through the layers
of her clothing. Thankfully the lovely new undergarments she'd purchased with Sofia's guidance were very
much lighter and didn't impede the explorations of a lover
nearly as much. Her nipples were hard and clearly Ritchie
could feel them so. "You weren't in this condition while
you were in church were you, you wicked woman? What
on earth would the vicar say if he knew? He might refuse
to officiate at our wedding if he knew you were such a
wanton."

"Actually," gasped Beatrice, closing her eyes and wriggling against the upholstery. She opened her legs, unable
to stop pressing herself hard against the horsehair beneath
her. "It might make him even more anxious to officiate.
I'm sure the sooner I'm a respectable married woman,
the better, in his eyes. That way I have a proper and sanc-
tioned outlet for my natural desire *and* I'm serving God's
law."

Ritchie laughed happily, and Beatrice's closed eyes
snapped open again to find that his were dancing with
mirth and provocation.

"Excellent! I'm pleased to learn that the God-fearing
respectability of marriage isn't going to interfere with
your commitment to the pleasures of the flesh," he said

jovially, still plying his fingers over her breast. "But I am concerned that you might get out of the habit of it if we have to wait until after the ceremony." He gave her a wicked look of poorly feigned anxiety. "The erotic arts require commitment. Constant practice. No slacking."

"But what about your ankle?" She cast a dubious glance at his carefully bound limb. "I don't want to hurt you." Desire warred with solicitude inside her, in a titanic struggle. Her breasts ached, her puss ached...her entire body ached for him. And yet the thought of causing him pain held her back.

"Oh, I think I'll survive," he murmured in her ear, suddenly reaching for her hand and directing it to his groin. Through the cloth of his dressing gown and his drawers, she felt him hard. "Perhaps not a wild sweaty gallop, but I'm sure between us we can find ways to pleasure each other in a more circumspect fashion." His lips settled against the side of her neck, feathering over her skin. "An imaginative young woman like you must surely have plenty of ideas."

His hand squeezed hers, pressing it against him.

Beatrice smiled. She couldn't help herself. She loved the feel of hot, hard life, the essence of her man. He might be temporarily lame, but this part of him was in prime condition and free from all impediment. Between her legs, her flesh trembled, as if calling to him.

"But the door is unlocked, Edmund," she protested. "Someone might come in while...while we're occupied with each other."

"No they won't. I've given instructions. Very clear instructions. Under no circumstances may anyone enter the room without knocking."

Beatrice shivered, but not from cold. Prickles of delicious yearning surged across the surface of her skin, both the areas that were exposed, and those covered.

"Polly's used to swanning in after just the most cursory of knocks. She might easily forget." Distracted for a moment, Beatrice smiled, but for another reason. An astonishing development had taken place, one which she thoroughly approved, despite its unconventional nature. "Especially now."

Two days ago, her brother had brought Polly to her in an endearingly formal manner, and announced to Beatrice and Ritchie that the two of them were going to be married soon, and henceforth, his fiancée should be treated as a member of the family rather than a servant.

After her initial surprise, it'd dawned on Beatrice that she'd been anticipating something like this. And that there was more to it than met the eye. She'd glanced at Jamie Brownlow, standing at the door, his face amused and watchful, and wondered just to what exactly she and Ritchie were giving their blessing.

Ritchie gave Beatrice an assessing look. "How do you really feel about your brother's impending nuptials? Not outraged that he's marrying your own former servant?" His eyes narrowed. "You do realize that there's more than just the happy couple involved, don't you?"

It was Beatrice's turn to smile, giving him an arch look as she massaged his magnificent erection with a little more vigor than before.

"I'm not blind, Edmund, and I'm not entirely naive." Delicately shaking his hand free of hers, she flipped open his robe and then attacked the buttons of his knitted cotton drawers. "I'm well aware that some people enter into somewhat *unconventional* relationships, and if all parties in this particular 'arrangement' are going to be happy together, well, I for one am delighted. Polly and

Charlie will do well together. She has a keen mind and a good heart, and I couldn't wish for a more amenable sister-in-law." She paused, her fingertips hovering. "As for Jamie...*I* don't know him very well yet, but if he has your complete trust, he must be a fine man indeed."

"He is," affirmed Ritchie, completely sincere, "and I believe they'll all muddle through in their strange triangle and be content."

For a moment, the two of them stared at each other, but after a beat or two, Beatrice had a sense of a line being drawn.

Ritchie spoke up again. "And now, can we return to our own arrangements, Miss Weatherly?" He glanced down at his tumescent groin, and her fingers so close to it. "We seem to be at rather critical juncture."

"Indeed we are." Beatrice was brisk and workman-like when she prized her fiancé's splendid penis out from amongst the folds of his linen.

"Oh, my angel," sighed Ritchie as she began to caress him, her fingertips as in love with the silky texture of the shiny, rosy skin that covered the hard core within as her heart was with the man in his entirety. She slid them up and down the length of him, exploring his intimate geography while she savored the low moans that issued from his lips.

There was no silent stoicism where Ritchie was concerned, and when she inclined forward and took the head of his cock into her mouth, he let out an oath of encouragement, his voice both raw and appreciative.

"Oh yes, my clever, wicked, beautiful one... That's it, my dear, that's it. Oh Lord, that feels wonderful."

He chanted as she licked. He gasped as she sucked. He sighed and then groaned long and hard and heartfelt as she attempted to do both at once, as well as fondle him with her fingers at the same time. Beatrice knew that she still had much to learn about the finer arts of love, but the way Ritchie responded told her that she was at least performing this act to his satisfaction.

Especially when she found his special sweet spot…and he erupted.

"My love, my love," he exhorted her, voice loud and intense, as he gripped her head, his fingers dislodging some of the pins that held her coiffure. Would the servants hear, Beatrice wondered vaguely as she received his silky seed upon her tongue and swallowed it down with enthusiasm and joy.

When he was finally spent, Ritchie subsided against the cushions with a long, happy gasp. His eyes were closed and there was an expression of purest satisfaction on his dear and handsome face. As carefully as she could, Beatrice dabbed both him, and her sticky lips with a handkerchief she'd had tucked in her sleeve, then returned his loins to a state of propriety.

My love. My love. You are so beautiful.

She smiled at him as he lay there, getting his wind back. He was the most precious thing in the world to her now, an unexpected love who she'd never thought to meet. How lucky she was to have found—or been found by—this special man.

And now you sleep, you wretch.

With a silent, indulgent chuckle, she let him rest and, out of curiosity, turned her attention to the many papers spread out before him on the table just to one side. It probably wasn't the done thing for a fiancée or wife to pry into her loved one's business dealings, but she'd already decided that she would be a radical, modern partner and take an interest in all matters that concerned Ritchie, whether personal or commercial.

Increasingly fascinated, she sifted through the thick pile of documents. Reports on a variety of his holdings, profit and loss accounts, bank and investment statements. Most satisfactory, as far as she could see with a nonfinancier's eye. She was going to be a very well set up wife indeed. Which was something she felt no guilt at the prospect of enjoying.

At the bottom of the heap, she found a paper that made her gasp aloud, and let out a cry of "Oh my goodness!"

Westerlynne! It was a bill of sale for Westerlynne, her old home, the happy home of her youth, purchased just two days ago by her future husband. An adjacent letter revealed that the new owners were as debt ridden as she and Charlie had been, and were relieved to accept such a generous offer from Ritchie.

She gave his shoulder a good shake, and his blue eyes snapped open.

"You rogue, when were you going to tell me that you've acquired Westerlynne? You can't possibly think I wouldn't be interested in this news?" She tried to sound stern, but this new, unlooked-for delight made that impossible.

He didn't look shamefaced. He simply looked disgustingly pleased with himself.

"I was about to tell you when you walked in, my darling, I swear I was. But then I'm afraid I became distracted by your beautiful face and the feel of your luscious body beneath that undeniably handsome bodice."

"Oh, do lay the blame at my feet." She grinned at him, unable to do anything else but. Her heart had already been brimming, but this new joy made it impossible for her to wear any facial expression but a smile.

"At your feet. At your shapely calves. At your sleek, delicious thighs…" Blue eyes twinkled, and darkened with lust. "At your sumptuous, heavenly puss, your divine breasts, and your embracing arms." Coming up, he reached for her. "At your perfect face, your fiery hair… your wicked, sweet lips…" He glanced at her mouth, and then down toward his own groin.

Beatrice melted. Every bit of her, lost in love and in lust at the sight of his handsome, ardent face and the devilish light in his eyes. She knew that look and she knew the pleasure that always ensued when she saw it.

"But I do think I should offer retribution for not informing you more promptly," he continued, murmuring against her ear now, his hands already at work, unbuttoning her bodice, "some recompense…" Unhooking the top of her corset, then plying open her chemise, he bared her breasts, then switching his attention lower, he commenced hauling up her skirts.

Then he kissed, he touched, he toyed with, and he aroused. His fingers made magic everywhere they settled, probing and stroking. It might be a little hazardous yet for her to climb aboard him while his ankle was still susceptible, but that didn't prevent him from wreaking heaven on her body.

Sucking her nipple and stroking her clitoris, he made her spend.

And then it was Beatrice's turn to slump against cushions, breathing hard.

"Oh my goodness," she breathed, laughing and a little stunned.

"Indeed," agreed Ritchie, stroking her hair.

A little while later, Beatrice asked, "And shall we live at Westerlynne, Edmund?" Straightening her clothing, she sat and faced him, calmer now. "It's very beautiful… a lovely home, and spacious too."

Ritchie smiled, his expression relaxed and open, hiding

nothing anymore. "I thought we might live there part of the year, and the rest of the time, the Season, here in London. Either at this house, or some other. I'm at your disposal, my love."

Beatrice reached for his hand and folded her fingers lightly around his. It was a slight embrace, but exquisitely sweet, perfect for the moment.

"That sounds extremely amenable. The best of both worlds." She paused, thinking of others in the house. "And what of Charlie and Polly…and Jamie."

After a moment's thought, Ritchie answered, "Well, I'll leave the decision to them, but if they wish it, I think they'll do well residing at Westerlynne and overseeing the running of the house when we're not there. Jamie is a countryman at heart, and I believe country society might be a more comfortable setting for your new sister-in-law." He hesitated, and gave her a wink. "Not to mention that it will be far easier for them to conduct their unusual arrangements away from the eyes of London gossips."

Beatrice nodded. He was so right. Despite the steadying influence of his new wife and his loving friend, Charlie was prone to temptations. But in the country at Westerlynne, he could throw himself into running the estate with the wise counsel of Jamie and Polly on hand to steer him.

"You think of everything, don't you?" she teased lightly, knowing that he knew she meant it as a compliment.

"I try to…I do try to." He smiled back at her, then lifted her hand to his lips, to kiss it passionately.

They were quiet for long moments, looking into each other's eyes.

"How did we come to this?" said Beatrice softly as Ritchie drew her back into his arms, an embrace of love now, the power of passion temporarily sated. "It's barely more than a month since I first set eyes on you, and I didn't even like you on that occasion."

Ritchie gave a low laugh. "That's true, my love. I could tell. But I couldn't help but pursue you once I'd met you in the flesh. I wanted to really get to know the woman who'd captivated me so powerfully from just a photograph."

Beatrice nestled closer. "And do you feel you know me now?"

He seemed to consider her words. "Yes, my love… to some extent." For a moment, he pressed his face into her hair, which had come unfastened and streamed loose over her shoulders. "But I think there's still much I have to learn in the many years that lie ahead…and I look forward to discovering a million wonderful secrets."

It was Beatrice's turn to chuckle. "I sincerely hope you won't be disappointed, Edmund. I'm really just a very ordinary woman."

"Nonsense," said Ritchie simply, kissing her neck. "You're a goddess and a siren, my dear, and you're well aware of that, aren't you?"

"Well, if you say so, my love, then I am indeed a paragon."

And so are you, Edmund Ellsworth Ritchie, so are you. For me, I do believe you're the perfect man.

There was no need to say it. Indeed, no need to speak a syllable for the moment. As Ritchie laughed again, she just held him to her, warm and close.

* * * * *

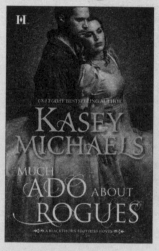

These cowboys are tough...but not too tough to fall in love!

In these timeless romances from bestselling authors

JAYNE ANN KRENTZ,
LINDSAY MCKENNA

and

B.J. DANIELS,

three women will discover that the West has never been so wild....

Available now!

www.Harlequin.com

REQUEST YOUR FREE BOOKS!

2 FREE NOVELS
FROM THE ROMANCE COLLECTION
PLUS 2 FREE GIFTS!

YES! Please send me 2 FREE novels from the Romance Collection and my 2 FREE gifts (gifts are worth about $10). After receiving them, if I don't wish to receive any more books, I can return the shipping statement marked "cancel." If I don't cancel, I will receive 4 brand-new novels every month and be billed just $5.99 per book in the U.S. or $6.49 per book in Canada. That's a saving of at least 25% off the cover price. It's quite a bargain! Shipping and handling is just 50¢ per book in the U.S. and 75¢ per book in Canada.* I understand that accepting the 2 free books and gifts places me under no obligation to buy anything. I can always return a shipment and cancel at any time. Even if I never buy another book, the two free books and gifts are mine to keep forever.

194/394 MDN FELQ

Name	(PLEASE PRINT)	
Address		Apt. #
City	State/Prov.	Zip/Postal Code

Signature (if under 18, a parent or guardian must sign)

Mail to the **Reader Service:**
IN U.S.A.: P.O. Box 1867, Buffalo, NY 14240-1867
IN CANADA: P.O. Box 609, Fort Erie, Ontario L2A 5X3

Not valid for current subscribers to the Romance Collection
or the Romance/Suspense Collection.

Want to try two free books from another line?
Call 1-800-873-8635 or visit www.ReaderService.com.

* Terms and prices subject to change without notice. Prices do not include applicable taxes. Sales tax applicable in N.Y. Canadian residents will be charged applicable taxes. Offer not valid in Quebec. This offer is limited to one order per household. All orders subject to credit approval. Credit or debit balances in a customer's account(s) may be offset by any other outstanding balance owed by or to the customer. Please allow 4 to 6 weeks for delivery. Offer available while quantities last.

Your Privacy—The Reader Service is committed to protecting your privacy. Our Privacy Policy is available online at www.ReaderService.com or upon request from the Reader Service.

We make a portion of our mailing list available to reputable third parties that offer products we believe may interest you. If you prefer that we not exchange your name with third parties, or if you wish to clarify or modify your communication preferences, please visit us at www.ReaderService.com/consumerschoice or write to us at Reader Service Preference Service, P.O. Box 9062, Buffalo, NY 14269. Include your complete name and address.